Kissing Frogs: The Thirteenth

Kissing Frogs: The Thirteenth

Jessica Lynn

NEW Reads Publications

Copyright © 2019 by Jessica Lynn

Library of Congress Cataloging-In-Publication Data

Lynn, Jessica.
    Kissing Frogs: The Thirteenth/Jessica Lynn

    ISBN 978-1-7335848-1-4

To those who pushed me and held me accountable, even when the river was dry.

Contents

1. Things Fall Apart, I Don't Have To

I've spent my entire life wrapped up in dreams,
To suppress the pain of reality, it seems. All the sounds,
textures, scents and things
Echoing emptiness, regardless of the sensations they
bring. I anchored myself away from these dreams,
wrapped my words in the softest satins and silks to bind
me.
And my tongue down and hide the lashes
And cuttings on the flesh of a disappointed dreamer
trying to break free . . .
But what is freedom . . . ?

~ Olosunde

It was a cold, and overcast Saturday in October, and I was sitting in front of my vanity pouting at my reflection in the mirror. I was feeling pitiful and frustrated by my disheveled appearance, but it had been a long night full of dreams and reliving the voice messages I had left on my newly ex-boyfriend's phone. My roommate, Erica, tapped on my door and popped her head in without invitation.

"Journey? You all right in here?"

I responded with an empty glance at her through the mirror, but I didn't turn around. She came all the way into the room and leaned against my vanity.

"You know you were too good for him, right? I mean, who just disappears like that?"

This time I refused to look at her at all; I just blinked and blinked, wishing she'd get out and let me be, but knowing she meant well. I blinked back the tears and took a shaky breath.

"I'm going to take a shower, and then we can go to Eatonville for breakfast. I need to eat. I need to work.

I need noise. I need distraction. I need to get the hell out of this house. Just… give me thirty minutes and I will be ready, okay?" I sounded stronger than I felt. I just wanted her out of my space so I could process my feelings. I'd do and say almost anything to get her out of my room.

"Okay," she said.

She bounced off the edge of my vanity and out of my room. She had melted down over many a guy during our friendship, and I was always there to help her sweep up her heart's broken pieces, but she wasn't a very big help when the situation was reversed, and I knew it. I was more determined to emotionally manage myself. I needed three days to feel and to wallow in the depths of whatever the feelings were going to be. I needed three days to examine all angles of the wound, and after the three days, I would push forward. This was my process, and dammit I needed my three days! I was only on day two. Erica was different; she would brood for weeks and months over a broken heart; I even think there's a guy she's been crying over for a few years. I couldn't live that way. I had been through way too much over the years, so my process was to spend a day analyzing the guy, a day analyzing myself, and a day mourning the loss of the relationship. After that, every other second of every other day was spent on healing.

I fluffed my curly hair on one side of my head until it stood on end. I tugged the other side down and finger-combed my way through the mass of bedhead I was sporting. I stood up, pulled my pink flannel pajama shirt up over my head, and my green striped pants down, and left them in the middle of the floor as I trotted off to the shower. Under the hot stream of water, I was safe to think, cry, and remember. Naturally, my thoughts drifted to Devin and the last time I saw him. I leaned into the stream of hot water, letting it wet my hair and run down my face and mix with my fresh tears, blinking as it dripped off my eyelashes.

***

Seven days ago, I'd had a nightmare that was so vivid and high definition that I woke up shaking. My reaction made Devin wake up and turn over next to me.

"Journey, what's wrong?"

"I just had this horrible dream that I was a man riding a bicycle down a street at night, but there were people walking around like it wasn't late or something. It was kind of like what you see in New Orleans. Then there was a shout, a screech of tires, and I was hit by a vehicle on my left side. I skidded across the ground so hard that the skin was scraped off the whole right side of my face and side, and I felt my limbs crack and break. I hurt so badly, I could hardly breathe. I think I was dying."

He looked at me with wide eyes for a few moments as he listened.

"It's okay babe," he said finally, drawing me into a strong, tight hug.

I was silently comforted by his muscled arms and his warmth.

"We don't live in New Orleans, and you don't even own a bike."

He laughed a little as he kissed my forehead and eyelids, and ruffled my hair. I smiled and rested my head on his chest, allowing the sound of his heartbeat to help regulate my own. His phone buzzed, and he reached over to get it off my nightstand.

"Hello? Hey... what! What happened to him?"

He shifted away and sat up with his back facing me, his feet now on the floor. There was panic in his voice as I listened to a woman's voice crying on the other end. I held my breath and watched the vein pulsing in his neck, wondering what was going on. I touched his shoulder lightly, supportively, unsure of exactly how to support him or what else to do. He listened for a long time, and I waited for him to finish his conversation. After what seemed like forever, he finally put the phone down. He dropped his head into his hands and sobbed from a deep, soul-wrenching place. I had never seen him or any other man cry like that before. His broad shoulders shook with the weight of his grief, and I instinctively knew that someone had died, but I continued to wait for him to tell me what happened. I climbed out of bed and walked around it to the other side to embrace him. He sobbed into my belly as I held him, rocking him from side to side and gently stroking his back, absorbing his tears into my pajamas and silently holding space for him. After a few minutes, I heard him finally speak, but his words were muffled by my closeness. I stepped back a bit.

"What did you say?"

"I said, my brother who lives in New Orleans is dead!"

"Oh, my God, I'm so sorry! I felt like it was something really bad by your reaction."

He looked up at me with accusation, "How did you know?"

"What do you mean?" I asked, confused by the question.

"My brother died the exact same way you saw in your dream. How did you know?"

His voice rose slightly with a hint of anger and what I identified as fear. Yes, he was afraid, and worst of all it sounded like he was afraid of me.

But I didn't know. I mean, yes, I had seen the man, but I had never even met Devin's brother. It wasn't the first time something like this had happened to me, but there wasn't much I could say.

"I'm so sorry, Devin," was all I could muster.

He pulled away from me, rising and yanking on his clothes.

"I have to get out of here," he muttered.

He was angry. He was hurt. The rest was just silent actions. Push legs through pants. Stomp feet into shoes. Jacket. Hat. Keys. Door. He was gone without even saying goodbye. I was so entirely shocked that I couldn't bring myself to interrupt him or encourage him to stay. It was a surreal moment for both of us, but for different reasons. He was rightfully mourning the loss of his brother while I was lost remembering the panic I felt waiting for my grandmother to answer the phone in the middle of the night three years prior. I remembered how she answered the phone cheerily at 4:00 a.m., asking me if I was okay.

"I just had a dream about you, Grandma, and I was calling to check on you."

"Oh, you had a dream I was dead?"

She said it with such nonchalance, but her words felt like bricks on my chest.

I was dead . . . I was dead . . . I was dead . . .

The words bounced back and forth inside my head until I placed both hands on my temples. I sat there in the center of my bed for a long time until John Legend started chiming on my alarm telling me, "Good morning, love," and crooning about our favorite love song, but I barely heard it. The peaceful energy that the alarm usually evoked was replaced by sadness, an echo of sobs reverberating off the walls, and the deafening proclamation that Devin's brother was dead. There was nothing more I could do but start my day.

***

I stepped out of the shower and wrapped a big, fluffy, yellow towel around my head and another around my body. I was humming *Melancholy Melody* by Esthero while rummaging through the drawers in my closet for something to wear, when Erica appeared, leaning against the closet doorway. I screamed, startled out of my own thoughts (again), and made a mental note that I was going to have to start locking my door like she does.

"What are you DOING?" I asked angrily, brushing my wet curls out of my eyes. "Why do you keep coming in here without my permission?"

"I'm watching you sing that same pitiful ass song you sing to yourself when you're in a mood. And if I waited for your permission, I'd never get in and I'd be waiting forever to leave this damn house so we can eat."

I ignored her rightness, "You scared the hell out of me! I don't pop up in your room cause you don't like it and . . . "

"You can't pop up in my room because I lock my door."

"Yes! Because you don't like it and even if you didn't lock the door, Erica, I would still respect that you don't like it! Now would you PLEASE stop sweating me and let me get my life together? Damn! We will be leaving soon!"

"Mmmmhmmmm."

She muttered something under her breath that I couldn't hear on her way out, but I didn't care. I huffed out of my closet holding a pair of black boy shorts and a black bra. I tend to feel like I have my life together when my panties match my bra. I sat down on the edge of my bed, and began rubbing shea butter on myself. I skipped the perfume, tugged on a yellow shirt, wiggled into my favorite pair of skinny jeans, and carelessly massaged some curl moisturizer through my hair. I put on my favorite brass peacock earrings and some comfortable, casual shoes, then changed my mind and put on my favorite boots instead. I wasn't concerned about how I looked since there was no one I needed or cared to impress.

I stepped out of my bedroom to find Erica lounging on the couch in black leggings and a very fitted black shirt with a dangerously low V-neck to show off her breasts. She was a pretty 5'4" woman with a smooth, chocolate complexion. I thought she was beautiful with her full lips, voluptuous figure, and sad, soulful, light brown eyes, but she never really saw herself the way I saw her. She had issues with her sense of beauty from years of being told that she was "pretty for a dark-skinned girl," raised to the power of being abused by her father, as well as other men, her whole life. She was creative and had a quick wit with a sharp tongue to match, but no one could ever truly love her enough, and that always hurt my heart for her. She reached down and pulled on her black Ugg boots, and I rolled my eyes at her with disgust.

"You aren't going to really wear those, are you, Erica?"

"What's wrong with my shoes?"

"Nothing, except that they're UGLY as ever and they destroy any outfit."

"Whatever, Journey! Can we go? I clearly don't have time for you and your depressive hangry moments!"

"First of all, I am NOT depressed, and second, did you just say HANGRY?"

"Yes, I did just make up a word. You know, hungry and angry makes hangry. Now let's GO! Your hangriness is contagious!"

I rolled my eyes and jokingly flipped her the bird. We laughed and left for a much needed breakfast outing.

Eatonville was packed with weekend brunch patrons. After driving through D.C. traffic and fighting for a parking spot that wasn't too far from 14th Street, we were more than happy to be seated and sipping coffee. I wasn't sure how many more back handed remarks I could take from Erica on an empty stomach, so the caffeine was essential. Our favorite waiter, Carlos, came over to our table smiling at us.

"Hello ladies! What can I get for you today?" he asked, serving us a smile.

"Hi Carlos!" we said in unison with matching smiles.

He was the restaurant crush for both of us. We came here for brunch often just to sit in his section and chat with him while he served us because he had great customer service, and he was the best eye candy. He was a caramel-colored Puerto Rican with the most perfect teeth and beautiful smile we had ever seen, a dimple on only the right side, black hair that he kept cut very low, and a tattoo that peeked indiscreetly out of his perfectly rolled shirt sleeves. He had told us what the tattoo was once before, but I couldn't remember, and I don't think either of us cared because we just liked listening to the way he rolled his Rs when he spoke to us. He was comfortable with us, so his accent would often slip out, and Erica and I would kick one another under the table and smile in silent appreciation.

"I will have my usual," I said, sipping my coffee.

"WE will have our usual orders, and we would like to indulge in the bottomless mimosas today. Journey has had a rough couple of days."

I kicked Erica under the table at the mention of my hard couple of days and shot her a warning look.

Carlos laughed at us, "Is everything okay, Journey?"

"I'm good, Carlos, thank you for asking. I don't know what's gotten into Erica." I shot her another look and rolled my eyes into my coffee cup.

"Nothing has gotten into me, but since we are on the subject of getting into me... do you have a girlfriend, Carlos?"

Erica flirted, leaning back a little and letting her breasts poke out a bit. I choked on my coffee and covered my mouth with my napkin, spitting coffee into it and struggling to catch my breath.

"I don't," Carlos answered with a smirk, "but I just got out of a relationship and we are in that weird limbo space."

"How sad," Erica fake pouted at him, sipping her coffee and leaning back a little more in her chair, crossing her legs sensually. "Well, if you don't get back together, you should give me a call sometime."

She wrote her phone number on the napkin and handed it to him. Carlos smiled, nodded and walked away.

When he was out of earshot, I kicked at Erica under the table, "Oh, my God! Awkward much, Erica?"

"What? He's fine, and we both know it. Somebody had to make a move!" she said, laughing at my expression that was a mixture of embarrassment and mild frustration.

"How weird and rare is it that we are both attracted to the same guy, and NOW you want to make it awkward by bringing him home with us so I can listen to you two getting your freak on across the hall from me? Ew, Erica! Just, ew!"

"Listen, chick, I know you're going through a rough time here, but I'm single and free, and if Carlos wants to pay a visit to casa de Erica, then who am I to stop him?"

I rolled my eyes at her again and sipped my coffee. I wasn't jealous, I just thought it was weird, and I didn't like the feeling of lusting after the man that my roommate was screwing under the same roof.

"So, Miss Journey, how many times did you call Devin last night? And don't tell me you didn't call him, because I heard you leaving heartfelt messages on his answering machine while I was in the living room last night."

"Oh, so you were ear hustling outside my door? Must you stir this pot right now? I don't want to talk about it anymore. I'm only on day two, and this outing is interfering with my process already."

"Yeah, yeah, you and your three-day purging process," she rolled her eyes at me and smiled at the approaching Carlos, who was bringing our mimosas and breakfast. She cut her eyes at him flirtatiously while I tried not to look at his slightly uncomfortable expression or expose mine. I sensed that he wasn't into her; Erica had come on to him a bit too strong, but he was being polite. He shifted his eyes to me and raised his eyebrows and widened his eyes a bit with a strange tight-lipped grin that I had never seen him make before, but I understood the gesture. Yeah, he wasn't into her.

He turned and moved away to another table, and I waited until he was back near the kitchen area before returning to my conversation with Erica.

"I don't judge you when you melt down over Adele songs and sappy movies because they remind you of whomever, so don't judge me and my three-day purging process."

My mimosa glass clinked against my coffee cup as I took a large gulp of the sweet, sparkling citrusy liquid and glared at her. Erica raised an eyebrow at me, her own mimosa glass cupped slightly in her palm and balanced carelessly between her middle and ring fingers.

"Oh, so you just want to start laying it all out there, huh? Well, for your information Miss Thing, I am just waiting for you to purge this negro so we can get you back to the guy you REALLY love. You knew Devin was temporary, and I never liked him for you anyway. You're always trying to fix these guys. It's like you meet the guy who has issues, you take him on as a fixer-upper project, you get attached and start dating him, and then your feelings are hurt when he falls short of your expectations. They're NEVER going to live up to your expectations, Journey! You need to just go get back with James. You were HAPPY with him! Your EVERYTHING would light up when you were together!"

Other patrons who were nearby were beginning to notice that we were having a tense conversation and began looking at us with shifting, judgmental glances. I cared, but I knew Erica didn't; she was never the type to back down. I decided not to match her energy and lowered my voice so that it could no longer be heard over "A Sunday Kind of Love" playing in the background. I leaned in toward her while plastering a fake smile on my face to deflect my irritation as I cut my fried green tomatoes into little bite sizes before slicing a bit of my salmon and cream cheese omelet onto my fork.

"While we are sitting here having a deep examination of my wounds and scars as if they aren't still VERY RAW, I need you to accept that James doesn't want me. HE walked away from ME, not the other way around. Now, for YOUR information, Devin was not a project. I really cared about him, and he is in a state of mourning which is why I keep calling him. I'm trying to be understanding and patient with his grieving process."

I chewed my food as she twisted her lips sideways, nodding as if in consideration of what I had said, and spread butter onto her French toast. She poured a little syrup into a saucer, and then cut the bread with her fork instead of using her knife. She dipped her toast into the syrup and chewed three slices of French toast. She always said she hated when her pancakes, waffles, or French toast were too soggy with syrup, so she dipped them in syrup rather than pour syrup on top. When she finished chewing, she pointed at me with a piece of bacon and squinted her eyes at me.

"Just because he is grieving doesn't mean he couldn't call you back, and he invited his 'best friend' who just so happens to be a woman he told you he used to sleep with to the funeral, but he didn't invite you. Don't you think that sounds mighty suspicious?"

She sang the last part as she waved her bacon for emphasis.

"Yes! It sounds suspicious, but I can't go around not trusting him because of what somebody else did to me, and I can't go accusing him of something that he might not have done or questioning his choices of whom he would prefer to support him right now."

I was getting upset. I could feel my heart beating faster, and my cheeks were feeling warm. I hated getting into uncomfortable conversations in public places, and I really wanted her to drop this.

"I just think you're being naive."

She muttered over a mouthful of French toast, as she dusted a bit of powdered sugar off her shirt and licked her lips.

"I saw it happen, Erica!" I defended.

I slumped in my seat looking around at the people who were turning to look at us as our voices picked up volume again. Erica was quiet for a second.

"Wait, do you mean you . . ."

"Yes."

I held the table and hung my head with the gravity of the confession.

"I saw his brother die in a dream. I woke up and told him about the dream, but I didn't know it was his brother initially because I had never met him before. A few minutes afterward, one of his relatives called him crying with the news. He is understandably freaked out now. I have to allow him to have his space and be sensitive to his process."

"Did he know beforehand that you have this gift of predicting births and deaths?"

"No, but we had a weird experience once about a girl he used to date when he was younger who passed away. Her name was Tiffany. He accepted that one, but I suppose this one just hit way too close to home. I mean, it was his brother, Erica."

"You are so damn accommodating! It makes me sick! I just want you to be mad at him, and be done with it!"

"Well, I can't do that. That's why I keep calling him."

"But he isn't answering your calls and he texts you hurtful things. Didn't that last text tell you to just forget him and let him go?"

"Yes, but I feel like if I could just talk to him—"

"Journey, sweetie, you need to just let it go," she gestured with both palms raised for emphasis.

Carlos appeared with our checks. I didn't make eye contact with him. I didn't feel comfortable admiring him anymore. I put my debit card in the bill folder and averted my eyes when he came to retrieve them from both of us. When he returned with the receipt to sign, I scribbled a generous tip, total, and signed my name. I almost missed the neatly handwritten message on the customer copy that read:

I'm actually more interested in you . . .
Give me a call.
(202) 232-7322

He had drawn a smiley face in the corner. My cheeks burned as I looked up inconspicuously from the receipt and found him watching me from across the room with a subtle smile on his handsome face. I shoved the receipt into my coat pocket, grabbed my purse, and walked out hurriedly with an oblivious Erica in tow.

We stepped out into the cold, autumn breeze with our heads slightly bent, trying to maintain our warmth with silence until we reached my car. As I waited for the engine to warm up, Erica started in about Carlos.

"How long do you think it will take for him to call me?"

"I don't know. He said he just broke up with someone, so he may need time."

I strategically omitted that he had given me his number and asked me to call, as I shifted into drive. I had enough to think about and didn't feel like adding him to the mix, regardless of how fine he was.

"Well, all I know is, if he calls me, I will happily help him forget whatever woman was fool enough to let him slip away. Mmph! Carlos!"

She twisted her lips into a smirk that insinuated lustful thoughts, but I pretended not to hear her and stared at the road ahead, very focused on driving. Maybe she got the cue to shut her face, maybe her social media account was exceptionally interesting, but we thankfully managed to drive home to our apartment without discussing Carlos any further.

***

Several hours later found me in the kitchen, wearing a yellow apron, preparing nutmeg chicken, scalloped potatoes, wilted greens, and a half dozen baby Bundt cakes. The entire apartment smelled sweet, warm, and savory as I busily hummed about the kitchen. Erica didn't cook in our house often, but she loved being my resident taste tester for any new recipe I wanted to try. I called her to me, and pushed a cake in her direction with a small, knowing smile on my face. It dripped decadently with cream cheese frosting that I had also made from scratch. She squealed and took a huge bite.

"Oh. My. Gosh. Journey, you're giving me a huge butt with all this baking!" she said over a mouthful of cake.

I shook my head and laughed at her without looking in her direction, "You're welcome! I am sure you aren't truly complaining."

"I'm not! Since we've been roommates, I have been getting way more compliments about my assets," she said, emphasizing the last word by shaking her butt at me.

"Well, I am not mad about helping you build your side selfie portfolio," I teased. "Can you grab that bottle of wine off the shelf? I want to have it with my food art creation."

She retrieved the bottle and began uncorking it, while I prepared our plates. She grunted and tugged for a few minutes, causing me to turn around and watch her straining to get the cork out.

"Here, let me see that," I said, reaching for the bottle.

I tugged and grunted for a few minutes as well but I couldn't get the cork out either.

"I know! Erica, you hold the bottom of the bottle while I hold the cork and corkscrew. I'm going to count to three, and then I'm going to pull up while you pull down. Try not to have one of your clumsy moments and spill wine everywhere."

We both laughed in nervous anticipation and held opposite ends of the bottle firmly as I counted, "One... two... three... PULL!"

We tugged with all our strength until the cork popped. I fell backward onto the floor while Erica managed to hold on to the bottle, but also ended up on her bottom, finding herself sprayed in the face with wine in the process. She was coughing and sputtering dramatically, and the two of us were laughing at each other and our clumsiness. Who says a little slapstick comedy can't distract you from a broken heart?

The next morning, I woke up to my cat pawing my face, demanding my attention, completely unconcerned about my sleep or whether I felt like petting him. "Get off me, Rico," I said as I removed him from my belly. I groaned at the sunshine streaming happily into my windows as I peeled myself from between my yellow sheets and sat up with my feet planted on the carpeted floor. My head was still spinning from too much wine I drank with Erica the night before. We killed two bottles together over a marathon of *True Blood* and way too many baby Bundt cakes. I exhaled deeply in astonishment over how much my head was still spinning. Ignoring Rico's purring and gentle pawing on my back in an effort to encourage me to pet him again, I stood up and made my way to the kitchen to get some water.

"A perfect start to my last day of mourning," I said aloud to no one.

Rico padded softly into the kitchen and sat in front of me, swishing his tail and then rubbing up against my bare legs. I guzzled my second glass of water as I rummaged through the cabinets for flour and baking powder. I heard Erica moving around in her bedroom and snickered to myself as I listened to her loud, long sigh after making it to the toilet. After I heard her washing her hands and her electric toothbrush began to whir from inside her bathroom, I tapped on the door, "Yo... pancakes?" I asked from behind the closed door.

"Yesh!" she replied, with a mouth full of toothpaste.

"Bet," I said, as I walked back toward the kitchen, adjusting a wedgie before washing my hands and donning myself with my apron over my T-shirt.

I whipped and mixed the pancake batter halfheartedly, and reached for my cell phone to turn my Pandora onto my Janelle Monae station, and immediately began bouncing and twirling my hips to the music.

"Yaaaaaaaaaas!" Erica exclaimed from behind me, identically clad in boy shorts and a t-shirt.

I stopped and turned to have a little dance session around the kitchen with her, laughing at her twerking with her hands on the island. The skillet crackled warmly as I poured the pancake batter into it, and then I bopped to the refrigerator to retrieve eggs and began to make the mixture for salmon croquettes. I wiggled a little to the next song as I blended the food and hummed to myself, internally acknowledging that I didn't feel the heavy sadness I had been prepared for anymore.

After a while, I called Erica into the kitchen to get her plate, and we sat at our round table to eat our food. Rico stared at us from beneath the glass table, waiting for someone to acknowledge his presence.

"Hey, mama's pretty kitty!" I exclaimed, as I stroked him with my foot.

He rubbed his whole body against my legs in response to encourage me to pet him more.

"Ugh! You and that damn cat!" Erica said with disgust.

I ignored her and continued to pet him with my foot as I ate my food, when the music stopped and my phone began to vibrate, signaling a phone call. I rose to see who it was and saw Devin's name on the screen. I snatched up the phone urgently and began to walk quickly toward my bedroom. Erica sensed who it was by my reaction and I saw her roll her eyes at me out of the corner of my eye as I shut the door for privacy.

"Hello?" I said with tenderness in my tone.

I wanted to be angry, and I knew that he didn't deserve any ounce of the sweetness I was prepared to give after the mean things he had said to me in the text messages he sent a few days prior, but I couldn't help myself.

"Hey," he said dryly. "I just wanted you to know I got your voicemails, and that I'm back from the funeral. It was nice, and they had a little parade for my brother through the neighborhood. Me and Angie just finished having breakfast, so I figured I should call you."

I twirled the curl at my right temple, mentally correcting his grammar as I listened, but rather than say so and potentially irritate him, I ignored it and the comment about his friend whom he chose to allow to comfort him instead of me. I turned, took a deep breath and leaned against the window, and then I exhaled slowly and quietly, watching my breath fog up the glass before I spoke.

"I'm glad that he was sent off properly. Devin, I—I think we should meet and discuss things. You left abruptly, and while I know you were hurting, you said some extremely unacceptable things to me and I think we need to clear the air before we attempt to move forward."

I sounded strong and firm, but I felt like anything he said back could crush me and leave me spiraling into despair again. I slid down the wall on my right shoulder down to the floor, drawing my knees to my chest as I cradled the phone between my left shoulder and ear as I began twirling the hair at my temple again.

"I know. I'm sorry about hurting your feelings, but I do think it best that we go our separate ways. I just don't think I can handle your abilities right now, and I need to focus on myself and my own healing for a while. I'll come by later to get my stuff from your place, if you are okay with that. If not, you can just let me know when a good time will be."

"Devin, I understand that you're hurting right now, but treating me as if this horrible event is my fault is cruel! I didn't kill your brother or have anything to do with his death in any way, and to treat me as if I did is totally unfair!"

I was angry and my voice raised slightly as I threw my hands up in frustration to an empty room. A room that was as empty as I felt.

"Cut the shit, Journey! I'm trying to be honest with you right now, and you begging me to deal with you beyond what I'm prepared or willing to is fucked up on so many levels! I don't want to talk to you! I don't want to see you! I just want to get my shit from your house and roll. If you don't want to be there when it happens, that's fine, but it IS happening. Matter of fact, I will send Angie and you can just give it to her."

My heartbeat quickened, and my armpits tingled as I raged quietly.

"You act like I'm trying to keep you from getting your stuff from my house when that's not the case! Cursing at me and disrespecting me won't bring your brother back, and while I'm sorry he died, I will not be your fucking punching bag! Don't talk to me like that, and you better not send your little friend over here unless you're looking to get her ass hurt!"

I knew I was flipping out and adding fuel to an unnecessary fire, but he had crossed the line by suggesting sending another woman to my house for his belongings.

"You know what, Journey, you can just keep that stuff or throw it in the trash. We don't have to talk ever again. Get the fuck off my phone!"

The sudden silence of him hanging up in my face left me with my words frozen in my throat and my heart racing as I threw my cell phone at the wall.

Erica tapped lightly on the door a few minutes later, and the door creaked open slightly as she stuck her head into the room. She didn't say anything as she watched me sitting on my bed with my head in my hands taking deep gulps of air as I tried to calm down.

"I take it that didn't go well," she said as she crinkled her nose slightly.

"He's such an asshole!" I shouted from behind my hands covering my face.

I let out what sounded like a war cry as I let the sound propel me off the bed. I began stomping toward the closet and thrusting things around in search of Devin's overnight bag. I was muttering and cursing him out under my breath as I shoved his clothes, toiletries, and other items of his into it carelessly. Erica came all the way into the room and watched me quietly.

"What did he say?" she asked after a while.

"Fuck him!" I threw back at her. "He can get his shit and get out of my entire life! I don't have any more room in my life for people to mistreat and abandon me at a whim just because life happened, they feel like it, or they don't know what they want! I'm done!"

I shoved the last item into the bag and zipped it hard enough to break the zipper.

"I'm going over to his house to dump this shit on his doorstep, and I dare that Angie chick to say anything to me!"

"Oh shit! Journey, I don't think I've ever seen you like this before. I'm coming with you in case you need backup. You can't be fighting and all that, and I have no problem punching anyone in the neck. I'm going to shower and get dressed and come with you."

"Fine, but hurry up. I'm trying to get this over with. So much for a good day."

"So much indeed," she muttered as she walked out of the room.

The ride to Devin's house was silent, save for the angry music by Prodigy I blared on the way. Erica didn't utter a single word as I drove carefully, conscious about not allowing my emotions to drive me. As I cranked the volume up a bit more and gripped the steering wheel tighter, she eyed me quietly, shifting her eyes between me and her cell phone every few minutes, doing a silent temperature check of how much I was raging inside. I didn't exercise any courtesy as I parked my car within inches of Devin's, and practically leapt out of the driver seat with Prodigy blasting from my open door. I snatched the overnight bag from my back seat and slammed the door, leaving the driver's door wide open.

Marching toward the front door of his town house, I stopped at the bottom stoop and hurled the bag at it, giving no fucks about whether not I broke the bottles of cologne when it collided. I immediately turned on my heel and stormed back toward my car, oblivious of the front door opening. Erica flailed her arms at me in alarm as I approached my car, and I whirled around in time to see who I could only assume was Angie running up on me scowling angrily. I stopped in my tracks to face her, intending to keep my distance, when she shouted, "You stupid bitch!" and swung at me.

I dodged the blow and took several steps back trying to catch my balance.

"This has nothing to do with you! I don't even know who you are, so you need to carry your ass back into the house before somebody gets hurt!" I yelled.

Erica had gotten out of the car and was walking up to the pending fight. Devin appeared at the door and saw the commotion and ran over in an attempt to calm Angie down.

"This is what you wanted, right Devin? You wanted to send this crazy bitch to my house so she could get a mud hole stomped in her ass, right?" I snapped.

"Who you calling bitch, Bitch? Devin is MY man now, and you don't bring your ass over here throwing shit and whatever! Don't let your mouth write checks your ass can't cash, cause you can get this work!" Angie shouted as she began taking her earrings off, throwing them on the lawn.

"You can have him!" I said as I stormed back toward my car, serving her my back. "Devin, we're done! Do me a favor and don't ever call me again. Erica, get in the car!"

I slammed the door and Erica got into the passenger seat. We screeched off, leaving the two of them on the sidewalk looking after us.

"You should've let me beat her ass!" Erica exclaimed as I merged onto the interstate. "I would have drug her ass down the block!"

"That's what she wanted. She's been talking shit about me since Devin and I got together, which is why we've never met. Besides, did you see her? If I'm going to fight someone, it isn't going to be the person who looks like they've already been beaten in the face with a pan. They clearly don't have anything to lose, and I don't have to prove anything by trying to fight someone twice my size. I mean I would defend myself, totally, but my beef wasn't with her. Let it go."

Erica laughed. "Girl, you ain't lying! I definitely wouldn't want to roll up on her in a dark alley. She's built like a refrigerator!"

We laughed as we rode the rest of the way home. By the time we made it to our apartment, Devin had called me ten times and left several text messages and voice mails, to which I had no intention of responding. We had our share of arguments over the ten months we had been together, but I had no interest in entertaining him any further after he allowed his new girlfriend to attack me the way he did, and I was now too angry and disgusted to be hurt. Maybe I would listen to his voice messages later, but not today. I was content to meditate, do some yoga, and release that whole fiasco into the universe. As far as I was concerned, now he was just somebody I used to know.

***

In the morning, I stood in my closet looking for a statement outfit. I was free and feeling powerful, and I wanted to let it show. I rummaged through my clothes and selected a green and gold African print pencil skirt with a white collared blouse and black cardigan. I slid my feet into a pair of black pumps, feeling like I was ready for the world as I fluffed my curls, trying to decide how I wanted to wear my hair for the professional development training I was about to host. I brushed my hair up into a high bun, smoothed my baby hairs down, and coiled the strands at the nape of my neck around my finger until they spiraled perfectly. I smiled at myself in the mirror.

"Good morning, everyone. My name is Journey Richards, and I'm your trainer for today," I rehearsed.

I grabbed my coffee from the Keurig, mixed the crème brulee creamer in, stroked my pretty kitty, and clicked my heels out the front door before Erica woke up. As I walked to my car, I rummaged in my purse for my car keys, and groaned as I realized that I left them on the hook in the front hall in my rush to walk out the door. "Shit," I muttered to myself as I turned around to go back to my apartment to retrieve them.

"Journey, can we talk?" I looked up to find Devin leaning against my white Ford Probe, looking fine as hell with an apology in his eyes.

My heart quickened and I huffed, "I don't have time for this, Devin. I have to get to work."

I spun on my heel and began to sashay away angrily.

"Baby, I know you're mad, but I really need you to hear me out."

"Fuck you, Devin!" I said, whirling back around to face him. "You let some other woman be the one you went to in your time of need when I never did anything but try to love you, and then to add insult to injury, you let her completely disrespect me outside your house! I have nothing left to say to you – and don't call me, Baby!"

I turned back around to walk away from him, but he followed me. I don't know why I let him, or why I didn't slam the door shut behind me when I went to grab my keys. I don't know what I was thinking to let him get close enough to kiss me. I don't know how I managed to allow his hands to find their way up my thighs, or how my lips ended up parting to allow his tongue to dance with mine when he scooped me up, holding me by my hips as he carried me into my bedroom and peeled me out of my clothes. All I know is that when he touched me and pressed his hardness into my soft wetness, I couldn't find it within myself to be angry with him or make him stop.

When I had finally descended from the sex cloud Devin had me on, I glanced at the clock on my dresser and realized that I would be late for my training seminar if I didn't leave in the next five minutes.

"Shit, Devin! I have to get out of here!"

I brushed my hair back into my bun, smoothing my edges and wiping any remaining remnants of the deliciousness that just happened before I yanked on my clothes and stepped into my shoes. He was still lying in my bed smiling at me.

"Don't look at me like that! You have to go, too! We are not good just because this happened. We are going to have a serious talk about everything, but now is just not the time! Get up!"

I pushed him out of the bed, tossed him a warm, wet towel to wipe himself off with, and motioned for him to put his clothes on, ignoring how good he smelled. When he was decent, I opened my door to find Erica standing in the kitchen, leaning against the counter holding her cup of coffee and smirking at me judgmentally. I ignored her as I grabbed my car keys. She shook her head at me and I picked my purse up off the kitchen floor.

"Let yourself out, Devin!" I shouted over my shoulder.

I shrugged my pea coat back on and clicked my heels out the front door wondering what the hell just happened, and what the rest of my day was going to be like. I half ran, half stumbled to my car, snatched my lukewarm coffee off the hood where I had left it in my exchange with Devin. I turned the engine on and sped out of the parking lot, shamelessly and unapologetically leaving the exhilaration of my morning indiscretions behind me until the end of my work day.

As I waited for the elevator in the building where I worked in Silver Spring, Maryland, I saw my colleague walking through the front door.

"Hey, Shayla! How are you, Girl?"

"Morning, Journey!" She finger-combed her hair and straightened her blue blazer. "I'm good, Girl! I had a nice weekend with Steve, and I'm just waiting until I can see him again next weekend."

The elevator chimed its arrival, and we walked into the empty car together. Shayla pushed the button for the eighth floor.

She continued, "I didn't think it was going to be as hard as this, but I'm considering moving to Atlanta to be closer to him."

I cringed at the mention of Atlanta because that's where James lived, and I had tried desperately to move back there several years before, but I had no success. I could understand where Shayla was, and she and Steve had been together for almost two years. Steve was offered a great job opportunity in Atlanta that paid him way better than his job in D.C. He took it and she supported him, but now six months had passed and the travel was adding up, while the time in between visits was becoming burdensome. One of them was going to have to make a move soon, and I couldn't judge Shayla for being willing to relocate before Steve gave her the incentive of proposing marriage.

"Have you been looking for job opportunities there?" I asked hopefully. "I know how hard it can be finding a gig in Atlanta. I used to live there, and if I thought it was hard while I was there, it was even harder when I wasn't there and tried to find one."

"I just started looking last week. I found a few positions I was interested in, and I sent out my resume and all that," Shayla said.

The elevator reached our floor and the doors slid open. We walked out of the elevator, lowering our voices so that no one would hear our conversation. It was no secret that the director of our office and her little flunky of an administrative assistant were prone to gossip and liked to lurk and eavesdrop. The last thing Shayla needed was one of them impeding her progress of trying to move on from the company before she could get a shoe in elsewhere, and they were known to blackball employees who tried to advance or leave for better opportunities.

"Well, it sounds like your relationship is becoming more serious," I said with a smile. "Do you think Steve will propose soon? I'd hate to see you make all these transitions for him, if longevity isn't even a factor in his mind."

"We have discussed the future at length, so I think I'm okay in that area, but you're right. I never thought of it through that lens before."

She rubbed her manicured nails through her brown hair saying, "I am willing to take the risk, but I do wonder why it's always the woman who has to take the risks up front in a relationship, you know? I would love for him to have proposed already so I have no doubts or worries about what will happen going forward, but that feeling doesn't silence the small voice inside telling me that I need to go get my man, you know?"

I nodded solemnly. I knew what she meant and I had been there before. It wasn't my place to impose my failed experience on her potential fairy tale, so I just listened to her and kept the bruises of my past to myself. I had met Steve many times, and he seemed like a keeper, so why wreck her flow by speaking fear into her heart over her choices?

"Well, I'm happy that you feel like you've found someone worthy of all the potential struggle, girlfriend. Let me know how I can help or support you going forward," I said as I left her at the door of her office and headed toward my own.

28. Jessica Lynn

When I reached my office and hung my coat on the hook in my closet, I opened my purse to check my phone for any messages and saw several texts from Devin and Erica. I didn't feel like answering Erica's potential questions or hearing her opinions about the utter decadence I had experienced with Devin that morning, so I opened his instead.

> I can't stop thinking about you. The way you smell and feel when I hold you close. You just taste so good. I'm at work and I can still smell you on me. I have the most massive erection right now. I can't wait to see you later.

I blushed slightly as I closed his text messages and ignored the warm, tingling sensation building between my legs. I adjusted my skirt as I sat down and tried to focus on the tasks of the day, when the office intern poked his head into my office.

"Good morning, Journey!" he offered with a smile.

I smiled back at him tightly, his presence interrupting my thoughts.

"Good morning, Brian. Were you able to touch base with Pembroke and Associates to schedule that training for this week?"

"Yes, they'll be sending their order to Regina later today to schedule your trip to Atlanta for their training, and they've confirmed your hotel and travel accommodations," he said as he stepped fully into my office.

"Thank you! How's your day going so far?"

I smiled at him sweetly. He reminded me of my younger brother in so many ways, and I always found his presence and attention to detail regarding the trainers uplifting. I hoped that when he was done with his internship, he would find a place at a good company that would appreciate his professionalism.

"I'm really good, thanks! How about you?"

"I'm doing well, Brian, thanks for asking. Are all the pamphlets and workbooks for today's training ready, or do I need to make copies?"

"They're already prepped for you; all you have to do is get to the location."

"I have to travel somewhere? How did I miss that detail?" I asked, scrolling through my inbox trying to find a message indicating a change in location.

"Regina sent it to me this morning, and I assumed that you received it also," Brian stated.

"All right, thanks," I conceded.

I groaned under my breath as I noticed the message from last night. Why did she feel the need to send out emails on weekends? Didn't she have anything better to do on a Saturday or Sunday than work? Ugh! Maybe that's why Regina was so uptight and all up in our asses all the damn time. She clearly needed some dick in her life. I pushed myself away from my desk and slid my coat back on. As I walked down the hallway, I bumped into the administrative flunky, Judy.

"Good morning," I said politely, as I passed.

"Hi, Journey! Did you receive your location for today's training?" she asked with a smirk.

I wanted to smack the smirk off her face and drag her down the hallway by her hair, but I just smiled and said, "Yes, thank you," and kept going. These smug moments were things that I just didn't have time for.

I rode the elevator down to the ground floor and got into my car, ready to make the thirty-minute drive to Laurel, Maryland to host the training session of the day. As I drove, I allowed my mind to drift back to my morning with Devin. He was just so fine and the sex was good, but I knew that I was going to have to address Sunday's issues, among other things, and I didn't want to. I just wanted to exist in the bliss that was his embrace, his touch, and his kiss. I sighed to myself and tried to shift my thoughts to the training ahead.

When I arrived in Laurel, I was twenty minutes early and I strode calmly into the office facility and scanned my badge at the door. The receptionist smiled warmly at me as I passed her, and I smiled back complimenting her hair. She beamed at me as I got on the elevator and went to the classroom that would be my stage for the next six hours. The people poured in after about fifteen minutes, and I rose to greet them, directing the early birds to the refreshments in the back of the room, when someone lightly touched my elbow, making me turn around to see an old college friend.

"Hey, J! How are you?" he said, pulling me into a quick, tight hug.

"Hey! Travis Howard! Long time! How are you?" I squealed.

I had always called Travis by his full name, and his smile broadened exposing his perfect teeth as he shook his head at me. He kissed my cheek, and I spent a few minutes asking him about his post-college life. He was a private contractor for a company in California now, and he was going through their onboarding process.

I reminisced briefly about our conversations from our early twenties and the fun we used to have at Florida A&M University, when my alarm chimed to let me know that it was time to start the training session. I excused myself with a smile and called the class to order.

***

After the session was over, I spent a few minutes conversing with some of the attendees who wanted to ask more questions or request my card for future training engagements for their firms. Travis lingered in the back, conspicuously waiting for my undivided attention. When the last person left, he strode over to where I was collecting the remaining booklets for people who didn't show up to the training and getting my belongings together.

"What did you have planned for the rest of the day?" he asked.

"I'm finished for the day. What about you?"

"I don't have anything pressing going on. Want to catch up over happy hour?" he offered.

"Sure!" I said enthusiastically, "Did you have a place in mind, or should I recommend a place?"

"I'm open to whatever, as long as it's with you," he replied, smiling suggestively. He was beyond handsome, but I had more than enough to sort through. So, I decided not to take the bait he was dangling, but I agreed to meet him at a place that was near his hotel. I sent him the location in a text message and we walked out of the building together, chatting and laughing as we walked toward our separate cars.

After about thirty-five minutes of fighting D.C. rush hour traffic, I parked my car in a spot down the street from the Apple Lounge. The wind was strong, blowing some of my curls out of my bun and around my head, and I shivered slightly as my heels clicked purposefully through the gusts. I climbed the steps of the lounge and untied my hair, fluffing it out as I looked at my reflection in the window. The hostess came over to seat me, and I sank into the plush leather couch as I waited for Travis to arrive. The waitress sashayed my way, smiling pleasantly, and I ordered a glass of Pinot Noir and lounged, tapping my foot to the music playing in the background.

Travis strode in ten minutes later with a gust of wind, making his trench coat flare out a bit around the legs of his tailored blue suit. He looked around and I wiggled my fingers in the air at him when he looked my way. He smiled at me as he started in my direction, and I felt a strange flutter in my stomach like butterflies as he approached, but I wasn't sure why. I resisted the urge to let my gaze linger on him and allowed my glass to serve as a distraction as I stared into my it, swirling the wine gently before taking a sip. He sat closer to me than I expected, and I scooted away slightly to give him room, but he scooted closer, strategically closing the space between us as he leaned in to hug me with one arm. He cupped my right cheek gently as he kissed the other side, letting his fingers stroke my hair slightly upon release. Surprise flitted across my face briefly, but I fixed my expression before he could notice. We were close once, but I wasn't expecting his level of familiarity after having not seen each other for so long.

"So, Journey, what has it been, four years? I'm surprised you're not wifed up somewhere with kids by now."

I rolled my eyes playfully and offered a small smile as I ran my fingers through my hair to smooth the area he had touched back into place. I could tell he was on the hunt, but we both knew that I wasn't the desperate type and wouldn't be easily impressed by his behavior. Some things never change, no matter how many years passed or what my relationship status was.

"Everything in its own time," I replied casually. "I could say the same for you, though. What have you been waiting for? You're handsome and you seem to be doing pretty well for yourself. You mean to tell me that there's no beautiful woman and adorable kid waiting for you in Cali or something? I mean, if memory serves me correctly, you're quite the ladies' man."

"I've had my share of romances," he offered, "but I haven't found the one yet."

I raised my right eyebrow slightly, indicating that I thought he was full of it, and he laughed in response.

"Seriously, J, I have been burned a few times since we last saw one another. That's neither here nor there, though. I want to talk about you. How have you managed to slip through the fingers of any man with good sense?"

"Good sense is like common sense; it ain't always common, nor is it always good."

He chuckled as the waitress returned to take his order. She flirted with him a little, cutting her eyes at me now that there was an attractive man present.

"These chicks stay trying to get chose," I said after she was gone.

He seemed to be oblivious to my comment as he watched her switch away, admiring her long legs and her round behind in her tight, black leggings.

I laughed out loud. "Some things never change," I said, chiding him.

"What?" he asked innocently widening his eyes in my direction.

"You should just lick her next time she comes by," I laughed, "maybe she will give us free drinks or something. It seems to work when the ladies flirt with waiters and bartenders."

"Hey, man, if I wouldn't get smacked for trying, I just might," he snickered, "but I'd much rather enjoy my company with you."

"Yeah, yeah," I dismissed with a wave of my hand as I laughed, "tell me anything!" I was feeling more comfortable and I continued to tease him for staring at the waitress. "You've always been a sucker for a big butt and a smile."

"Journey!" he exclaimed, holding his hand over his heart dramatically. "I'm shocked by your opinion of me! I guess I have to do better at providing you with a sounder impression of the type of man I've become."

"Whatever, Travis," I admonished. "Stevie Wonder can see you haven't changed much!"

The waitress appeared with his drink and asked us if we wanted to order a hookah. We declined and she offered to refill my glass.

"Yes, please," I said politely, handing her my glass.

I leaned back into the couch a bit as I let one shoe slide off and wiggled my toes. Travis stared at my toes and his eyes met mine for a second as he licked his lips in a gesture that made my cheeks warm slightly. I slid my foot back into my shoe, thankful for the dim lighting.

"You have such pretty feet. Let me see."

It wasn't a request, and he didn't wait for me to comply as he reached down, cupping my ankle in his hands pulling my foot into his lap to appreciate my golden polished toes more closely. I tugged my skirt down as I adjusted my body on the couch, unsure of what the heck he was going to do. He stroked the arch of my foot gently, his thumbs warm against my cool skin. He pressed the ball of my foot firmly and squeezed my toes together, as his eyes drifted up my legs and body and met mine for a second. I stared at his hands as they moved to my heels and he kneaded them with his thumbs. I looked at his face as he pulled his bottom lip into his mouth and pressed his fingers into the top of my foot and his thumbs stroked the bottom. I gasped slightly as he applied a little more pressure and bit his lip.

"Can I be next?" the waitress asked, appearing at his side, watching us with a smirk on her pretty face.

I had no idea how long she had been watching, and I was suddenly conscious of all the other people in the room amid the lowered lights. I giggled slightly, embarrassed by my reaction and that this was even happening, as I slid my foot out of Travis's grasp and planted it firmly back in my shoe.

"Sorry, sweetheart, this is just for her," he replied sensually. She pulled her lips into a flirtatious pout and placed our drinks on the table.

"Well, let me know if you change your mind and you feel like sharing," she said as she walked away.

"Ummm… thank you," I muttered shyly to Travis.

My defenses were clearly lowered, and I rose awkwardly, tugging my pencil skirt back into place.

"Excuse me," I said as I strode around the table, so as not to have to squeeze past him, heading toward the ladies' room. I was more conscious than ever of his eyes on my ass as I walked away, and I watched him watching me in the mirror as I slipped into the restroom.

Thankfully, there was no line, and I stepped into a stall and locked the door behind me, exhaling deeply.

What the heck was that about? I thought as I wiggled my skirt up and my panties down, ignoring the clear moisture that was lingering in the seat of my panties. I used the bathroom quickly, wiping my underwear before pulling my panties back up and my skirt back down. When I stepped out of the stall to wash my hands, the waitress was standing in the mirror applying lipstick. She smiled at me as I dried my hands.

"You better get him before someone else does," she said boldly.

I changed the smile I had originally offered back to her into an exasperated eye roll as I walked out of the bathroom to join Travis on the couch again. He was scrolling through his phone when I approached, but he placed it on the table when I sat down and the smile returned to his face.

"Listen, Travis, I appreciate you coming out with me and all that, but I have to get going," I said as I reached for my purse to pay for my drinks.

I suddenly felt the need to get out of there, and fast. He placed his hand on top of mine to stop me.

"No worries, J. I apologize if I made you uncomfortable. Please just finish this glass with me, and I will walk you to your car," he urged. "Drinks are on me."

I hesitated for a beat before placing my purse back down with a sigh of concession. I picked up my glass and sipped my wine as an awkward silence fell between us.

"You may as well hand me your other foot so I can rub it, too. No sense in walking with one tense foot."

He held his hand out, beckoning at me to hand him my other foot. I smirked into my glass, and against my better judgement, I let him rub my other foot while I sipped my wine. This time he didn't bite his lip suggestively, but I sensed that his actions served him as much as they served me. When he was finished, my glass was empty, and he sipped the last of his drink as I put my coat on. Travis paid the waitress and we walked out of the lounge together. I ignored the waitress as she winked at me on the way out.

Outside, the wind wasn't blowing quite as hard, but Travis put his arm around me as we walked to my car in silence. I realized that my feet felt much less tense as we reached my car and he opened the door for me.

"Thank you for taking me out, Journey. I enjoyed your company, as usual, even though I made you feel a little uncomfortable. I apologize again, that wasn't my intention," he said as he hugged me warmly.

"It's okay, Travis. No harm done," I said as I returned his embrace and lowered myself into my driver's seat. "I suppose I just wasn't expecting it and I didn't know how to react, but you're very talented. You might have a bright future as a traveling masseuse," I laughed.

"You have no idea," he replied as he closed my door gently and took a step away from my car.

I shook my head, smiling slightly at his comment as I turned on the engine. He tapped on the window and I rolled it down.

"Can I call you sometime, J?"

"Sure. You have my number."

"All right," he said with a small smile. "Get home safely."

"You, too," I said as I rolled up my window and drove away.

I felt a sense of emotional unrest the entire drive home. I had so much stimulation to process between the amazing morning with Devin and happy hour with Travis. I knew I should chill, but my body was buzzing and tingling with relaxation from the foot massage.

I never should have let his fine ass touch me.

I scolded myself as I pulled into my parking spot, slightly surprised by how quickly I managed to get home with my mind on autopilot. When I walked into the apartment, Erica was lounging on the couch reading with Rico curled up next to her on the couch.

"Hey, Boo! I'm home!" I announced.

"Well, you're rather exuberant, aren't you?" she said dryly.

She didn't look up at me as she turned the page of her book. I caught a glimpse of the front cover and rolled my eyes exaggeratedly at her response as well as at the fact that she was reading one of those ridiculous romance novels again. Not a realistic love story. I could respect romance novels in general, but she was addicted to the ones with some muscled, half naked man and his buxom enchantress on the cover. It wouldn't matter so much if it wasn't for the fact that I had deduced that her lens on love and a lot of her behaviors in relationships seemed to be influenced by the books she enjoyed so much.

I took my shoes off at the door and hung my pea coat in the hall closet, not once responding to her little quip about my demeanor because I knew she was fishing for an opportunity to give me shit about this morning. I poured food into Rico's bowl, refreshed his water dish, and padded softly away to my room, closing the door behind me. I locked it, imagining that Erica heard the sound on the other side and looked after me with a surprised expression.

Musing to myself over that possibility, I unzipped my pencil skirt and stepped out of it, leaving it in the middle of the floor. I walked toward my bathroom while I shrugged off my cardigan and unbuttoned my blouse, leaving them both in a trail behind me. I stood in front of the mirror above my sink and stared at myself for a few minutes, assessing my brown eyes, lips, and ran my hand through my hair. I unhooked my bra and dropped it to the floor, examining my breasts and appreciating my reddish brown areolas as I caressed the soft skin, remembering Devin's hands and mouth on them earlier. I shivered a bit at the memory and stepped toward the tub, turning on the shower, stepping out of my panties and into the hot water. I inhaled the steam and exhaled the stress of my day as I slid on my yellow shower gloves and lathered the lightly fragrant soap into them.

I scrubbed myself as I reflected on the training session, smiling a bit as I thought of Travis and the way his smile left me feeling those delicious butterflies in my stomach. I rested my foot on the edge of the tub and flipped my hair to the side so that I could scrub my legs and feet. I rose and stepped back to let the hot water massage my scalp as I rinsed the soap off myself and the gloves, sliding them off and hanging them on the towel rack inside the tub. I took the shower head off the holster and directed the stream to my back and watched the ripples of soap rush off my honey brown skin and down the drain.

I adjusted the intensity of the water stream and turned the heat down a bit as I turned the shower head and directed the rhythmic water stream between my legs, opening them slightly as I leaned against the tile on the wall. The warm rhythm pulsed against my clitoris, and I arched my back slightly with pleasure. The water vibrated against me for a few minutes and ran down my legs. I sighed and bit my lip as the orgasm built and fluttered in my abdomen, exhaling a soft moan as I gyrated my hips lightly and gave into the rainbow-colored sensation that careened down my thighs to my calves and finally curled my toes. Panting lightly, I readjusted the shower head again to the soft stream that I used to bathe, and hung it back in the holster. I turned the water off and wrapped myself in a towel, stepping gingerly onto the bright green bath rug and patted myself dry, feeling sexy and delicious after a much needed release. I appreciated sexual encounters as much as the next woman, but it's just as important to know how to give yourself an orgasm as much as it is nice to share one with another person.

I unwrapped the towel from my still damp body and wrapped it around my head instead as I strutted my nakedness to my vanity where I kept my shea butter and carried it to my bed. I scooped some out and began smoothing it into my skin. I leaned back on the mattress as I lifted one leg into the air spreading the moisture into one foot, and then the other. I sat upright again and stood to select some pajamas out of my drawer when I heard my phone ding softly from somewhere on my bed. I ignored it as I slipped into a simple white t-shirt gown and walked to the bathroom to detangle the mass of hair that fell to my shoulders when I took off my towel. The phone dinged again as I applied curl cream, parted, and twisted my hair into four neatly sectioned ropes on my head and rinsed the remaining product off my hands.

I walked back to my bed and picked up my phone to find four text messages from Devin, and two from Travis. Travis let me know he had made it to his hotel safely and wanted to see me again on Wednesday for dinner, if I was free. I kneeled onto my bed and rolled over onto my back as I called Devin rather than respond to his many texts about how he had been missing me and thinking about me all day.

"Hey, Baby," he answered warmly, "I was just thinking about you."

I smiled a little, "Hey. How are you?"

"I'm great, now that I'm talking to you. How was your day?"

His southern accent drawled slightly, and I could tell by the sound of his voice that he was lying down as well.

"It was good. Long. I didn't hurt anyone in the office, although Judy was being her regular annoying self. Anyway," I said before he could inquire further, "we really need to talk about what happened this morning."

"I know," he groaned slightly, "I just had to see you and let you know that Angie and I aren't together. She just said that shit to piss you off, and you were so upset that I really didn't have the chance to explain before you left yesterday."

"Yeah, but she was trying to fight me, and you didn't seem to mind that either. That was a major violation, in my opinion, and after all the fucked up shit you said to me, I didn't really know what to think anymore."

"She wasn't going to hurt you, Baby, she was just being protective," Devin tried to explain.

"Protective? Of what? I hadn't done anything to hurt you, therefore you must have been speaking negatively about me while you were together at the funeral," I concluded.

"I apologize, Journey. I did tell her about your dream, and you have to admit that it's a rather jarring experience."

"Well, yes, but that doesn't justify her behavior one bit. Not to mention, you told me that it was over between us, and you said some pretty hurtful things to me as if I wanted to see your brother's demise. I've never even met him! Did it ever occur to you that I might have some feelings of fear or anything about witnessing it myself? I mean, I understand you were and are still grieving, and I am not trying to take that from you, but you were very hurtful toward me. This is who I am, Devin, and you can't vilify me every time the gift reveals itself."

"You're right, Baby. I'm sorry I hurt you. You tried to be there for me and I pushed you away . . ."

"And you let another woman disrespect and attack me in front of you."

"Yes," he said begrudgingly, "I was wrong. How can I make it right again?"

"I'm not sure that you can, Devin, and I never want to feel like that ever again. I know when I saw Tiffany's spirit and told you about it, you were freaked out, but this is different, and the way you treated me in this case was a little abusive. I don't have any room for that in my life right now. You caught me in a very vulnerable place this morning, for a plethora of reasons, and I just don't know whether we can come back from that. I think I need some time."

"I respect that. I don't like it, and I don't want to lose you, but I know that I was wrong. I really hope you can find it in your heart to forgive me," Devin said with remorse.

"That's the problem, I DO forgive you," I told him, "but I just don't know if this relationship is for me anymore. I need time."

"Well . . ." he exhaled softly, "I can't argue with that. Take the time you need, and I will do the same, and hopefully we can make this thing right again."

"Okay. Well, I'm going to go. I have to make dinner and finish some work from today's training. Maybe we can talk more later in the week."

"All right," he mumbled, "I will talk to you later. I love you, Journey."

I hesitated for a second and then said, "I love you, too, Devin. Good night."

"Good night."

I hung up quickly before he could say anything more that might make me retract my statements and find him in my bed for the second time today.

I bounced up off of my bed and passed the living room where Rico was still curled up on the couch, but Erica was no longer there with him. I entered the kitchen and began preparing the curry chicken that I had been marinating since last night, and boiled a pot of water for the couscous and another pot for collard greens.

2. Outside Looking In

I have walked the fiery road of anger and
indignance;
Swam   through the swamp of sadness, disbelief and
confusion.
Now I'm half flying, half falling into numbness,
And as the wind whips the tears from my face, stealing   my
breath away . . .
All I can wonder is what's beneath me, and whether
someone will be there to catch me,
Or at least be kind enough not to desecrate my broken
body when I land.

~ Olosunde

"One of these days Journey is going to wake up and see that she's wasting her time with that clown," I told Rico as I turned the page of my book.

I could hear her talking to Devin on the phone in her bedroom. I sighed and kissed my teeth. I couldn't understand why she didn't just drop his ass and go back to James. I remembered when I first met them at karaoke when we lived in Atlanta, and his very presence would make her shine like someone turned on all the lights on a Christmas tree. I tolerated the guys she tried to find happiness with after we left Atlanta, but no one was like him. She thought she had it all figured out, but I sincerely felt like she was just biding her time until he came back for her.

Devin seemed cool at first — helping us move, being handy, and putting furniture together and all that. He even passed the little test I created when I tried to see if he would be loyal in her absence on a trip to visit her family in Chicago. He didn't take the bait, but I still didn't think he was right for her. I couldn't directly put my finger on why, but even our other friend, Sydney, agreed with me. Who did Journey think she was fooling, with her, 'I need more time,' bit. I was itching for her to just let him go.

I got up off the sofa with irritation in my gait and went to my room when I heard her end her conversation with him. I didn't want to talk to her after the sexcapade I witnessed this morning, and I sensed that she didn't want to talk to me either. As I sank into my mattress and listened to her banging pots and pans in the kitchen, undoubtedly cooking dinner, my newest flavor called me on Skype. I rolled over to my open laptop and plugged the headphones into my ears.

"Hey, Chocolate Star!" he said sexily.

I loved his voice, and his lips just made me want to melt onto them, but I hated when men made pet names revolving around my complexion. I twisted my lips in disapproval and his grin widened, exposing that gap between his front teeth.

"What's up?" I asked without emotion.

"Damn, Baby, you and those breasts... I just want to come over and put my lips on 'em and lick those pretty ass nipples until they stand up for me."

I smirked a little. He knew how to get me going.

"Just my breasts?" I asked, slipping my shirt off seductively, showing my cream-colored bra that barely hid my nipples through the lace.

"Damn..." he mumbled in appreciation. "What time you want me to come over tonight?"

"I don't know," I told him, leaning back so he could get a better view of the girls. "If you come by soon, I might let you taste me while I ride your face."

He licked his lips as if he could already taste my juices filling his mouth, "I'm still at the job, but I get off soon. I gotta go slide some money to my son's mother, but then I'll be on my way."

"Don't make me wait too long," I warned. "If I fall asleep, the window will have closed on you for the night."

"Don't worry Baby, I will be over there tonight, and if you're asleep I'll give you a nice ride to wake up for."

He gestured to the half-mast erection building in the pants of his security uniform.

"You bring that on over here and I'll make a mess all over you and these sheets," I told him enticingly, "and I might even let you spend the night."

I heard another voice in his background and he told his partner he would be there in a minute.

"I gotta roll, beautiful, I'm gonna hit you later."

"All right. Bye." I hung up before he could say anything else, and went to take a shower and shave my legs.

When I got out of the shower, feeling like I could surf my soft skin off Darryl's lips, I wrapped my braids in a towel and squeezed out the water, and then pulled it off carefully, whipping them to the left and right a few times, letting them slide against my shoulders slightly. I hung the towel on the rack, and wiped the sink and toilet with a Clorox wipe while I let my skin air dry. I pulled the simple clear shower liner back into place thinking of how colorless my bathroom looked in comparison to Journey's. She had a green and bronze decorated bathroom, complete with pretty little silk ivy vines hanging over her mirror, and I didn't have any of that. I didn't see the point in decorating my bathroom like that. I mean why did people feel the need to extensively decorate the room that they used to shit, shower, and shave anyway? It seemed like a waste of time and money. I lay the small, white towel that I used as a shower mat across the side of the tub and put my toothbrush in the medicine cabinet.

I could smell the curry dish Journey was preparing and my mouth watered despite my desire to steer clear of her. She knew how to reel me in by my stomach, and I put my night shirt on and stepped out of my bedroom with nothing underneath to see if she was done cooking or not.

"Hey, Girl! I thought you were gone!" Journey said as she stirred the couscous.

"Nah, I was eavesdropping on the couch for a bit, then I went to take a shower," I responded, intentionally omitting the conversation with Darryl and that he would be paying me a visit later that evening.

Journey didn't like when I brought home people she didn't know, and I always felt like she was judging me when I chose to have a roll in the sack with someone new. I didn't have time for all her armchair therapist bullshit, although I knew she meant well.

"Well, your plate is almost ready, Boo, so don't go too far."

"All right," I muttered over my shoulder as I retreated to my room.

I scrolled through my social media accounts, liking photos of friends, memes, and statuses when my breath caught in my throat sharply. I lingered on the newest photo of my former best friend, Sabrina, and my ex, Angel, hugged up in a photo. They looked happy on a balcony someplace exotic and tropical. I thought of how years ago he refused to apply for his passport so he could travel with me, and the next photo showed them sharing a kiss as the ring on her engagement finger twinkled in the sunshine. The caption read, "The future Mrs. Harris," and I felt my heartbeat quicken as chunks rose in my throat. I rushed off to the bathroom, thankful that I had just cleaned my toilet, and let the chicken salad sandwich I'd eaten a few hours ago empty into the bowl before I had a chance to raise the seat. The strong smell of the bleach I poured in hours before made me wretch and gag as I held onto the sides of the seat. When I was finished, I wiped my mouth with a few squares of toilet paper and sat on the floor.

Journey tapped at my door, "Erica, are you okay?" I grimaced and spat into the toilet.

"I'm all right. I'll be out in a minute."

"Okay. I'll make you some tea."

I tossed the paper into the toilet, mad at her for her nurturing and her concern, as I pulled myself off the floor.

After a few minutes, I finally came out of my room and slumped into the dining room chair, sighing deeply.

"Are you okay?"

"I'm all right. I think I just ate something that didn't agree with me."

"What did you eat?" she asked with genuine concern furrowing her pretty, manicured eyebrows.

"Chicken salad sandwich," I answered. "I'll be fine."

She stared at me for a few minutes while I avoided her gaze and focused on steadying my breathing.

"Come here," she said approaching with one outstretched hand. "Let me touch you to see if you have a . . . "

"I said I'm all right, Journey! Damn! Give me some space! Shit!"

She stopped in her tracks, snatching her hand back as if I had burned her with my words.

"Okay . . ."

She hesitated a few seconds, still assessing me from where she stood before turning around and returning to preparing our plates.

"Do you think you'll be able to keep this down?"

I put my head in my hands and rubbed them down my face, inhaling and exhaling deeply.

"Yes," I said finally, "I can eat."

She set my plate down on the table in front of me and took her seat on the opposite side of the table. We ate in uncomfortable silence for a while.

"I know something happened," Journey said. Typical of her problem-solver self. "I understand if you don't want to talk about it yet, but I'm here for you, Erica."

I thought I would be able to ignore her, but the emotion rose in my chest and took over, "Why do they hate me so much?" I sobbed into my collard greens and couscous.

She stared at me, and I imagined the confusion on her face as I melted down, but I dared not look up at her.

"Who, Erica? What are you talking about? What happened?"

I looked up at her to find the very expression that I expected staring back at me.

"Sabrina and Angel are getting married," I wept pitifully. "I just don't understand why they did this to me. I loved him so much! She was supposed to be my best friend! How could they do this to me?"

Journey got up and walked over to the kitchen and poured two glasses of wine and sat back down, placing one in front of me, and sipping hers before resting her chin on her hand. The lip gloss she wore emphasized the dimple in her bottom lip as she pouted at me empathetically. She was quiet, waiting on me to continue. I wiped my eyes again and let out another deep sigh.

"Where did you hear about this?" she asked.

"I saw in on my timeline," I vented. They posted pictures of him proposing to her on some white ass, sandy fucking beach. He never wanted to travel before, but now all of a sudden, he finds it in himself to recreate the proposal I envisioned and told him about, for Sabrina of all people! Why? There has to be a special place in hell for people like them!"

She was silent as I continued to rant my envious word vomit into my plate, and I was glad. Journey tried to rescue me from myself by dragging me to D.C. after Angel had broken up with me for Sabrina. She had tried to help me cope for months after the breakup while we were still in Atlanta, but I kept going back and trying to fix things. She never said, "I told you so," no matter how many rejections I received in my efforts, and she never threw my weakness up in my face when I tried to use sex to make him choose me again, no matter how many times she tried to advise me otherwise.

The wine stung my throat as I swallowed it down quickly and I made a face, but Journey just refilled my glass and listened. There wasn't much she could say to heal this wound, and we both knew it, so instead she got up and pulled me out of my chair into a supportive embrace.

I hated hugs, but I let her hold me for a few minutes. I was holding back my tears by holding my breath until she stroked my back in a circle and squeezed me as she whispered, "Breathe..." into my ear softly. The dam of defiance and contempt I was holding broke and I wept into her shirt as she rocked me from side to side.

A knock at the door startled us, and we released each other. "Who is it?" she called.

"It's Darryl," came the voice from the other side of the door.

My eyes widened in panic, "Shit! I thought he wouldn't be here for at least another hour!"

"Who is Darryl?" she asked.

I waved my hands at her frantically, "He's a friend. Let him in, but… ummm… stall him a bit."

I pranced off to my bathroom to wash my face and get myself together. I didn't want him to see me like this, but I was definitely in need of some sexual healing now.

Journey sighed, "All right. But don't leave me out here with him for too long. You know how I feel about strange folks coming to our house."

I ignored her as I closed the door and turned on the cold water in my sink to try to lessen the puffiness of my eyes.

"Hello…" I heard her say cautiously, "Erica is in the bathroom, but you can come in and wait for her in the living room."

"Thanks," Darryl said. "You must be Journey,"

"Yes, I am. Ummm… would you like a glass of water or something?" Journey offered. "We have wine also."

"Nah, I don't really drink wine. I'm more of a dark liquor type of guy," Darryl said.

"Oh, well, all we have is water and wine, unless you'd like some tea."

"Water is fine. It sure smells good in here! What are you ladies eating?" Darryl sniffed the warm air.

"Curry chicken, collard greens, and couscous. There's plenty left if you'd like a plate," Journey said as she walked toward the kitchen.

"Maybe later."

"All right, well, have a seat and I'll get you some water. Erica can make you a plate later if you want it."

"Thanks," Darryl said as he settled onto the sofa.

"Not a problem," Journey said warmly.

I held a cold towel over my eyes as I listened to Journey trying to be hospitable, knowing she was internally freaking out, reading and processing his energy to establish just how uncomfortable she was with his presence, and how much saging she would be doing later, if at all. She was a trip with her empath issues. I took the towel off my eyes and saw that they were still a little puffy, but the redness was mostly gone.

"Journey!" I shouted through the closed door. "Can you come here a second?"

She slipped into the bathroom with me with alarm on her face, "What's the matter?"

"My eyes are all puffy and I don't know how to fix it!" I whispered in a slight panic.

"Did you try a cold compress?" she asked softly.

"Yes. What do I do?" I moaned, shaking my head.

She bit her lip as she thought, "I can get you some ice."

"Ugh! I don't even want him to be here now. Can you get rid of him?" I whined. "I don't want to answer any questions right now. I just want to be by myself."

"Ummm, I don't know him. What should I say?"

"I don't care, just get him out. Do something!" I urged.

"Ugh! Okay, Erica. I will try." She slipped back out into the living room.

"Hey Darryl, I don't think Erica is feeling well. She apologizes, but she ate something that upset her stomach and she says she's sorry, but she doesn't want to keep you waiting," Journey explained, thinking quickly on her feet.

I coughed and gagged loudly, pouring water from the cup on my sink into my toilet to make it sound like I was throwing up for decoration.

"See? Maybe you should go, I will have her call you later," Journey said as she handed Darryl his coat.

"Damn. That sucks. All right." I heard him get up and walk toward my bathroom door.

"I'm going to head out, Baby," he called, tapping on the door softly.

"Okay, Darryl. I will talk to you later," I called mournfully and poured more water into the toilet as I wretched and gagged again.

"Yuck," I heard him mutter, and I smiled to myself at our combined genius.

"Call me when you feel better, Erica. Take care of her, Journey. It was nice meeting you," Darryl said as he shrugged into his coat and turned toward the front door.

"You as well. Good night," Journey replied.

The front door opened and I heard Journey lock it behind him. She waited a few minutes before jerking the bathroom door open and cackling at me. I slid off the edge of the vanity where I was holding the towel to my face again.

"You still want some ice? Maybe some facial cream will help, too," Journey offered as she leaned against the doorframe.

"Nah, I don't have to impress anyone now," I said dryly. "I'm just glad he's gone."

"Well, come on outta here so we can binge watch our show," she said as she jerked her head toward the direction of the sofa.

"In a minute," I said, taking a cleansing breath.

"All right. Don't keep me waiting all night," she said.

"You will wait!" I joked.

"I will, but I don't have a problem watching without you!" she sang back at me as she closed the door.

About fifteen minutes later, I finally emerged and found Journey stretched out on the sofa with Rico resting on her belly, the television watching them as she was texting on her phone with a light smirk on her face.

"Don't tell me you're texting that deadbeat again," I huffed as I slumped into the chair. "I thought he was officially Black History."

"Nah," she said without looking up, "I'm talking to an old college friend I bumped into at work today. He was taking my onboarding class for the Wilson Company. You know, the one for compliance and security?"

"The one where the CEO cheats on his wife with the receptionist?"

"Yeah. Which is sad because I like her, and he always seems so happy when he's with his wife, but he flirts with anything with tits," Journey lamented.

"Men suck," I brooded, "can't trust any of them completely."

"I don't know about all men, but he's definitely a serial adulterer," she replied.

I turned my lips up into an expression of disgust.

"We watching our show or not?" I asked.

"Yes, Girl, hold on." She finished her text and propped herself up on the pillows, pushing Rico off of her. "Okay, let's go!"

We watched the next four episodes of our favorite vampire series, *True Blood*, and I woke up a few hours later to the, "Are you still watching?" alert on the screen. Journey was sound asleep, so I covered her with a blanket, and then I crept off to my bedroom and shut the door quietly. The clock read 11:32 as I crawled into my bed and pulled the covers up over my head.

***

When my alarm woke me, I hit the snooze button and I turned over on my side, curling up into a ball without closing my eyes. I reached for my cell phone and opened my social media account where the photo of Angel and Sabrina was still smiling about their new engagement. I didn't want to admit it, but I respected Journey's three-day process. I envied her ability to guard herself from those who would hurt her repeatedly. I sighed to myself as I reluctantly rolled out of bed. I could smell the coffee Journey was brewing in the kitchen, thankful that I knew she would prepare enough for us both, even though I didn't always drink it. I trudged to the bathroom to shower, stopping to pee and tie my hair into a pineapple on top of my head first.

I washed quickly and chose a sweater dress and leggings from my closet to wear, laying them across my bed as I rubbed lotion into my skin. I chose a chocolate brown bra and matching thong from my drawer and put them on, stretching the black leggings on and pulling the heather grey sweater dress over my head, adjusting the fabric over my breasts and then around my hips. I found my grey ankle booties with the wedge heels and put them on, zipping them up on the sides, and grabbed my purse on my way to the kitchen.

Rico stood up from his hiding place under the dining room table and looked as if he wanted to rub up against me.

"Don't you come over here, cat!" I said, stamping my foot at him.

He ran away toward Journey's door, looking back at me reproachfully. Journey opened the door to step out of her room as Rico darted past her at his first opportunity to escape into the safety of her bedroom. She looked after him and laughed, and then back at me.

"Good morning, Beautiful!" she chirped.

"Good morning," I replied without enthusiasm.

"I have to run, but there's coffee on the counter for you. I figured you'd need it as much as me this morning."

Her curls were loose and bouncing as she tugged a burnt orange blazer over a black pantsuit and adjusted an orange and gold necklace around her neck properly.

"You look cute today!" she offered.

I felt shitty although I didn't say so.

"Thanks. Do you think you can swing by the office to pick me up after work?" I asked, hoping she'd say yes.

"I can't, I'm meeting my friend right after work for dinner. If you want to tag along, I'm sure that will be fine. You can meet me in the city and ride home with me from there."

"Nah, I hate being a third wheel," I said, disappointed.

"You look great today, Girl! I'm sure you can find a handsome guy who will be happy to flirt with you at the bar. You don't have to sit with us, although you know you're always welcome," she encouraged.

"I'll think about it. If Jared isn't being a jerk towards his trusty administrative assistant and my mood improves, I just might."

"All right! Text me and let me know what you want to do."

She blew a kiss at me, grabbed her coat, coffee, and keys, and walked toward the door as she scooped her purse off the counter.

"Bye," I muttered.

I poured coffee into my travel cup, stirring in the sugar. I hated integrating my coffee, so I didn't add cream. I noticed the time, screwed on the lid, shrugged on my coat, and grabbed my bag and keys and headed to the train.

It was overcast and drizzling slightly as I walked to the train. I pulled up my hood as I stepped outside and headed to the train station behind our apartment, avoiding eye contact with the other people milling about as I paid my fare and rode the escalator down to the platform. The train pulled in about ten minutes later, and I pushed past the other passengers and sat in the first double seat I could find, setting my bag down next to me so no one else could sit there. I pulled my book out of my bag and began to read, allowing myself to become lost in a world where women were pursued and desired deeply, men were strong and handsome, love making was always passionate and vigorous, and endings were always happy.

Romance novels were my escape from the harshness of the real world where women were coveted as petty, aesthetic arm accessories, men were always conflicted liars who didn't do what they said they would, and you just never knew what to expect. I liked knowing what to expect from the characters, and I could always identify with the reckless abandon with which they loved. My grandmother used to collect romance novels, and she shared her rather impressive stock of them with me when I was a teenager. I used to store them under my bed when my mother sent me to live with my father, until he found them one day and destroyed them after beating me with the thickest ones until the spines were broken. Now I kept a collection of them in a trunk in my closet. If our apartment were on fire, they were the only thing I cared to save. I had repurchased most of the ones my grandmother had given to me, and even though they didn't smell like her, I still imagined what she thought or felt as she inhaled them, romancing each page like its own special little love story.

"Erica? Is that you?"

Upon hearing my name, I looked up from my page and into the face of Gary, the IT guy who worked across the hallway from the legal office I worked for. I didn't feel like smiling, but his smile was so sincere and the familiar feeling I got whenever he stood near me, like the ocean pulling the sand into the depths of the abyss with each wave, was so strong that the corners of my mouth turned up into a grin that was all his. I didn't smile like that for anyone, past or present, and I noted that I always had this reaction to him as I did so.

"Good morning, Gary. I didn't know you rode the train to work."

"Good morning. Yeah, I usually don't, but I'm having some car trouble right now, so I had to do what I had to do to get to work. You know how it is," he explained.

"I do," I said, still smiling. "Have a seat," I invited, moving my bag out of the seat beside me and onto the floor.

He sat down and reached for the bag, holding it in his lap along with his own.

"You shouldn't put your bag on the floor, Ms. Williams, it's filthy down there," Gary gently admonished.

I looked at him with surprise. Most men I knew didn't pay attention to things like germs on a train, or whether I put my bag on the floor or not. The fact that he was holding it in his lap didn't bother me the way it would have if he were someone else. I suddenly realized that I wanted to give him everything.

We talked easily all the way to our Foggy Bottom stop on the train, and I wondered why I had never given him the opportunity to converse with me previously. Maybe it was because I hated my boss so much that I was always more focused on getting in and out of the office than I was on building relationships with coworkers, or anyone else in the building for that matter. I learned that Gary was thirty, he had an adorable daughter named Michele, and that he was originally from Trinidad. He had a slight accent that I picked up on throughout our conversation as he got more comfortable, and I smiled a little bit every time I heard it. By the time we got to our floor in our building, we had exchanged numbers and he invited me to a bonfire shindig at his house that coming Friday.

As I sat at my desk, Jared walked over and offered a confused looking smile as he delivered the blue folder of tasks that he always put on my desk every morning.

"Good morning, Erica," Jared said. "You're looking pleasant today. How are you?"

"Good morning," I replied. "All is well. Why do you say that?"

"Well… you're smiling. I don't believe I've ever seen you crack a smile the entire time you've worked here."

"Really?" I said, looking over his shoulder at Gary who was waving at me through the glass window before walking into his office across the hall. I smiled at him without waving back, stating, "I never noticed."

He followed my gaze to the door closing behind Gary.

"Ooooh! You're checking someone out! I see! Well, whatever brings out that beautiful smile of yours is something I support fully. I could get used to it."

I straightened my face abruptly as I adjusted in my chair and looked at him.

"Well, don't get too used to it," I replied, rolling my eyes slightly and looking inside the folder. "What do you need from me today?"

"Take your time today, Erica. You can have that to me tomorrow."

He tapped my desk with his fingertips twice before walking away. I looked after him but said nothing more as my phone buzzed twice from my bag. I pulled it out and saw a text message from Gary that read, '*Have a fantastic day, Beautiful.*' I smiled again and slid the phone into the center drawer of my desk as I leaned back into my chair. Yes, perhaps today was going to be a fantastic day after all.

3. Journey of Seduction

How the day starts versus how the day finished . . .
How the beat builds versus how the hope's diminished . . .
I've got fire in one palm, and water in the other to
replenish.
What you do with either is your decision.
Your choice.
Whether you love or lose . . .
Or win this . . .

~ Olosunde

It had been a long day at work, but I was looking forward to seeing Travis for happy hour and dinner. As I parked my car in the parking garage and walked in the rain with my umbrella up, I was glad that my hair was natural and I didn't have to worry about it frizzing up or my hairstyle messing up. The hostess at the restaurant opened the door for me and asked me how many were in my party. I saw Travis waving me down from the table where he had been waiting. I thanked her and pointed to him in a gesture indicating that I had a seat waiting for me. She conceded politely and moved aside so I could join him. I walked toward him to the rhythm of an upbeat, hip-hop instrumental I didn't recognize.

"Hey!" I greeted breathlessly as I sat down, taking off my coat. "I'm sorry I was late, but traffic was horrendous!"

He stood up and hugged me warmly, kissing my cheek as I sat down on the sofa beside him. "It's all right. I ordered some calamari. I hope you like it."

"I love calamari," I replied.

The waitress arrived and we added a pitcher of sangria, empanadas, and salads with shrimp and avocado to our order. Travis leaned back in his seat and stared at me for a few minutes with a look that I had never seen from him, but one with which I was very familiar. He had something on his mind.

"What's up?" I asked him with a smile, as I rested my right elbow on the back of the sofa.

He had been texting me since we last saw each other and it was good to see him and hear his voice. The waitress returned with our order, giving him a minute or two to collect his thoughts.

"I'm just happy to see you again. I missed you a little bit."

He chuckled a little nervously and picked up his glass of sangria, sipping it as he looked off towards one of the televisions playing ESPN in the back, avoiding eye contact.

"Just a little bit?" I smirked as I touched his chin softly, gently encouraging him to focus on me.

"No. But that's all I'm going to say for right now."

He flashed a dimple at me and glanced away at the television again.

I reached over to his palm, resting on his knee, overturning it so that I could walk my fingertips up his hand toward his wrist. I circled the inside of his wrist a few times and watched him try to resist the sensation of my touch.

"I stalked your pictures on social media for a while today," I said. "I liked a few of them... they were pretty old, but I liked them anyway, rather shamelessly in fact."

"Shamelessly, huh?" he laughed, finally returning my gaze.

The eye lock made my cheeks burn and I bit my bottom lip slightly before smiling again. I toyed with my earring as I sipped my sangria.

"Yeah. I was thinking, 'let me find out that Travis had that whole Al B. Sure thing going on back in the day.'"

He laughed at me again and sipped his sangria as he turned his open hand over to return my touch, fingertips to fingertips.

"You're handsome now," I continued, "but 2009 to 2011 Travis was really cute."

"Is that right?"

He licked his bottom lip and grazed it with his perfect teeth as he looked at his fingertips caressing mine, and then back at me.

"Yes... I don't know if we could have been friends back then. I would have been flirting with you all the time."

I exhaled softly, feeling myself getting turned on.

"Well then, I would have been flirting right back," he said.

There was a hint of seduction in his tone as he held my gaze while continuing to stroke my hand with his fingertips.

"I can imagine that I would have made your fans mad."

"Not as mad as the women who saw you walk in and sit down after I was here waiting for you for a while."

"Really? Who?" I looked around for other women, "I didn't even see anyone looking at me when I walked in."

"It doesn't matter, love, I saw them." He said softly, turning my chin back toward him, "You're wearing that outfit, by the way."

"Thank you." I blushed, feeling a throbbing sensation stirring in my belly.

"The pleasure is all mine." He tilted his head to the side, "Do you still cook like you used to?" he asked.

"I do! I can't believe you remember me cooking for you!" I smiled.

"How could I possibly forget? You were walking around my house in that sundress, and a brother was thinking some thoughts."

He closed his eyes as if he were visualizing me in the past.

"What thoughts were you thinking?"

I giggled like a teenager and widened my eyes with curiosity.

"You were wearing that sundress! I could never forget."

"You're too much!" I giggled. "You've probably talked some poor, unsuspecting young woman out her sundress a time or two. You didn't even say anything that indicated that you were into me back then."

"Oh, I was into you." He nodded, "That's for *damn* sure. Like I said, I had some thoughts."

"What kind of thoughts?" I asked again, arching my eyebrow.

"I was thinking about you being in the kitchen in that sundress and you reaching up for a measuring cup that was just out of your grasp, and me walking up right behind you and whispering with my lips gently brushing on your ear, 'Let me get that for you,' knowing you couldn't reach it. In my mind, you eased off your tippy toes as the top of your ass and the small of your back slid down the front of my pelvis down to my top of my legs. Then I turned you around as I looked in your eyes, and I leaned in to kiss you, but not your lips. I kissed your cheek first, then your soft lips that I had been looking at since you walked in, followed by your collarbone . . . twice.

I didn't feel close enough, so I lifted you up on the counter and slid your dress to the tops of your thighs so I could get as close to you as possible. I kissed your lips, and then raised your dress to the top of your breasts. As I stared at the perfection that is your body, I kissed each rib, which led me to kiss that spot right below the tattoo on your right side that you only kiss when you're ready for a woman to put both of her legs over your shoulders so you can taste how sweet she is. I had been anticipating that since the moment you walked through the door strutting around in that sundress that hugged you so tightly. Maaaaan, I tell you what . . . " he trailed off.

I stared at him openmouthed for a few beats, blinking in astonishment. I didn't know what to say back, but his intentions were clear. He had been thinking about this for a long time, and I had practically forgotten the moment he recalled in such detail.

"Wow," I whispered finally, "I wasn't expecting that."

"What can I say, J, I'm full of surprises and if you'll let me, I promise I will make you feel like nobody else ever has. I've had a lot of time to think about it, and when I saw you yesterday, I just had to see you again. I know I was a little forward with that foot rub, but I enjoyed it as much as you did. I haven't stopped thinking about your sweet shea butter scent since then, and I just want more," Travis said earnestly.

"Is that the end of your thoughts, or was there more?" I asked, raising my eyebrow slightly.

"There was a bit more to tell," he said with a tilt to his head and a twinkle in his eye.

I took another sip of my sangria as he continued painting the picture of his thoughts.

"Since I could tell how wet you had become from the moisture on my beard, the rest of me wanted feel it as well. I pulled you down from the counter top and turned you around so I could finally see what had been covered by that striped sundress all morning. I kissed the back of your neck as I spread your legs just far enough that I could pull down my basketball shorts and softly rub the tip on the outside of your lips. Tempted by the moisture I could feel running down your thighs with my other hand, I slid the rest of me into you, only to hear a slight moan filled with the sexual tension that had been building for quite some time. As you arched your back leaning over the counter to invite me in deeper, I let you feel every inch of me as I slowly stroked you until I decided it was time to carry you off to the bedroom and continue something that I had been thinking about for years."

" Once in the bedroom, you pushed me down and climbed on top of me so I could see the tattoo on the small of your back. You grabbed me and sat up and proceeded to slide down my already soaked shaft, leaning over grabbing my shins and looking back, grinning at me, slowly grinding, giving me plenty of time to admire the ass that I thought was a work of perfection. I could imagine me just getting a chance to put two hands on it to bring you in close to kiss me," he finished.

"Wow," I said again, "you HAVE been thinking about that for a long time. You put a lot of imagination into that."

The waitress appeare with our entrees, and I used the excuse of her presence to slip off to the bathroom where, once alone, I leaned against the sink and let out a deep sigh that came from my soul. I was beyond speechless as I washed my hands and fluffed my curls, trying in vain to settle myself before I went back out to where Travis was waiting.

He was a problem waiting to happen, but I asked, "What would Erica do?" aloud to myself as I smiled at my reflection in the mirror and went back to join him.

4. Bittersweet

Alone doesn't equate lonely.
However, sometimes the loneliness of aloneness allows
those sneaky,   insidious voices to creep up against me.
Pressing into the curve of my shadow.
Placing a hazy hand that only I can see over my mouth.
Holding the other over my belly like a lover's embrace as
it whispers to me to listen.
I do.
In spite of my better judgment,
Because who am I to judge what the subconscious has to
say?
But now the voices are speaking every day,
and my smile is shrinking . . .
I am shrinking . . .
My light is shrinking . . .

~ Olosunde

I felt like I was spiraling out of control. I had lost my younger brother, and somehow managed to allow myself to destroy my relationship as a byproduct of my grief from that loss, and I didn't know who to turn to. Journey had a gift that she had been vulnerable enough to share with me, and what did I do? I fucked that up by blaming her for something that wasn't the least bit her fault.

***

I remembered the first time I met her. She was singing on stage at a restaurant on karaoke night, and I was with my friends watching a football game. Her hair flowed out of her head like a curly lion's mane and framed her face like a halo as she demanded the attention of nearly everyone in the room with her sweet voice. I don't even remember what the score was that night because of how captivated I was by watching her. She was enchanting, and I was completely disarmed by her smile when she walked off the stage, humbly accepting the applause of the other patrons in the restaurant. She had a mean walk to boot, so I remembered staring at her hips sway as she unintentionally enticed any man who saw her pass, yet she had a modesty about her that I didn't encounter often.

She wore blue jeans that hugged her behind, black boots, a black sweater that hung loosely behind her and offered the occasional peek-a-boo as she walked. I told myself I wasn't going to approach her, but then her friend, Erica, walked up to where my friends and I were sitting at the bar and struck up a conversation with my friend. She invited him to sit at their table to chat, and I took the opportunity to go with him. Journey had an irresistible glow about her that was working on me before she even looked up at me from her phone where her thumbs were working away at a text message.

When I slid into the seat next to her, she glanced up at me with alarm, her light brown eyes asking, "Who are you?" and at that moment I felt a feeling I had not felt since I was a teenager talking to a high school crush for the first time. The pupils of her eyes drew me in with the intensity of an event horizon, and I couldn't help but stare. Then she smiled, and I knew I needed to know her. We all talked easily until the restaurant closed, and I knew I couldn't let her leave without trying to speak to her and potentially see her again, so I gave her my phone number without asking for hers. I wanted her to want to talk to me, and to feel like she was in control.

For three days, I didn't hear from her, and then I bumped into her again at the hardware store as she was buying brackets and frames for mounting pictures at her apartment, and trying to determine the correct ones for what she needed. It had to be fate that she had all the wrong items, and we spent about twenty minutes finding the correct combinations of frames and brackets that she liked.

I offered to come over and help her hang the heavy frames, and she looked at me for a long time before smiling and agreeing. I followed her to her apartment in my car, and when I stepped in, there were boxes strategically placed like she was still unpacking from moving in. Her dresser was in pieces, her bed frame was put together, but the mattress wasn't on it yet, and yet somehow the place already seemed homey.

"I'm sorry for the mess. Erica and I just changed apartments to get more space and to move from beneath our old neighbor who was always loud," she explained.

"It's cool. If you want, I will help you put these furniture pieces together," I offered.

"Really?" she beamed. "I would really appreciate that. I mean, I have put my stuff together before, but this is a new piece from Ikea, and I just haven't had the time this week."

"I'd be happy to," I assured her.

"Thank you! I'm going to cook really quickly, and then I will come and help you."

"I don't need any help," I laughed, "I know my way around assembling some furniture. You go ahead and do what you need to do. I got this."

She stared at me for a few minutes, as if she was trying to determine whether I was sincere.

"Thank you, Devin." she said as she smiled and walked away to the kitchen.

She made me dinner that night and managed to unpack about three of her big boxes while I tightened her bed frame, put her mattress down, and hung her pictures. Around eleven o'clock, she was starting to look tired, so I told her to go to bed.

"You look like you're fading, Journey. Why don't you get yourself some rest?"

"I'm okay. I will wait for you to finish," she said.

I sensed the hesitation in her tone. She had good reason, considering that I was still basically a stranger, and she was already taking a risk by inviting me to her house to help her.

"Girl, I'm not going to bother you. Go on ahead and go to sleep. I'm off tomorrow, so I will just stay out here in the living room and put this together, and if it's okay with you, I will let myself out when I'm done. Just promise you'll call me tomorrow. You can even lock your bedroom door if that makes you feel safer."

She smiled again.

"That's really sweet," she said softly. "Okay, well, I will let you do that, but please don't stay up all night doing this. If you get tired, please take a break. If you want something more to eat, you can have whatever you like from the fridge. Erica is out on a date, but I will just let her know that you're here so she's not surprised if she comes home."

"Okay. Good night, Journey," I said as I waved her toward her bedroom.

"Good night."

She walked away and shut her bedroom door, locking it behind her. I turned my music on from my phone and worked for an hour or two putting her dresser together. It had glass slabs on the front and decorative handles that required a little bit of careful handling to get them in just right, but I finished.

I looked around and noticed she had shelves that needed to be put together, so I assembled those as well. When she woke up at about five o'clock, I was still working on them. She opened the door, rubbing her eyes sleepily.

"You're still here?" she asked in surprise.

"Yeah, but I'm almost done."

She looked around, noticing that I had assembled more than just the dresser, and looked back at me with wide eyes.

"You did all this?"

"I figured you could use some help," I replied.

"My goodness! I don't know how to thank you!" Her face lit up with a huge smile.

"Your reaction was thanks enough," I said, feeling tired, but satisfied.

"Did Erica ever come in?"

"Nah, she didn't. I guess she had a good date."

I laughed as I finished screwing the legs onto her couch and chairs, and stood up.

"Well, Miss Journey, I appreciate you letting me be of service to you. I'm finished now, so I think I will be going. Besides, you look like you need to get ready for work."

"Yes, I do. Well, please let me return your kindness. Let me cook dinner for you or take you out or something," she offered.

"That sounds like a plan. Give me a call and let me know what you'd like to do," I said, reaching up to the sky in a stretch.

"I will."

"Okay. Well, good morning. You have a good day."

I stood up and put on my coat, and kissed her cheek before letting myself out, looking back only to see her smile at me as I closed the door.

***

I blinked in the now as I shook off the memory of how I first met Journey and sipped the cold whiskey in my glass. I had been nursing several glasses most of the evening and resisting the urge to call her to apologize again. I wanted to show up at her place and ask her to talk, but she had asked for time and space, and my pride wouldn't allow me to risk rejection. I scrolled through her photos in my phone instead, as the sick feeling in my stomach increased. She was so beautiful and I had lost her. I tossed the phone on my bed and leaned farther back in my computer chair.

When the phone alerted a text message with a soft chime, I hopped up and dove for it, hoping it was her. It was Angie. I groaned and threw the phone back on the bed, slumping back into the chair. I didn't want to talk to her. She had potentially destroyed my happiness with her foolishness, and I had ripped her a new ass hole after my last conversation with Journey a few days before. We had been friends for a long time, and although we had had sex once before, I had no desire to be with Angie. She never liked any other woman I ever dated and always found a reason to have a problem with them, but Journey was different. I saw a future with her, and I had been looking at rings and thinking about proposing to her for a few weeks before my brother died. She made me a better man, but when things got complicated I threw that away.

I decided to go to the gym and sweat out some of my frustration, so I grabbed my gym bag and my keys and trudged out the door favoring a hoodie over my coat.

I had just finished a thirty-minute run on the track and was scrolling through a playlist on my phone, when my phone started ringing. It was a number I didn't recognize, but I answered it anyway.

"Hello?"

"Hey, Devin."

I recognized Erica's voice on the other end. "Hey, Erica, what's up? Is everything okay? Where's Journey?"

"She's fine. She's on a flight to Atlanta. I wanted to know if you were busy and if you'd come pick me up?"

"Oh, okay. Where are you?"

"I'm at the house."

I hesitated a minute, wondering how she got my number, then recalled that she had it from a previous situation when Journey was out of town and Erica was locked out of the apartment.

"I don't think that's appropriate. I'm not trying to get into it with Journey, and the last time I helped you out, you tried to come on to me."

"Well, you two aren't together now, so whatever happens, happens . . ."

"Nah, I'm good. You should probably just find another ride," I said as I wiped sweat from my forehead with a towel.

"That's real fucked up, Devin. You wouldn't want me to tell Journey about how you and I had that hot night while she was in Chicago."

"Yo, are you trying to blackmail me? That's shady as hell. You know damn well you came in from drinking with whoever you were out with and tried to climb into bed with me. I wouldn't touch you if you were butt naked in front of me. We aren't cool like that, either, so please don't call me again." I shook my head at her audacity.

"I hope Journey feels the same way," Erica threatened.

She hung up, and my heart raced. I hadn't told Journey about the incident before, and I didn't know what Erica's angle was, but she was always jealous of my relationship with Journey and would always talk shit about her behind her back. I called Journey, but she didn't answer.

Shit. She was probably still in the air.

I put my headphones back on and started doing reps at the lateral press machine, thinking about how I was going to do damage control. This shit could get ugly, and I needed to get in touch with Journey.

5. Don't Listen, Don't Speak

A quiet jealousy rushes through me.
I see it, but that's not who I want to be.
You crop me, store me, shelf me,
But your words are full of adoring.
Even if I tried,
I can't have or replace for you where you've been . . .
What you've seen.

~ Olosunde

I checked into my hotel in downtown Atlanta and rode the elevator up to the fifth floor. When I opened the door to my room, I took off my boots and jeans, happy to wiggle my toes and be free of the confines of those garments as I checked my phone. I texted Erica to let her know I was safe and sound, and ignored the voice message from Devin asking to talk.

It had been three months since our last conversation, and I wasn't in the mood to go back down that road with him where he would try to get me to rehash old issues and whatnot. It had been over for four months now, and I just preferred to let sleeping dogs lie. I couldn't understand why he felt the need to reach out now, and I wasn't trying to invest emotional energy trying to find out. It was a new year, and I had been dating Travis for a month. Things were going well, and I was in a good place. I texted Travis next to say I was in Atlanta, and then headed to the shower to wash off the day of travel.

One of my favorite parts about my job was the travel. I loved being able to connect with people in places outside of D.C., and inspire and educate them beyond the scope of what their companies paid me in the various trainings I provided. So many people would email me to tell me how much our conversations following training or the creative flair I brought to sessions helped them. I loved my job. My phone dinged and I saw Travis' message as I slipped into my pajamas.

What room are you in?

I smiled and responded to his text with the room number. Not five minutes later I heard a soft knock at the door. I opened it to find Travis standing on the other side holding a bouquet of calla lilies and wearing a smile on his handsome face. I melted inside as I smiled back, stepping aside to allow him in.

"What the heck are you doing here?" I asked, in slight shock.

"I know I have been busy and missing in action lately, so I reached out to your assistant, Brian, and he gave me the details of your itinerary. I had to bribe him heavily for about two weeks, and promise him that you wouldn't disrupt his internship before he gave me the information, but he helped me get to you," Travis explained.

"Oh, my gosh!" I exclaimed. "I wondered why he kept asking me questions about my plans outside of work on this trip. I thought he was just being attentive. He's so great!"

I took the flowers from Travis and filled a water pitcher to keep them in for the next few days. I felt a little nervous with Travis being there since we hadn't done much more than kiss and FaceTime in the past month. I was very particular about allowing myself time to heal between relationships. Whenever he was in town from San Diego, we would spend time together and go on dates, but our past friendship wasn't enough to get me into bed with him. I trusted him, but I had to be careful. I didn't want him to be my rebound or share myself with him before I truly felt like I was over things with Devin. Anytime things got too heavy, I would politely find a reason to leave, and I knew he knew why. The fact that he had put so much effort into finding out where I was and surprising me was working on me in a very real way.

"J, I know you have been dealing with letting that other dude go and all that, and I don't want to put pressure on you in any way, but I wanted to make it very clear to you that I'm not him, and I want to love you in the best way," he said while looking me directly in the eyes.

I blushed a little and sat down on the little sofa in my hotel room, pulling one of the throw pillows into my lap. He walked over and sat down next to me before cupping my face in his hands and kissing me. I kissed back hesitantly at first, clutching the pillow in my lap, until he pulled it from my hands and let it fall to the floor as he moved in closer and deepened the kiss. His lips touched my right and then my left cheek before moving to my neck. I arched my back and allowed him to wrap his arms around me, and I embraced him tightly as he lifted me off the couch and carried me to the king-sized bed, pulling back the duvet before laying me down.

Before I knew it, he was pulling off the baby t-shirt I planned to wear to bed. As he slipped it over my head, I continued to wonder if I was moving too fast, even though he did go through quite some trouble to find me, and I knew he was really into me. In the middle of my thoughts, I realized it was too late. Right before the shirt was over my head he stopped and started to kiss me on my lips. I could tell he had been wanting this for a while just by the way he kissed me. I brushed my hair out of my eyes so I could see again, and he had already moved down to my collarbone, licking a slow wet line down to my breasts. I moaned softly, which seemed to motivate him even more.

He proceeded down my stomach just as he had talked to me about before in his dream. I clenched my legs slightly and held them together because of the sensation I felt building between my thighs, only for him to part them and slide my pajama pants and boy shorts down at the same time, right down my ankles and over my feet. Before I knew it, I could feel his beard tickling my thighs, and his lips were kissing the lips that had been wet since he walked in the door with those damn flowers.

I exhaled and inhaled sharply as he bit my thigh, soothing the pain with his tongue. I clamored away from him toward the other side of the bed, but he gripped my leg and pulled me back toward him as I arched my back again with pleasure.

There was no sound except my heartbeat racing in my ears, and his lips wet from my wetness as he buried his face into me, his tongue doing gymnastics while I sighed and breathed his name and my hips found a rhythm that matched his. My fingertips found my mouth as I rolled my hips into the slow strokes of his tongue, and he reached up and pulled my hand from my mouth, placing it on the back of his head. My thighs shivered and I gasped, arching my back, resisting the desire to scoot away from him.

"Give me that, Baby," he murmured into my thigh before circling his tongue around the supple, sensitive flesh there until I clamped my legs shut over his ears. He didn't stop when I started to shiver and shake as the orgasm built and curled my toes.

Then it happened. I knew where this was headed, and I knew I wasn't ready, despite the orgasm that had just commenced. It was as if we were one mind thinking the same thing, and he lifted his head up, beard soaked, as he kissed my stomach, then my lips and cheek.

He looked at me and said, "I've been thinking about this since the moment I saw you, and we have plenty of time for the rest of the things I have planned for you; no need to rush anything, I'm not going anywhere anytime soon."

I smiled, kissed him again, and drifted off to sleep.

When I woke in the morning, Travis was holding me closely, and I reached over to turn off my alarm on the nightstand. I slid from underneath his arm and leg and stood up, stretching with a smile on my face as I watched him sleep peacefully. He stirred and opened his eyes briefly before rolling onto his back.

"Good morning, Beautiful," he said.

"Good morning, Love. How did you sleep?" I asked as I continued stretching.

"I had the best sleep I've had in a long time; especially since I was next to you," he said with a smile.

"Well, then I suppose we will have to do that more often," I whispered to him before tiptoeing off to the bathroom.

I washed quickly and brushed my teeth, humming softly to myself so as not to wake Travis. When I came out of the bathroom, my clothes were out my suitcase and the wrinkles were ironed out of the things I had forgotten to hang up the night before. My dark purple and grey pencil skirt and cream sweater were lying on the bed with my grey heels standing next to them.

"Awww! Thank you!" I exclaimed. "I appreciate you doing that!"

"I figured you could use a few additional minutes this morning."

I was already moisturized and wearing my underwear, and I only had to put on my pantyhose and get dressed while he brushed his teeth and showered. A few minutes later, he emerged from the shower, wearing only a towel and a grin.

Room service arrived at the door with a steaming bowl of oatmeal, toast, and a bowl of fruit for both of us. He brewed coffee for me in the hotel room's coffee maker and served it to me just the way I liked it while I enjoyed mouthfuls of the oatmeal.

"Thank you, love. That was really thoughtful of you."

"I just wanted to make your day starts off right," he said, "and breakfast is the most important meal of the day."

He smelled so good that it was hard for me to not want to pounce on him.

"Thank you," I blushed into my coffee. "What do you have planned for the day?"

"I have a meeting with a client at ten o'clock, but then I'm free to have lunch with you around two, if that's okay with you," he said after he chewed and swallowed a strawberry.

"That sounds fantastic!"

"Great, I will send an Uber to your training session, and I will meet you there."

"Okay!" I said enthusiastically.

I kissed him goodbye after I gathered my things and prepared to head out the door.

It was so hard to leave him and I just wanted to spend more time with him, but duty called and I went out to start my day.

The training went by quickly, and the attendees were eager to get out and have lunch. When I texted Travis to let him know I was done for the day and ready to meet him, the car didn't take long to arrive to take me to him.

We had lunch at the Sundial Café not far from where I was training, and I was impressed by his choice in location. We spent hours there laughing and talking about everything and nothing, and took a shuttle back to the hotel we were staying at for the next few days.

When we reached the door to our room, Travis pulled a silk scarf out of his pocket and a pair of Beats headphones out of his bag, dangling them in front of me with a mischievous grin.

"What's this?" I asked, my interest piqued.

"This is the start of a great night."

He wiggled his eyebrows at me knowingly and unlocked the door, revealing a trail of sunflower petals on the floor leading from the door of the room to the bed where a bucket of ice and chilled wine was waiting for us. He uncorked the bottle and poured me a glass, handing it to me. I sipped the wine and smiled at him.

"Wow! Somebody put some thought into what he wanted this evening," I observed.

"Proper planning promises positive performance," he said as he sipped from the glass he poured for himself.

I took a couple more sips before he took my glass from me, tying the blindfold over my eyes and sliding the headphones over my ears. I grinned and submitted to the element of surprise. Before he turned on the music, he instructed me not to take off the headphones or blindfold, no matter what happened. I was a little surprised by the command, but I said okay, silencing the small fearful voice inside.

He raised the blindfold and looked deep into my eyes and told me, "You are not in control of what is about to happen, sit back and relax, and let me handle this."

I coached myself that he wouldn't harm me, considered that maybe I should suggest a safe word, but I ultimately ignored all of that and nodded as he carefully pulled me out of my sweater and readjusted the headphones as he pressed play.

The first song was an old favorite, "Anytime, Anyplace" by Janet Jackson, and from then on, I had no idea what to expect. For a few seconds I felt nothing and just enjoyed the music, and then he kissed my lips. It startled me at first, but that passed quickly. He guided me onto my back, reached under my pencil skirt and began to massage my thighs in a soft, circular motion, and with everything drowned out around me, my remaining senses were in overdrive. There was a river flowing in my panties almost instantly, and I silently appreciated my healthy water intake. I could feel him pulling down my pencil skirt, pantyhose, and underwear, wiggling me slightly from side to side as he pulled the garments over my hips. He kissed the soles of my feet and I giggled softly at the sensation of his beard against them. With a soft, but firm touch, he caressed me up my ankles, calves, knees, and hips, stopping to spread his large hands out fully across my belly, kissing it as he rubbed his face against my hip bone. I responded with an encouraging, "Mmmmm." He trailed his tongue and lips to my navel and I struggled not to squirm away.

Unhooking my bra as he ran his fingers down the middle of my back, I shivered a bit, arching my back to give him room to unwrap me and kiss my cool flesh with his hands on my breasts. He stroked my waist and kissed my hips again while walking his fingertips down to my inner thigh. His fingers found their way down to the moisture collecting at the middle of my lips, spreading it from top to bottom, right before he slid one finger inside me, followed by another and curved his fingers up toward my g-spot as I moaned and bit my lip with pleasure. I then felt him part my legs wider, sliding his head down between them, where he let his tongue meet my clitoris. I flailed my arms and gripped the sheets briefly, grabbing his head to pull him in closer, but he held both of my wrists and removed them.

To prevent me from touching him and attempting to control anything again, he turned me over, and propped me up on my knees with my chest and head resting on the bed. Brushing my hair away from the back of my neck, he kissed and licked me there before tracing his tongue down my spine to my tail bone. I squirmed and writhed as he pulled back for a few beats. He resumed kissing me, first on my side, then my left butt cheek, and then the back of my right thigh as I trembled. He spread my cheeks and aimed his tongue directly inside of me. I grabbed the sheets, gasping sharply, twirling my hips onto his tongue as the orgasm built inside me. He pulled away and I felt nothing again for a few seconds until both of his knees brushed up behind me on the inside of my feet and he pulled me closer to the edge of the bed. I felt something warm and soft rubbing between the moisture on my lips, however, this time it wasn't his finger. It was the tip he had promised to rub on me in the kitchen scene he told me about.

I inhaled and grabbed at nothing, as I was blinded by the scarf. He pressed into me slowly, as far as he could, until my knees gave out and I collapsed prostrate onto the bed. He grabbed me by my hips and pulled me back into formation and began stroking me slowly while I breathed, moaned, and sighed his name with his movements. We found a rhythm and I dipped my spine to allow him more depth and space to maneuver. My mind was spiraling with the lack of sight and sound, but I was liking the way he was handling me. I began to rock my hips, bouncing back at him, and could faintly hear the wetness over the music as our bodies connected and separated again and again. I clutched at the blindfold in effort to remove it, and he paused in the backstroke to turn me onto my back and pull me toward him with his hands crooked under my knees.

He slightly lifted the headphones off my right ear. "I thought I told you that you are not in control," he breathed into my ear as he slid himself back inside me to the hilt.

I arched my back and dropped my head back in ecstasy. We continued at that pace as he slow stroked me at the edge of the bed, until he pulled out of me and guided me to the middle of the mattress where I could feel him position himself under me. Accordingly, I lifted my leg facing away from him, letting him slide under me, and then I lowered myself down. However, once I sat down, I didn't immediately let him slide in, I decided to tease him a bit. I sat on his shaft and bounced up and down slightly as the moisture allowed for no friction, stimulating my clit as he caressed his hands up and down my spine. I leaned forward slightly, unable to help myself anymore, as I rolled my hips and dropped down all the way with my hands on his knees. It was my opportunity to control this situation for once, and I was going to take full opportunity. Although I still couldn't see or hear, I knew this is what he wanted, and I was going to give it to him.

I tapped into my ancestral rhythm and primal desires as I rocked my hips harder, twirling in a circle on the upstroke, hearing only music and his manly moans that encouraged me. I felt him shiver a little and nudge my walls, and I knew that he was getting his. I rose to a squatting position on my feet and began to bounce softly at first, then harder and more determined as I felt him grip my hips and breathe in spasms into my hair that was now loosely falling into his face over my shoulder as I rode him in reverse, determined to return the pleasure and energy he had been giving me for what I assumed was the last hour or so. He held me tightly and I felt him release in ecstasy into the barrier that separated us. I didn't stop rocking and twirling my hips for him as I rode him, varying speed as his hands on my hips and thighs increased in intensity. It was feeling good to me, and I climaxed on top of him in a shuddering heap of sweat and strands of hair, dropping my back onto his chest as he held me close. We lay there with each other for a few minutes, engrossed in our own separate but equal pleasure. He stroked my belly with his fingertips like a guitar, and I climaxed again as I felt him pulsate inside me again and again with spasms from the pleasure that he had received as well as that he had given.

I rose up off him and pulled off the blindfold, intending to get a warm, wet towel from the bathroom, and noticed that the condom was no longer on him.

"Shit!" I exclaimed, dropping down onto my back beside him and reaching my fingers inside me to find the edge of the condom, but I couldn't reach it. With a panic-stricken countenance, he fished for it inside me also, but was equally unsuccessful. I pushed his hand away and hopped up, rushing to the bathroom. I squatted on the toilet for a few minutes, clenching and releasing my vaginal muscles until his seed oozed out of me and into the water with several faint plopping sounds. I finally reached the edge of the condom with my fingers and pulled the flaccid barrier out of me. It was filled with creamy, white semen, but the outside was still covered with it. Travis appeared at the bathroom door as I finally retrieved the condom with a slight look of alarm on his face. We both seemed to process the situation at the same time.

"Shit, J! I didn't know it was stuck. We need to get to the pharmacy fast for the Plan B pill."

Being that we were in Atlanta, neither of us knew where the nearest pharmacy was. We found one that was ten minutes away on the GPS of his phone, but it was after nine o' clock, so it was closed. I cringed internally and put my face in my hands, breathing into them as I tried to calm myself. All the pharmacies within thirty minutes of us were closed, and the one just outside our radius was out of the pill when we called them to see if they had any in stock. Travis rubbed his hands down his face in exasperation.

"I can't afford to have another kid, Journey," he murmured. "We have to handle this as soon as possible."

"Another?" I asked sitting cross-legged on the edge of the bed. "What do you mean another?"

"I have a son, and I'm not trying to have any more children right now, especially out of wedlock," he reluctantly explained.

I stared at him in disbelief, "The fuck you mean you have a son?" I asked, my voice rising in volume with every word.

"I have a son in San Francisco. He's three and lives there with his mother."

My mouth fell open in an 'O' and my brows knitted together as I realized he had lied to me months before when he said there was no woman and child waiting for him somewhere. I stared at him incredulously as my mouth opened and closed with panic reeling in my chest. What kind of shit was that to tell me now, of all things? I rubbed my feet and ankles as I sucked in deep breaths and tried to calm myself from the desire to slap the taste out of his mouth like I was his mother. After all this waiting and healing, this man had lied to me about having an entire child with another woman. *This can't be my life right now*, I told myself as I rocked back and forth

"You should go," I said to him finally.

"Journey, I'm sorry but — ,"

"You should go!" I repeated firmly, anger in my tone.

He sighed like a man defeated, and began to put his clothes back on silently.

"How could you keep something like that from me?" I stood, whipping my hair out of my face. I was getting loud, but I didn't care.

"I was going to tell you, but I . . . "

"Shut up! Just stop talking and get out!" I raged at him, my eyes welling up with tears. "Get dressed and go! You've been playing games with me this entire time! I trusted you, and now you pull this? After all I've been through, Travis?"

"I was going to tell you, J, I was just waiting for the right time."

"The right time? What kind of shit is that? I directly asked you if you had someone in California! That was clearly the right time! You lied to me!" I was getting louder and angrier by the word.

Travis pulled his shirt over his head and packed his belongings in silence. He opened the door to my hotel room.

"I know you're upset, but just give me a chance."

"A chance to deceive me more?"

"Baby, I love you. I've loved you for so long and I just didn't want to mess things up. I'm sorry. You've gotta believe me," he pleaded.

"No! Don't try to tell me what is and isn't now! You lied to me!"

I stood up, wrapping myself with the bed sheet, regardless of the fact that he had been caressing my skin for however long, and ushered him out the door. I didn't know whether he had a room in this hotel, but I needed him out of my space, stat.

When he was gone, I sat on my bed with my head in my hands for a few minutes grappling with my mind, fighting with all the orgasms that my body had just received over the time we had spent together.

"I could have kept my panties to myself for this shit," I said to myself, standing up to go to the bathroom to try to push more of him out of me.

After about thirty minutes of sitting on the toilet panicking internally, I logged onto my health care provider's website and scheduled an appointment for when I returned home. All I needed was to have a baby with a liar. I didn't throw shade at single moms, but that wasn't the life I envisioned for myself.

I got up and walked back over to the bed. I lay in the center of the mattress and wrapped myself up in the bedding and cried bitterly, feeling like I had taken three steps back from the place I had been in the three months prior. I fell asleep with the lights on and the television watching me, dreaming fitful dreams about babies who wanted a consistent daddy that would never arrive. I woke up several hours later and turned off the lights and an infomercial that was advertising a system for baldness, curling back up in the blankets as I inhaled the scent of Travis' cologne and drifted back to sleep.

When I woke up, I walked to the pharmacy nearest my hotel to buy the Plan B pill. They didn't have it, so I went to another one that was near my work site. I walked down the aisles, shamefully. I kept telling myself that these things happen to everyone, but I couldn't help but feel irresponsible and foolish. I found the magic pill that I hoped would ease my shameful emotions, grabbed a bottle of Figi water from the refrigerator, and erased my glorious indiscretions for a solid fifty-four seventy-nine. I was done with that, and I hoped I'd never lay eyes on Travis again.

***

When I returned to D.C., after my two weeks in Atlanta, I took an Über from the airport to my apartment. Erica was nowhere to be found, and I was happy for that since I could use the alone time. I refilled Rico's food and water dish and went to the bathroom to wash the day of travel off of me. After tying my hair into a pineapple on top of my head in a white satin scarf, I lay down in my bed, stroking Rico's soft golden fur and tickled his little white feet until he tired of my shenanigans and moved away from me to rest at the foot of my bed, purring me into a peaceful slumber.

When I woke in the morning, I opened the blinds and stared into the sunshine. It was a Saturday, and I was just thankful that I didn't have anything pressing to do. I flounced back onto my mattress, ignoring Rico's weight on my belly as he returned to demand attention. He kneaded my shirt with his front paws and rubbed his face up against my shoulder from his nose to the corners of his mouth, marking his territory as his eyelids lowered in contentment. I stroked the golden brown 'M' on his forehead with my fingertips and stroked his ears.

"In my next life, I want to be someone's pampered cat," I told him.

He licked the inside of my wrist with his rough tongue until I giggled and lifted him off me. I hadn't spoken to Travis in a week, and I didn't want to. I was feeling betrayed and foolish for trusting him in a way that I wouldn't have if he hadn't been someone with whom I was so familiar. I rolled over onto my belly and picked up my cell phone and listened to the voice messages from Devin that I had been avoiding for months, with my head resting on my arm. I closed my eyes in nostalgic appreciation at the sound of his voice.

There were eight messages, but the last three were more recent and he sounded stressed. I lifted my head sharply at the last one and replayed it, hearing urgency in Devin's tone as he asked me to call him immediately about Erica. My ears tingled and, instead of deleting the message as I had the last seven, I called him back.

"Hello?" he answered.

"Hey, Devin. What's up?"

"Yo, I need to talk to you about your girl," he said, sounding serious.

"Erica?"

"Yes, fucking Erica."

"What did she do?" I squeezed my eyes shut with dread.

He sighed a frustrated sigh, "J, remember what I told you she did when you were gone to Chicago?"

"Yeah," I said, unsure of where he was going, but I held my breath as a knot formed in my stomach, expecting the worst.

"She doesn't know that I told you about when she came on to me, and she's trying to threaten me with telling you. I just don't want you to think I tried to do anything with her."

"Devin, all other shit aside, I don't think that you came on to her," I assured him.

"Well, she called me while you were away last week and tried to threaten me with telling you that I tried to fuck, and I just don't want you to take that shit seriously. I was mad as hell."

"I would know if you did, Devin. I believe you."

He sighed and I imagined the vein pulsing in his neck the way it did when he got mad.

"Yeah, okay. I just don't want no shit."

"Tell me what happened."

I listened to him relate the story of her calling him again trying to rope him into picking her up, and how he thought it was another attempt to proposition him for sex in my absence, and my heart sank. I knew she was in serious need of some healing and that, aside from me, she had no one here to support her. I had ignored her previous foolishness with Devin because I knew he wasn't interested in her. Above all else, I knew she needed the stability that our situation provided. I didn't have the heart to put her out, as foolish as it seemed. Maybe my heart was too big— maybe I wore too many bright colors, but I didn't take offense to her behaviors or her trying to betray me because I had a soft spot for what she had been through in life.

"Thank you for letting me know," I told him finally.

"Watch your back, J. I know you think she's your friend, but I don't trust her. I can't tell you who to be Captain Save-a-Friend for, but watch her," Devin warned.

"Thanks," I told him.

"I'll talk to you later, Babe. I'm about to finish this next set in the gym."

"All right. You take care."

"You, too."

He hung up and I got up to scramble myself some eggs and eat some toast. I knew I needed to eat, but I was feeling queasy, and I didn't want to ruin my day by upsetting my stomach with heavier food. I scarfed down my light breakfast and followed it with some tea as I went into my room to put on some sweats and head to the gym in my complex.

I ran a mile on the treadmill, stretched a little, and then did some yoga with earbuds in my ears until I realized two hours had passed. I used the bathroom mirror in the gym to fix my hair back into the bun I had tied on top of my head, and put my jacket back on to walk back to my apartment. When I made it home and walked into my apartment, Erica was lounging on the couch with a man I had never seen before.

"Hey, Journey!" she exclaimed. She seemed strangely happy, but I didn't try to throw shade. Everyone deserved to be happy, in my opinion.

"Hey, Babe. Who is this?" I asked nodding toward her visitor.

"This is Gary. Gary, this is Journey, my roommate," Erica said, making introductions.

She trotted through the living room in a t-shirt and very short shorts. I nodded and waved, giving her a slightly judgmental eye slide as I walked away to my room. I never understood why she felt the need to bring every dude she liked home with her, but I didn't say anything as I closed my door, leaving the living room to her and her guest.

Halfway to my bathroom, I felt a sharp pain in my abdomen, strong enough for me to double over and hold the wall for balance. I tried to stand and another wave of pain overpowered me, causing me to sit down on the floor. I pressed my fingers into my belly for relief, bit my lip hard to redirect the pain, and crawled to the bathroom door. I felt dizzy as I tried to pull myself up the doorframe and stand upright.

Another wave of pain hit me, buckling my knees and I called out to Erica as I slid down the doorframe and blacked out.

When I opened my eyes, I was in a room with monitors and beeping all around. Disoriented and thirsty, I had no idea how long I had been there, or where "there" was, but I figured it was a hospital. Erica jumped up from a chair nearby when I stirred and I turned groggily to face her.

"Journey? Journey? Are you okay? How are you feeling?" she asked in a rush.

I licked my lips to answer her, but no sound came out. A woman in scrubs entered the room on my left, and I knew I was in a hospital.

"What happened?" I managed to ask Erica.

She walked to the side of the hospital bed, facing me to explain. "You fainted in your room, and I found you sprawled out on the floor. I called the ambulance and now you're in the hospital. We are waiting for a doctor to come and tell us something now. What happened?"

"She had an ectopic pregnancy," another voice announced. I looked toward the voice to see a woman in a white coat who was nearing the nurse checking the IV bag that was attached to me.

"Ectopic pregnancy! What the hell?" I heard Devin's voice and turned to look at him with earnest eyes in the chair in the corner of the room.

"Ms. Richards, when was the first day of your last menstrual cycle?" the doctor asked.

"January fifteenth," I muttered, feeling disoriented and dehydrated. "Am I okay?"

"You will be," she said blandly. "Your hCG levels are dropping and we managed to control the bleeding, so we may not have to perform surgery, but we are going to want to keep you for observation for a while after we give you an ultrasound to see how things are looking."

I licked my lips again, wearily scanning the room, taking note of the panic on the faces of Erica and Devin standing beside me.

"How long was I out?" I asked.

"Just a few hours. You're lucky, Ms. Richards. Some women end up in here knocking on death's door without even knowing they're pregnant. I'm going to ask you a few questions about your habits and whether you want us to notify anyone other than your roommate and your boyfriend here."

I took a deep breath, processing Devin's presence, as I recalled that I had listed him as an emergency contact on my medical benefits. He looked as scared as I felt. I spent the next half hour answering invasive questions about my most recent sexual encounter, explaining that I had taken the Plan B pill a week or so before. The attending nurse took notes of my statement and vitals, and both she and the doctor left me to rest with Erica and Devin by my side.

"Should I call Travis?" Erica asked, looking at Devin slightly, then back at me.

"No," I told her. "He isn't important now. I don't want him here."

I struggled to sit upright and Devin helped me as I attempted to get my bearings. The IV in my hand was itchy and uncomfortable as I pulled myself fully into a sitting position with his assistance. I was slightly embarrassed, and didn't want to look at the worried look in his eyes. He didn't ask me any questions or make any judgments. He seemed to be genuinely focused on my well-being, which made me feel worse for having avoided him for the past few months. I hung my head, avoiding his gaze, and looked at my wrist, focusing on the tube that connected to the bag of fluid hanging beside me.

A few hours passed, and Erica had gone home with her friend, Gary, but Devin stayed behind at the hospital with me. The night nurse came in to check on me, and she was pleasant and tried to make conversation.

"Good evening, Ms. Richards, how are you feeling?" she inquired.

"I've been better," I said unenthusiastically. "You can call me Journey."

"Journey, that's pretty."

"Thanks." I told her, "My mom loved to travel before she had me."

"Your mom? Have you spoken to her? Should we call her?" she asked.

"No," I scoffed, "she's been deceased for years now."

"Oh, I'm sorry to hear that," she replied.

"You didn't kill her, cancer did."

She looked at me for a second, and then squeezed my hand supportively before leaving a small container of pills and a glass of water by my bedside.

"What are these?" I asked.

"Methotrexate to help you pass the fetus, a multivitamin, and Ibuprofen," she listed.

I grimaced and swallowed the pills separately with several gulps of water.

"Let me know if you start to feel queasy, okay?"she said.

"Okay."

She walked out, leaving Devin and I alone with the sound of the faint beeps of the monitors around us, and the television playing something that neither of us were watching in the background.

"I didn't know your mother died," Devin said. "How come you never told me that?"

I sighed, "You spend enough time with people feeling sorry for you, and you just omit shit, I guess."

"Wow. J, we dated for almost a year, and I always wondered why you didn't talk about your parents. You have shown me pictures of your teenage and college years, but you never talked about your immediate family or your childhood. Why?"

"My father was abusive, and my mother left him when I was two years old after he hung her out of a window, threatening to drop her if she tried to take me away from him. She remarried a decent man and had another child, but my stepfather died in a car accident when I was ten and my younger brother was two. She developed cervical cancer two years later, and when she died, we were sent to live with my stepdad's brother, Felix, and his wife, Loretta.

He was a pedophile who abused me until I was sixteen. His wife pretended it wasn't happening, and probably because I wasn't related by blood, treated me as a burden. When I tried to speak out about it, I was put out. She eventually found me living with a friend and brought me back home. Part of me hoped things would change, but it didn't. I ran away to my friend's house again and ultimately Loretta sent me to live in a group home until I turned eighteen and could go to college.

I had decent grades in high school and was on the debate team, as you know, and I got a full ride to school. I did my best to keep good grades and make good decisions so I could keep my scholarship. My Aunt Loretta died a few years ago, and my brother is in college now, but he didn't have the same experience as I did, so he was glorified as the prodigal nephew, and we have been estranged for years. I've been on my own for a long time."

Devin sighed like he had been holding his breath the entire time. "Damn, J, that's deep. You might be one of the strongest women I know."

"I made a choice long ago not to let my past define my future, and not to look like what I've been through, no matter how hard things got."

"Thank you for sharing that with me," he said.

"I apologize that it took for us to break up for me to do so. I suppose I thought that if I was more open about it, you wouldn't view me the same way. I work hard not to illicit pity from others. The group home was my saving grace. If it weren't for the counselors and the connections I made, I might not be who I am today. I don't have room for feeling sorry for myself. I just have a greater arsenal of compassion for others as a result."

"Erica...," he whispered.

"Exactly. Please don't share what I've told you with anyone else."

"I wouldn't dare. I feel like I have seen you for the first time. "

***

When Devin finally gave in to my urging him to go home and get some rest and left, I sat with my eyes closed for a long time, trying in vain to find sleep. He had awakened some feelings and thoughts that I had successfully pushed into the black box of my mind for years. I tried everything, but I suppose that all the sleep I had earlier that day from the meds had thrown off my sleep cycle.

I decided to call my brother. The phone rang four times before he picked up, sounding like he was in a party.

"Hello? Journey, hold on! I'm going to go outside," he said loudly.

I waited silently as I heard the noise lessen and I assumed he was away from the noise.

"Hello?" he said again.

"Hey, Mikey."

"Journey! Hey! How are you big sis?"

"I'm okay," I lied. "I just wanted to check on you."

"I'm all good, just celebrating my homeboy's birthday," he said, sounding cheerful.

"Sounds like fun." I tried to sound upbeat, but I was failing.

"What's wrong? It's been months since I've spoken to you."

"Nothing, Baby. I just wanted to hear your voice."

The loneliness that hearing his voice created welled up in my chest, as a tear fell down my cheek.

"You're lying," he said after a long pause.

"I'm okay. Just not feeling well. I was missing my baby brother, is that a crime?" I flicked the tear away.

"No, but I know you, even though you keep yourself from me."

"You don't know nothing," I chided, "you just think you do."

"Yeah, okay. Hampton isn't too far away. I don't have a problem kicking somebody's ass about you if I need to."

I laughed a little. "That's sweet, but unnecessary. I just missed you."

"I miss you, too."

I covered my mouth as the sadness took over and I gave in to crying. I cleared my voice and forced myself to sound chipper.

"Well, okay, Baby, just call me when you have time. I know how the college life can be."

He was quiet a minute, no doubt processing my lies.

"Okay, Journey. I will hit you up tomorrow."

"All right."

"All right. Journey?"

"Yeah?"

"I love you."

"I love you, too."

I hung up the phone and let it fall on the bed beside me as I covered my face with my hands and cried. His childhood had been different from mine, and it just seemed wrong to corrupt his image of his uncle when he had given him so much. Families tended to love their sons and raise their daughters, and I hadn't been seen as a daughter in the house that loved him.

The nurse came back with the doctor in tow.

"Ms. Richards, you seem to be in good condition. We can't find the fetus in your ultrasound, so it must have passed. Everything looks good with your fallopian tubes and your uterus, and you will be able to carry a pregnancy to term in the future, whenever you're ready. We are going to be releasing you tomorrow if you can find someone to take you home."

"Really? That sounds great! I was worried I'd be laid up in here for the rest of the week. I hate hospitals," I said with relief.

"Well, we appreciate your faith in us, and someone will come by tomorrow and give you the necessary documents to release you. Please take care of yourself and don't hesitate to come back to us if you feel any pains or experience any bleeding."

She shook my hand and the nurse lingered to remove my IV. When she was gone and I had full range of my body without dragging a cord with me everywhere, I took a much needed shower, and lay down to sleep.

Devin arrived in the morning to collect me from the hospital, and I was so grateful that he had thought to stop by my apartment and gather an outfit and shoes so that I wouldn't have to go home in the same sweaty clothes I had come in.

We stopped at Bob and Edy's for breakfast before heading to my place, and I scarfed down chocolate chip pancakes, eggs, hash browns, and cheese grits. I felt like I hadn't eaten in forever after trying to stomach the food the hospital provided. He eyed me with a look of concern and was adamant about me taking the medicines that the doctor had prescribed before discharging me. I hated pharmaceuticals, so I argued with him, insisting that I didn't need the Ibuprofen any longer. We compromised on the antibiotics and the multi-vitamin, and I swallowed them with my coffee, opening my mouth and shifting my tongue from side to side to show that I had swallowed them. He laughed at me and stuffed his mouth with pancakes soaked in syrup.

"I've missed you, Woman."

I looked up from my coffee cup into his eyes, feeling a softness for him that I hadn't felt in a long time.

"I find it hard to admit, but I've missed you also. I'm sure the past few days have been hard for you, what with me being pregnant by some other guy."

"Nah, love. You're perfect in my eyes. You can do no wrong. You do so much for other people and hold space for other people's craziness, mine included. I was just worried that you weren't going to be okay. Now that I know you are, I'm hoping that we can at least discuss our differences and move on from them. If that turns into us getting back together, so be it. If not, I am man enough to respect it and still be here for you. I can't promise to be your most platonic friend, since I know you biblically," he laughed, "but I'm always here for you. You're everything to me, and I plan to make sure that you know it from here on out."

"That's a lot, Devin. I don't want your pity."

"Who said anything about pity? I love you, J. That's it."

"I guess."

"Well, let me reassure you until you know. Shit happens, J, and life ain't pretty, but your soul is the most beautiful I've seen in a long time."

I blushed and sipped my coffee, avoiding his eyes, but I felt that he was sincere.

When we were finished, he paid the waitress, and we left without speaking. I felt a silent appreciation for him, and although I didn't say so, I couldn't imagine a better person to support me through the process I had endured. He was much better than Erica or I had given him credit recently, and I felt a slight twinge of embarrassment for the way I spoke about him through his storm of losing his brother.

When I got home, Rico was all over me, and Erica was gone. Devin sat down on the sofa and let me get myself together for a while before stepping into my bedroom.

"Journey, ummm, I'm going to let you have some space. I want to stay, but I feel like I shouldn't out of respect to you and what you're dealing with."

"I would prefer you to stay, but I understand if you need to leave."

"I want to stay, but I know that I want more than what you're prepared to give right now," he explained.

"Fair enough. Well, I suppose I will see you later."

My heart ached to let him go, but I didn't want to have him there when he might be feeling something that I just didn't have room to process. He had already done a lot, and I didn't want to ask him for anything that I might not be willing to give him. I let him out and went back to my room to do some yoga and meditate. I had been through a lot in the last couple of days, and I needed to center myself in preparation for work the next day.

6. No HanD.C.uffs on My Heart

I won't get mad at you if you walk away.
How can I be when you're not here anyway?
You harden the soft spot I left for you . . .
                              ~ Olosunde

I loved her, and I yet I knew I couldn't obligate her to me. She had been through so much in a short time, and I could only imagine it was an effort to try to get over me. I felt shitty because things wouldn't have been that way if I hadn't mistreated her when my brother died.

Nobody would argue that I had the right to feel however I felt about that, but she deserved better. Journey was always bending over backward for others, and I felt a deep sense of protectiveness toward her after she told me about her own family. I never knew that the woman I loved so deeply had so much in common with me. When she saw Terrence's death, I didn't exactly blame her, but I've never known a woman with that gift since my grandmother passed. In my mind, gifts like that were reserved for the elderly, or the weirdos that I saw in solitary confinement at work who would slowly self-destruct with visions and messages from who knew where. I didn't readily expect or accept it coming from someone her age or with the type of life I expected a woman like her to have. Time and again, she proved herself to be different in so many ways.

On the other side, I felt a sense of what I could only describe as disappointment about her choosing not to share her childhood with me, although I knew I hadn't given her a reason to discuss that with me. I had selfishly rested my burdens on her since we had gotten close. She knew about my stepfather and his abuse. She knew about my promiscuity and the nearly two hundred women I had been with before her, yet she still embraced me with a sense of purity and nobility that made me feel like I was worthy of her love. I never knew that it came from the fact that she was dealing with her own demons and monsters under her own bed.

As I drove home from her place, I fought the urge to turn around and go spend the rest of the night holding her and letting her know that she was everything to me. She deserved that, but timing was everything, and now wasn't the right time. I knew she needed to process the experience with Travis.

Travis...

I didn't know who he was, and yet I couldn't be mad at any man who thought she was as amazing as I thought she was, but I definitely wanted to know what had happened there. I felt jealous of her pregnancy with him, although I knew I had no grounds to express that to her. I found myself imagining different details to the stories she had yet to tell, and I told myself that I would spend more time letting her share with me going forward. I didn't know where our relationship would ultimately lead, but I knew that she deserved to be vulnerable with someone and not feel like she had to wear her mask with me. I wanted her to know that it was okay to relax and let somebody take care of her sometimes, let her guard down and feel comfortable about doing so and know without a doubt that she had somebody there for her who would listen to her and protect her heart.

I threw my keys on the table and hung my fitted hat on the hook before dropping my weight into the leather sofa with my arms out at my sides, and taking a deep breath. The past twenty-four hours had been stressful, and I wasn't happy to be home. I wondered what Journey was doing. I picked up the remote and turned on the television where the Celtics were playing the Bulls, and watched for a few minutes without sincere interest. I got up off the couch and went to the bathroom to take off my clothes and have a shower.

When I was finished, I wiped the steam from the mirror with a dry towel and stared at myself in it, examining the tattoo on my chest. The "My Brother's Keeper" was still slightly red and healing across my heart as I rubbed ointment into the skin and went to find a t-shirt to put on. After stepping into my boxer briefs, I returned to the couch in time to catch the highlights of the Celtics game while I sipped a beer.

My phone was resting on the sofa beside me and began to vibrate with a phone call. I saw that it was Erica from the "Shady Bitch" notification on my screen. I didn't want to answer her, but I worried that something else was going on with Journey, so I picked up.

"Hello?" I answered warily.

"You need to get over here."

"Is something wrong with Journey?"

"No, Devin, there's something wrong with me. I'm feeling a little unable to keep our little encounter a secret any longer, and Journey is sitting on the couch looking so unaware that I might not be able to keep it to myself if you don't come stop me by giving me what I want."

"Listen, nothing happened between us. I don't know why you keep acting like it did, but you're clearly sick in the head. You need to chill," I demanded.

"Well, when she sees these pictures I have of us in bed together, I don't think she's going to believe that, so you better get here."

"Pictures? What pictures? Girl, I've never touched you! What's your problem? Why are you so determined to come between us? We aren't even together anymore," I exclaimed.

"Because you pose a threat, and you were supposed to be mine all along. You just don't know it. She stole you from me. I was watching you all that time and you got caught up in her light skin and long hair. I'm just as attractive as her, and I wanted you, but you can't make her happy. You can make me happy, though."

"Erica, I swear to God, I'm going to snatch the life out of you if you don't stop with these games!"

"Mmmm... I like it rough. See you soon, Devin." She hung up.

I punched the wall and came away with plaster on my fist. I had never had anything like this happen before, and I needed to fix this shit before it got any worse. I put on my sweatpants and a hoodie and drove back to Journey's house to set things straight.

I jumped out of my car at Journey's house with rage pulsating through my veins. What I wasn't going to allow was Erica to disrupt the peace I had worked to repair with Journey any longer. I pounded on the door three times like the police, and when it opened, I was surprised to see Journey. She looked confused, but she smiled at me.

"Did you forget something, Devin?"

"No! Tell that crazy bitch to come out here!" I pushed past her and into the kitchen, looking around like a canine seeking blood. "Erica! Bring your ass out here!" I commanded.

"Ummm, Devin, she's not here. What's going on?" She placed her hands on her hips, raising her eyebrow, and I could feel an attitude brewing in her.

"She called me again talking about she was going to tell you that we had sex. She claimed to have pictures of us in bed together!"

"Devin... I'm not sure what's really going on between you two, but I already know you didn't sleep with her, so unless you suddenly have an alternative story to tell, I think it's safe for you to calm down," she said.

"I'm sick of her shit, J! I don't like someone trying to accuse me of things I didn't do!" I proclaimed.

"Devin, please stop yelling. I know you're upset, but she's not even here. You're starting to freak me out."

I wiped my hands down my face and growled from a primal place inside.

"I'm sorry, J. I just lost it a little. Can I sit down for a minute?"

"Yeah, sure. Would you like some water? You're over here turning colors and whatnot. I think you need to get some rest."

"Yeah, you're probably right. She's just so crazy."

"It's okay. Have a seat, I'll get you some water."

I tried not to watch her walk away, but the jiggle going on under her nightgown had me staring hard. The arch in her back as she retrieved the glass from the cabinet drew me in, and the curve of her backside slayed me as the silhouette from the refrigerator light showed that there was little to nothing underneath. I cleared my throat and adjusted my sweatpants before having a seat on her sofa, telling myself to chill because now wasn't the time to be thinking such thoughts.

I avoided looking at her as she walked over with the water, trying to collect myself, when I heard a key in the door. Erica walked in and my heart began to beat faster as the rage I felt previously returned.

"Hey, Journey, Girl!"

She seemed to be drunk as she held the doorknob and rotated her hips to the music that nobody could hear but her.

"Hey, Erica. You seem... wasted," Journey said.

"I might be." She giggled and shut the door completely, before turning around as if she was just noticing my presence.

"Heeey Devin!" she said exaggeratedly, "How you doin?"

"I've had it with your shit, Erica. Stop calling me and texting me! We ain't cool, and your jealous ass is just trying to hurt Journey!"

"Hurt her? Why would I want to do that? She's my best friend! I love her!" She blew a kiss in Journey's direction, while Journey just looked on in silence.

"Show me the pictures, Erica. You keep calling me and talking shit, let's see what you have," I insisted.

"You mean these pictures?"

She pulled out her cell phone to reveal images of us lying in bed together with my arm around her. I balked and Journey's mouth opened as she saw the pictures also. I was confused and angry. I took the phone from her and threw it on the floor, cracking the screen. Erica giggled drunkenly until she fell on her butt on the floor. She continued to laugh as Journey and I looked back and forth from her to each other.

"Devin, what's happening?" Journey asked.

"I don't know, Journey! I swear I never laid a finger on her!" I insisted.

"These pictures would confirm that's a lie!" Erica continued to cackle from the floor.

"Erica, what did you do?" Journey demanded.

"I made it so you could see what a jerk he really is! You spent nearly a year getting close to a man who ain't shit and clearly doesn't love or respect you as much as you thought he did after I drugged him!" she confessed.

"Drugged him! Erica, why would you do that?"

"Why?" She pointed her finger at Journey and then me in accusation.

"Because your light skinned ass thinks you're better than everyone else." Swiveling toward me she said, "and you ignored me when I liked you because she has light skin and long hair! I'm so sick of people like you and your friends telling me that I'm 'pretty for a dark skinned girl' and I decided to make you pay for it."

Journey turned and looked at me with wide eyes, "Devin did you say that to her?"

"No! I didn't like her because she wasn't my type. I don't discriminate on complexion like that."

"Bullshit!" Erica exclaimed, pulling herself up and weaving from side to side as she held onto the kitchen island. "Your friend told me that shit on the night we met and I told him I was more interested in you. 'Devin doesn't really date dark skinned women,' he said. I was so insulted. You were supposed to be mine!"

"Erica, how many times have I told you that you have to stop with these color issues? We are all black, sweetie," Journey admonished.

"Fuck that! He didn't even look at me twice after he saw your ass!"

"Yes! Her ass is what I saw first, not her complexion! Sorry, Journey, I mean no disrespect," I said.

"None taken," Journey replied with a small smirk. "Erica, I think it's time you went to your room and sobered up. I'll bring you some water."

"I don't want any fucking water! You're always acting like you know everything and have all the answers! You don't know everything! You don't know what I go through looking the way I do!"

"Erica, I always tell you that you're beautiful, don't I? I can't make you believe it, but I don't think my relationship with Devin has anything to do with you not being a certain complexion."

"Fuck you, Journey! Since we've been friends, men always ask me about my 'pretty light skinned friend.' I'm so sick of that shit! He was supposed to be mine!" Erica shrieked.

"You need to get some serious help, Erica," I said. "Who drugs somebody to take pictures of them in their sleep? What did you give me anyway?"

"That's not important. I proved my point. I don't have time for this shit anymore. Journey, I'm moving out. I found another apartment, and I don't need your charity anymore! I can make it on my own," she declared.

She stumbled away to her room, leaving Journey and I looking after her long after she slammed her door shut and locked it. We heard her go to her bathroom and start vomiting.

"I'm so sorry, Devin," Journey apologized, "you've been saying that she was harassing you for a long time, and I didn't listen."

"It's okay, Baby. I know she was your friend, and this was a difficult situation for you, even more than me."

"That doesn't make it right, though. I should have taken your concerns seriously. Can you please find it in your heart to forgive me?"

Journey took a step in my direction, placing her right hand over her heart.

"I already have. I'm going to go. That was a lot to deal with, and I have a headache now."

I grabbed my keys from her counter and started for the door, but she blocked my path.

"Wait... Devin, will you please come meet me tomorrow after work? I want to make this up to you. Let me buy you dinner or something."

I smiled at her and touched her cheek softly, cupping her chin before kissing the corner of her mouth, avoiding her dimpled bottom lip.

"Whatever makes you happy, Baby."

I walked out of the apartment and down the hall, torn between being furious at Erica, and hopeful for any possibility to repair things with Journey. Everything happens for a reason, right?

7. To Err is Human, To Forgive is Divine

It's sad when you want to save someone you love,
But watching them self-destruct is like watching an
airplane crash from a distance,
In slow motion.
When you find them, they're so far down in their dark,
miserable hell,
That they can't see the rope you're swinging above.
~ Olosunde

I went to bed with my mind swirling and asking questions that may never receive answers. How could Erica do something like that to Devin? It seemed almost laughable, but she had been targeting him for her sick vindication for months, and I wondered about all the things I ever shared with her in the past about him and any other man I dated. How many times had she done this? How long had she been tormenting herself about the one thing she couldn't really change? How much had I contributed to her ultimate unraveling? I wanted to be angry with her, but I could only find a sense of pity. I was glad the truth was out and I felt a slight relief that she decided to move out, or so she said. I wondered who in the unseen world I had pissed off to be experiencing so many tumultuous relationships all at once. It literally felt like my world was unraveling, and I no longer knew who to trust.

I pulled Rico in close to me, holding him as I drifted off to sleep. I dreamt a dream that I hadn't had in a long time. I was floating, prostrate in the air through what appeared to be a starry sky. My grandmother's necklace came unclasped from my neck, and fell below me as it created ripples in the stars, which let me know I was floating over water that reflected a star-filled sky. My body began to turn from the prostrate position to an upright, standing position as I floated. A warm glow began in my abdomen, swelling and pulsating steadily inside me as I hovered over the water. It was as if I was the sun itself, bringing dawn over the water. Soon, the light was nearly as big as my entire body, and I hovered in the center, allowing the light to radiate through me as morning light kissed the surface of the water beneath me, illuminating mountains and grassy plains in the distance. My light glinted off something triangular in the distance that looked like a pyramid, and the reflection touched me, making me spasm and quake as the light came out of my mouth, ears, eyes, hands, feet, and the top of my head. A strange, unfamiliar chord rang out of me, mixed with a scream, and echoed off the surface of the water and the landforms around me and I was so amazed by the brilliance that my body couldn't handle it.

I flashed into blackness, stillness caressing me all over with a sublime peace I had never felt in my life. I felt like I was sleeping, but when I opened my eyes, I was lying on what appeared to be cool, glinting sand. I stood, looking around at enormous sand dunes whipped into pointed hills by a wind that I didn't feel. It wasn't hot, yet there was something like a twinkling sun glinting overhead.

"You are the sun," I heard a strange voice whisper to me.

I dusted the sand off my white skirt, lifting it slightly to reveal pretty, jeweled beads secured from my big toes and strung around my ankles like thong sandals. There was a leather strap hanging from my waist, fastening a leather water gourd to it. I wasn't thirsty, but I opened the gourd and looked inside, finding it empty. I stretched my arms, letting the sand fall from the sleeves of my white blouse, before walking toward a small plateau in the distance.

After what felt like hours, I reached the plateau, and a soft wind blew past me.

"Time is of no consequence here," it sighed as it beckoned me from the bottom in a swirl of sand.

I squinted my eyes as sand shimmered like diamonds in the small gust. I climbed the plateau slowly, appreciating the soft grass that protected me from rocks bleached white and rounded into smoothness over time unmeasured. When I reached the top, I found a grassy field and a fountain that poured its water into a pool. I bent to admire flowers of a species and hue I had never seen before, but as I reached out my fingers to touch them gingerly, my hands passed through them as if they were merely composed of light and energy, like a hologram. Curious, I approached the fountain as I had when dreamed this before, and uncorked the gourd hanging at my hips, lowering it into coolness that wasn't wet, but was the most brilliant blue that I could have ever imagined. My gourd swelled and I lifted it out again, finding no moisture on the outside or on my hand. I lifted my gaze to see the pyramidal structure before me in the center of the grassy surface of the plateau, guarded by two majestic-looking lions resting peacefully outside the entrance.

I approached the pyramid slowly, with respect for the lions guarding it, but without fear in my heart. When I reached them, I squatted down, stretching my arms out in front of me as they yawned and rose to lope in my direction. I unscrewed my gourd, amazed to find water in it, as I poured a little into my hand. The lions lapped at it thirstily, and I poured more, somehow knowing that this was my payment for safe passage into the pyramid. When the water was finished, the two lions rubbed their faces against my hands and then each other, finally resting on their haunches with bowed heads, as if to say, "You may enter."

I stroked the tawny mane of one lion as I passed him, continuing slowly through the dark doorway. There was no sound or light at first, as I used my hands to guide me through the darkness. I felt a slight twinge of fear and uncertainty tugging at my subconscious as I groped along until I saw a faint purplish light flickering in the distance. I followed the light carefully until I reached a great room with five chairs that looked like thrones lining the walls. In the center of the room was a large table with a huge, pointed amethyst crystal in the center. I noticed there were mirrors at the head of each throne as I approached the table to examine the crystal.

I touched the pointed tip of the crystal, and it began to glow with a warm purple light. I snatched my fingers away as it spun slowly, then picked up speed as I watched. I felt like I was being hypnotized by the stone as it began to rise up off the table, increasing in speed and the glow gaining intensity. Faster and faster it spun, the glowing light becoming too bright to look at, until there was a loud whooshing sound followed by a bright purple flash of light, and I heard several voices that were layered in a melodic chord all singing at once. After a few seconds, they settled into one.

"Daughter, sister, mother, friend, here you are. We meet again."

I blinked as I tried to gain focus on the images in white robes seated on the five thrones. They were hazy and unclear, but their voices were one layered melody as they spoke in unison.

"You are the princess, but you must crown yourself queen. You have been given the gift of sight and knowing, but you have not yet learned to trust it.

We are your mothers and are with you, always, but you must be obedient. This is your destiny. Turn and see."

I turned my back to the thrones and saw an image of myself before me, dressed in a beautiful white dress with a crown atop my head. Before my eyes, my hair grew like a curtain of curls from my head and then wove into the base of the crown with invisible hands until it was all in place on top of the crown. The voices spoke again.

"You are fortified with knowing, and your responsibility is great. Maintain a gentle character and a soft tongue. Go forth with your gifts and heal. It is through healing others that you shall prosper. It is time."

There was another bright flash of light, and they were gone as mysteriously as they had come. I stood openmouthed, with a great sense of responsibility weighing in my chest like I had never known. I exited the pyramidal structure easily as there was a lighted path now, and I could see words on the wall that read, "*Discipline is freedom. Knowing is the light.*"

When I stood outside again, one lion remained. I didn't know where the other had gone, but the one who lingered padded softly over to me and bowed his head, touching his wet nose to my feet as he licked them with his rough tongue. When he looked me in the eyes again, I noticed they had a familiar roundness and an amber, green tint to them like Rico's. He turned around and planted his bottom on the ground, turning around on his haunches to look at me as if telling me to climb on. I did so, and he rose with me on his back, and began to descend the plateau. As he carried me, purring, I felt a great sense of sleepiness and I leaned my head into his mane, stroking it the way I would Rico's fur. I slipped into a peaceful slumber as he carried me across the sand until the day became night.

When I awoke, Rico was nowhere in my bed, and I felt rested and empowered to begin my day. I came out of my bedroom dressed in a white pantsuit, golden belt and shoes, and ready to walk out the door a little earlier than normal. It was intentional, as I didn't want to see Erica or start my day with any of her negative bullshit. I realized that I was always accommodating her as much as she hated that I accommodated Devin and anyone else. For the first time, I wondered if it bothered her because my accommodating and holding space for others meant that I wasn't doing so for her, and she craved my attention like a child who felt that any amount of attention, good or bad, was better than none at all.

I skipped the coffee and breakfast routine that I was accustomed to, grabbed my purse and keys, and walked out the door. I went down the steps of my building to the leasing office to discuss transitioning to a one bedroom apartment, and saw the last person I expected to see there.

"Carlos?"

"Journey! What are you doing here?"

"I live here," I said laughing. "What are YOU doing here?"

"I just signed my lease. I'm about to move into one of the one bedroom lofts today," he explained.

"A loft, huh? That sounds snazzy! I'm actually thinking about changing my apartment from a two bedroom to a one bedroom also."

"Really? I thought you and Erica were roommates," he said, looking puzzled.

I made a face, turning my lips up in response, but said nothing more.

"I see," he said, "trouble among friends, huh?"

"You could say that. I'm not in the mood to talk about it right now," I responded.

"Understood. Well, you have my number. If you decide you'd like to come by or whatever, just let me know."

"Thank you. I will keep you in mind, new neighbor. Welcome to the community."

"Thanks! I'll catch you later," he said with a smile.

"Later."

He kissed my cheek in a quick embrace, and walked away.

I found the agent sitting at her desk sipping her coffee while staring into her computer screen. I tapped the door frame, so as not to scare her, and she looked up and smiled brightly.

"Ms. Richards! Good morning! How can I help you today?"

"Good morning, Ms. Jones."

"Please, call me Yasmin!"

"Yasmin, I know I just came here less than a year ago to transition from my first two bedroom unit to another with Erica, but I have reason to believe that she will be moving out soon. I came by to see about downsizing to a one bedroom unit, rather than paying a fee to break my lease."

"Oh! Hmmm, okay, let me see what I have here." She turned to her computer screen and began opening my file and looking at available units.

"I have you in a twelve hundred square foot unit right now. There is a nine-hundred and sixty square foot, one bedroom apartment available at the end of the month, another similar unit available at the start of March, and a one thousand twenty square foot lofted unit in another building that is open at the end of this week. When were you looking to move, and which would you like to see?"

"I don't mind moving as soon as possible, but I'm open to seeing all three."

"Well, the units that are available at the end of this month and in March aren't empty yet, but I would be happy to show you the models. The loft is open now. Would you like to see that one?" she offered.

"Absolutely. Thank you!"

"My pleasure, sweetie. I just need your driver license and we can head out as soon as I get the keys."

I handed her my license from my wallet and sat in the chair on the other side of her desk to wait for her as she exited her office to get the keys.

When she came back, keys in hand, we walked out into the cold air and to the newer building with the lofts. I smiled at the smell of the newness and the artsy décor in the lobby.

"This unit is on the fifth floor, which is at the top of the building," Yasmin explained. "There's a private pool on the balcony with an entertainment center on the other side. If you want to rent it out for small parties, you just let the leasing office know, and we will give you the keys to it. Access is included in your amenities fee for residents in this building, but all other residents have to pay a fee."

She unlocked the door to unit 515W and I noted the repetitive number five as I recalled my dream of the five women. As the door swung open, I was met with shining wooden floors, high ceilings, and all the sunlight I could ever desire. I gasped and smiled with appreciation, stepping past her into the space. There were granite countertops and stainless steel fixtures in the kitchen, a mosaic backsplash behind a gas stove with six burners. The chef in me squealed a bit as I walked my fingertips along the cool, hard surface of the granite.

"There is a full master bathroom in the bedroom, and a half bathroom accessible from the living area. The balcony has a retractable awning for shade or sun, and there is a bookshelf built into the wall in the living room."

Yasmin narrated from the kitchen as I roamed around the loft.

She said, "You'll find an operating fireplace and a staircase that leads to an open office space upstairs. The bedroom itself isn't too different from what you already have in your own master bedroom in your apartment, except there is more closet space in place of the vanity."

I nodded silently, mentally decorating the space.

"How much is this unit?" I asked.

"It's the same as what you're paying for your two bedroom unit," she stated.

I nodded again. "I really like this, Yasmin! I don't want to see the other models. I will take this one."

"Fantastic! In that case, let's head back to my office and draft up your new lease. Oh! You can also sign a two year lease for a cheaper cost, and that will lock in your monthly rental fee for that two year time frame."

"I love it! Let's go!"

Yasmin grinned and we left the loft together as I rattled on about how I was excited to move now.

Back in the leasing office, I signed the roommate release forms and the new leasing agreement, thankful I didn't have to pay another fee since I already lived there.

"You'll have to get Erica's signature on the release form for when she vacates the property so you won't have any responsibility for damages to the unit after you move out. Another agent or I will do a walk-through of the unit you're already in, whenever you're ready, to assess the condition of the place, and you can just schedule that appointment at your convenience. Would you like me to email the release form to Erica, or would you like to get her signature yourself?"

"You can email it to her. She's an adult. She doesn't need me to handle her business for her."

Yasmin paused and looked at me for a second.

"Did something happen between you two? I know that you're really good friends from the amount of time you've been here. I don't mean to pry, and I know it's none of my business, but I'm just curious."

"We are parting ways for ethical differences, and I no longer consider her a friend," I said with as little emotion as possible.

"I'm so sorry! Well, best of luck to you, Journey! I won't ask any more questions."

She handed me a yellow envelope with all the documents inside, and walked around her desk to wrap me in a kind embrace.

"Have a fantastic rest of your day, and thank you for being a part of our community!"

"Thanks, Yasmin!" I said squeezing her back. "By any chance, do you know what unit that guy, Carlos, is moving into? He's a familiar face, and we might bump into each other from time to time."

"Oh! Yeah, he's cute, isn't he?" she said.

"He is!" I laughed.

"He's actually on the other side of your floor in 515E. Your unit faces the sunset and his faces the sunrise." She winked at me and shook my hand.

"Come by on Friday and I will give you the keys to your new unit so you can move over the weekend, okay?"

"Okay, great! Thanks for everything, Yasmin!"

I left the leasing office and went back to my building where my car was parked so I could grab some breakfast and coffee somewhere on my way to work.

As I pulled out of the parking garage, I saw a call come in from Erica, but I declined it and continued to listen to music instead. I hadn't been good at establishing boundaries with her up until now, but today was a new day, and I didn't have to show up to every fight to which I was invited. We were done as friends as far as I was concerned.

I didn't have any appointments that day, so instead of setting up new sessions or following up on the ones I had in Atlanta, I spent the morning adjusting my mailing address online, changing the emergency contact on my lease from Erica to Devin, and removing her as a dependent from my health insurance. It was a cold day, and the warmth in my heart no longer existed for Erica or her bullshit. I researched cheap moving services and decided to reach out to Devin instead.

"Hello?" he answered.

"Hey, Devin, how are you?"

"I can't complain. What's up, J?"

"I signed a new lease to move into a single unit in my community this morning, and I was hoping you weren't busy this weekend and could help me."

"Sure, just let me know what time. Do you need any help packing?"

"Yes, but I didn't want to ask you for too much. Erica will still be in our current apartment for a while, and I didn't want to create friction," I replied, feeling a little awkward.

"Journey, just ask for what you need. If I can help you, I will. You don't have to ever worry about asking me for too much again," he assured me.

I smiled at his comment. "Okay then, I will keep you posted. Thank you."

"You're welcome, love. I will come by when I get off and help you get ready."

"Okay. See you then."

"Bye."

"Bye."

I ended the call feeling a peace I hadn't felt in a long time. Something about having Devin's support made me relax, and I decided to surprise him at his job with lunch from his favorite restaurant.

8. The Middle of May

Like a flower of my favorite hue, I'm missing the kiss of the sunshine too.
My petals rustle.
My stems, green and strong . . .
My face full towards the sky . . .
My eyes watching God . . .

~ Olosunde

It had been months since Erica and I had parted ways. I had tried to handle her fairly, and with respect, but I think she was so embarrassed or angry — or maybe both — that she stirred the shit pot and ended up having to lick the spoon.

***

On Wednesday, I came home from work the day I signed the new lease, she had taken all my dishes out of the cabinets and smashed them on the floor and put a hole in my flat screen television. I found my couch and chair out on the balcony covered in eggs and coconut milk. She had locked Rico in the poorly ventilated dryer room with the dryer on high and the face broken off the knob so it wouldn't stop drying. She had put the best of my pots and pans inside the dryer, and when I finally got home he was dehydrated and scared from the loud banging sound, cowering in the corner as he cried piteously.

She had stuffed the drain of my tub with several bloody tampons, and wrote *"High yellow bitch"* on my mirror in my lipstick. She poured red, blue, and green food coloring all over the carpet in my bedroom, and water and flour all over my bed until it seeped into my mattress. She had attempted to start a fire with the toaster by putting it in the gas oven and turning the oven on, and she filled the kitchen sink with ammonia and bleach. I found her bedroom and closet empty, and all her other belongings were gone.

I was horrified, but I took pictures and called the leasing office, which promptly filed a police report and pressed charges for criminal vandalism. Devin was kind enough to let Rico and I stay with him until the weekend when we moved my clothes and anything that wasn't damaged to my new place. Erica had fled D.C. and returned to Atlanta, where she was apprehended by police and held there until she was returned to D.C. for trial.

The apartment complex was run by a wealthy firm who had her imprisoned for six months, and she would face another six months of probation when she was released in August, provided she didn't do anything to extend the sentence while she was there. Thankfully, I hadn't had to face her in court, but I had filed a restraining order, and renter's insurance paid out a nice sum of money to replace my damaged belongings.

***

I blinked twice in the present, releasing the crazy memory with a deep sigh, as I sipped the last of the homemade sangria in my glass while watching the Saturday evening sunset from my new white, leather sectional. The balcony doors were open with a warm breeze blowing the sheer, golden and cream colored drapes. Rico was propped up against the peacock feather pillow on the other end of the sofa, enjoying some feline dream as his ears twitched rhythmically and his paws clutched one another.

Carlos came out of the half bathroom and sat down beside me on the couch, rubbing his bare feet on the blue, cream and gold sankofa bird print rug as he picked up the pitcher of sangria from the mahogany table in front of us and refilled his glass and then mine.

"I love sunsets from your place, Journey. It almost makes me feel like I'm back home in Miami with your ocean meditation track playing."

I smiled and nodded in agreement at his statement without looking at him as I sipped more sangria.

"This is good, Carlos! You have to share the recipe with me."

"Nah, lady, this is a family secret. My aunt owns a restaurant back in San Juan and she made this recipe, but I will be happy to make it for you anytime."

"I wish I had a collection of family recipes to call upon, but my grandma passed and my aunt took all of her belongings, recipe books included, and hoarded them all in her basement. Not long after, the house burned down and took everything that Grandma left behind up in flames. All I have left of her is this necklace and ring that I never take off and that urn on my mantelpiece."

"Damn. That's sad, Journey," Carlos lamented, shaking his head.

"Yeah, but she's still with me. I see her sometimes when I go through difficult things, and she brings me peace or tells me what to do," I shared.

He stared at me a moment, his glass turned toward his lips, but not actually drinking its contents. He put the glass down and looked me straight in the eyes.

"Are you saying you physically see your deceased grandmother?"

"Yeah, and I talk to her when I do. Why are you looking at me like that? You think I'm a weirdo or something?" I said, feeling a little self-conscious.

He laughed softly, shaking his head, "Actually, no. It sounds like something my Aunt Marisol back home would say. Have you ever heard of Santeria?"

"Yeah, here and there, but I'm not really well versed on the topic," I admitted.

"I'm going to visit my cousin this coming weekend. She practices it, and could maybe tell you more. Would you like to meet her?"

"Sure. Just let me know."

"Okay. I think you'll really like her, and maybe she will give you a reading."

"What's a reading?" I inquired.

"Well, she's a priestess, and sometimes she has clients who pay her to consult with the spirits about different things like their past, future, health, jobs, even relationships. She's really good at connecting with people's ancestors, and she does a lot of healing work," he described.

"So, she's like a psychic?"

"No, she's a priestess. There's a difference, I think."

"You think?"

"Well, I've never gotten involved beyond doing whatever ritual or bath or whatever she prescribed me to do, so she could explain better than I could," he said.

"Hmmm . . . okay."

The sun had finally set, and Carlos got up and slid his feet back into his sandals.

"I have to go, Journey. I have a date." He smiled mischievously, wiggling his eyebrows.

"Ooooh! What's her name?" I asked, sipping my refreshed sangria.

"Vanessa. I'm taking her to the festival of lights at the harbor. You should call Devin or Sydney and go. It's supposed to be a big deal!"

"I just might. Thanks for the sangria. Do you want me to help you carry the pitcher back or anything?"

"Nah, you can keep it. I will get it from you next time," he said as he extended his hand to help me up from the sofa.

"Okay," I said walking him to the door. "Have a great time!"

"Thanks!" he kissed my cheek and walked down the hall to his apartment, and I went back to the sofa and texted Devin to see if he was free. He said he had plans, so I asked Sydney next, but she said she was going on a date as well.

I decided to go solo instead. No need in sitting around the house by myself on such a beautiful night. I looked up the details of the event on the internet, and got up to go change my clothes and fix my hair.

I stood in my closet for a few minutes trying to decide what to wear. The temperature was supposed to be warm, but being close to the water was bound to create a bit of a breeze, so I chose a pair of skinny jeans, a simple white tank top, and covered it with a sheer, crocheted orange shirt that hung off the shoulder and draped in front and behind me in a V shape. I pulled my hair up into a high ponytail, and hung a pair of seashell chandelier earrings in my ears, then slid my feet into my new zebra print flat shoes and smeared on a golden tinted lip gloss. I went upstairs to my printer and tucked the ticket I printed for the festival into my purse before walking out the door.

By the time I made it to the harbor, there was already a zoo of patrons out walking slowly in the middle of the streets as if cars don't hurt when they smack into human bodies. I clenched the steering wheel tightly and twirled a long strand of hair that had come undone at the nape of my neck in effort to calm myself. I parked my car in one of the garages instead of spinning my wheels trying to find a parking spot on the street. I would pay for the convenience before I stressed myself out with people milling about aimlessly. I exited my car and walked toward the crowd of people, pushing past bodies that were standing around without moving, in effort to get closer to the water.

I walked into one of the restaurants and ordered a glass of wine to calm my nerves, and then sat on the balcony where I could watch the festival without a crowd for a while. Eventually, I went outside to the open space where couples and families were sitting on lawn chairs and blankets. I was trying to find a place to lay my blanket so I could watch the fireworks, when I literally ran into Travis.

I balked as I stumbled backward, and I blurted out, "Travis" before I saw the woman sitting on the blanket with a little boy about three or four years old, who was digging in a bag for snacks.

"I'm sorry, do we know each other?" he asked.

It was then that I noticed the ring on his left ring finger and my face turned five shades of red. This Negro was MARRIED! I stood there silently for a second as he stared at me with eyes widened, silently begging me not to cause a scene. I turned to his wife, a pretty, racially ambiguous woman, and shook her hand politely as I introduced myself, "Hi, I'm Journey."

I glared at Travis for a few seconds before turning to walk away, then I turned back to stand in front of him again. When I knew his wife was looking, I reached all the way back to *The Color Purple* and slapped him. Hard. So hard the swing almost knocked me off balance.

Then I looked over to his confused wife, smiling, and said, "Welcome to D.C.. Y'all have a nice evening," before walking away into the sea of people and back to my car.

When I was settled into my car, I shrieked loudly with rage. I rested my head on the steering wheel for a few seconds before I sped to the turnstile of the parking garage, and squeaked my tires out of the parking lot. I uncharacteristically allowed my emotions to speed me all the way home, without any fucks to give about whether police would pull me over. I had smoke coming out of my ears and tears streaming down my face when I finally parked my car in my space in the garage of my apartment building.

I got out slowly, now that I had spent so much energy driving with anger, and walked a slow, steady walk of shame towards my door, wishing that I had a mother or grandmother to call and lay this weight on. Since I didn't, I went in my house and took an extra-long shower, crying under the stream of water until it ran cold, forcing me to get out. I dried off in the sheets of my bed as new tears replaced the ones that I rinsed off in the shower, neglecting the shea butter and pajamas routine, and fell asleep feeling sorry for myself. I knew I wasn't to blame and that Travis was the king jerk of all jerks, but I felt stupid for believing him. How else should a woman act when she just wanted to be loved by someone, and all she got was fuck boys to entertain her?

When I woke up in the morning, I had several texts from Devin and Carlos. Apparently, Carlos had seen the altercation with Travis from a distance, but was too late to catch me before I walked away. Devin wanted to come by tomorrow and introduce me to a woman he was dating. I texted Carlos that I was fine and told him to stop by when he was awake. I sent

Devin a text back to agree to have him and his friend over later the next evening for dinner.

I went to the bathroom and brushed my teeth and by the time I hung my toothbrush back in the holder, I heard a knock at my door. Thinking it was Carlos, I put on some yoga pants and a t-shirt, and walked to the door to peer through the peephole. When I opened the door, Carlos' expression was urgent as he wrapped me up in a tight hug.

"Journey, are you okay? I saw you last night and I was worried about you the rest of the evening, but I couldn't chat because of my date."

"I know, Sweetie, it's okay. I wouldn't have wanted to interrupt your time with Vanessa on my account anyway. Thank you for worrying about me," I said as I closed the door behind us.

"What happened?"

"I saw that asshole, Travis, at the harbor and he was with his wife! He was MARRIED, Carlos! I asked him if there was a woman in California waiting for him, and not only did he LIE, he was MARRIED!"

Carlos' mouth dropped open in shock. "Are you sure he was married then? I mean he could have just gotten married recently."

"That's just as bad! That means he was ENGAGED during that time, and he still had a child that he didn't tell me about. That boy looked like he was at least three or four!"

"Damn. I can't argue with that, Love. That's pretty valid, " he agreed.

I shook my head angrily, trying to process my rage.

"When can I meet your cousin? I have questions for her?" I asked.

"We can go today if you're free. I mean, I was supposed to go see her this weekend, but we can go sooner. She's home."

"Okay cool. Set that up, please. I'm going to go get dressed. You're welcome to wait here, or I will come by when I'm ready."

"Okay, come through when you're set."

"Perfect," I said.

He hugged me quickly and let himself out as I went to go get dressed. I needed to gain some clarity on things I was pondering, and allow myself some peace that I hadn't truly had in a long time.

When we arrived at Carlos' cousin's house in Virginia, I was buzzing internally, wondering what would happen. I had so many questions, but I played it cool at first. She opened the door and greeted us warmly, kissing us on both cheeks before asking us to take off our shoes at her door. I stepped out of my zebra flats from the previous day and sat on the sofa where she invited me to sit in the front room.

"Your lady friend is very pretty!" she exclaimed as if I wasn't there.

Normally, I would have been offended, but I just thanked her and let Carlos do the talking.

"Carmen, this is Journey, and she's interested in a reading from you and maybe learning more about Orisha."

"I see! Well, we can do that! Let me go to my shrine room and prepare. Would you like some water or anything to eat while you wait?" she offered.

"No, thank you," I said.

"We will have some water and whatever you're cooking," Carlos told her, ignoring my comment without looking at me.

When she walked away to her kitchen, Carlos whispered, "It's rude to decline food or drink in Latin culture. Just eat a little bit."

"Oh, I didn't know. I apologize."

"It's okay. She's not offended, but you should at least eat a little bit."

Carmen came back with plates for both of us and set them on the table before walking away to return with two glasses of water. She walked away again as I sipped my water politely. I grasped my fork and nibbled on rice and black beans smothered with a delicious chicken and onion mixture. It was well seasoned, and better than many Latin restaurants I had been to. I complimented her cooking and polished it off more quickly than I expected. *Maybe I was hungrier than I thought I was*, I thought to myself.

Carmen returned from her shrine room and held her hand out to me, beckoning me to come over to her.

"Come, Journey. Tell me about what's going on that brings you here for a reading."

I looked at Carlos for a second, uncertainly, but he just smiled and nodded in her direction. I stood up and followed her out of the front room. She led me through a nicely decorated dining room, into a room with a white curtain hanging over the doorway. There were many shelves with pretty pots on them, decorated with beautifully colored fabrics lining the walls. Some of them had statues or dolls beside them or plates with food. Incense burning on the bookshelf lingered in the air, giving the room a hazy look. She invited me to sit on a soft ottoman-like cushion on the floor on one side of a mat while she sat on the other side, smiling at me warmly.

"What brings you here today?" she asked.

"Well, I've had some really challenging experiences lately," I began. "My ex-boyfriend, Devin, had a death in has family; it was his brother, but I had never met him before. I dreamed about his death on the night of his passing and told him about it before he got the call. He was reasonably rattled by that, but it wasn't the first time I had an experience with him and spirits. The first time was when a woman he used to love came to me in a dream, except she had been deceased since he was about eighteen. He was okay about the first time, but I suppose the second time hit a little close to home. He ultimately broke up with me because he was afraid and confused, which left me devastated."

"A few months later, I had an ectopic pregnancy, and he came to see me in the hospital and we decided to remain friends, but we aren't together anymore. After that, I lost my friend with whom I was roommates because she drugged Devin and took and took pictures of herself with him in my bed to make me jealous. She has some issues," I said with a dry laugh.

"Clearly, she does," Carmen replied with a wide-eyed expression.

"Anyway, afterward, I had a dream that I met these five women on five thrones with mirrors on the back, dressed in white gowns, who told me that I was the princess, but I must crown myself queen. They told me that I had the gift of knowing and that they were my mothers. After that, I saw the guy I had the pregnancy with and found out he was married to another woman and had a son. I feel like I'm supposed to understand some responsibility I have, but I don't know how. Carlos told me about you, and I decided to come and see whether you could help me understand my gifts and what I'm supposed to do with them."

"Well, that is some kind of tale, young lady!" she exclaimed. "You have some serious kind of talent! Let's see what the spirits say."

She pulled a white sack from a basket on her bookshelf and poured a bunch of cowrie shells into her hand. She poured fragrant, greenish water onto them and rubbed them between her palms vigorously before dropping them onto the mat in front of her. She touched a few shells, examining them where they lay, and placed her fingertips to her chin thoughtfully as she grabbed a book off the shelf, opening it to a page near the center of the book.

"What was the ex-boyfriend's name again?" she asked without looking at me.

"Devin."

"Hmmm... what was the name of the man you were pregnant by? The one with the wife."

"Travis," I whispered, watching her intently.

She gathered the shells, throwing them again. I watched her study them closely, then refer back to the book she had retrieved from the floor.

"Did you make love to Devin after the death of his brother? Sometime before the encounter with Travis?"

"Yes," I said, my eyes widening with disbelief that she could possibly know that. I wished I could see the book, understand her thoughts, read her mind. I hated not knowing what was going on. She looked up at me and leaned back on one arm, stretching her legs out away from the shells.

Carmen leaned back on the opposite arm and sighed, "Travis wasn't the father of the child, Devin was. Have you ever been pregnant before that?"

I sat upright, stiffly, "Yes, when I was twenty-five."

"You terminated that pregnancy," she said nodding. "You need a cleansing to heal your womb. You should not terminate any pregnancies in the future, so be mindful of your dealings. You will be able to have children in the future; however, you may not hear the call of motherhood for some time."

My eyes welled up with tears at the memory of the terminated pregnancy. When I had the ectopic pregnancy, I had internally beaten myself up because of the abortion I'd had years before. *How could this woman know such a thing*, I wondered?

"Journey, you come from a long line of seers and healers, and you will benefit from initiation to the Orisha and learning more about the spirits. They come to you to share messages and your ancestors protect you. Your mother is with you, and she used to be a priestess. Did you know that?"

"No. I had no idea. She passed when I was young," I shared with Carmen.

"I'm going to teach you how to erect a shrine for your ancestors so you can communicate with them and begin honing your gift. This is a great responsibility for you, and it is your destiny."

I just stared at her in silence, unable to wrap my mind around what she was saying to me.

"You've been seeing spirits all your life and you have experienced much clairvoyance over the years. Did you ever think that there was a purpose for these abilities?"

"No," I told her, "I thought I was just a weirdo who happened to know things from time to time."

"Someone abused you when you were a child. We are going to do a cutting ritual to cleanse you of all the hurt and negativity you've experienced in your life so far to open your roads for your future. It is a very bright future, indeed. You will marry and have many children. You will have three husbands, but your final husband is a seeker; someone you have yet to meet. He is a man who travels far and wide. A man who will lift you up like the brightest jewel in his crown." She sat back and stared at me for a few seconds with a smile.

"That's it?" I asked with hesitation.

"That's plenty. You have to make some hard decisions going forward about what you want and your obedience to the spirits will be your fortitude and your freedom."

I was shocked to hear the exact same words from her that I had heard in my dream. I thanked her and she rose from her mat and embraced me before leading me back into the room where Carlos was waiting. We found him napping on the couch with his feet crossed at the ankles.

Carmen touched his shoulder, waking him, and said, "Carlos, I need you to bring Journey back over in a week so I can perform some cleansings for her."

"Okay," he said sleepily. "How much does she owe you?"

"This consultation is free. She just needs to come in clothing that she doesn't mind never wearing again, and another outfit to wear home."

"You got that, Journey?" he asked, looking at me earnestly.

"Yes," I replied softly, still feeling shocked by what I had been told.

Carlos ushered me to the door where our shoes were and kissed his cousin goodbye while I slid my feet into my flats. Carmen hugged me, thanking me for visiting her. I thanked her for her reading, and left, following Carlos down the hall and out of Carmen's apartment.

When I was seated in his car, I turned to Carlos exclaiming, "Your cousin is amazing!She knew things

I've never told many people. She also told me that the baby from the ectopic pregnancy was Devin's, not Travis.'"

"I have to admit I thought that for a while myself," he said as he pulled into traffic.

"Really? Why?"

"Well, I'm no expert, but based upon what you told me, you hadn't been with Travis long enough for the child to be his. Plus, you went to the hospital two weeks after the time you were in Atlanta. I read online that it takes longer than two weeks for an ectopic pregnancy to be apparent, but you had been with Devin four months prior, and some women still have regular cycles during their pregnancies, especially when they're ectopic."

I sat in silence, thinking about what he was saying. He made a good point, and I wondered why I had never thought of it before. Perhaps with the breakup and everything else that had happened the past few months, I hadn't considered the alternative possibility that the child wasn't Travis'. We rode in silence for about thirty minutes before Carlos turned to me and asked if I was willing to swing by his bar with him for a while. I agreed, and we got off the traffic-filled highway and drove to a quaint little restaurant.

He introduced me to a few of his co-workers, and invited me to have a seat at the bar and have a drink while he handled some business in the back. The bartender, Kwesi, handed me a menu and talked to me about the drinks on it.

"You should try the Kissing Frog," he said. "A lot of ladies like it. It has rum, triple sec, lime, cordial, sweet and sour mix, mint, and prosecco."

"Ooooh! I think I will try that!" I exclaimed. Kwesi nodded with a smile and went to mix the drink.

He came back with a sexy, curvy glass with green liquid inside. I sipped it and smiled.

"This is good! Thank you!"

"My pleasure," he said as he moved away to serve other patrons.

I sipped my Kissing Frog, contentedly swinging my legs from the bar stool, listening to reggaeton as I waited for Carlos. After about twenty minutes, he came to find me at the bar, working on my second glass.

"What are you drinking?" he asked with a smile.

"Kissing Frog," I shouted over the music. "It's delicious!"

"Kwesi made that?"

"Yeah! I've never had this before! I think I've found a new favorite!" I exclaimed.

"Go easy," Carlos warned, "Kwesi is a little heavy handed on the spirits."

"I don't mind at all! It's so refreshing!"

"Mmhmm," Carlos mumbled with a smile. "Kwesi, will you make me a Long Island?"

Kwesi nodded from the other side of the bar and walked away to make the cocktail. Carlos and I chatted about my reading in more detail, and I learned about the kinds of cleansings he'd had over the years for different things ranging from crazy ex-girlfriends to health issues. He'd had an interesting experience, and I envied his cultural awareness. We talked more about his childhood and what it was like growing up in Arroyo, Puerto Rico.

All economic challenges aside, it sounded like a childhood in paradise. I swooned internally over his tales of coquito frogs and island life. I told him about my experiences in group homes and losing my parents, and even shared the abuse story of my step-uncle. He listened with wide, compassionate eyes, and rubbed my shoulder supportively. I finished my third drink before we went out to Carlos's car and headed home.

I was very talkative in the car after the three Kissing Frogs, and I rambled along incessantly about whatever thing caught my stream of consciousness along the way. When we parked at our apartment building, he walked me to my door, took my purse from me, and opened it with my key, guiding me in carefully with one hand on the small of my back. I dropped my purse on the island in my kitchen and stepped out of my shoes as I plopped down on the sofa. Carlos brought me a glass of water and a slice of bread as he sat down beside me, encouraging me to take both from him.

"I'm fine, Carlos! I just really enjoy your company! Come sit by me," I said as I patted the sofa beside me. He sat down beside me carefully.

"Journey, I think those Kissing Frogs were a little stronger than we thought. You've only eaten once today, to my knowledge. Eat this bread, please, Sweetie."

I took the bread from him and pulled it apart, popping pieces of it into my mouth. I sipped some water at his request and leaned my head onto his shoulder, enjoying the musky scent of his cologne. We sat that way, me with my head on his shoulder watching the sunset for a while.

"Thank you for introducing me to your cousin today. I appreciate that," I said after swallowing the final bite of bread.

"You're welcome," he whispered to me, as he stroked my arm delicately.

I turned my face up to look at him for a long moment, and he stared back, brushing the curls out of my face and tucking them behind my ear. When he lowered his head to kiss me the first time, it was the most gentle, genuine kiss I think I had experienced since my first kiss when I was fifteen. It was innocent and unassuming, and full of compassion. When his lips parted mine with his tongue for the second kiss, my heart fluttered in my chest, and I relaxed in his embrace as he pulled me closer. He lifted my chin gently, cupping it as he sucked my bottom lip lightly, and I turned toward him, facing him as he pulled me into him more, deepening the kiss.

We kissed for what seemed like hours, until I needed water, and reached for my glass to finish what remained.

"It has been a long day, Journey, and you've had a nice amount to drink. I don't want to take advantage."

"I don't want you to leave," I told him.

"I will stay. I just don't want to take things too far," he replied.

Undaunted by his nobility, I kissed him again. He kissed back and wrapped me up in a tight embrace. We lay on my couch kissing each other lightly until I fell asleep.

I woke in the morning with Carlos still beside me, his arm draped across my waist. I shot up sharply, unsure of where I was, as he pulled me back into his chest.

"You're safe... nothing happened. I just stayed like you asked me to," he reassured me.

I relaxed slowly into his embrace and put my face into his chest, breathing him in.

"Good morning," I said to him.

"That it is..." he whispered back.

9. Life, Death, and Rebirth

Some people don't see your worth,
Just your novelty.
Some people are infatuated with the idea of your
potential,
Rather than where you are, or what you might do for
yourself.
Some people recognize that you are everything that they
should want,
But have no clue how to meet you with the same efforts,
So that you want them in the same way.
Fan my flame.
Don't snuff me out.

~Olosunde

I had no one to blame but myself for my most recent actions, but I was still angry. I was angry at my parents most of all. My disgust for my father and him treating me like his property by dressing me in boys' clothes for years to hide my curves, only to sneak into my bedroom at night to violate that which he claimed to wanted to protect. My quiet resentment toward my mother for sending me to live with him and abandoning me later when I tried to return home to her, swirled with that disgust like hot lava beneath the surface of my skin, and now I was forced to face it.

"I was sent to live with my father when I was fifteen," I told the jail therapist.

"Why Erica?" Dr. Bronson asked me.

"Because my mother had remarried and had a child, my brother Jeremiah, with a horrible man who was a deacon at our local church in Georgia, but he beat my mother anytime she did the slightest thing to upset him. Whenever I would step in to try to protect her, she would attack me and tell me that I was being disrespectful. My father was a police officer who would make negative comments about my complexion, and he would beat me in places that no one could see when I upset him.

What's worse is I was so dark nobody could see the bruises, and I couldn't convince anyone I was in danger. It went on that way for years until one day when I was seventeen he found some hidden love letters I had from a boy I liked at school, and he beat me so badly that I could hardly walk. The letters weren't even sexual, he just really liked me. Anyway, I collapsed in gym class, and my friend, Josh, carried me to the school nurse. From there, I was taken to the hospital, where my dad managed to have me released to him because he was an officer. I don't know what he said to them, but they didn't question him at all. I ran away to my mother who drove me right back to him, rather than risk conflict with her husband."

Dr. Bronson looked at me with wide eyes as she waited for me to continue. She had been scribbling notes and asking me questions for an hour. In our previous court mandated therapy sessions, I hadn't given her much, but I wanted out of this place, and I was willing to give her whatever she needed to help me achieve freedom at this point. I had been seeing her for weeks since my physical altercation with another inmate in the ladies' room of the jail.

"I'm so sorry that happened to you, Erica. How did you ultimately get away from your father and his abuse?" she asked me in between sips of her tea.

I clasped my hands and took a breath before continuing.

"I graduated high school and went to a military college. I lost my virginity to my own father, and he treated me like I was filthy and detestable as a result. I always felt like his actions were a result of his inability to hold on to my mother and control her, but she had just gone from one abusive man to another."

"I see. How was your college experience?"

"I was good at school, but I got pregnant by the first guy I opened up to, and ended up having to leave the school when he lied to everyone and said that the child wasn't his. He just disappeared into thin air one day. I called and called him and he just never responded. I finished my first year of school, and spent the latter parts of my pregnancy alone with my mother. My son, Jason, lives with my mom."

"Have you spoken to Jason's father since then?"

"No. I was really depressed for a long time after his birth. I would never hurt my son, but I left him with my mom in Athens and I moved to Atlanta when he was one so I could work and try to give him a stable life," I explained.

"Wow! How old were you then?"

"I was twenty. Since then, I've just been trying to stabilize my life so I can get him back. I tried to go back to school, but I just didn't have the money for tuition with the hosting and waitressing gigs I had at the time. My mother's horrible husband died and she got married again to a guy named Lawrence. She got pregnant by him at the same time I was pregnant. When she had my little sister, Leilani, she had to start her motherhood experience all over again. After a while, I decided that it was better for Jason to have a stable life than to be with me full time. I visit him, mostly for holidays, but I've slacked off lately because of my finances and because I don't want to own up to the fact that I'm not the mother I should be. My mother has full custody of my son."

"I see." She scribbled some more notes in her notebook and looked up at me with a sad smile.

"I'm sorry, but our time is up, Erica. I'm going to be back next week to talk with you some more. I think that we may be able to get you out of here and seal your records so you can go on to live a normal life for your son."

I thanked her as the guard came to collect me. I'd had time to think about my life and what I wanted it to look like from here on out, and I just didn't want Jason to think that his mother had failed him. I didn't want him to carry the same regret or anger that I had all these years. I hadn't spoken to him for the past six months; my mother had told him I was working and that I would be home soon. I knew I needed to get back to Georgia and get my life together for him and for myself. Since my sentence was almost finished, I wanted to go back to Georgia and start over.

Dr. Bronson helped get me released three weeks earlier than I expected, without probation. I went to be with my mom in Georgia, but I had to see a therapist in Athens twice a week to help me deal with my depression. I probably never would have considered that I was dealing with actual depression all these years and was just undiagnosed, but then again very few black people sought therapy for mental illness. Most of the time we are told to go to church and pray, or given the "stay strong" speech by someone close to us. Talking out our problems with professionals is culturally frowned upon for the most part.

The Sunday of my release came quickly, and I took an early bus from D.C. to Athens the morning I released, and my mother and Jason were waiting for me at the station that evening wearing identical smiles. I didn't have any bags underneath the bus, just a carry-on with a toothbrush, deodorant, and the few items I had on me when I was arrested six months ago.

"Mommy! Mommy! I'm so happy to see you!" Jason squealed, bouncing up and down like he had springs in his shoes.

I hugged him tightly, swallowing the lump in my throat as I kissed the top of his curly head. I had been waiting for this day for months, and I continued to hold him and hug him, enjoying the warm scent of him. He smelled like warm cocoa butter, fabric softener, and the faint lingering of a little boy who had played outside earlier that day. He had grown so much since I had last seen him, and I stroked the top of his head that now reached just below my breasts.

"I missed you, too, Baby," I told him as I leaned in to embrace my mother briefly.

Jason's arms were glued around my middle, squeezing me tightly, and I looked back down at his sweet face and saw that he had begun to cry a little. Unable to hold myself together anymore, I scooped him up in my arms and held him tightly as I rocked him from side to side, his legs swinging, with my own tears flowing. My mother stood by smiling, letting us have our moment.

We walked to my mom's car together with Jason chattering excitedly about everything from school to his room décor. He wanted to show me his toy car and action figure collections when we got home. I just smiled and nodded at him because I couldn't get a word in edgewise.

Jason fell asleep on the car ride to my mom's house, and after she parked, she stepped outside the car in the driveway of the white bungalow with blue shutters, beckoning for me to follow her. When we were near the trunk of the car, she hugged me tightly and rocked me from side to side, releasing me to hold both sides of my face in her hands gently as she looked me in my eyes.

"I didn't tell Jason where you were, so don't feel obligated to do so. Lawrence doesn't know about it either. As far as anyone in this house knows, you've been working for a company that had you doing a lot of traveling. You can fill in the details as you see fit. I will support whatever story you tell. This is a mother and daughter situation, and I will be your greatest advocate from here on out."

"Thanks, Mom," I told her softly before attempting to move toward the backseat to get Jason, but she pulled me back to her, holding my hands in hers.

"I know I wasn't there for you when the situation happened with your father," she began in an emotion-filled voice. "I'm really sorry, Baby. I have been beating myself up about that for years, but I know that doesn't change what you went through. I know Lawrence was abusive to me for a long time, but he's better now. I want you to know that you're welcome to stay here for as long as you need to. I failed you when you needed me most, but I will do everything I can to make that up to you. Take your time, see your therapist, do whatever you need to do. When you're ready, I won't fight you over custody for Jason. He's your son, and I can only imagine what these past seven years have been like for you."

I was floored and filled with an awkwardly unfamiliar sense of emotion. I didn't know what to say to her. Part of me wanted to be angry with her, but the other part of me was exhausted with fighting and resentment, so I just hugged her tightly.

"Thank you, Mom. That really means a lot to me for you to say," I said as I squeezed her.

She nodded when I released her, and we went to wake Jason and walk into the house to prepare dinner. Leilani, my little sister, came bounding down the steps with a squeal and launched into my arms when I walked in the door.

"Erica! Erica! You're home!"

"Hey, little sis!" I said with a broad grin, hugging her tiny seven year old body to myself.

"That's my mommy! Let her go!" Jason teased, tackling her to the floor. She bested him, climbing on top of him and tickled his ribs until he squawked loudly.

"I'm your auntie; you better let me see my sister!"

I didn't realize she had so much personality, and I laughed at them rolling around on the floor, play fighting over me.

"Hold on, guys!" I shouted playfully, "There's enough of me to go around and I'm not going anywhere anytime soon!"

"We know!" Leilani said matter-of-factly. "Mom says you're going to stay for a while! Jason and I are sharing a room so you can have your own room. Aren't you excited, Jason?"

"Not really," he grumbled. "I would rather be in my own room or at least share with my mom than have to room with a girl."

"Well, you can bunk with me for a while," I told him. "I snore a lot, though. I fart in my sleep sometimes, too. If you can deal with that, you'll be the perfect roommate. I'm also a girl, though."

He made a face as he digested this information.

"I guess it's me and you, Leilani!" he said.

We all laughed.

Who knew these kids were so witty?

My mom's voice from somewhere in another room sobered our play.

"Erica, come help me in the kitchen, please. Leilani, you and Jason go in the basement with your daddy until dinner is ready."

"Okay, Mommy!" Leilani replied. "Come on, Jason! Let's play hide and seek downstairs!"

"You always cheat!" he said.

"I'll let you hide first this time," she bargained. He smiled and ran off toward the basement steps with Leilani in tow.

With Leilani and Jason out of our hair, my mom and I started cleaning and seasoning chicken to be fried, and pre-heating the oven for my mom's famous hot water corn bread. She opened a can of greens and set them to boil on the stove. It wasn't the health-conscious food Journey made, but at least it wasn't jail food. I was happy to be cleaning the chicken alongside my mom in the kitchen. The window was open and the cicadas sang in the distance as a warm, summer breeze blew into the windows over the sink.

"Jason pretends to be mad about sharing a room with Leilani, but when Lawrence and I were setting it up, he was thrilled. I'm sure he will want to give you a grand tour soon."

"As if I didn't live in this house for years," I laughed. "They're cute, though. I'm glad he got to grow up with Leilani, even though it was weird being pregnant at the same time as you."

"These things happen," she said, laughing. "They love each other like siblings, though. Leilani likes to pull the auntie card on him from time to time, which never fails to rile Jason's ego."

I laughed softly as I seasoned the chicken and dipped it in egg before rolling it in a mixture of flour and cornmeal.

"Thanks for taking care of him, Mom. I don't think I've said that enough over the years."

"He's my grandbaby. I'd never leave him out to the wolves. I know I upset you when I took custody of him, but that was Lawrence's influence. I just wanted to make sure you and Jason were okay, especially after I abandoned you. It was the least I could do."

I was quiet for a minute, nodding as I processed her statements. I never knew she felt that way, and this moment in the kitchen with her was really healing for me. I felt like I would be able to set aside my resentment for her and start a new chapter.

"Hey, Wife."

We both jumped as Lawrence appeared in the kitchen, startling us.

"What are you making for dinner?" he asked.

"We're making fried chicken, mustard greens, and hot water cornbread, Honey. Is there something you need?"

"I just came up to see this pretty thing in my kitchen making my dinner," he replied, smacking her on the butt.

Mom giggled, but I bristled and turned my head away at the gesture, remembering how the hits weren't so playful in the past.

"Hi, Lawrence," I mumbled over clenched teeth.

"Hey, Young Gal!" he called from behind me. "Welcome home! I haven't seen you in a long time! Look at you all nice and filled out!"

Mom swatted at him with a kitchen rag saying, "Lawrence, leave her alone! She's had a long trip and she's helping me make dinner. Go on back down there with Leilani and Jason. Keep them from tearing up the basement."

"All right. How long before the food is done? I'm hungry."

"I will let you know," she dismissed without looking at him as she mixed the cornbread batter by hand before pouring it into the pan.

He left without any further comment, and I felt the hairs rise on the back of my neck in a way that made my stomach churn with foreboding. I knew my days were numbered by him, and I needed to find a job and get myself and my son out of there as soon as possible.

When dinner was finished being cooked, my mother called Jason, Leilani and Lawrence up from the basement to eat. We prepared plates and set the table for five before sitting together. We all held hands as Lawrence blessed the food, although I hadn't said grace in ages. I held my mother's and Jason's hands anxiously, as I bowed my head. When we all said "Amen" and sat down to eat, an awkward silence came over me. Everyone else was chatting away happily, but I just felt forlorn. Maybe it was the fact that I had been away for so many years. Maybe it was the fact that I just didn't like Lawrence, but I just couldn't settle into the warmth and acceptance around me.

When the kids were sleeping soundly and the kitchen was clean, I lay in my bed for hours, staring at the ceiling. I replayed the way I trashed the apartment I shared with Journey in D.C., and I felt sick inside when I recalled the rage I felt. It was so unnecessary. She didn't deserve that. I tossed and turned in bed the way I had in jail for months, until I decided to take advantage of my freedom and go outside on the front porch.

The temperature had dropped a bit, but the humid air felt good to me. I sat in one of the two rocking chairs for a while, lost in my own thoughts, until my mother came outside with a glass of wine in each hand and handed me one as she sat down silently beside me. The gesture reminded me of Journey, and I smiled slightly with a twinge of guilt tugging in my heart as I sipped my glass. We rocked in silence for a long time until I heard my mom snoring. I got up and stood over her for a few minutes, watching her breathe softly as she dozed. I noticed the faint lines in her face; the laughter around her cheeks and mouth, the worry around her eyes, and I leaned forward to pay my respects to her struggle as I kissed her forehead.

I realized this woman I knew as my mother had a story I had never heard. There was forgiveness and appreciation in that kiss as I whispered, "Good night," to her before turning to go in the house.

"I love you, too," she whispered as I opened the screen door, and I smiled as I went inside to find my bed.

***

I woke Monday morning to the busy bustle of my mother's house as I heard her transitioning from rousing, to coaxing, to threatening Jason and Leilani out of bed.

"If you two miss this school bus this morning and make me late to work, I'm going to pour buckets of water on you! Get up! Get up! You spent all that time talking when you were supposed to be asleep! You think you're slick, but I know you two!"

I snickered to myself, recalling how many times she had said the same things to me, only they weren't empty threats. I could hear Leilani and Jason protesting and begging for five more minutes. I decided to get up and help her lay down the law.

"Jason, I know you're not giving your grandma a hard time in here. Come on and get up out of that bed. You, too, Leilani. You two have to get to school," I said as I arrived in the doorway next to my mother. She smiled and winked at me in gratitude, folding her arms across her chest as she glared at the kids.

"But Mommy, we don't have school today. It's a teacher institute day today," Leilani explained.

"What? Why didn't I receive a note?" she asked with raised eyebrows and crossed arms.

"I forgot to give it to you," she said hopping up and digging in her backpack, handing a folded sheet of paper to my mother before returning to her bed. "See? We don't have school today."

My mother's lips moved as she read the paper.

"Leilani and Jason, you have to tell me these things so that I can prepare!"

"I'm sorry, Mommy. I guess we both forgot because we were so excited that Erica was home," Leilani apologized, with Jason co-signing with vigorous head nods.

"Erica, do you mind looking after Jason and your sister today?" she said turning to look at me.

"Of course not! I'd love to get some time to myself with these two little rascals. I'll even make breakfast."

"Yay!" they both cheered from their beds.

"Can we have cinnamon pancakes?" Jason asked with hope-filled eyes.

"I'm sure I can make that happen," I agreed.

"Thank you, Baby. I thought the year-long school would be different, but they have days off and early releases at some of the most random times," my mother said.

"It's my pleasure, Mom," I reassured. "Go ahead to work. I will look after them."

"You guys can sleep until breakfast is ready," I said, pointing to the kids in their beds.

Mom and I left the two of them snuggling back under their covers as she went to her room to finish getting ready for work, and I trotted to the kitchen to make them pancakes.

Living with Journey had its benefits. I knew how to make pancakes from scratch and I brewed some coffee for my mom and I, which was something else I hadn't known how to do before being her roommate. The butter sizzled in the skillet as I mixed the batter into ripples and poured it into the hot skillet. After a few minutes, Lawrence came into the kitchen wearing a navy robe and slippers.

"Oh! Good morning! I didn't expect to see you down here making the kitchen smell so good! What are you making there?"

"The kids wanted pancakes for breakfast. I have enough batter for more if you'd like some." I was a little surprised by my good mood and my offer, but I didn't show it.

"Sure! That sounds great! Is it too late to get a little of that coffee also?" he inquired.

"Not at all." I poured him a cup and handed the yellow mug to him across the breakfast table.

"Thank you. Are you making anything else, or are there only pancakes on the menu?" he asked with a smile.

"I can scramble some eggs and make some bacon if you want," I said as I opened the refrigerator door.

"Thank you."

"No problem." I pulled the bacon and eggs out of the refrigerator and two more skillets from the cabinet.

A few minutes later, the kitchen smelled warm and tasty as Leilani and Jason came bounding down the steps. I prepared plates for everyone while the kids chattered to each other about how excited they were to go to the park. My mother's heels clicked into the kitchen and she stopped short with a broad smile.

"Oh, Erica, you went all in! Thank you!"

"You're welcome," I said as I slid a plate onto the table in front of her. "Do you want cream and sugar for your coffee?"

"No, Baby, I like mine black."

"Me, too!" I told her, "I don't think I ever knew how you liked your coffee."

"Just a little sugar is enough to get me going," she told me.

"I've got some sugar for you, Sweet Thang," Lawrence flirted.

They laughed and kissed as Jason, Leilani and I made grossed out faces.

"Ewww!" the kids exclaimed, turning their heads away.

I laughed a little as I cut my pancakes into little neat squares and poured syrup on top. I skipped the eggs and bacon. Eggs always gave me gas and I didn't eat pork. I felt at home in my mother's house for the first time in over ten years, and I was happy for this moment as I sipped my coffee and enjoyed my pancakes. Today was going to be a good day.

When breakfast was over and my mother was gone, I sent the kids up to get dressed as I went to enjoy a hot shower. Lawrence was retired, so he disappeared into the basement to watch ESPN, or whatever he did down there. I found a razor and shaved my legs, intending to wear the shorts my mother had bought me. I pulled my hair into a high ponytail on top of my head and tucked the ends under into a little bun. I needed to find a good salon to get my hair braided down here now that Journey wasn't around to braid my hair for me anymore. I made a face at my reflection at that thought, then dismissed it. I'd have to start over here, and that wasn't such a bad thing.

10. Summer Soulstice

Let me be your water.
Let me be your air.
Let me be your heartbeat pulsing deep with love and
care.
Let me be your lyric.
Let me be your song.
Let me be your culture so you can know me your whole
life long.

~ Olosunde

I sat in a booth on the rooftop of a restaurant with Carlos, Sydney, Devin, and Devin's new girlfriend, Alora. The August evening air was moist, and the music was a loud, steady, pulsing sensation in my chest. The table was covered with a beautifully fragrant spread of Lebanese food and there was a glass raised in each person's hand as Carlos gave a toast in my honor.

"Journey, may your voyage through this thing called life be as happy and free as the cool river waters that dance waves into the deep blue sea. May you ride the crest of these waves for all of your days, and as you go forth from this birthday, remember that if you cannot be with the ones you love, love the ones you're with, and may they love you in return with reckless abandon... Cheers!"

The glasses clinked all around me and everyone smiled and said "Cheers." I noticed a funny little look play across Devin's face as Carlos kissed my cheek and hugged me, but I ignored it.

Sydney flagged down the waitress and she came over holding a huge slice of tiramisu with a candle sticking out of the center. The plate had 'Happy Birthday' written on it in emerald green glaze and was garnished with strawberries and whipped cream. Everyone broke out in song as I sat smiling, thankful to be surrounded by even a handful of friends for my birthday. I was so accustomed to lonely or dramatic birthdays with just Erica and Rico to accompany me. Results of being a foster child, I guess.

Devin ordered a round of shots for everyone, and I looked at Carlos somberly, letting him know that I wouldn't be having multiple shots of anything. He nodded at me, wordlessly, as he slid out of the booth to go to the bar to order me another Kissing Frog.

"What's that drink?" Alora asked me over Devin's arm.

"It's called a Kissing Frog," I shouted over the music and the restaurant's patrons' voices.

"Really? It looks yummy! What's in it?"

"You have to ask Carlos," I said pointing to him across the room by the bar. "His co-workder made it for me once, and now it's all I order whenever I'm out."

Alora wiggled past Sydney and out of the booth, making her way toward Carlos.

"I'm going with her!" Sydney exclaimed. "I want to try some of that, too!"

When both ladies were gone and Devin and I sat alone, I took the opportunity to do a temperature check on him.

"Hey, you," I said. "I appreciate you coming out tonight. It was really nice getting to meet Alora. I'm sorry I was unable to have you two over for dinner when you asked before. I had a lot going on."

"It's all good, J. I'm just glad you're happy," Devin said, glancing away.

"I try to stay happy. Is everything okay with you? I noticed a strange vibe earlier during the toast."

"Like I said, J, I'm just happy you're happy."

He adjusted his fitted hat and straightened his jeans, but that telltale muscle working in his jaw let me know something deeper was going on. I leaned forward and put my elbows on the table.

"Devin, I hope you aren't uncomfortable with me inviting you. I think that Alora is beautiful, and she seems nice. I was more worried that she would feel strange about being here with our history."

"Nah, she's good. She'd never be weird about that," he replied.

"Really? Well, then she's a special kind of lady!"

"No . . . I mean she is, but she wouldn't trip because I didn't tell her," he confessed.

"Wait, what? You didn't tell her that we used to be in a relationship?" My eyes widened and I sat back as I had a flashback of Travis.

"Nah. I didn't want to create any animosity or anything. You're too important to me for that," Devin explained.

"So, she just thinks that I'm someone you know and are friends with?" I questioned.

"She thinks you're an old friend from college. I never told her anything more."

"Devin, that's not the best lie you could tell. We didn't even attend the same college. What if she and I become friends or if she asks me something about your college days? What am I supposed to say?"

"It doesn't matter. She's nice, but she's temporary," he said a bit dismissively.

My mouth dropped open to hear him talk about his date whom he had been introducing all evening, as well as discussing in previous conversations, as his girlfriend.

"Devin, I — "

"It doesn't matter, okay? Besides, you're with Carlos now, so it doesn't matter. It shouldn't matter, as far as I see it."

"But Carlos and I aren't — "

My comment was cut short by Sydney and Alora returning to the table.

"This stuff is good, Journey!" Sydney shouted as she started sliding back in the booth.

Alora stood in front of the table looking at Devin, then at me, then back at him again. Her green eyes lowered into angry little slits, and she whipped her hair as she turned around and stormed away.

"Shit!" Devin cursed as he got up from the table to go after her, pushing past Sydney.

"What the hell? What was that about?" Sydney asked.

"He told Alora that we never dated, and I guess she read his lips or something and figured out the truth," I explained.

"No, Girl, she was standing near here for a while. I didn't know what she was doing, but she must have been listening while you two were distracted. When I walked up, she had already been there."

Carlos slid back into the booth, "Hey ladies! How are those drinks coming along?"

"Delicious!" Sydney told him.

"Great! You okay, Journey?"

"I'm all right. I think my happy, peaceful birthday is about to be short-lived, though."

"Why?" Carlos asked with a puzzled expression.

"Because Devin didn't tell Alora that we used to date, and she heard me talking to him about it when we weren't looking. Apparently, he told her that we were college friends and she stormed off with her glass when she heard the truth."

"Oh, shit! Where are they now?"

"I'm not sure. They walked that way," I said, pointing in the direction I saw him follow her.

"I'm going to go check things out. You stay here with Sydney."

"Okay, just be careful. Devin seems to think that you and I are a couple, and he seemed a little irritated about that," I warned him.

"Okay," Carlos said, shaking his head. "I'll be right back. Sit tight."

He left us at the table silently sipping our drinks.

The deejay announced karaoke on the microphone, and I turned to Sydney and said with a squeal, "Let's go sing!"

"I'm not getting up in front of all these people to howl at the moon! You go, I'll watch," she replied, waving me away.

"Ugh! You party pooper! It's my birthday! You're supposed to be a good sport!"

"And I will be, from right here," she told me with one hand in front of her face. "I don't do public singing."

"Come oooooooon!" I begged her. "Just one song!"

"No, ma'am! Go ahead, J. I'll cheer you on!" she said with a smile.

I huffed my disappointment and walked up to the booth to retrieve a song book from the deejay. After about ten minutes of scouring the pages, I chose three songs and wrote them down on three little slips of paper. I saw Carlos out of the corner of my eye as I left the deejay booth and returned to my seat. He was there waiting when I got back to our table and got up to let me scoot past him to my seat in the center.

"What's going on out there?" I asked him.

"Alora and Devin are having a screaming match on the front steps of the restaurant. I tried to mediate, but there are some other things going on out there. I left them to it and came back up here."

"Damn. I just knew this birthday was going to be different," I said, pouting as I sipped my drink.

"It will be. Don't let them ruin your evening," he said, patting my shoulder.

"Yeah, Girl! We are here, you've had an awesome time so far, don't let them ruin it with their little spat. Besides, you're about to sing!" Sydney chimed in.

"You guys are right. I won't let them dampen my good time," I resolved.

"That's the spirit!" Carlos offered.

Just then, the deejay called my name, and I scooted back out of my seat and made my way to the stage.

"Everyone put your hands together for the birthday girl! Who better else to kick off the karaoke round tonight than her? Give it up, everyone, for Journey!"

I looked back at Carlos and mouthed to him to ask if he told the deejay it was my birthday, and he winked mischievously in response.

The other people in the room clapped politely, while Sydney and Carlos hooted and howled supportively from our table.

"Thank you. Thank you," I said. "Today is my birthday, and I have some of the best friends in the world! Thank you, guys, for being here with me. I'm ready."

The deejay nodded and started the Janelle Monae song I chose and I started to rock my hips a little as *Q.U.E.E.N.* started to play. After a few minutes of singing, I started to really feel the song and I came off the stage and started dancing with people in the audience. They ate it right up and started clapping loudly to the music. I danced around the perimeter of the audience, and then jumped back up onto the stage when the song ended, smiling, sweating, and feeling high off the energy of the crowd.

"That was great!" the deejay exclaimed as I hung the microphone back on the stand.

The crowd applauded and I smiled, thanking people I passed on my way back to my seat. I saw Devin lingering by the front door and I adjusted my course to make a beeline for him instead.

"Hey, are you two okay?"

"I'm good," he sighed with frustration. "Alora took a cab home. She was pretty pissed off."

"I'm so sorry, Devin! What happened?" I asked, giving him a sympathetic look.

"She heard our conversation!"

"How much of it did she hear?" I asked, feeling sorry for him.

"Enough, apparently. She said she never wants to speak to me again. I don't think it really has everything to do with me, though," he explained, shaking his head.

"Damn. Well, I'm not sure how you're feeling, but you're welcome to stay here with us, of course, but if you want to leave I totally understand."

"Yeah, I'm going to stay. I'm just sorry I brought that shit to your party. I didn't expect it to blow up like that."

"It's okay. You're among friends. These things happen," I reassured him.

"I guess...," he said, taking a step in the direction of our table.

I put my hand up to halt his movement.

"Well, I do want to clarify something before we go back to the table. Carlos and I are not an item. We are just friends and we have known each other for a while. I don't know what led you to think otherwise, but that isn't the case."

"Carlos is in love with you, J. You might not see it, but the way he looks at you, the way he treats you... he definitely has feelings for you," he replied.

"I know he loves me and cares for me, but I don't think it's what you're thinking it is. That's a conversation for another day, though. Come on and sit down. Have a drink or two and let's just have fun, okay?"

"Okay."

He followed me with reluctance in his stride, but Sydney and Carlos were warm to him and he slowly adjusted.

Two or three other groups of people got up to sing before the deejay called me for my second song. People clapped for me as I walked up to take the microphone again.

I closed my eyes as I took a deep breath and started singing.

"When I feel what I feel, sometimes it's hard to tell you so. You may not be in the mood to learn what you think you know."

The crowd waved their hands in the air and a few people let the lights on their cellular phones shine in appreciation.

I crooned, "But at your best, you are love. You're a positive motivating force within my life. Should you ever feel the need to wonder why, let me know. Let me know."

I swayed from side to side and had a little romance with the song as couples kissed and cuddled up with one another. When the music faded out, I placed the microphone in its holster again, and tiptoed off the stage.

"That was amazing! My gosh, Journey! I never knew that you could sing like that!" Carlos exclaimed when I got back to our table.

Devin rolled his eyes a little and Sydney stood to squeeze me briefly. I hugged her back as I poked Devin discreetly and mouthed for him to fix his face. He cracked a smile at that and I wiggled past him and Carlos back to my seat.

"Journey, you're going to be signing autographs by the time you leave here tonight! Great job, and respect to Aaliyah!" the deejay shouted into the microphone.

I blushed modestly and mouthed "thank you" at him as I sipped my third Kissing Frog and settled into chatter with my crew.

The next group up sang "Bohemian Rhapsody," and we cheered them on. The next singer sang a song we didn't know, and the next two sang N'Sync and Spice Girls songs to which Sydney and I belted the lyrics shamelessly, as Devin and Carlos chided us about showing our age by knowing all the words.

The deejay called me back up, but he also announced, "This time she will be accompanied by Sydney!" The crowd cheered, and Sydney cringed, her face turning red.

"Don't worry, you only have to do the rap part at the beginning. If you want to run away at the end, I won't be mad," I said, giving her my best puppy dog eyes.

"Ugh! Okay, Journey! You better be glad it's your birthday!" She whipped her long locks over her shoulder as she rolled her eyes.

I squeezed her in a tight embrace, and urged her out of her seat. The crowd cheered us on as we walked up to the microphone, and the deejay handed me an additional microphone. When the song "Whatta Man" came on the screen, she turned and smirked at me and shook her head. She knew I knew she knew the song like she knew her name, and when the music started, she turned right on cue. I smiled broadly and stepped back a little to give her the limelight.

Devin and Carlos cheered and yelled things we couldn't hear over the rest of the crowd. I sang the EnVogue parts and the second Salt N' Peppa verse, the way we usually did when we rode together in the car. When the song ended, everyone cheered and we hugged each other on the stage before returning to our seats. Carlos and Devin were all smiles and hugs as we got back to the table.

"Ow! That was fun! Let's get outta here and go to some other places! Let's do a club crawl like we're twenty-two, or until we can't feel our feet from dancing!" I shouted.

"Whatever you say! It's your birthday!" Sydney shouted back.

"Let me pay the tab and you got it!" Carlos agreed.

"Let's split the check," Devin offered.

"Cool! Thanks!" Carlos said with a smile, fist-bumping Devin.

They walked away together to pay, as Sydney and I gathered our purses and met them at the door.

"All right, J, where to next?" Devin asked.

"It doesn't matter to me!" I exclaimed. "Let's just go to the places on the street that are playing the best music!"

"Sounds like a plan to me," Devin agreed.

Carlos and Sydney nodded, and we all turned to walk down U Street. We walked into Society Lounge and climbed the stairs until we could feel the music pumping inside our chests. We had a round of shots of something Devin ordered, and danced until we were sweating. Everyone knew the only rule I had was no vodka. I didn't do well with that and I didn't want to get sick by mixing too many different liquors.

Sydney and I took turns sandwiching Carlos, and then Devin, between us on the dance floor. After a while it got too crowded to move with all the college students milling about, so we left there and went a few doors down to Marvin's Room. They were charging a twenty dollar cover for guys, so we drifted on to Patty Boom Boom where the reggae beats were encouraging people to dance in the street.

Inside, we all had another round of shots and enjoyed a local band that was performing onstage. We vibed to about four songs in their set before finding our way back outside where the air was less thick and humid. The breeze picked up and I pulled my hair into a bun on top of my head, fanning myself and wiping the sweat off my hairline with my hands. My white, sleeveless, tunic-style dress clung to my waist, and I adjusted my gold belt to allow some air to blow up under it a bit.

"Girl, it's hot in there!" Sydney exclaimed. "My vagina is sweating! Let's go to Pure next so I can adjust my undies!"

"Ok, cool!" I agreed.

"You're not sweating your panties off in that dress, Girl?" Sydney asked.

"What panties?" I giggled, fanning the long hem of my dress. "This is my favorite dress to be free in. No color of underwear goes unseen under this dress, so I skip them altogether."

We laughed as Carlos and Devin shook their heads at us, laughing at our drunken confessions.

Inside Pure, I held the bathroom door closed for Sydney so she could adjust her wardrobe without someone pounding on it or opening it while she stepped out of her underwear. I passed her the pack of wet wipes I always carried in my purse.

"Ooooh! Cucumber melon!" she exclaimed from behind the door.

"Yeah, I infuse them with a little peppermint extract, too, so they may make you tingle a little bit afterward," I warned.

"Ooooh! Fancy!"

We laughed and she tapped the door three times to let me know she was ready to come out. We giggled again for no reason as she washed her hands. She swayed her hips from side to side in her orange dress as she dried her hands off and threw away the paper towel.

"This feels niiiiiiiice!" she whooped as she fanned the hem of her dress. "I need some of these wipes, Girl!"

"I'll get you some the next time I go buy them," I promised her. We giggled again as we stepped out of the bathroom and back onto the loud dance floor.

Carlos and Devin were by the bar with another round of shots.

"This is my last one, guys!" I said as I cringed into my glass.

"Me, too!" Sydney agreed.

"Neither of you are driving, so drink up!" Devin encouraged.

"That may be so, but I fear a hangover in my near future," Sydney told him.

We all laughed and downed the shots. I flagged down the handsome, bearded bartender with the neck tattoos for some water. He smiled at me and winked one hazel eye at me in agreement and returned with four tall glasses of water. I lowered my gaze slightly as I took them and walked them over to my friends. I thrust glasses at Devin and Carlos, silently demanding them to drink the water without argument.

Sydney accepted hers and sipped half of the glass down before pulling me close to whisper, "Bartender cutie is a certified life-ruiner! Fine as hell for no reason. He's the type with four baby mamas, who will leave you with no edges, bad credit, and a bill from the abortion clinic."

I laughed at her, swatting her away from me as I bent over so as not to spit my water all over her. I came up coughing over my giggles and wiping tears from my eyes.

We danced together for a few songs, while Devin and Carlos lounged on the bar stools watching ESPN on the huge flat screens on the walls.

"My feet hurt, J," Sydney complained. "It's nearly three in the morning. Are you ready to go yet?"

"Yeah, Girl, we can roll out of here," I agreed.

I flagged Carlos and Devin across the room, signaling that I was ready to go home. They nodded and we all headed toward the exit after they paid the tab at the bar.

Outside the club, Sydney and I hugged one another, and then I hugged Devin while she hugged Carlos. We parted ways in pairs, as Devin was driving her home, and Carlos was driving me home since we lived in the same building.

"Text me when you get home!" Sydney called over her shoulder as she and Devin walked away. I waved at her, indicating that I would, as Carlos opened the car door for me to get in.

When he was in the driver's seat and we were pulling out into traffic, he glanced at me with a smile.

"Did you have fun?" he asked.

"I sure did! Best birthday ever!"

The warmth of his hand on mine made me smile back as I squeezed it and laced my fingers with his.

"Good," he said, "I'm glad I could help with that."

I let my seat back a little and closed my eyes slowly. The shots had long since kicked in, and I was feeling relaxed and pleasantly dizzy as he drove. I woke up about twenty minutes later to Carlos squeezing my knee softly.

"Journey, we're at home. Wake up, Sweetie."

I blinked twice and accepted his help as he guided me out of the car. My gold strappy heels were killing me as I tiptoed around the car toward the door.

"Let me help you," he offered, scooping me up sideways in both arms.

I giggled as he respectfully tucked the length of my dress underneath me and carried me to the door of my apartment. When he put me down in front of my door, I unlocked it and immediately unlaced my shoes and stepped out of them, letting out a sigh of relief as my soles relaxed onto the cool floor.

Carlos followed me in, closed the front door, then took my hand and pulled me to the kitchen. Not bothering to turn on the kitchen light, he reached into my refrigerator, pulled out a bottle of water, and handed it to me. I took it from him and drank it down quickly, resting my palms and then my head on the cool granite counter.

"Are you okay?" he asked.

"Yeah, this counter just feels so nice and cool. I just want to lay here a minute."

He didn't say anything for a few minutes as I enjoyed the coolness against my head. When I lifted my head, he was standing beside me, watching me intently.

When he stepped closer, I felt his warmth radiating off of him, but there was something else. Something like desire that made the fine hairs on my arms raise and small goosebumps appear. He touched the back of my outstretched hand and raised it to his lips as he turned it over and kissed the palm and then the inside of my wrist, staring into my eyes.

I blinked twice in the darkness of my kitchen, trying to convince myself that this wasn't some drunken fantasy playing on my sexual frustration that I would roll over from in the morning. Using the wrist he was already holding, Carlos pulled me gently into him and embraced me, strumming the base of my spine with his thumb. I inhaled his scent and shivered a bit at the sensation.

He kissed my forehead and lifted my chin to kiss my lips. The first two kisses were soft, almost as if he was reading my response. At the third kiss, he flicked his tongue against my bottom lip and pulled me in closer, holding me more tightly against him. We kissed for a few minutes more as his hands traveled down and squeezed the softness of my behind, and it was evident that I wasn't against allowing him to explore me in any way he wanted to. I pressed my pelvis against his and he made a sound, gripping me sharply by my hips and reluctantly pushing me away.

"Journey, I have to go."

"What? Why? You can stay . . ." I stammered.

"I know, but... you told Devin we were just friends, and I want to be clear about my intentions with you. I have no desire to do this and remain just friends. I've wanted you since you first strolled into Eatonville with Erica. Besides, you've been drinking and while nothing would make me happier than to scoop you up and spend the next few hours making love to you the way you deserve on your birthday, or any day for that matter, I want you to want this with a clear mind. I don't want to take advantage or make you regret this in any way afterward," he explained.

I stared at him for a few moments, speechless. He smiled at me and kissed me on the lips again.

"Good night, Journey," he whispered as he stepped around me and opened my front door.

"When you're ready to be more than friends, you let me know," he said as he closed the door softly behind him.

I stared at the door, listening to his footsteps walking away and toward his apartment down the hall. I heard a soft mewing from Rico, and his silky fur rubbing against my legs seemed to unglue me from where I stood.

I walked quickly to the bathroom to shower and process what Carlos had just said. When I got out, I wrapped myself in a soft, emerald towel and stood in front of my mirror. Staring at my foggy reflection in the glass, I wondered aloud, "Why not?"

I had chosen Devin, who with all his good qualities wouldn't be honest with his girlfriend about our past. Travis was also a liar. James had dropped me when our proximity ceased to be convenient for him, even though he had spent over a year being with me before I had to relocate from Atlanta to D.C..

Carlos didn't have children, he was mature, he respected me, he hadn't told any lies — that I knew of — and he was clearly patient and willing to resist engaging his carnal desires with me to maintain the friendship we had already established. He was single, stable, successful, disciplined, and he protected me and took care of me when he didn't have to. He was exactly the type of man I should want.

By the time my image was clear in the mirror, I had made my decision. I unwrapped the towel from my body and used the dry parts to squeeze the excess moisture from my hair. I rubbed a little curl cream through it and combed it through evenly. I rubbed shea butter into my skin, and reached for the small bottle of perfumed oil I kept for when I needed to make a lasting impression. It was a sweet and musky fragrance that I made myself, and it lingered behind when I left a room. I poured five drops of it into my palm and pressed my hands together, careful not to rub them together. I patted my palms strategically against the insides of my elbows, the backs of my knees, the insides of my thighs, the back of my neck, and underneath my butt cheeks. I rubbed the excess under my breasts, down my abdomen and all the way down my legs. I poured five more drops into my palm and pressed my hands together again, bent over so all my hair hung in a curtain in front of my face, and rubbed the oil into my hair and the center of my scalp. I padded into my bedroom and pulled a white, silk negligee out of my dresser, slipped it over my head, and slid my feet into a pair of slippers. I grabbed my keys and left my apartment, making my way to Carlos' door.

The hallway was cool and my heart raced a little with anticipation as my knocking echoed softly. The television was on and I heard Carlos' footsteps approaching the door. The peephole darkened and he opened the door with a surprised expression.

"Carlos, I know it's late," I began, jingling my keys nervously, "but I thought about what you said and I . . . "

He interrupted my words by kissing me.

"Come in here," he said, leading me across the threshold by the hand and closing the door behind me.

"Sit down," he commanded softly, following me into the living room.

"Would you like some water or anything?" he offered.

"Yes, thank you."

I rested my keys on his table and my body on his plush black sofa. He returned with a bottle of water and turned the television off before sitting down on the sofa beside me.

"Now, I already have an idea of what you were thinking based upon the fact that you're here, but please continue," he said before drinking his own water.

"I was thinking that you're right," I said. "I've been hurt a lot over the past few years, but you're different from the men I've previously dated or been in relationships with. You're exactly the type I should want. You're right about everything you said tonight, and I appreciate you not taking advantage of my being drunk."

He leaned back a bit and motioned for me to lean into him as a smile slowly played across his face. His summer-bronzed skin seemed to pull me into his exposed chest and I scooted closer to him and lay my head on it. He brushed his fingers through the other side of my curls and my fingers found their way to the soft hairs on his chest.

"Journey, are you sure you're ready to be in a relationship?"

"I know we have gone on a few dates and we have maintained this friendship without sexual benefits for a few months. Aside from the two times we've kissed, there hasn't been any advancement in that direction, and you've treated me with the utmost respect. I'm willing to see where things go. So, yes, Carlos, I am."

"That's exactly what I wanted to hear," he said as he pulled me into his lap.

"Now come on and let me give you this birthday sex," he said with a sexy grin as he picked me up and carried me off to his bedroom.

***

In the morning, I pulled myself from beneath Carlos' arm carefully, trying not to wake him, and tiptoed to the bathroom. The need to pee was so urgent I feared I wouldn't make it in time as I practically ran the last few steps and plopped down on the toilet. I wiped myself and ran the water before flushing so as not to wake him with the noise. When I returned to the bedroom, he had barely stirred, so I climbed back into bed and snuggled back into the spot that was still warm from our body heat. He smiled a little as he pulled me close, and I kissed his eyelids, cheeks, and lips. He moved a bit at the last kiss and opened his eyes slightly, serving me a full smile.

"Good morning, Beautiful."

"Good morning, My Love," I responded.

He squeezed me around the waist and rested his palm on my ass.

"It isn't every day I wake up to an angel in my bed. I must be living life right these days."

I laughed. "I guess you are. Are you hungry? I certainly am."

"Yes," he said, rolling over onto his back and stretching. "What do you want for breakfast?"

"What do you have here? I can cook something at my place, or I can bring food from my place and cook here."

"Nah, it's Saturday. Let's go have breakfast out somewhere," he countered.

"Okay. Should I choose a place, or did you already have something in mind?"

"Let's go to Ted's Bulletin or The Front Page," he suggested.

"Cool, well, let me go home and get dressed." I started to get out of the bed, but Carlos pulled me back in.

"Noooo! Stay a little while longer, please. I just want to hold you a little more."

I giggled as my head hit the pillow beside him again. We kissed a little as Carlos took advantage of my nakedness, caressing me under the sheets.

"You smell so good," he inhaled my hair and kissed my collarbone gently. "What *is* that? I've never smelled it on you before."

I didn't answer as I absorbed his kisses that were moving toward my breasts. He didn't need to know everything and I was good for keeping my arts of seduction to myself.

11. Emerging from the Chrysalis

Looking out the corner of my eyes,
Smiling my smile,
Maintaining my disguise,
Quietly slipping notes into my mental files,
Seeing through the lies.

~ Olosunde

I had a job interview in Atlanta and my mother was letting me borrow her car. I was sweating like crazy in the car, even though the air conditioning was blasting. I was grateful that my criminal record had been sealed and I was able to start over again, but I knew the stakes were high to get myself and my son on track. I wanted to be a better mother to him and heal from my past more than anything.

I had landed an interview at Emory University as an administrative assistant to the dean in the school of business. I smoothed the curls on the side of my head that were trying to escape the pinned-up hairdo I was rocking and drummed my fingertips nervously on the steering wheel. This job paid enough for me to move into the city and enroll Jason into a school in Gwinnett County. My girlfriend, Tracey, had a nice condo that she was willing to rent out to me when I found a job, and it was close enough that I would still be able to see my mom and Leilani and not separate Jason from them too much.

I was grateful for my mother's support and that she wasn't trying to stop me from moving away. In previous years, she had made her disapproval of my moving to Atlanta known, but now she said she just wanted to see me be my best self and give Jason his best chance.

An hour later, I parked my car on campus and adjusted the hem of the blue pencil skirt I wore. The striped blazer was a little snug around my breasts, but the white blouse I wore fit well, so I didn't worry too much as I tiptoed gingerly through the grass and into the building. I waited in the front of the office and tried to find calm as the receptionist paged the dean to let him know I was waiting for him. If I had to choose between a job interview and a root canal, I would choose the root canal every time. I hated the questions and the fact that I had to wear a mask to make people like me.

"Dr. Jones will be with you shortly," the woman behind the desk told me.

"Thank you," I replied politely with a stiff, uncomfortable smile.

It was fake. She huffed softly and rolled her eyes, returning to whatever she was doing on her computer screen. I toyed with the stitching on the black leather binder I carried with me. My mother had helped me update my resume for this job three weeks ago, and this was the sixth interview I had been on. I had forgotten how much nepotism surrounded the hiring process in Georgia, and Lawrence was fraternity brothers with Dr. Jones, so I hoped I wouldn't have as hard a time in this interview as I had at the others.

I inhaled deeply, held my breath for a few seconds, and then released it slowly, the way I had learned in therapy, as I tried to command my heart from beating out of my chest. The old air conditioner in the window hummed loudly as it dripped into a plant that appeared to be strategically placed below it. A few minutes later, a short brown skinned man with a round belly came from around the corner and smiled at me with an extended hand.

"Ms. Massey! How nice to meet you!"

I smiled the most genuine smile I could muster, responding, "Thank you, Dr. Jones, it's nice to meet you as well."

"I've heard such good things about you! Please follow me into my office."

I rose and adjusted my skirt again before following behind him into a cool hallway where there were five doors that were closed. He opened the one at the end of the hallway, and found I it much larger than I expected.

"Please, have a seat," he gestured to one of the empty chairs on the other side of his desk. I lowered myself into the blue and gold cushioned chair and folded my hands in my lap on top of the binder. He sat down across from me with the same smile on his face.

"So, Erica, Lawrence has told me that you've relocated to the area and are looking for a job. I've reviewed your resume, and you appear to be well qualified for the administrative assistant position. This interview is merely a formality, as I owe Lawrence more favors than I care to admit." He laughed a little as he leaned back in his chair and adjusted his tie over his round belly.

"The position pays fifty-five thousand annually, and you'll have benefits and a gym membership on campus."

"Are you serious?" I asked with wide eyes. I wasn't expecting to hear such good news.

"Yes! As serious as can be! You're also able to take courses on campus at a fraction of the cost of other students. Here at Emory, we strive to help all students and employees advance themselves to reach their goals. Is that something you'd be interested in?"

"Of course!" I replied with excitement.

"Perfect! You'll have a week of training beginning next week, and you start the following week," he explained.

"Oh, my goodness! Thank you!"

"The pleasure is all mine. We've gotta stick together around here, and Lawrence is like family to me. I'd offer you a tour, but you have on heels. Next week, I will show you around and help you get acclimated," he offered.

"Thank you so much!" I clutched the black leather binder to my body, smiling in gratitude.

He waved a hand at me as if it were nothing and rose to shake my hand.

"Check your email this evening, and you will find a few documents to sign. You have to pass a drug screening before you start. Here's the address to the facility," he said.

He handed me a sheet of paper with an address and directions on it.

"If you call now, they may be able to take your specimen today, and the sooner we receive those results, the sooner you can start."

I took the paper from him, grinning from ear to ear as he walked toward his door. I followed him out and back to the lobby.

"It was a pleasure meeting you, Ms. Massey, and I look forward to having you join the Emory family," Dr. Jones said in farewell.

I thanked him again and practically skipped out of the building and back to the car.

When I was seated in the driver's seat of the car again, I called my mother to tell her the good news.

"Hello?" she answered.

"Mom! I got the job!" I shouted in exhilaration.

"That's awesome, Baby! I'm so happy for you! Lawrence's connection with Rodney came through! I was praying for you all morning. I just knew Jesus would make a way!"

"Thank you so much for asking Lawrence to help, Mom! I wouldn't have been able to do this without you two!"

"That's what family is for, Baby."

I wiped the tears that were starting to form in the corners of my eyes.

"This means so much to me, Mom. I am so grateful for you and all you've done for me and Jason. I promise to make you proud from here on out."

"You make me proud every day, Baby. You've been through so much in your life, and this is your time to blossom into the amazing woman I've always known you would become."

Her words made me cry harder as I sat in silence and absorbed her encouragement.

"I have to schedule this drug test," I told her when I could speak again. "I will see you when I pick you up from work later today."

"No need, honey, Lawrence is going to pick me up. Keep the car and go celebrate. I put some money in your account earlier today, so after you get gas, go treat yourself to a manicure and pedicure somewhere. You deserve it."

"Thank you, Mom."

"You're welcome. I will see you later. I won't tell Jason the good news. I'll save that for you."

"Okay, Mom. Bye."

"Bye, Sweetie."

I called the drug testing facility after hanging up with my mom and scheduled an appointment for noon. Then I did a quick search on my phone and saw there was a nail salon nearby on Howell Mill, and after reading some of their reviews, I decided to go there while I passed the time until my appointment.

I chose a soft, sparkly purple color and followed the nail tech to a spa chair. It wasn't the Mimosa Salon I used to go to with Journey in D.C., but it was nice. I texted Tracey the good news and invited her to meet me for drinks at happy hour. She agreed and suggested a tapas lounge in Buckhead that she knew. We made plans to meet after she got off work.

The nail tech's name was Erica also, and we chatted about our sons; I learned about her experience as a military brat to a Vietnamese mother and American father. She told about how she had lived in California for years before moving to Georgia, and how her mother managed to open this salon. Her family had owned and managed it for years. It was a family business and her teenaged son worked the register during the summer.

When she was finished, I tipped and paid her at the register, and walked down the block to take my drug test. I waited in the lobby for thirty minutes while a woman with old weave and a bad attitude popped her gum at the front desk. A man came and led me to the back where I was instructed to put my purse and other belongings in a locker before being given a cup to urinate in. By the time he arrived to get me, I really needed to use the bathroom, so I came out quickly with my specimen in hand. I placed it into the cabinet where the rest of the labeled cups were and retrieved my belongings from the locker. The woman at the front desk didn't even look up as I left, but I didn't care. I was on a cloud because I knew I had secured a job that would allow me to start a new life for Jason and I.

When I reached my mother's car and sat down, I realized I was hungry. I hadn't eaten breakfast because of how nervous I was, and I'd only had coffee so far. I decided to go to Atlantic Station to have lunch. I chose an outside table at Boneheads Grill, and as I sat down to enjoy a red snapper sandwich, I saw James walking into the restaurant with his friend, David. I made a face at the sight of David, but I smiled and waved at James when he saw me. He waved back and pointed to me as he spoke to David, who made a face that mirrored mine when James started in my direction.

"Hey, Erica! How are you?" James asked.

He greeted me warmly with a tight hug and a kiss to the cheek.

"Hey, James! I'm good. How are you doing?" I tried to ignore how handsome he was in his light blue button up shirt and dark blue slacks with a welcoming smile on his caramel face.

"Can't complain. What are you doing here? I thought you were in D.C.," he said as he straightened and stood across from me at my table.

"I was, but I've moved back. I'm trying to start over and get my son back from my mom," I explained.

"That's awesome! How long have you been back in town?"

"About a month. I'm staying with my mom and her husband in Athens. I just got a new job today, so I will be moving out this way soon."

"That sounds great! How's Journey doing?"

The question was bound to come up, but it made me uncomfortable all the same. To my knowledge, they hadn't spoken since he broke up with her nearly two years ago. I remembered the sound of her wailing and crying herself to sleep for days afterward and how much she went through in effort to get over him. I blinked away the memory and smiled tightly.

"I really don't know. We haven't spoken in months," I admitted.

"Really? You two had a falling out?"

"You could say that," I said nervously as I recalled the time I spent in jail. I shivered in the September heat. "I'm sure she's well, though. You know Journey."

"Yeah, I do. Well, since you're back, hit me up sometime. Here, let me put my number in your phone."

I handed him my phone, and he handed me his. After the exchange was complete, he smiled at me again.

"Don't be a stranger, Lady."

He winked at me before walking back toward David who was still looking at me with a disapproving gaze. We had butt heads a time or two during James' and Journey's relationship, and we didn't get along.

I ate the rest of my lunch in solitude, watching the people milling about. When I finished, I headed over to Ikea to look at furniture models for the new place I was going to be renting, and by the time I was done there, it was nearly four o'clock. I decided to head over to the restaurant where I would be meeting Tracey because I knew rush hour traffic would be fierce.

After sitting in traffic for an hour, I walked into the tapas lounge to find Tracey already there and holding a table for us.

"Hey, Girl!" I said with enthusiasm.

"Hey, there, Miss Newly Employed! Congratulations!" she said with her arms stretched out for an embrace. I hugged her, smiling.

"I know, right? I'm so excited! I can finally start my life over. I enjoyed spending the last few weeks with my mom and Lawrence and getting to be with Jason and Leilani, but it is time to move on, girl!" We sat down and I hung my purse off of my chair.

"Yes! I will definitely drink to that! So, tell me about the new job!"

"It's an administrative assistant position at Emory."

"Really? How'd you land that?" Tracey inquired.

"Lawrence is frat brothers with the Dean of the School of Business, and he owed him a favor," I said.

"Girl, nepotism at its best. Thank God, though!" she said as she waved her hands in the air for emphasis.

"Absolutely! It pays well, I have benefits, I can join the campus gym, and they offer classes to employees at a reduced price. I was thinking I might want to finish my degree or just start over on something else if my credits don't transfer from Georgia Military College."

"That sounds fantastic! I'm really happy for you Erica!" Tracey beamed.

"Thank you! I am so excited! I needed this break. I've been through so much."

"Yeah, you have, Friend. So, when do you think you'll want to move? I'm dying to put the chick who lives in my condo out, although her lease is up at the end of the month."

"Probably at the end of October. I need to save up to move and get a truck, and I want to transition Jason smoothly," I said.

"Oh, Girl, don't worry about a truck. My brother has a truck and I'm sure we can find a few guys to help move you," she assured.

"Well, I have to buy some furniture for myself first, and I know you'll need a security deposit."

"Forget about that! You're my homegirl and as good as family! I know you aren't going to skip out on rent or destroy the place. You can move in as soon as I clean the unit out and handle repairs. In fact, once I'm done, why don't you move in first, and then once you're settled you can research the nearby schools for Jason?"

"You're right. It's going to be a bitch driving all the way from Athens to Atlanta every day. I just don't want to leave Jason."

"You can stay with me throughout the week and go back to your mother's house on weekends if you want. I have a guest room in my townhouse, and it's not too far from Emory," she offered.

"Okay! Thanks, Girl! I really appreciate that!"

"No problem! When I left my husband, and moved out here from Alabama two years ago, my line sister helped me the same way. We all need somebody."

"You ain't lying."

Our waiter arrived, and we both ordered margaritas with sugared rims and ate empanadas with guacamole until we were stuffed. After three margaritas, Tracey paid the bill, refusing to let me split it with her, and insisted I let her treat me in celebration of my new job.

Afterward, we strolled over to Tongue in Groove, grabbed a small table, then went to the dance floor and danced a while. Someone brushed the back of my arm and I turned around to see James' fine ass.

"Hey, Girl," he said casually.

"Hey, James. Twice in a day? If I didn't know better, I'd think you were following me."

"Maybe I am," he said with a smirk.

"Where's David?"

"He just left. His daughter isn't feeling well, so I'm solo."

"Oh, that's too bad," I offered with a slight raise of my eyebrow.

"Lies," he said laughing. "You still don't like each other, so you were hoping he wasn't here. Admit it."

"True," I admitted with a chuckle. "I can't stand him. It's always good to see you, though." Tracey two-stepped closer to James and I.

"You, too. Who's your friend?"

"Oh, that's Tracey. Tracey, this is James. James, this is Tracey," I introduced.

They both waved at one another. Tracey winked at me and motioned conspicuously that she was going to the ladies' room. I laughed at her a little and gestured that he wasn't a big deal. She smiled, ignoring what we both knew was a lie, and moonwalked away to give me a few minutes alone with James.

"She's funny," James said with a chuckle.

"Yeah, she's acting weirdly wired right now from all the margaritas we had, but she's funny in general. So, how've you been getting on since . . . the last time I saw you?" I said as we walked off the dance floor to the table Tracey and I snagged earlier.

I wanted to say, "since you broke up with Journey," but I didn't feel right about discussing her with him, especially after what I had done to Devin.

"It's been about two years since I was last in D.C., and I've switched jobs since then. I was working in IT for an insurance company for a while until they let me go. That actually happened right after Journey and I broke up."

"Really? Why'd they let you go?"

"I got caught up in a stupid DUI situation, and based upon the contract I had with that company, an arrest or a 'no call, no show' is grounds for immediate termination. After that, I had a bad car accident in the rain that totaled my car. I flipped over three times on the highway when a truck veered into me and I swerved to avoid it. I'm lucky to be alive. I lost my apartment and had to stay with David for a few months until I found another job as a private contractor for another company, but then that contract ended unexpectedly and I was out of work for another few months. Now I have two contracts that complement each other, and I'm in my own spot near Moreland Ave," he explained.

"Wow, James! That was a lot! I'm so happy that you could pull through! Hell, I'm happy you're alive!"

"Me, too!" he laughed. "I definitely had a few moments where I thought that I wasn't going to make it."

"I can totally imagine that!"

"Yeah... so where are you two heading after you leave here tonight?"

"She's going to her house, and I have a long ride home to Athens."

"Athens? That's like an hour away! You may as well stay with your friend!" he suggested.

"Yeah, but I've got my mom's car."

"I see. Well, please let me know when you get home safely tonight. It's a Friday, and folks tend to act a little crazy on the roads."

"I sure will. Thanks for worrying about me."

A loud, breaking noise caught our attention, and we both turned in time to see Tracey stumble into a table while all the glasses on it crashed to the floor. A white man who appeared to be a little drunk shouted angrily at her and shoved her hard back to the ground as she started to stand again. James ran toward the man while I ran toward Tracey. As I helped her up off the floor, I noticed that she was bleeding from her hands and knees. I rushed to the bathroom to get paper towels for her, but when I returned, I saw a huge piece of glass stuck in her thigh where she had fallen.

"Oh, my God! Somebody call 911!" I shouted.

I looked around for James and saw him and the guy who had pushed Tracey being pulled apart from their grappling and then restrained outside by security for fighting. I snatched a cell phone out of the hands of some moron who was recording the incident, and called the police.

When they arrived with an ambulance in tow, I grabbed both our purses off the table I had been sharing with Tracey, and followed the stretcher outside to the ambulance. As I walked, I noticed the police were about to handcuff James, and the man who pushed Tracey was being guided into a police car.

I rushed over frantically yelling, "Officers! Officers! This man is my friend and he isn't responsible for the accident. That man over there shoved my friend to the ground because he was mad she bumped his table and knocked over the drinks. My friend was only pulling him off my girlfriend when he tried to fight him."

"Is that true?" the officer asked the man who had pushed Tracey. I shot him an evil look that dared him to lie to all the officers present.

"Yes," he admitted, reluctantly, rolling his eyes at me. "I pushed her fat ass on the floor because she knocked over all our drinks!"

"I see," the black officer replied with a disapproving scowl. "We are so sorry, sir, for the inconvenience," he told James. "Please have a safe rest of your evening." He removed the handcuffs from James and shook his hand.

"Thanks, Officer! We have to go!" I shouted, pulling James by his free hand until he began running behind me.

"Let's take my car and follow the ambulance to the hospital," James suggested.

"Okay, cool."

I followed him to his car and we rode closely behind the ambulance until we arrived at Grady Memorial Hospital. James let me out at the ambulance entrance, and then went to park his car. I followed the stretcher inside and let the nurses who began working on Tracey know that she and I were together, giving them the personal information I knew about her. They refused to let me in the back while they extracted the glass from her thigh, hands, and knees and tried to stop the bleeding.

When James arrived in the waiting area of the ER, I updated him on Tracey's condition. She was stable and had received fifteen stitches, but we couldn't leave until the police finished taking her statement. The man who had pushed her apparently had prior charges for domestic abuse, and this incident violated his probation, so Tracey had to decide whether she wanted to press charges.

When the officers were done with her statement, Tracey limped out into the waiting room. I sprang up when I saw her, rushing to let her lean her weight on me.

"I'm good, Girl. It doesn't hurt that bad, this bandage is just making it hard to maneuver."

"You sure you don't want a wheelchair to get you to the car?" I asked.

"No, I'm okay. I think I look a lot worse than I actually am thanks to all these bandages."

"All right. Well, at least let James and I help you so you don't lose your balance."

I cut my eyes at James to get his ass in gear and help me with Tracey. He was hanging back looking like he was trying not to intrude or overstep his boundaries, but he snapped out of it and came over to help.

We walked Tracey to James' car and lay her on the back seat so that she could stretch her legs out and be comfortable. As we drove back to Tongue and Groove, we decided James would park his car and drive Tracey home in her car while I followed them in my mom's car, then I would drive James back to his car.

When we pulled up, we didn't see her car anywhere. We got out and hit the panic button to see if maybe all the commotion had made Tracey forget where she parked, but there was no sound to lead us to her car. We noticed there was a lot of glass on the ground in the space where Tracey said she had parked her car, so we feared it was possible that someone had stolen it. I found my mother's car where I had left it, so we decided to take Tracey home, and I followed James to Tracey's house.

When we arrived and were walking her into the house, Tracey told me that she had called the towing company for the area we were in and discovered her car had been towed.

"Do you want me to stay the night and take you to pick it up in the morning?" I offered.

"No, Girl, Chris is going to be here in about an hour when he gets off work and he will take me to get it tomorrow. You are welcome to stay if you want to, though. It's late for such a long drive back to Athens tonight."

"Yeah, but I wouldn't want to interfere with your alone time with your man," I told her. "I'm going to text my mom and let her know I'm okay and just get a hotel room."

"You can stay with me, Erica," James offered. Tracey smiled a little and slid her eyes in the opposite direction as she raised her eyebrows. She had been saying James was into me all evening, so she was eating this right up.

"That's okay, James, I wouldn't want to inconvenience you in any way. You've already done so much already. You almost got arrested because of us, and . . ."

"And you helped me by talking to the officers, so let me help you now. I insist."

Tracey's smile broadened as she looked back at us, and she interrupted our exchange.

"Well, Erica and James, I really appreciate the two of you going out your way for me tonight, but I'm ready to take these clothes off and get comfortable. Chris will be here soon enough, and you two obviously have some tension to work out before the sun comes up. Erica, I love you, but I'm putting you out now. Good night!"

We all laughed and James and I reluctantly left Tracey on her couch.

"I will text you my address in case we get separated in traffic," James told me as he walked me to my car. I nodded and glued my eyes to the ground, swallowing a smile. I had a weird feeling about him and I didn't know whether it was a good thing. He smiled at me as he shut the door of my car and walked to his. My phone chimed when I received his text message.

I texted my mom to let her know I was okay and that I would be home tomorrow rather than drive home as late as it was. I didn't expect her to answer because she was likely asleep, but I knew she would see it in the morning. I put James' address in the GPS and followed him to his house.

When we pulled up at James' townhouse half an hour later, I parked my car in the driveway behind his. His house was nicely decorated in shades of blue, grey, and green. I saw the picture that Journey had given him of a man holding the world on his shoulders on the wall, and I immediately felt a twinge of guilt about being there.

"Do you want anything to drink? I have water, wine, beer, juice, or I can make you a mixed drink" James offered.

"Some water will be fine, thanks."

"Water it is. Have a seat. Make yourself at home." He gestured toward the living room.

He walked away toward the kitchen and I found a spot on the sofa. When he returned, I was sitting with my feet tucked underneath me. He held two bottles of water in his hands. "Do you want refrigerated water or room temperature water?"

"Room temperature, please. It's kind of cold in here," I said with a little shiver.

"Oh! Okay, I'm going to turn the air down for you."

"Thank you," I said, opening the bottle he offered me and taking a few sips.

"No problem. Do you want to watch a movie or something?" he asked as he adjusted the thermostat..

"Sure. I don't know if I will make it through a whole movie, though. I'm a little tired."

"That's okay," he laughed. "I'll get you something to sleep in and you can wash your clothes so you can take them home tomorrow."

"Okay."

He disappeared into his bedroom and returned with a pair of grey sweatpants and a t-shirt in one hand, and a towel and wash cloth with an unopened bar of soap on top.

"You can take a shower and change. There's a new toothbrush for you in the bathroom."

"Thank you," I said, surprised by his hospitality, and went to the bathroom to shower and change.

I unpinned my hair and stepped into the hot water, letting the stream pour down over my hair for a few minutes. There was a bottle of conditioner on the ledge of the tub and I poured some of it into my hands, finger combing it through evenly. I washed slowly, enjoying the water pressure on my skin.

When I was clean, I hung the wash cloth on the rack inside the tub and wrapped myself in the grey towel James had given me. I rummaged through the cabinet for some lotion, and found some cocoa butter. After rubbing it in, I stepped into the sweatpants that were too big, and tied them at the waist. I rolled the waistband down a few times to help them stay up and pulled the blue t shirt over my head. I fluffed my hair with the towel a bit and then hung it on the rack also.

When I finished brushing my teeth and stepped out of the bathroom, James was lounging on the sofa in a pair of grey sweatpants and a white t-shirt, sipping something brown while watching Sports Center. He smelled like men's body wash, so I knew he had showered while I was showering.

"I poured you a glass of wine, but if you don't want any that's fine," he told me when I sat down.

I thanked him and sipped the wine as I got comfortable on the couch next to him.

"What do you want to watch? I have Netflix."

"Let's see what's on," I suggested.

We flipped through the options on the screen as we laughed and argued over which *Friday* film was the best. Eventually, we agreed on one of the Katt Williams standup films. Soon, we were laughing and leaning into each other over his act. I stretched my legs out and James grabbed my foot and squeezed it.

"You're freezing! Do you want some socks?"

"Sure, thank you," I replied, wiggling my cold toes.

He got up and went to his room, returning with a pair of socks that were big enough to swallow my entire foot, but he didn't give them to me.

"As much as I like to see a woman in heels, I don't know how you do it. I couldn't imagine walking in those things all day," he said, settling onto the sofa.

"It takes practice. I personally hate wearing heels."

"I don't blame you," he told me as he squeezed my toes and applied pressure to the ball of my foot.

I didn't realize how tense my feet were until he started massaging them. I dropped my head back and let out a deep sigh, and James laughed at my reaction.

"You clearly needed this."

"Ugh! I didn't realize how much. Thank you."

"No problem." He kissed the bottoms of my feet and winked at me as he put the sock on my right foot, and then the left.

I blushed and sipped my wine again, and tried not to look at him.

"What's wrong?" he asked.

"Nothing," I mumbled into my glass.

"You ain't gotta lie. Talk to me."

"I just feel a little strange being here with you like this since . . ."

"Since I used to date Journey," he finished my thought.

"Yes," I said, looking up to meet his eyes.

"Well, she and I aren't together anymore, and you two aren't friends anymore, so I don't see anything wrong with you being here."

"Yeah . . . I guess it's just a little weird to me."

"I understand that. I'm not going to lie and pretend I'm not attracted to you, but I don't want to make you uncomfortable in any way," James said.

I fidgeted a little with the stem of my wine glass. I was attracted to him too, but after the fiasco with Journey and Devin, and remembering how Angel and Sabrina made me feel, this felt forbidden somehow.

James scooted closer to me and put his arm around me.

"I promise I won't do anything you don't want me to do, but I do want to spend time with you, and if it turns into something, I think we deserve to see where that goes," he said.

When I turned to look at him, he cupped his hand underneath my chin and kissed me gently. I hesitated at first, but when I kissed back, I felt a guilty pleasure that I hadn't known since the boy who used to write me love notes in high school. We made out on the couch until Katt Williams went off. James reached for the remote and turned off the television.

In the dark, he stood up and reached for my hand saying, "Let's go to bed."

I allowed him to lead me off the couch and up the stairs to his bedroom.

He didn't turn on the lights, but my eyes were already adjusted to the darkness. He pulled the blankets back and sat me down on the bed. He sat beside me and kissed me again. There was less hesitancy in my kiss now, and his hands drifted up my shirt and caressed my skin.

I leaned back with him onto the mattress and wrapped my arms around his neck as his hands found their way to my breasts. He pulled the shirt over my head and lowered his warm mouth onto one erect nipple, and then the other, making circles around the areolas with his tongue until I moaned softly and arched my back. He trailed his tongue between my breasts and up to my neck until I shivered and bit his shoulder softly.

I pulled his shirt over his head so that I could enjoy the warmth of his skin against mine. He unrolled the sweatpants I was wearing and untied them while he kissed my other breast again, reaching his hand into my pants. He stroked the wetness building between my legs as his lips made their way to my navel and I writhed beneath him breathing in short gasps.

"I think she likes me," he said as he pulled the pants off of me and spread my legs as wide as they would go. "I think it's time I had a little conversation with her."

I giggled and then gasped as he twirled his tongue around my clitoris. He lapped gently at the river flowing from between my legs, and I moaned and sighed.

"Hold on a second," he told me as he propped a couple of pillows under my lower back and lowered himself back between my legs. "Now back to our conversation."

He licked and licked my clitoris gently until my legs shook and I tried to wriggle away from him, but the leverage was all his. He held me in place with his arms under my legs, and laced his fingers over my belly as he pushed the hood of my clitoris back with his top lip, exposing more of it. He flicked his tongue against it unhurriedly until my moans transformed from soft, low, and almost melodic to a higher, gasping, staccato sound. My knees trembled erratically and I felt like I couldn't breathe, but he didn't stop or release me. He removed one arm and slid his thumb inside me, pressing the soft pad into my G-spot softly at first, and then building with intensity while he continued to flick his tongue against my clitoris. I felt a pressure build at the center of my forehead and then spread across my entire scalp. I was practically convulsing and screaming now, but I couldn't stop or even care about how loud I was. There was a sudden gush and I inhaled sharply, loudly, as I held my breath and all my muscles locked up as my legs collapsed onto the pillows beneath me. James rose and smiled, wiping the wetness I left on his beard after I squirted on him.

I trembled and stared at him with a look of surprise in my eyes. I'd had my share of orgasms, but I had never had such an intense orgasm in my life. He calmly stepped out of his sweatpants and smiled as I gasped at the intense erection he was sporting. However, when he stepped closer to me, I tapped into my star player and turned him around, pulling him down onto the bed.

"My turn," I said smiling and licking my lips.

I bent down and licked him from the bottom of his shaft up to the head. He moaned and propped himself up on his elbows and watched. When I had licked all sides of him, a vein began to bulge and pulsate in a steady throb as the pre-cum slid down the delicious curve of his erection. I twirled my tongue in slow circles, mixing my saliva with the pre-cum that continued to ooze out of him. He reached out and gently grabbed my chin in one hand, pulling my mouth away from him.

"Listen, you're obviously good at this, but I really want you to come sit on this dick. I know you're wet as hell, and if I have to choose between getting some head and stroking that wet pussy, I'll choose pussy any day. Bring that ass up here," he commanded with a hungry gleam in his eyes.

I smiled as he pulled a condom from God knows where and masterfully rolled it down with one hand. Facing him, I slid slowly down onto him, my walls spasming as I held my tongue against my top lip and gasped.

I rocked my hips back slowly, raised up, and came down hard. He reached behind me, gripping my hips in both hands as he guided me back up and down in a deep thrust. I leaned forward, resting the weight of my breasts against him as we kissed. We settled into a steady grind that ended in hard, wet thrusts echoed by our moans. I sat upright and pulled myself into a squat, resting my weight on my feet as I began to bounce, riding him hard.

His face crumpled into a slight frown, and he held his bottom lip between his teeth before pulling my torso back into him and flipping me over onto my back. He lifted my legs up over his shoulders and kissed my lips and neck while he pounded into me. I licked his neck and bit into his shoulder as he continued to thrust. The orgasm that exploded between us left us looking like a heap of sweaty brown limbs as we lay kissing each other.

After a few minutes, he got up and went to the bathroom to dispose of the condom, returning with a warm, wet washcloth. He wiped me gently, front to back, and took the towel back to the bathroom. When he returned, he pulled the blankets up over us and held me close, kissing my forehead and then my lips. I smiled with heavy eyelids and yawned as we both slipped into sleep with the pink sunlight peeking between the blinds.

12. Journey is the Destination

As the shooting star passed,
I let go of the last.
I'm a little scared of the future,
But can't live in the past.
No need to look backward like the Sankofa on my spine.
Change is inevitable,
It's only a matter of time.

~ Olosunde

"I have this philosophy that people show you degrees of their red flags of craziness in thirty day increments," I told Sydney as I tried on the third dress for her approval in my living room.

"Spin, Girl, spin! Let me see you walk in it to make sure it doesn't start inching up. You know how badly I talk about chicks who have to tug their skirts or dresses down every three steps!" Sydney said.

I walked from the front door over to her in my heels and the dress didn't budge, although it hugged my hips. I spun in a circle and popped my booty at her a few times until she giggled and cheered.

"Yes, Girl! Work! I love it! You definitely have to pack that one! Now what do you mean about these thirty day increments? You always have these crazily deep philosophies to share."

"I think that when you first meet a guy, you get to see their mask or representative self," I said. "That's not who they really are, though. That's them playing nice so as not to run you away. After thirty days, you get to see how attentive they are and how much they're willing to accommodate you and your quirks in exchange for your company."

"After sixty days, you will have usually gotten to see how they handle conflict with you as well as others, and you will have had at least one difference of opinion with them. Unfortunately, some women ignore the red flags at this point and continue along with the relationship, even if the man has exhibited certain aspects of his being unstable, emotionally unavailable or underdeveloped; especially if the sex is good."

"After ninety days, most people feel comfortable enough, and the image they've been projecting for all that time starts to weaken and the real person starts to show. That's how I handle my ninety-day rule. Mine is less about physical intimacy and more about personality and energy," I explained, smoothing my dress out and sitting beside her on the sofa.

"How long have you and Carlos been together now?" she asked.

I felt a smile forming at the corners of my lips as I thought about him, and then pulled it back in a bit, so as not to seem too thirsty in front of Sydney.

"Next week will make six months. The first few months was just us getting to know each other, but we didn't have a sexual encounter for more than ninety days because I just wasn't ready to share myself with anyone."

Sydney narrowed her eyes at me and smiled mischievously, "So, is this a pleasure trip, or is there something more you're keeping close to your chest? I know how secretive you can be. Nobody knows your business unless you're ready to tell it," she pried.

I lost the battle of trying to control my feelings and smiled broadly.

"Carlos has invited me to Puerto Rico to meet his family. They're having some kind of family reunion type of event there and he asked me to go."

"Travel really tells you a lot about a person, and he has been nearly perfect. We have had minor disagreements and differences of opinion, but he's so patient with me and I love his masculinity. He doesn't try to silence me, he protects me, respects me, and listens to me. He doesn't talk at me, and he apologizes when he's wrong."

"I love that he isn't controlling and he compromises when we don't agree. It's a different level of maturity than I have ever experienced with a man. I am in such a place of peace with him. I don't feel the need to challenge him or get mad at him at all. I really love him!"

I looked out the window, avoiding eye contact and the feeling of what it was like to say that out loud.

"Aww! J!" she wiggled her hands at me, "I'm so happy for you! You know I love me some Carlos! How long will you be gone?

"A week. I'm really excited!" I said, bouncing a little on the sofa.

"I bet you are! Hell, I'm excited for you!" she high-fived me.

"Thanks, Girl! Let me go put on this other outfit for you!"

I pushed myself up off the sofa and clicked my heels back into my closet to try on a series of other outfits for her approval. I lay the outfits she liked across my bed for packing later, but we were almost finished.

"When are you leaving and how is Devin handling your relationship with Carlos?" Sydney asked.

She called to me as I rummaged through my closet for the next outfit.

"I've wanted to ask that for a while now," she said.

"Tomorrow afternoon." I called back. "We have a nonstop flight to Jose Aponte Airport, and then we are driving to another part of the island from there to wherever his family lives. I think we are spending a few days at a resort before we come back, but the first few days will be at his family's house."

"As for Devin, we had a long talk about things between us, especially after he figured out the baby I miscarried was his," I said. "He was a little hurt at first, but eventually he wished us the best. We still see him occasionally, but I think he's been playing the background and entertaining another woman now. He hinted at it, but he hasn't directly told me about a new relationship."

I stepped out of the closet briefly so I could see her.

"You told him about the baby?" She asked incredulous. "I just knew you were going to keep that quiet. I figured he'd flip after that. I know how serious he was about you."

"Yeah, he was there for the hospital visit, but he has some soul searching to do. I don't think it's fair to me to ignore such a good thing with Carlos because of Devin. I mean he might love me and all that, but he's not ready to commit like I am. These are things I just don't have time for."

I waved my hand dismissively and walked back into my closet.

"I can totally understand that," she said, "Well, this trip sounds nice! How much was the flight?"

"I found one for two-hundred dollars roundtrip. I've never been to Puerto Rico, so this is a big first."

"Do you speak Spanish?"

I stepped back out to look at her again, "Not really, but I know a few words and phrases. I don't think that will be much of an issue with Carlos. His family speaks English as well as Spanish, and I don't plan to be away from him to have too much of a hard time with it."

"Bring me back something nice!" She grinned excitedly.

"You know I will, Girl!" I grinned back.

I lugged my suitcase into the living room and began folding my outfits together to fit neatly inside my carry-on. I hated checking my luggage after having airlines lose my bags while traveling. I tried to pack as smart as I could and leave anything I didn't absolutely need at home.

I stuffed a tote bag in the front pocket of the carryon so I could carry home any souvenirs in there.

"Well, if you leave me your keys, I will come by every couple days and feed Rico and pet him," Sydney offered as she put her purse on her arm and grabbed her keys. "I know how much he will miss you."

"Thank you! I'd really appreciate that. I was going to buy one of those feeders that let the food come down as he eats it, but I was honestly afraid he would overeat and have an empty bowl before I returned."

"You know he can be particular about his food and whatnot with his spoiled self."

"That would be fantastic! I have a spare key in my room. Hold on, I'll get it for you before you leave."

I went to get the spare key from my nightstand drawer.

I returned to Sydney and said, "Here you go. You don't have to come tomorrow, but if you could drop by Wednesday and Friday, that will be great. We will be back on Sunday."

"Coolness!" Sydney exclaimed. "Have fun! I will be praying for you to have a great time and safe travels."

"I appreciate you, Girl! I'll see you when I get back."

We hugged at the door as she left and I went back to packing.

Carlos came by later that evening to make sure I was packed, and cooked seared scallops, quinoa, and mixed vegetables for dinner. We spent the rest of the evening cuddled up on the couch watching television until we both fell asleep.

In the morning, we checked and double checked that everything we needed and called a cab to take us to Ronald Reagan Washington National Airport. Carlos was all smiles and excitement. This would be our first Valentine's Day together, and I hadn't really celebrated that holiday with anyone before.

The nervous energy I felt made knots in my stomach as I slipped on the socks I carried in my purse for the security check at TSA. I hated walking my bare feet through that area, and I always felt my inner germaphobe cringe at people who didn't care. Carlos accepted the socks I packed for him with a chuckle and slipped them on his feet as he walked through the security check as well.

We bought coffee and breakfast near our gate and commenced to people watching as we waited to board our flight. There were couples enjoying their breakfast, military travelers, and families trying to keep their children in line as they waited in the airport. It was like watching hundreds of people who were all completely engaged in their own universes amid the travel announcements that could barely be heard, save for the woman with the Trini accent somewhere at one of the gates.

A mother with two children who appeared to be under the age of two was having a difficult time holding her youngest child in her lap while the oldest resisted her hand clasping his wrist trying to prevent him from running away. A thought crossed my mind as I watched the man who appeared to be the husband and father sitting nearby with his eyes glued to his phone, seemingly oblivious of the struggle going on beside him. I turned a thoughtful gaze to Carlos.

"Do you ever want to have children?"

"Me?" He asked pointing to himself. "I don't know. Once upon a time I wanted to have quite a big family, but after seeing my friends and family have children, I think I'm okay with waiting until I'm married to the right woman," he said.

"What's your idea of the right woman?"

"Someone who loves children and is nurturing. Mothers are amazing and a child's first teacher, not to mention that a mother is God in the eyes of her child, so I have been careful of the type of women I have chosen to lay with and potentially share my seed."

"Hmm . . ." I mused quietly. "So, hypothetically speaking, you'd want children with a nurturing woman to whom you were married?"

"Yes," he answered, "someone like you would do nicely."

His smile made me smile and I continued to watch the mother struggling with her oldest child.

"What type of father do you think you'd be?" I continued.

"What do you mean?" he asked.

"Would you be hands-on in the parenting process, or would you be distant like homeboy over there with his eyes on his phone, looking like he's messaging his side chick or watching the game while his wife struggles with the kids?" I nodded my head in the family's general direction.

"Well, my father was awesome," Carlos said. "He changed diapers and helped with all things child rearing, so I was socialized not to leave the brunt of the work on my wife. I mean my mother was a supermom in her own right, but my dad wasn't the type who was only around for providing or disciplinary purposes like some other fathers I know."

"My dad is my hero. I think you'll like him. He's charming as ever, though. I may have to watch you around him."

He chuckled and I swatted at him with a napkin as I laughed, too.

When we boarded our flight, Carlos let me have the window seat so I could see the island and the ocean as we landed. I accepted giddily and settled into my seat as he hoisted our bags into the overhead compartment. My heart raced with anticipation as the plane took off as if I hadn't been on an airplane a million times before. I couldn't sleep, but he let his seat back and rested his hand on my knee as he napped through the three-hour flight.

As our plane was preparing to land, I marveled at the expansiveness of the ocean, and I felt so small as my spirit vibrated. I couldn't wait to touch those beaches and soak up the sunshine! I was practically glued to the window as I gasped and cooed over how green everything looked. It was such a different view from the cold, cloudy skies we had left behind. The plane landed smoothly and I could hardly wait to get off and into that warm ocean air. Carlos smiled at me endearingly and squeezed my hand as we walked through the airport with our luggage.

Once we were through customs, Carlos turned his phone on and called his uncle who was picking us up from the airport. As we exited the airport, a tall man walked over to us with a smile and embraced him tightly.

"Carlos! Welcome home," the tall man said. "Ooooh! You brought your lady with you! She's so beautiful!"

I smiled shyly and thanked him as he embraced me and kissed my cheek.

"Do you guys have all your luggage?" the tall man asked.

"Yeah, Uncle Rafael, you know I only bring carryon luggage when I come home!"

"Great! Let's go," Rafael said, turning in the direction of his car. "Your mom and sister are dying to see you and meet this beautiful woman you've brought with you!"

I suddenly felt anxious, and I worried whether I'd make a good impression. Carlos squeezed my hand as if he felt my nervousness and kissed the top of my head as he led me out toward his uncle's car. It was about an hour-long ride to Yabucoa where Carlos' family lived, but it felt shorter with the conversation and stories Rafael told about Carlos and his sister growing up there.

By the time we arrived, I was less anxious and hungry as hell. Uncle Rafael wasn't exaggerating about everyone being excited to meet me, and I don't think I had been kissed and embraced so much since I was a kid. I barely walked through the door before I was introduced to a ton of people whose names I didn't get to process before being embraced by another pair of arms. It was nice to be around so many warm people who had heard so much about me already. It felt good to know that I was important enough to Carlos that he had spoken highly of me to his family.

I felt myself quietly longing for the connection of family, but with my life and childhood being what it was, I just didn't have that. For the first time, I began to wonder in depth about what it would be like to have that family structure through Carlos. I felt butterflies inside as I watched him playing with his nieces, nephews, and cousins. The children flocked to him, begging to be picked up, demanding his hugs and kisses, and squealing as he lifted them up and spun them around. I felt myself falling more and more in love with him by the minute.

Carlos hadn't lied about his father, who was extremely charming, but his grandmother was the real matriarch. Anytime she spoke, everyone stopped to listen and cater to her. Her small, elderly voice was the most respected in the house, and all conflicts appeared to cease at her command. She had raised ten of her own children and had three times as many grandchildren who were curious, yet well mannered.

The amount of food I ate that evening was unbelievable, and I enjoyed every bit, even though it differed severely from my normally health-conscious routine. I danced, looked at family photos, played with children, and nobody allowed me to lift a finger as Carlos' special guest. He had apparently never brought anyone home before, so my presence was a bigger deal than I had anticipated or ever imagined. We all sat in chairs in the yard around a large, wrought iron dining table with a glass top.

"She's much better than that woman you dated before, Carlos!" his aunt commented. That made me a little uncomfortable, and Carlos laughed nervously.

"Oh, I sense a story!" I teased.

His sister and aunts laughed.

"Marisol, why do you always have to bring that woman up?" he asked.

"Because I told you she was no good and you didn't listen to me. You know I know things, nephew." He sighed and looked away from her.

"What happened?" I asked.

"He proposed to her and she ran off with his ring and never came back. When we heard from her again, she was pregnant and married to another man."

"Carlos was devastated about that for a long time. She was beautiful to look at, but she had a cold heart. Carlos is more of a lover than a ladies' man, and she didn't appreciate him one bit."

"I see. Well, he's been the most wonderful man to me," I told her. "I have a hard time believing any woman wouldn't want him. I imagined he would have been beating the ladies off with a stick here."

"He really is a good guy, Journey," Marisol said.

"I'm right here, ladies, do I need to leave so that you can discuss me in peace?" he said with a chuckle.

"Oh, no! We prefer you to hear all that we have to say about you," she joked.

We all laughed at that and I pulled Carlos in for a kiss that made him blush a little.

It was dark and the citronella fragrance of the candles flickering and the coquito frogs singing made me aware of how far away from home I truly was. I yawned dramatically to signal to Carlos that I was tired and wanted to wind things down a bit.

"Are you tired, Baby?"

"A little. I think I need to shower and lay down. I fear I'm turning into a pumpkin soon."

"Let's go get you a shower, then," he said as he clasped his fingers between mine and pulled me up.

The children were already in bed, and it was nearly midnight. I hugged and kissed all the aunts and uncles who were still outside and followed Carlos into the house.

Inside, there was a bedroom with blue and green walls that had a private bathroom. Carlos told me how he and his uncles had built the additional bedroom and bathroom onto the house when he was in high school to accommodate the family members who had left for the states and would come back and visit. He told me that his father rented the room out to tourists when family wasn't visiting.

The bathroom had seashell wallpaper and ocean colored tiles. There were towels laid out for us, and Carlos turned on the shower while I dug my body wash and shower gloves out of my suitcase. I undressed quickly, and when I walked into the bathroom, he was naked and waiting for me with a ponytail holder in his hand. He beckoned to me and scooped my curls up on top of my head when I approached. When he finished tying my hair up, he took my gloves and body wash from me and pulled back the shower curtain, popping me on the butt as I stepped past him and into the stream of water. I looked back and smirked at him as I waited for him to step his gorgeous frame into the tub with me.

He put the gloves on and poured the shower gel into his palm as I enjoyed the warm water ponding the tension out of my shoulders. He turned me around so that my back was facing him and scrubbed it firmly in circles the way I liked. I leaned into him as he brought his hands around and cupped my breasts, kissing the side of my neck. He scrubbed my arms and belly, and I pressed my back into him encouraging the erection that I felt growing against my backside. He stepped back a bit and stooped down to wash my hips and thighs, eventually making his way down to my legs and feet. I leaned my head forward so that the water hit the back of my neck and between my shoulders.

When I felt his tongue against my tailbone, making its way up my spine, I arched my back in invitation. He pressed his lips against my neck, licked my ear, and bit my shoulder as he pulled me into him and slid himself inside me. I exhaled and bit my lip as he filled me up from behind, slowly at first, and then building as I became more wet for him. The roughness of the gloves against my neck as he held my head up while he stroked me made me whimper with pleasure as I tried to be quiet because I had no idea whether anyone could hear us. He turned me around to face him, pressing my back against the wall as he lifted my legs up over his arms and kissed me deeply until I felt like I couldn't breathe. I let a deep loud moan slip out, to the point where I felt the need to cover my mouth in fear of being heard by whomever was in the room nearby.

He shut the water off and stepped out, leading me behind him before bending me over by the sink in front of the mirror so he could see me as he stroked me slowly, over and over again. He enjoyed seeing the unrehearsed faces I made as I enjoyed every single thrust. I felt like I had let him control it long enough, and I started rocking my hips and strategically throwing my slightly damp ass into him as deep as I could. Right when he began to close his eyes in complete pleasure I sped up just to let him know the business he was giving could be reciprocated just as easily. He spread my cheeks to get even deeper and I could feel him pulsing inside me every time he slid in and out. I admired the veins protruding in his arms and neck as he bit his lip and moaned deeply.

He stepped back a bit and turned me around to face him again as he kissed me and picked me up, carrying me to the bed. I giggled as I scooted away from him toward the pillows, and he crawled up toward me, hunting me with a primal look in his eyes. I stopped him for a second and handed him a condom from my toiletry bag that was on the bed. After all I had already been through, I wasn't trying to have any unplanned pregnancies. He smiled and kissed me again before sliding it on and I sank into the pillows as he sank into me. He stroked me a for a few minutes before he grabbed my right leg and placed it over his shoulder, looking me deep in my eyes, and as he leaned in closer to kiss me, he penetrated deeper and deeper.

We were both so into it that it took me some time to realize that my foot had been repeatedly kicking the blinds the whole time, but none of that mattered as he stroked me as if he hoped we broke the blinds above the bed, the headboard, and anything else close to us. I could've kicked the whole window out and it wouldn't have mattered, it was all about us and the pure ecstasy we felt. He made love to me as if it would be the last time he would be able to do it, and I was more than happy to match his intensity.

Before he slowly backed out of me, he glared at me and whispered into my ear, "I forgot to taste you," and slowly slid down to my waist where he placed both thighs over his shoulders and began licking circles around my clit. T h e sensation provoked me to grab the sides of his head with both hands as his beard tickled my inner thighs. He slid two fingers inside me while he licked, pressing against my g-spot and beckoning in that 'come here' motion until I pulled the pillows over my face, crying out softly as I came for him. He snatched the pillow from me with his free hand

and didn't stop as I arched my back and breathed sharply over and over. When he finally came up for air, his hand was wet all the way to his wrist. My eyes widened in surprise as I stared at him openmouthed. He advanced toward me, but I placed my hand on his chest and tried to squirm away.

"Baby, hold on, I have to pee."

"Oh, no," he growled at me.

He snatched me back to him and thrust himself back inside me, plowing away until I squirted at him. His face was buried in my neck as our bodies made a loud, wet slapping sound, and all I could do was hold on to him as I orgasmed again and again. When he finally climaxed, he collapsed on top of me with my trembling legs lying limply over his arms. We kissed lazily as his erection became less and less intense, and finally slid out of me on its own; we almost simultaneously slipped into a post climactic slumber.

***

In the morning, I woke feeling dehydrated, sweaty, and starving for the delicious smelling food that was being prepared in the kitchen. Carlos stirred slowly after I wiggled from beneath his heavy arm, and we both smiled at each other in silent appreciation of the events of the night before.

"Happy Valentine's Day," he whispered, pulling me back into him.

"Happy Valentine's Day, Baby," I said back. "We smell like sweaty, yummy sex," I said as I giggled and hopped up to take a shower.

He peeled the used condom off and threw it away as I pulled the ponytail holder off of my hair and fluffed it out. My curls were piled crazily on top of my head in a slightly dampened mass, and I finger-combed conditioner through them in the shower. Carlos stepped in behind me and kissed my shoulder.

"Oh, no, sir! I need to eat and hydrate before I let you turn me up all over again!"

He laughed as I teased, and I kissed him and slid my shower gloves on. They were slightly stretched out by his hands being in them last night, but I didn't care. I washed quickly as soap careened down my legs and I rinsed the conditioner out of my hair. When I stepped out of the tub to let Carlos finish his shower while I did my hair, I smiled at the lighthearted happiness I felt. I hadn't been this happy in a long time, and I was glad I had made the decision to be with him and to come spend this time with him in Puerto Rico.

"I'm taking you on an adventure today," he told me from behind the shower curtain. "Don't start asking questions, okay? It's a surprise."

He peeked out from behind the curtain and winked at me, smiling mischievously.

"I can't wait!" I squealed. "What should I wear?"

"Something comfortable. Don't wear heels. Wear the most comfortable sneakers you have," he instructed.

"Okay!" I replied, bouncing excitedly to get my toothbrush and toothpaste out of my bag.

I brushed my teeth as I hummed to myself. When I was finished, I rubbed on shea butter and my new lime peppermint deodorant, and stepped into a yellow and white romper before putting on some little white canvas sneakers with pineapples on them.

"Well, don't you look cute!" Carlos said when he emerged from the shower with a towel lazily wrapped around his waist.

His hip was slightly exposed and the water clung to the hair on his chest and dripped down his belly. I walked over to him and trailed my fingertips from his chest, down his belly, to his navel and kissed him before snatching his towel off and running away from him. He laughed and chased me out of the bathroom, caught me by the waist, and pounced his wet body on top of me on the bed. We laughed and kissed each other as his hands wandered up the bottom of my romper. I managed to wiggle away just as he realized I wasn't wearing anything underneath it, and he smiled another devilish smile as I slipped out the door.

"Really? I'm going to get you sooner or later!" he called from the other side of the door as I cackled because he couldn't follow me out while he was naked.

"Good morning!" his mother sang from behind me, scaring the shit out of me as I whirled around.

She laughed at my surprise and pulled me by the hand into the kitchen.

"I made breakfast for you guys. I hope you like it! Would you like some coffee?" she offered, gesturing for me to sit at the kitchen table.

"Yes, please!" I beamed, as she fixed a plate for me and poured coffee into a mug. "I really enjoyed spending time with you all yesterday! I don't think I've eaten so much delicious food in my life. Thank you!"

"You're welcome! We are all just so happy to have you and Carlos here. I'm not supposed to tell you where you're going today, but I think you'll have a great time!"

"You know about this adventure, too?" I chuckled. "Does everyone know but me?"

"Everyone who can keep a secret knows," she offered with a wink.

I sipped my coffee and smiled back at her as Carlos appeared in the doorway.

"Don't let me catch you slipping, Mom," he told her as he walked in and kissed her on the cheek. "Good morning. Do you need any help or anything?"

"No worries, Mijo, you sit down and eat. I have this," she said as she began fixing Carlos a plate.

"Thanks, Mom."

Rafael walked in with an unlit cigarette in the corner of his mouth.

"Good morning," he said. "You guys going to be ready soon, Carlos? I brought the car."

He kissed his sister and accepted the cup of coffee she handed him.

"Don't you light that cigarette in this house, Rafael! You take that outside!"

"I wasn't going to!" he told her.

He muttered something under his breath in Spanish. She swatted him with a dish rag in response, and they both laughed as he handed some keys to Carlos.

"You guys have fun. I will come get the car back from you tomorrow evening."

"Thanks, Tio," Carlos said as put the keys in his pocket and winked at me before he continued to eat his breakfast.

After we finished eating, I insisted on helping wash the dishes before Carlos ushered me out the door to the car.

After an hour of driving, Carlos drove past a sign that welcomed us to the El Yunque National Forest. We drove through a maze of canopy trees surrounded by greater trees in the distance. I gazed at the beautiful rainforest with my mouth agape until we reached the welcome center. Carlos parked the car and grabbed a backpack from the backseat before opening my door and guiding me out by my hand.

The air was moist and balmy as we climbed the steps to the welcome center. I took a quick moment to use the bathroom while he ordered tostones and

Medallas from the food stand nearby. We settled at a high-top table and ate while our conversation was accented by the sounds of tropical birds and coquito frogs in the distance.

When we were finished with our light lunch, Carlos led me up a path through the trees. The higher we climbed, the more out of shape I felt, but he took his time and didn't walk too fast so I wouldn't collapse. Neither of us had a good phone signal at this height, but that didn't stop us from taking lots of pictures along the way.

"Where are we going, Carlos?" I panted between breaths.

"It's a surprise. Don't worry, we will be there soon enough," he promised.

"I don't know how much farther I can go. Can we stop for a few minutes?"

"Sure. There's a rock up ahead that you can sit on and rest on for a bit."

We sat together on the rock as I slid my shoes off and my feet into the small stream that was flowing along the side of the path. There were so many plants and flowers I had never seen before that for a few minutes I felt like a fern gully fairy queen sitting on my stone throne. I said this to Carlos, and he chuckled and tucked an orange flower behind my ear, whispering, "Your Majesty," before kissing me. I grinned and blushed as I put my shoes back on, feeling refreshed for the rest of the climb.

After another thirty minutes of hiking, we reached an open road that Carlos told me was for park vehicles. We were so high up that we could see the clouds just above, and my hair was becoming damp from all the moisture in the air. We pushed along farther until we were standing in the clouds themselves, and I could see the whole island and the ocean beyond. The sight of the afternoon sun glinting off the blue water was so beautiful that my eyes filled with tears as I wished my mother could be there to witness it. It was the highest up I had ever been on land, and the closest to God I had ever felt in my entire life.

Carlos walked up behind me as I stared out into the distance, lost in my own thoughts for the moment, and wrapped his arms around me. He held me in silence for a few minutes before pulling me away so that we could keep climbing. We passed a clearing with what looked to be a little house slightly hidden behind some trees. I gasped with excitement and skipped ahead a bit to explore the new sighting.

"Wow! What is this?"

"A lookout post. There are lots of cannons down in Old San Juan that tell the history of the structures. I can take you there one day before we leave if you're feeling adventurous."

"Okay! That sounds exciting!"

"Yeah, this island has some really deep history, some proud, and some painful. I don't really venture into those areas too often, but I'll take you."

"I can't wait!"

"Come on, there's a little more ground to cover," he urged, and I followed him without argument after taking a few snapshots of the post.

When we reached the highest point of the mountain, I gasped with deep appreciation. I could see all sides of the island from this point and we were above the clouds with a nice, cool breeze ruffling our clothes.

"Journey," Carlos said quietly, making me turn around to face him. He lowered himself down on one knee in his khaki shorts waiting for my attention.

I gasped and my eyes widened as I came closer to him.

"Journey Richards, you've been the most influential woman in my life since my own mother, and I love you. I have been daydreaming about you since I saw you in the leasing office, and you suddenly seemed more than just the beautifully unattainable woman in my section at Eatonville. I wake up every day now with you on my mind, and I can't wait to get next to you every moment we are apart. It is my deepest desire to spend the rest of my days making every moment better than the last. I want you to be my wife and the mother of our children. Will you marry me?"

The tears started flowing down my face before he could even finish, and I said, "Yes," over shaky breaths and sniffles. He slid a beautiful ring on my finger, stood, and kissed me until I was breathless. All I could think was , to date, this was the most beautiful and happy day of my life.

I walked on a cloud for the rest of the time that we were in the rainforest. I held Carlos' hand and kissed him too many times to count whenever the mood hit. It took us about an hour and a half to make our way back to the car and my hair was frizzy and damp. I pulled it on top of my head in a bun after I sat back in the car. We held hands and smiled goofy loving grins at one another all the way back to the house.

When we arrived, everyone was waiting for us in the backyard. When we walked through the house and out the back door, all the family members there cheered and clapped loudly. A few people walked up and hugged me and congratulated us both. The best part was when Carlos' grandmother kissed both of my cheeks and said, "Journey, welcome to the family!" I embraced her as I blinked back fresh tears from her warmth and welcoming.

I texted my brother a picture of my ring and settled into enjoying the food and stories about how long the ring had been in the family, and how Carlos had figured out my ring size from the ring I usually wore on the ring finger of my right hand. It was a smidge too big, but I didn't care. I had spent Valentine's Day with the man of my dreams and I was finally happy.

13. The Slippery Slope of Disaster

I loved the one who had me at hello,
But he didn't wear a halo.
His smile gave me butterflies,
But his flow was false like day-glow.
Now it's spring and love is in the air,
My heart's white slate like Anglo.
Bags packed in the vehicle of the past.
Pour the gasoline,light a match, and watch it blow.

~ Olosunde

James and I had been seeing each other regularly for eight months, and I was feeling good about the time we had been spending with each other. He had taken me on some of the most memorable dates I had ever experienced before, and I was having some of the best sex of my life, but I wasn't ready to introduce him to Jason or my mom yet. I was enjoying myself with him, and the guilt of breaking woman law was receding as the weeks and months went on. Journey always said that guilt was a useless emotion, so I grounded myself in that as I gave myself permission to be happy with James.

Thanks to Tracey, I found an apartment in Gwinnett County, and I was enjoying my new job at the university. Things were going so well, I was having difficulty divorcing myself from the anxiety I felt at night when I was alone with my own fears, doubts, and memories of all the fucked up experiences I had managed to survive. I had never experienced so many positive shifts in my world at once. I hated to acknowledge that I was worried something could go wrong.

James interrupted my thoughts as he appeared behind me on the wooden deck of the marina, wrapping one arm around me and kissing the back of my neck.

"Oh! Hey!" I said in a startled greeting. "You scared the shit out of me!"

"Who else would be coming up behind you to kiss you on the back of the neck?" he asked with a naughty grin and a raised eyebrow. "Sorry I'm late, love. There was so much traffic."

"It's okay. I wasn't waiting too long," I said in a forgiving tone as I kissed him like I missed him.

We walked away from the marina and toward the yacht party that was on Lake Lanier. I had never been on a yacht, let alone to a yacht party, and I tucked away a little grin as he wove our arms around each other on our walk toward it.

James had been invited to a dinner party on this yacht for his job, and he asked me to be his date. He bought me a sleeveless, white dress with a sheer, flowing exterior to wear, and he wore a pair of white linen pants with a white linen shirt. I felt like a princess as we walked onto the yacht and were escorted to our seats by a pretty Latina hostess.

There was a live band and an open bar to compliment delicious Caribbean food. We both ate jerk salmon with rice and peas and steamed cabbage while the band played. After a hour-long set, a deejay began playing line dancing songs while the emcee encouraged everyone to get up and dance. We danced to a few songs we knew before the emcee began teaching new dances we had never seen before. We stumbled over each other without coordination through one song before I suggested we go step away from the crowded dance floor and rest.

We walked to the railing of the boat and stood in silence for a long time staring at the moon. It was so full and bright that it seemed to light up the whole sky. The wind blew my hair away from my face as I took a deep breath and exhaled as I closed my eyes, smiling to myself in appreciation of the moment.

I could feel James shifting beside me and a faint chiming made me open my eyes and look at him as he fished his phone out of his pocket. He declined the phone call and wrapped his arms around my waist as he stood behind me and inhaled my hair and neck before planting a suggestive kiss on my shoulder, and then my neck. I turned my head slightly in the direction of his kiss and smiled. His phone chimed again and again, but he ignored the call.

"Somebody really wants to talk to you," I teased.

"Forget about that. The only thing I care about right now is this moment with you."

At that, I turned around to kiss him deeply as the wind ruffled the hem of my dress, and I imagined that no one was there but us for a few minutes. We kissed passionately as his hands drifted down to caress my hips and cupped my behind as he pulled me closer.

"James, Hi!" a male voice snatched us out of our little world as James turned around to look at the person who spoke. A short, stocky Caucasian man approached us and extended his hand to James.

"Will! Hey! Good to see you!" he said shaking his hand.

"Likewise! I'm glad you could make it! And who is this beautiful woman you've brought with you?" Will asked, looking at me.

"Uh, this is Erica. She's my date. Erica, this is my manager, Will," James introduced us.

"Hi, Will, nice to meet you," I said, extending my hand to shake his.

"You are absolutely lovely," he said, grasping and turning my hand over to kiss it. "It's a pleasure to meet you."

"James, if I can steal you away from this gorgeous creature for a few minutes, I'd like to chat with you about this week's meeting."

"Certainly!" he told Will, before turning to me. "Erica, I will be right back, sweetheart."

"Okay," I agreed as I watched him walk away.

When he was out of sight, I turned back to the water and the sky and marveled at the stars for a while, enjoying the song of the crickets and cicadas in the breeze.

After a while, I returned to our table where I found James' phone and keys, but no James. I sat down and listened to the band's second set. I was lip synching *Red, Red Wine* when I heard James' phone chime indicating a text message. Against my better judgement, I looked at the screen and saw several messages from someone named Zara. The most recent read, *So you're just going to ignore me now?*

I raised my eyebrows a bit as my curiosity piqued, but I didn't touch the phone before the screen went black again. I moved to turn around and direct my attention back to the band when the phone began to ring.

I ignored the call and continued watching the band while looking around discreetly for James. I felt a growing sense of dread brewing in my chest, but I pushed it down, dismissing the nagging desire to know what was going on. Who was Zara, and why was she so pressed to speak to James? Should I ask him? Did the time we had been spending together give me the grounds to inquire? Why did I care at all? I was there with him, right? Right? Right.

I was coaching myself to trust him and mind my business when the phone suddenly exploded with the ring of a FaceTime call. *Mind your business, Girl*, I persuaded myself. I turned away from the phone and tried to focus on the band. What song were they playing? The ringing stopped and I exhaled deeply, glad to have the distraction silenced. A few seconds later, the FaceTime rang again, obnoxiously snatching my attention back to the screen. Before I knew it, I tapped the green button to answer the call.

A pretty woman whose brown curls spilled down onto one side of her head scowled at me on the screen asking, "Who the hell are you and where is James?"

"I'm sorry, but he's unavailable right now."

"Tell James I said get his ass on this phone! I tell him I'm pregnant and he just ignores me? What the hell? Who does that? Who are you? Where is he?"

She was belligerent with anger, but before I could say anything more, James appeared behind me, reached over, and ended the call.

"What are you doing, Erica?"

My cheeks burned and my ears rang. "Who is Zara and why is she so upset with you?"

He sighed and put the phone in his pocket.

"Let's step outside," he muttered softly.

"No, tell me right here, James!" I shot back, getting loud.

"Shhhh! Please keep your voice down! I work with these people. Please just step outside with me and I will explain," he said, looking around anxiously.

I stood, reluctantly, and followed him toward the exit of the yacht with attitude in my gait. The music grew softer as we stepped off the yacht and onto the dock. When we had reached the marina again, I whirled around confrontationally.

"Who the fuck is Zara, James?"

"She's a woman I've been seeing on and off over the past few months," he explained apologetically. "We had a conversation earlier this evening when I was on my way to you, which is why I was late. She called me to tell me she's pregnant."

"Pregnant? Pregnant! What the entire fuck, James? How pregnant is she?" I asked, flabbergasted.

"Twelve weeks . . ." he hung his head shamefully, knowing I could do the math as well as anyone else.

"Are you fucking kidding me, James? I know I wasn't sweating you about titles or exclusivity, but wow . . . just wow!" I was practically shrieking at him, but I didn't care. "You have unprotected sex with everyone or what?"

"Erica, it wasn't like that. She came over and I was drunk. She just kinda took it."

"Took it? You must think I'm stupid!"

"I don't think you're stupid, Erica. I wasn't expecting things to develop between us the way they did. She and I were broken up and she just came over. I thought it was for closure, but it turned into something else before I could stop. I haven't touched her since then. You should know from the amount of time I've been spending with you."

I just stared at him for a few minutes, realizing I didn't know who this man was.

"Take me to my car, James. I need to get out of here."

"Baby, just listen . . .," he started.

"No! What is this, *Dirty Dancing*? I'm not your fucking baby! Walk me to my car right now so I can go home. I don't have time for this shit! I've been feeling like you were too good to be true for weeks now, and I've been pushing back my guilt about being involved with you because of your history with Journey, only for you to hit me with some shit like this. Just take me to my car."

He was silent for a few seconds as he rubbed his hands down his face and released a sigh of defeat.

"NOW!" I shouted at him before turning on my heel and storming away into the darkness toward the parking lot where my car was.

He followed behind me quietly, leaving a safe distance between us as he saw me to my car. My heels clomped dangerously, echoing off the wooden planks and trees until I reached my car. I unlocked the doors and threw my purse inside angrily before dropping my weight into the driver's seat. I was furious and yet I knew I couldn't be angry at anyone but myself. I felt embarrassed and humiliated, and I just needed to get out of there.

"Erica, wait!"

"Don't say shit to me! Just get away from me! I never want to speak to you again! Lose my fucking number!" I shouted at him before slamming my door shut and screeching my tires off into the darkness, leaving James standing there alone.

As I drove down the path, surrounded by trees, I fought back tears. My hands were trembling as I raged while trying to find my way back to the main road. *Coffee* by Miguel was playing on the radio and I screamed as I slapped the radio erratically with one hand in effort to turn it off because it was James' favorite song for me. I swerved onto the main road, and then onto the highway, as I made my way home.

I hadn't driven ten miles before I saw cop lights in my rearview mirror. I realized I had been speeding as I pulled my car onto the shoulder of the road. A female officer got out and walked over to my vehicle with a flashlight and she shined it into my car before she tapped on my window.

"License and registration, please," she said blandly.

"Officer, I'm sorry, I know I was speeding. I just found out my boyfriend got another woman pregnant and I was driving emotionally," I explained in a rush.

"You were doing ninety miles per hour in a sixty-five miles per hour zone. That's not only considered reckless driving, but also warrants a ticket for super speeding. License and registration, please."

I balked and continued trying to reason with her, "Officer, I'm sorry, but I was upset. Can you please just let me go with a warning or even a regular speeding ticket? I was beside myself, and I will drive safely for the duration of my trip. I just want to get home to my son."

"Miss, if you don't give me your license and registration, you're going to have problems greater than you already do."

I conceded with a sigh and gave her my license and registration, in an effort to not become a Sandra Bland statistic, and said nothing more. She took my documentation rudely and walked back to her car.

After a long time, she returned to my car and tapped the window so I could roll it down.

"Erica Massey, you have the right to remain silent. Anything you say can and will be used against you in a court of law. You have the right to speak to an attorney, and to have an attorney present during any questioning . . . "

I turned my car off and rested my forehead on the steering wheel in defeat before I stepped out of my vehicle, allowing the officer to handcuff me and lead me away with my dress billowing dramatically behind me in the evening breeze as she guided me into the squad car.

All the cars passing us seemed to happen in slow motion in the gleam of the police lights, as the officer put a notice on my car for impounding before returning to the squad car and pulling off into the darkness. I wondered helplessly whether one of the cars passing was James, and I fancied I was truly abandoned and forsaken as a single tear rolled down my cheek.

I was placed in a holding cell in the Lanier County jail for six hours as I was booked, and waited even longer for my opportunity to call my mother to let her know what happened. She came early in the morning to post bail of twelve-hundred dollars. She was tightlipped as she and our family lawyer walked me out into the morning sunlight to her car.

Tracey was keeping Jason, so he wasn't aware of what happened, and I was too numb to cry anymore as we drove to the impound lot to retrieve my car.

"I'm sorry for disappointing you, Mom," I told her before getting into my car.

"You owe me twelve-hundred dollars, Erica," she said quietly before walking back to her car and driving away.

I watched her car until I couldn't see it anymore before starting my car and driving home.

I was lucky the lawyer managed to prevent the court from reporting the violation of my probation and sending me back to prison. I knew my mom was disappointed. She didn't have to say it, and I knew no explanation would be sufficient.

I drove along the highway, surrounded by trees, feeling sorry for myself and angry at James. The last thing I expected was to hear he got another woman pregnant. I dug in my purse for my cell phone and called Tracey to let her know I was on my way to pick up Jason. She didn't answer because it was still early, so I left her a message for when she woke up. An hour later, I was at home and anxious to get out of that white dress and into the shower.

Tracey called me back around eleven o'clock, and we met at Flying Biscuit for brunch with Jason. I beat them to the restaurant and was sitting at a table near a window enjoying a much needed cup of coffee. Tracey breezed in wearing a blue sundress and flat shoes with a pretty blue-green necklace and bangles. Her hair was pulled up into a high bun, and men eyed her as she passed. She looked beautiful, and I told her so when she hugged me.

"Ma'am! You are wearing this blue dress! You look like you're Queen of the Ocean or something!"

"Thanks, lady! You look fantastic, as always!" We air kissed each other's cheeks so as not to smear makeup anywhere, and Jason waited patiently behind her for his hug.

"Mom! Miss Tracey took me to the movies to see *Spider Man*!" he squealed as I squeezed him.

"Really? Was it any good?"

"It was so good! You and I should go see it again today!" he said, bopping with excitement.

"We might be able to make that happen," I told him with a wide grin.

I loved to see him smile.

"Baby, why don't you go to the restroom and wash your hands. Do you want French toast and creamy dreamy grits with sausage?"

"Yes! Thanks, Mom!" he exclaimed before walking away to the restroom.

When he was out of earshot, I turned a conspicuous gaze toward Tracey to signal that there was something important to discuss.

"Girl, I got arrested last night for speeding, and as if that wasn't bad enough, I found out James has a baby on the way by some woman named Zara."

Tracey's mouth dropped open in shock. "Girl! You have got to be kidding me! I was wondering why you called me so early! Are you okay?"

"I'm not in jail anymore, so yes, but I am upset about James."

"I can only imagine! I'm so sorry! Oh, Jason is coming back, let's talk about it later."

"Thanks. I didn't want him to know."

"I figured as much. Tell me about it later."

"I love this necklace! Where did you get it?" I asked, changing the subject as Jason sat down.

"I found it at the Martin Luther King festival last summer. I think I still have the card for the woman who sells them," Tracey played along.

"Bet! I need that!"

"Okay, I will check for her card when I get home. Send me a message today to remind me, 'cause you know I forget things."

"No problem, Boo!"

The waitress for our table came over, and we gave her our orders. When she left, Jason asked, "Mommy, how was your date at the lake?"

I resisted the urge to roll my eyes at the mention the fiasco of an evening I had.

"I had a really nice time, Sweetie," I lied. "We danced all night and the food was amazing. I may take you sometime."

"That sounds like fun! Can Grandma and Leilani come, too?"

"If they want to."

I personally didn't care if I never saw that fucking lake again for as long as I lived, but I'd do anything to keep Jason smiling.

"Great, cause Pop Pop loves to fish and he would probably like to come, too. I'm good at fishing."

"Well, maybe we can go for Labor Day weekend or something. I will look into it."

"Okay cool! Miss Tracey, do you like to fish?"

"I like to eat fish, does that count?"

We all laughed at that.

"No! You have to actually catch the fish. You can eat the fish Leilani and I catch."

"What about me, Grandma, and Pop Pop?" I asked.

"He's better at fishing than us. He can catch fish for everyone else."

We chuckled again as we enjoyed our breakfast the waitress had dropped off. Tracey and I split the check and we decided to walk out by Piedmont Park awhile.

Jason ran ahead, collecting rocks and petting dogs that ran up to him. I loved how free he was, and I felt a familiar pain in my heart for all the years I missed with him.

"So, tell me about your night," Tracey said, snatching me from my thoughts.

I watched Jason play with a group of boys who were kicking around a soccer ball. I sighed softly as we walked the park path and then sat on a bench in a slightly shady spot where we could see Jason without me looking like a hovering helicopter mom.

"This asshole and I were having a wonderful time together. We danced, ate, and were kissing on the outside of the yacht when . . . "

"Wait! You were on a yacht?" Tracey interrupted. "Yaaaas! That sounds fabulous!"

"It was nice until his phone kept ringing. He went to go talk to his boss and left his phone on the table."

"Whoa! You went through his phone? Erica, that's not cool." She shook her head disapprovingly.

"Yes and no. Just listen!" I held up my hands in defense.

Tracey nodded, "Okay, my bad! Continue."

She looked away and shielded her eyes from the patch of sun as she watched Jason running in the distance. I turned to watch him also as I continued.

"The phone kept chiming from texts from this Zara person, and I was trying to ignore it, but then she FaceTimed him twice. I ignored it the first time, but the second time I picked it up because I thought it might be an emergency," I explained.

Tracey stopped watching Jason and turned her eyes back toward me, twisting her mouth to the side as if she didn't believe me.

"NO really! This woman had been messaging him for hours and he was totally igging her. Anyway, I answered and she was like 'Who the hell are you?' and then he popped up and ended the call."

"What? Why?" she leaned back, making a confused face.

I shrugged. "I don't know. I guess he knew what she was calling about and wasn't prepared to deal with it. He claimed that he didn't know she was pregnant, and she had just told him earlier that day."

"Do you believe him?"

"Girl, I don't know. I don't know anything anymore. I'm just happy you're here and I can process this shit now. You know you're my only friend."

"Girl, bye! You know you have friends!"

"Not really. My other friend and I fell out before I left D.C. She's the reason I was arrested and on probation before I moved back home," I confessed.

Tracey's mouth opened in a big O as she listened. "Your FRIEND had you arrested?"

"Yes, but I did some real shady, fucked up shit to her and I deserved it."

I averted my gaze back to Jason who had found some other children to run around with.

"What did you do?"

"I don't want to even talk about it." I shook my head and looked at the ground. "That's a conversation for another day over lots and lots of alcohol."

"Damn, Girl . . . " Tracey said, shaking her head.

"Yeah. My whole experience before I got here was nuts."

I looked back at her and shifted until the sun was out of my eyes.

"Well, what did you do when you found out about the pregnant woman?" Tracey asked.

"I snapped on him, but not as hard as I could have. I ultimately left to go home, but I was speeding because I was upset. The cop pulled me over and ran my plates and license. Since I'm technically still on probation, I was arrested and had to spend the night in jail. I was doing ninety in a sixty-five miles per hour zone, so I couldn't really argue."

I threw up my hands in defeat and crossed my legs away from her, resting my elbow on the bench.

"Damn, Girl. I'm glad you're okay. How did you get out?"

"My mom called our lawyer and they came to get me out. She had to pay twelve-hundred dollars. My mom is pissed, and now I'm afraid she will try to take Jason back from me."

My eyes teared up uttering my fears out loud. I had worked so hard to prove myself to be a responsible adult, and now I felt like I was completely failing at life and motherhood.

"Well, at least you were able to get out. What did your mother say?'

"She told me I have to pay her the twelve-hundred dollars back and drove home. She's very disappointed at me. I don't know what I should do to get her to forgive me."

"Well, you didn't really do anything wrong. You reacted the way anyone would have. It sounds like you were just in the wrong place at the wrong time," Tracey reassured me.

"It's just that I promised her I would get my shit together, and I know the look on her face wasn't good. She's upset."

"She'll forgive you. That's the nature of being a mother; ask me how I know. You'll recover from this, Girl. What are you going to do about James, though?"

"I don't know. I told him I never wanted to speak to him again, but I'm hurt."

"You have every right to be. I don't know what I would have done in your situation. Just take your time and process how you feel. I'm here to support you however I can."

"Thanks, Tracey. I thought I wasn't going to see my son again. I was devastated. All I could think of was him. I'm too old for this foolishness."

She rested a supportive hand on my shoulder, "I understand. Take your time and process this before you speak to your mom. Whenever you speak to her again, just be humble and know that she loves you, but she may not see it through your lens. I think you should tell her what happened."

"Yeah, I don't know. I'm not really ready to confront her judgement yet."

"You never know. We as women all deal with cheating ass men from time to time. I'm sure she will be able to understand where you were. Besides, she's been your age before, you've never been hers. There may be a greater wisdom there that you don't see yet."

I pondered over this advice from my friend and reflected on what I knew of my mother's whole life, and her choices. I decided to judge my mom less harshly and hoped that when I had the opportunity to speak with her again, she would be more compassionate of my circumstances. There was much healing to be had, and I was ready to bloom.

We called Jason back over to us and made our way back to our cars in silence. I was grateful for the quiet and opportunity to process my feelings without judgement or interruption. I needed to do better as a person and a mother, and I was grateful for the positive reflection that was Tracey to help me see myself in the best light. We hugged each other with promises to catch up later, got in our cars and went our separate ways.

14. Journey to the Center

*I don't know whether it's your eyes or the way your smile
lights up the place,
B u t I feel like a flower blooming under the sun
whenever I see your face.
Each time you come close enough, my lips and fingertips
long to touch.
Start the fire, take us higher, because no height is too
much.
Listening to your thoughts and dreams breathes life into
my own.
I find my courage, engage my endurance and I never feel
alone.
Our story is strangely separate, yet we've been connected
for years,
Through experiences, both good and bad, and smiles
we've shared through tears.
I love you from an unconditional place, free of space and
time.
I appreciate that you are my reflection in this place, and
I'm blessed to call you mine.*

~ Olosunde

I dreamed I was standing on a dock in the middle
of the ocean. There was a sword fight going on around
me as I stood beside Carlos, and a man who appeared
to be a minister was performing marriage rites. There
were two ships, one of which was mine, off in the
distance, and six dinghies anchored to the dock.
Everything was happening in slow motion, but I looked
at Carlos standing beside me and I was happy. The
happiest I had ever been in my life.

Suddenly, everything froze, and the only things
moving were myself and seven men who were wearing

uniforms that matched the sails on my ship. The water began to churn and bubble as if it was boiling, and a huge bubble that appeared to be made of glass rose from the depths, encasing a humungous mermaid. She was at least twenty feet tall with hair that was so black that it appeared to be blue, and a little boy with a fish face on her shoulder. He had a large seaweed rope around his waist holding up pants that looked to be made of old burlap, and the rest of the rope was wrapped around the mermaid's arm. She didn't speak, and her face was beautifully emotionless as the fish boy hopped down from her shoulder and planted his webbed feet onto the smooth, sun bleached, wooden dock without popping the mermaid's bubble. He had whiskers like a catfish and sharp teeth as he smiled at me with his wet hair slicked back into a little coil, the front making a widow's peak above his slanted eyes that were too far apart. He blinked twice and beckoned a webbed hand to me in a large gesture before diving beautifully back into the water.

"I think he wants you to follow him," muttered one of the men in my crew.

"I'm not following some weird fish boy into the ocean," I refused.

We all looked up at the mermaid, who never made eye contact with us, but stood like a statue staring into the setting sun behind us.

"Miss, she scares me," another crewman whispered.

"I don't care, I'm still not about to follow some fish . . ."

My words were cut off as I felt myself snatched up by the waist and submerged in cold salt water before I could scream or react. I saw my crew floating haphazardly behind me inside the mermaid's bubble as she dragged us deeper and deeper under the ocean. I screamed in spite of myself as bubbles escaped my lips. I could feel myself panicking as water filled my lungs, but I couldn't cough. I flailed my arms frantically, unable to break free from her clutches, when I heard a familiar collection of voices in my head.

"If I wanted to kill you, you'd already be dead. Relax and you will find that you can breathe just fine."

I looked over at the huge mermaid's face who issued me a stern smirk of her lips, and I stopped fighting her. I was still afraid, but I relaxed a bit, and noticed the most beautiful aquatic life I had ever seen. There were fish of species and color that I had never seen in any aquarium or episode of *National Geographic*. She swam easily and relaxed her grasp slightly as I marveled at the water world of bright coral and fish around me.

As we descended, the ocean became darker and colder, and I shivered slightly. She swam and swam until there was nothing but darkness around us. She carried me for what seemed like hours, until my eyes adjusted to an eerie blue-green glow. We approached what appeared to be the ocean floor, and I panicked as we picked up speed again. I didn't scream, but I covered the top of my head as we sped toward the ocean floor. It opened to reveal a small circular chute that sucked my crew and I inside. I was falling and falling into darkness until I realized we were lying on a wet surface inside of a room.

"Where are we, Miss?" someone whispered fearfully into the darkness.

"I don't know, but I think we are at the bottom of the ocean," I whispered back.

Seconds later, small, soft lights began to glow from the walls, revealing some sort of chamber. The walls were all circular and there were windows that revealed the depths of the ocean along the walls. Dark sea creatures slithered and swam past them as we looked on in a collective mixture of awe and terror.

"Relieve your crewmen and enter the chamber on your right," a voice echoed softly off the walls.

It wasn't a request, and the lights in the walls illuminated a hallway to the left and a doorway to the right. The crew nodded to me silently and made their way down the hallway as I went to the doorway. When I approached it, it opened on its own to reveal a gorgeous, plush bedroom and wardrobe. There were mirrors on the walls, interrupted by seven windows to the ocean where seven giant mermaids hovered, watching me.

"We've been waiting for you. Now is your time. You must prepare. Cleanse yourself in the sweet water of the pool and get dressed."

A blue light illuminated a pool in the center of the room, and I disrobed and stepped into the water, surprised to find it warm. I bathed while the mermaids looked on silently from the windows, ignoring them, yet wondering what this was all about. When I finished, I stepped out of the water.

"Stand before the mirror and see yourself as you truly are," they commanded.

I obeyed.

As I stood before the looking glass, my curls wove up on top of my head by unseen hands, and a beautiful blue and white gown materialized on my body. It appeared to be a wedding gown made of the most soft, gorgeous satins and silks I had ever seen. It hugged my hips like a mermaid's fin and flared out behind me in a long train. I smiled at my reflection in the mirror before turning toward the windows for their approval. They didn't smile, instead pointing in unison to a shelf at the back of the room. There rested a jeweled crown that I lifted nervously and placed on top of my head. When I turned around to the windows again, all the mermaids lowered their heads in reverence.

"Come," they commanded. "It is time to look upon Olokun . . ."

The floors began to glow with a warm golden light that lead toward a doorway I hadn't noticed before. I hesitated for a few seconds before opening it to a brightly lit roomful of people who cheered loudly. Part of me wanted to run away, while the other part was frozen in place. I blinked into the lights feeling disoriented, when someone walked over to me and kissed my hand before kneeling before me. He then stood and held me by my shoulders and whispered, "Journey . . . Journey . . . Journey . . ."

"Journey . . . Journey . . . Baby, wake up. We have to go. We're going to the beach today! Get dressed!" Carlos stared at me earnestly, "Baby, are you okay?"

"Yeah, I was just having the craziest dream. Something about Olokun," I said groggily, as I rolled over onto my side and hid my face with my arm.

"Journey, Baby, get up." He pulled my arm away from my face and kissed my temple.

"Five more minutes?" I negotiated with a pout.

"Now, Baby, come on!" He chuckled.

"But I'm still trying to process my dream. You didn't even let me tell you about it."

He made a strange face, rolling his eyes at me. "You can tell me all about in in the car. Come on, we have to get going!"

I shrugged the dream off and jumped in the shower, brushed my teeth, and got dressed. By the time we got in the car, I had forgotten all about the dream.

The ocean breeze slapped me in the face as Carlos and I rode the Jet Skis from his cousin's business on the beach in San Juan. I had my arms wrapped around his waist as I clung to him, squealing as we passed over short waves. A big wave came up on one side and Carlos turned away from it and onto a calmer area of water. We had been enjoying a day at the beach, eating seafood and sipping tropical drinks in the sun. I was at least three shades darker from this day alone, and my tan lines were deep.

We saw fish swimming beneath us, and I squealed with an excitement that was drowned out by the sound of the engine of the Jet Ski. I was too scared to ride alone, and I felt the urge to use the bathroom after a spray of salt water splashed me in the face. I nudged Carlos and waved my crossed index and middle fingers in front of him to signal that I needed to take a break. He nodded and drove us back to shore. I hopped off and waded through the shallow water back to the service desk for the restroom key. Carlos shouted that he was going back out for a bit and would come back in a while to scoop me up again. I nodded and brushed my hair out of my face with wet hands.

"Where's Carlos?" his cousin Freddie asked me from behind the desk.

"He said he was going back out for a while. I have to use the bathroom," I told him.

He handed me the key and I trotted off to the lavatory. It smelled like ocean and old rum in there, so I made it quick, stopping at the mirror to tie my hair into a high bun after washing my hands. The water made it easier to pull my hair up and smooth it down in the wet ponytail holder I had been wearing on my wrist.

"I'm going to need a serious deep conditioning after today," I said to my reflection as I noticed the highlights the sun had left in my curls.

I heard a shrill whistle being blown in the distance as I walked to exit the bathroom door. I didn't think anything of it at first, until I got outside and saw a group of people gathered at the shore waving their arms while the life guards seemed to be running in slow motion toward the red emergency speed boat. I started to jog slowly toward the crowd that was growing and watched the fingers pointing out to the waves.

"What's going on?" I asked a guy who was beside me.

"Some guy was riding a Jet Ski and he fell off. Someone said they saw a shark and the lifeguards rode out to try to rescue him,." he said.

The lifeguards still hadn't made it out to the area where the abandoned Jet Ski was, and everyone was still watching. It seemed as though the entire crowd was talking at once. The rescue boat was closer to the Jet Ski, but no one was approaching it. Suddenly a head broke the surface of the water, and a brown tattooed arm followed before slipping beneath the surface again.

"Oh, my God! That's Carlos!" I shouted to no one, because no one was listening to me.

My heart lodged in my throat and my entire body went cold with fear.

"There he is!" A woman shouted.

She pointed a finger out toward where the head had emerged again. The rescue boat got closer and as one of the lifeguards was about to dive in, the waves turned a bright shade of red. Everyone on the shore gasped and screamed, and several cell phones came out of hiding to record the incident. The rescue diver dove in, and a deathly hush came over all of us on the shore as if everyone was holding their breaths, waiting for the rescuer to emerge with the victim.

The victim... The victim.. Carlos! Somebody save him!

The voice inside my head screamed frantically, but I was glued to where I stood on the shore as I waited helplessly like everyone else. Only I wasn't like everyone else. The man I loved was bleeding and possibly drowning. The pounding in my ears continued as my eyes searched the surface of the water for the rescuer and Carlos.

A few minutes later, he emerged from the depths, pulling a limp and unresponsive Carlos out of the water gripped tightly against him. The other lifeguards helped pull Carlos and the rescuer onto the speedboat and the female lifeguard waved her arms frantically from the boat to the guard on the shore who radioed for help. The engine of the speedboat whirred loudly as it neared the shore, and the lifeguards commanded everyone to back away.

A scream bubbled up in my throat as tears poured down my cheeks as they carried Carlos off the boat. I ignored the commands of the lifeguards who kept trying to keep me from Carlos' limp, lifeless body as I rushed toward him. Someone pulled me out of the way as the rescue team tried to resuscitate him. The sounds of the hollow thuds of them pounding on his chest echoed my wails as two lifeguards performed CPR and another dressed his wounds. His foot was mangled and bleeding, his thigh had a huge gaping wound, and his right hand was folded into a loose fist while his left was ripped open and bleeding. It looked like he'd tried to punch the shark or something. I realized it was Freddie who held me back in a tight restraint as they worked on Carlos.

"What happened?!" I demanded as I pushed him back from me, only for him to clasp me again in a rocking embrace.

"I decided to go out and join him while you were in the bathroom. We were riding and racing together, when I saw the sharks circling and there was a wave coming on the other side. I yelled for him to get away. He didn't get away fast enough, and I guess he panicked or was distracted. A big wave hit him and knocked him off the Jet Ski and into the water. I thought he climbed back on, 'cause Carlos can swim like a fish. I just knew he was behind me heading back to the shore, but when I didn't see him, I blew the whistle to alert the lifeguards."

A few seconds later, Carlos coughed up ocean water, and the crowd released a collective sigh while some people applauded.

"Sir, what's your name?" one of the lifeguards demanded after a few moments.

"Carlos," he coughed.

"Carlos!" I shrieked, as I rushed to his side. "Baby, are you all right? I'm here!"

His eyes swam around a bit before connecting with mine.

"Olokun . . ." he sighed before his eyelids fluttered and didn't open again.

"He's going into shock! Where's the ambulance?" one of the lifeguards shouted.

"No! No! Noooo!" I screamed as he was lifted onto a stretcher and rushed to the ambulance by the EMTs.

"I'm his fiancé!"

I shouted at one of the EMTs who attempted to hold me back. Freddie and I were waved into the ambulance, and the sirens were nearly deafening as we were whisked away to the hospital.

The fifteen-minute ride to the hospital seemed like fifteen years as the siren wailed deafeningly. Carlos was losing a lot of blood quickly in spite of the EMT trying to stop the bleeding. My knuckles were white as I gripped the side of the stretcher, willing Carlos to just hold on until we reached the hospital. I caught a glimpse of my reflection in some metal panel on a cabinet in the ambulance, and I looked stricken, covered in sand. I barely recognized the woman staring back at me, and I didn't think I had ever felt so panicked in my life.

How could this be happening to me and the man I love.

When we arrived at the emergency room, Carlos was rushed out of the ambulance and through the doors. Nurses took over and ran him into a little room, snatching the curtains closed as they worked on stabilizing him. Another pair of nurses prevented us from going into the room, and escorted Freddie and I away to the waiting room. We waited for four hours before Carlos' parents arrived in the waiting room, and Freddie and I stood to embrace them both. We spoke in hushed tones about not knowing anything about Carlos' progress. Carlos' mom had brought me a maxi dress, underwear, shoes, and my toiletry bag.

"Thank you so much, Mrs. Rivera," I said as she pulled the items out of her bag in a plastic grocery bag and handed them to me.

"Sweetheart, why don't you go to the restroom and get changed," she said kindly.

I looked down at my bikini top, shorts, and beach shoes and thanked her as I walked away to find the nearest ladies' room. I had barely noticed I was still in beach attire, and was thankful for her maternal and feminine instinct to care for me in this moment that was tragic for all of us.

The shirt I wore to the beach was still there, but I didn't care. I wouldn't have cared about my current attire if it weren't for the fact that I was freezing my ass off.

I pulled the washcloth and bar of Dove soap out of the bag and wet both until I had created a lather. Thankful it was a single bathroom, I washed my entire body from the sink, grateful to have the salt water off me. I rubbed cocoa butter onto myself, applied deodorant, stepped into clean underwear, and snapped my bra onto myself before pulling the yellow dress over my head and letting it fall over my body. I pulled off my beach shoes and washed my feet, dried, and moisturized them before sliding them into a pair of white crocheted flat shoes. When I was finished, I put the wet towel and all the other wet items into one plastic bag and all the other items into my toiletry bag. I rinsed my hair in the sink as best I could and brushed as much sand out of my hair as I could, and decided to let my curls air dry as they bounced around my shoulders.

As I walked the long hallway back to the waiting room, I replayed how handsome Carlos was on the Jet Ski before I left him to use the bathroom. The warmth of his body against mine, the sinew of his muscles as I held onto him while ocean water sprayed my face. He was so perfect, and I wondered if he'd be the same after this experience.

When I approached the waiting room, I saw a doctor walk over to Carlos' mom and dad and slide his hands into his pockets. He had a somber countenance as his lips moved to deliver news about Carlos. I hesitated for a few seconds to watch what response was had before I walked up. I was terrified, but curious to hear about Carlos' progress. My fear was more prominent than my curiosity, though, so I held the wall and held my breath.

When Carlos' mother's face crumpled and she turned to his father to cry into his arms, I knew something had gone wrong. My heart skipped a beat and I started frantically in their direction. Something was wrong, and I could feel it. My hair blew out behind me as I approached the family and embraced Carmelita as she collapsed into me, and her husband held us both up.

"What happened?" I asked with dread.

"He's in a coma! They said he's stable, but the lack of oxygen to his brain and the severe loss of blood left him in a coma. Oh, my poor baby! What am I going to do? Jose, what are we going to do?"

Jose held her and stroked her hair as he tried to soothe her.

I was in a state of shock and didn't have any words as I sat on the ugly tile floor without regard to the germs. Whatever would I do without my love in my life? I couldn't imagine a world in which he didn't exist. I wept silently until Freddie pulled me up off the floor and held me in a tight embrace.

15. Picking Up the Pieces

A storm is building slowly in me.
The lightning flashes, the tides come in, and the waves
toss in the sea.
I'll stand in the wet sand catching the lightning in my
hand,
Unharmed by the flash, turning sand into glass.

~ Olosunde

I lay in bed with the windows open, staring at the ceiling fan. The cicadas and crickets sang outside in the early summer evening breeze. Jason was asleep down the hall, so I had time to just lay and think. My mother was still avoiding me, although it had been two weeks since my arrest. I was still avoiding James and trying to make sense of my garbled feelings about learning he had a child on the way. I smoked the blend of shisha and marijuana from my hookah that rested on my nightstand beside me, otherwise not moving on my queen-sized bed. My hips tingled slightly, and I exhaled smoke after a few seconds.

Journey would have told me that this entire experience was my karma for breaking Woman Law and sleeping with her ex. I scrunched my face and kissed my teeth, wanting to ignore that her distant, unspoken wisdom was truth. Being that it had been nearly a year since the situation with her and Devin, I was surprised that I was still in a similar place. I asked myself why I hadn't grown beyond my connection to her and thought about things I knew she would say.

I rolled over onto my belly, settling into the body high that was building inside me, and looked at my phone. Why was this so complicated?

Because you hurt her on purpose, you never apologized, and then you turned around and fucked the one man you knew she loved more than anyone else.

You're reaping what you've sown.

I sighed deeply at my conscience, frustrated by the truth. Out of all the men in Atlanta, I chose the one man who made her soul light up, and I didn't have to. No amount of charm could make that right. I realized I needed to atone for my transgressions, but I didn't know how.

I scrolled through my unanswered text messages to my mother, apologizing for disappointing her and being irresponsible. That shit left me feeling helpless. Before I knew it, my spirit had me typing one of few phone numbers I knew by heart. Once the number was keyed in, I began a text message:

> Journey, this is Erica. I know we haven't spoken in a while, but I'm sure you understand why

I deleted the second sentence entirely and rested my head on my arm as I thought about how I would have to be more honest than that.

> I know I hurt you, and I'm really sorry. I hope you can find it in your heart to forgive me. I treated you badly, and I don't deserve your friendship at this point, but I'm in a low place, and I hope you can forgive me.

I held the phone in my hand for a long time with a tear sliding down my face before I finally hit send. Nothing happened for the next five minutes. I inhaled more of the marijuana and shisha concoction before resting my forehead on my arm feeling defeated.

Nobody knew me better than she did, and I was praying she would find enough grace in her heart to respond. Another ten minutes passed with my head beginning to spin slightly, when my phone finally buzzed and dinged in my hand.

I forgive you.

I blinked back tears as I read the three words that gave me a sense of peace I knew deep down I didn't truly deserve. She didn't even know the extent of my passive violence against her, but being who she was, she readily offered absolution.

> You don't know how much I appreciate that you responded. I messed up really badly, and I know I did.
>
> > You did, but there are greater things than that.

She had no idea how right she was.

> I really appreciate that you responded. I admit that I've done some things that you wouldn't be proud of lately, but I have been trying to be right. I am beginning to wonder whether my moral compass is faulty.
>
> > Lol! I can believe that. I wish you well, Erica. Whatever you're going through isn't bad karma on my part. I've forgiven you.

I smiled and thanked her, turning back over onto my back with a smile on my face. Journey was a special kind of person. Although I hadn't told her about James, the fact that she felt nothing but compassion and forgiveness toward my transgression with Devin made me feel at peace. I knew I'd eventually end up having to come completely clean, but today was not the day.

254. Jessica Lynn

***

When I opened my eyes, I was lying face down in my bed clutching my pillow closely. I dreamed crazy dreams about being at a class reunion for my graduating eighth grade class. A boy whose name I couldn't remember was the last thing in my memory from the dream, and I rubbed my eyes before rolling over on my side toward the window to squint at the light shining through.

I could hear Jason using the bathroom down the hall, and was silently glad that I had a kid who was old enough to pour his own cereal and milk for breakfast without waking me. That thought took me to James and the child he had on the way, and I sighed deeply as I sprawled on my back and closed my eyes in frustration. My heart began to race as I lay there in silence, just monitoring my breathing until I felt calm again. *How did I get here*, I wondered for the millionth time.

I rose and wrapped myself in a robe, trudging into the living room where I could hear Jason watching something on television.

"Good morning," I greeted sleepily.

"Good morning, Mommy!" he said back, without turning around to look at me.

"I'm going to make some eggs and turkey bacon. Do you want some?"

"Nah, I'm good, Mommy."

"All right," I said before heading to the kitchen to make myself breakfast and coffee.

Soon the smell of turkey bacon filled the house while I sipped my coffee in wait of the warm, savory flavors.

"Mommy, your breakfast smells good! Can I have some?" Jason asked, appearing in the kitchen.

I laughed, "Boy, you better be glad I made enough for you, too."

"Thank you," he said, giggling. "Why were you sad last night?"

I hesitated. "What makes you think I was sad?" I asked without turning toward him.

"You just seemed like you were feeling sad when I went to bed."

"I just had a lot on my mind, son."

"Hmmm . . . I guess . . ." He walked back to the living room and sat on the couch without further comment.

I scrambled my eggs and thought of James' situation. How would I react if it were me who were pregnant while he was with another woman, I wondered? I decided that I would at least respond to his text messages.

I put my eggs and bacon on a plate, grabbed a fork, made a plate for Jason, and curled up on the couch next to him. We watched some superhero cartoon together On Demand until I had enough and got up to go shower and get dressed.

"We are going out, kiddo. I will be back in a bit." I kissed his forehead and headed to the bathroom.

Under the weight of the shower stream, the heaviness in my heart didn't feel quite so unbearable. I scrubbed and scrubbed myself until the hot water nearly stung my chocolate skin. I wished I could scrub James off me. If bleeding him out of my veins were possible, I probably would have attempted that also. When the water started to feel cold, I reluctantly turned off the faucet and yanked back the periwinkle curtain angrily. I exhaled slowly, encouraging myself to garner peace, as I wrapped myself with a white, fluffy towel.

When my body was mostly dry, I wrapped the towel around my head and went to my bedroom to moisturize and dress. I slipped into a white romper, with navy blue flowers embroidered on the front and silver sandals. I fluffed my curls out and rubbed moisturizer into my ends to keep them soft in the heat. I walked out to the hallway that separated my bedroom from Jason's and tapped on the door.

"You ready, kiddo?"

"One second, Mommy," he responded.

I walked into the kitchen and began washing up the dishes I used for breakfast, and jumped slightly when I felt two warm arms embrace me from behind.

"You look so pretty, Mommy!" came Jason's voice.

"Thank you, Baby." I put down the sponge and dried my hands a bit on a towel before turning around to give him a squeeze in return.

He held me longer than I expected.

"Is everything okay?" I asked, looking in his brown eyes.

"Yes . . . I just miss grandma and Leilani," he admitted.

"Well, is that all? Let's go pay them a visit!" I sounded more cheerful than I felt.

"Really? I'd like that, Mommy. Can Leilani spend the night? She hasn't visited yet, and I want to show her my new room," he said with excitement.

I cringed inside, but I said, "Yeah, we can ask Grandma and Pop Pop if they don't mind. But she can only stay for one night if they say yes, okay?"

"Okay."

I grabbed my purse and keys and we walked out together, Jason bouncing alongside me talking a mile a minute.

When we pulled up in my mom's driveway, Jason bounced out of the car, full of excited boy energy. Before I could turn off the engine, he was running up to the front door screaming, "Grandma! Grandma!"

I chuckled, as I moved more slowly behind him. No matter how many times I begged her to stop, my mother always left the front door open in the daytime. I resisted the urge to chastise her as I hugged her in the kitchen. Who knew where Jason and Leilani were, but the smell of apples was strong in the house as my mother checked on the pie she was baking.

"Hi, Mom, how are you?" I smiled.

"I'm all right, Erica. How are you?" She returned the smile, but she looked a little confused.

"I'm okay. Can I help you?" I asked still smiling.

"No, thank you, I'm almost done with this pie." She turned away to focus on the dessert she was preparing.

"Okay . . ."

I hesitated, unsure of what to say since I knew she was still upset with me. "Jason said he missed you and he wanted to visit."

"You know you two are always welcome," she sighed softly.

Her back was to me, and I knew there were pages and volumes of detail behind that sigh.

"Thank you. Well, he wants to know whether Leilani can spend the night. He misses her and wants to show her his new room."

I leaned against the counter, resting my elbows on the surface.

"I'm sure she misses him, too, but I think not. I can't risk her being in a situation where she has to learn that her sister was arrested for some foolishness."

She continued to prepare the pie without looking at me.

I moved and sat down at the kitchen table, "Mom, come on. You never even allowed me to explain what happened. I can't believe you're just going to be judgmental and keep them apart over me," I protested.

"Oh, no, Jason is welcome to stay the night here, as are you, but I'm not risking another child to you and your irresponsibility," she said without turning around to look at me.

"Mom, I know I upset you, but please just listen to my side . . ."

I stared out the window into the yard so as not to feel the rejection of her not wanting to look my way.

She paused and turned her head in my general direction, but still didn't look at me.

"Erica, you cost me twelve-hundred dollars and potential embarrassment with your stepfather after you promised to get it together."

"Mom, I was out on a date with James, and this woman called him and told him she was pregnant. I didn't fight her, I didn't cuss her out, nothing like that. I yelled at him and I left. I was upset and I was speeding because of it, which is why I was arrested. The officer was rude, but I would never do anything to purposely embarrass you or my family."

"Wait, what?" she finally turned all the way around to look at me. "James? Who is James?" she asked. "I didn't even know you were seeing anyone seriously."

I bit my lip as my eyes started to fill with tears. She was looking at me, so I couldn't hide it or pretend. I opened and closed my mouth, searching for the words to explain what the past few months and weeks had entailed. Wordlessly, she stepped closer and embraced me, and I wept the way I wanted to weep when I first found out about the other woman's pregnancy. Like all the transgressions and betrayal I had experienced in my life to date were all pouring out of me at once.

"Let's go for a walk," she suggested, "there's obviously a lot I don't know."

I nodded silently. She turned to take the warm, golden apple pie out of the oven, covered it, and led me out the side door by the hand.

We walked out to the backyard and sat on the little wicker sofa under the magnolia tree.

"Talk to me, Erica," she said. "Tell me what happened."

I sipped several gulps of humid air, as I began to tell her about Journey, Devin, and James. I told her how I had met him in Atlanta on the day I went to my job interview at Emory, the fight at Tongue in Groove, the hospital visit, the first night we spent together, the guilt I had been dealing with in silence for so long, and finally the date night on the yacht during which I found out he had gotten Zara pregnant. When I finished my story, she stared at me for a long time in silence.

"I'm so sorry you've been dealing with so much in silence, Babygirl. I'm sorry for putting so much pressure on you, and for judging you without all of the details."

I wiped my face and sniffed softly. "I'm sorry for disappointing you, Mom. I'm more disappointed in myself that you could ever be, and I need you to know that."

"Oh, Baby, you've been through so much. I know I don't have to tell you where you were wrong, but have you spoken to Journey since you've been out?"

"Yes," I sniffed again, "I spoke to her last night through text message."

"Did you tell her about James?"

"No, I was so sad, I just apologized to her about Devin and I left it there."

"Well, Baby, what's done in the dark always comes to the light, so if you are going to keep talking to her, you're going to have to come clean. Otherwise, stop talking to her and leave James alone. Out of all the men in the world, you chose hers . . . twice! Baby, why?"

"I don't know, Mom. I guess I was jealous."

"Jealous of what, exactly? I mean, she's done everything for you. Why would you hurt her like that?"

"I don't know, Mom. She just always seemed to have all the answers. She's got that whole light skinned privilege thing going on."

Mom sighed, "Baby, you're both black. At the end of the day, white people might offer her a pass in some ways that you get denied, but if she's using that privilege to be her darker sister's keeper and loving you honestly, you have to let that hate go."

"White folks have been trying to use that color stigma to separate us for generations, but how does her ancestors being raped more than yours make her better? You have to be able to recognize the difference between a light skinned woman who thinks she's better than you from one who stands by you at all costs."

I had never thought of it that way. I had experienced being passed over for lighter women my entire life, but the whole aspect of how they became lighter never occurred to me.

"We as black people suffer from ancestral trauma, baby. We have difficulty recognizing the face of the enemy is not each other. It is deep seated and we behave negatively, all the while giving white folks reason to laugh behind closed doors about how they have us scrambling against one another for power for no reason. Your friend Journey seems like she held you up and you didn't know how to take it when she told you truths that made you uncomfortable, but how is it any different than things I've told you?"

I didn't say anything as I processed my mother's wisdom. I knew I had been less than a friend to Journey, but I had never looked at my transgressions and violence against her through the lens that my mother provided.

"Leilani can spend the night with you and Jason. She's been missing and asking about him a lot lately."

"Thanks, Mom. That will mean a lot to Jason, and to me."

"I know. I'm sorry I shut you out all this time. I will do better at making an effort to listen to you in the future."

"It's okay, Mom. It's okay."

We hugged each other under the magnolia tree until Leilani and Jason came out of the house, chasing each other around. I wiped my face and snuck off to the bathroom before either of them could ask any questions.

When I came outside again, Jason and Leilani were competing to see who could do the best cartwheel and had my mother judging their efforts. I hung back a bit to watch without being seen, when Lawrence appeared beside me.

"They're good kids," he said with a soft chuckle. "Leilani has really missed Jason. I'm glad you and your mom worked things out and you brought him over. They need each other."

"Yeah, they're like brother and sister more than anything else," I said.

"Exactly. Did your mother tell you about your brother?"

"No, what's up with him?"

"He's got a little girl on the way."

"Really?"

"Yeah, she doesn't like the mother, but you know she won't say it right away."

"Of course not. She loves him in a totally different way. He was always her favorite." I rolled my eyes at the last sentence.

"Actually, you were always her favorite, but she was able to keep him closer because he was from a different man. When she looks at him, she sees his father, and she sees yours in you, for better or worse."

I didn't say anything, but I wondered about the deeper secrets my mother kept. Jeremiah's father died before he was born, which came with its own challenges as a single mother of two, but he wasn't abusive to my knowledge. How many times had love knocked my mother down? How may frogs had she kissed before choosing Lawrence? What made her make the choices she had made? Only she knew.

Jason and Leilani played outside until well into the afternoon before we told her that she was sleeping over with us. Leilani squealed and ran upstairs to pack an overnight bag. I took them to Slice for dinner, and then skating at Cascade. It had been years since I had been on roller skates, and I hugged the perimeter of the rink, so as not to fall. They laughed at me and kept trying to coax me into the center of the floor. I wasn't going to embarrass myself, but I encouraged them to skate together.

After a while, I gave up and returned the skates I was wearing to the counter and put my regular shoes back on. The lights were flashing red and blue lights steadily while *My Boo* by Ghost Town DJ's blared from the speakers and the whole place smelled like a cacophony of hot dogs, pizza and nacho cheese. I looked around and saw my friend Naomi with her two daughters and walked over to say hello.

"Erica! How are you?" Naomi exclaimed. "It has been about three or four years since I've seen you!"

Naomi hugged me. Teenagers laughed loudly nearby, and I shouted slightly over their volume and the 90's music.

"I know! I'm doing well, how are you?" I smiled warmly.

"I'm good, Girl, just dealing with these expensive tweens I have." She rolled her eyes sarcastically.

"Oh, I totally understand," I laughed.

"How's Journey doing? I heard her fiancé is in a coma and she's a wreck. Is she pulling through?"

I was surprised, and my face showed it. "A fiancé? A coma? Wait, what? She and I haven't spoken in a while. What happened?" I asked.

"Apparently, he had some sort of accident at the beach the day after he proposed to her in Puerto Rico. Why don't you talk to each other anymore? Did you two have a falling out?"

"Something like that. How is she holding up?" The guilt rose in my chest, and I pushed it back down.

"She's as well as can be expected. I feel sorry for her. I just knew she was going to marry James. It's so sad! She's such a sweetheart. Maybe you should reach out to her."

"Yeah, maybe I will. Well, it was good seeing you, Naomi. Hit me up sometime."

"Will do!"

We embraced and went our separate ways. I spent the next two hours watching Jason and Leilani skate while I wondered about Journey. She hadn't said anything to me about a fiancé or him being in a coma when I texted her, not that I could blame her. I thought better of reaching out to her, and flagged Jason and Leilani down to let them know it was time to leave.

When we were at our apartment, Jason gave her a grand tour that ended at his room. They played with his toys for a while, and then went to watch scary movies in the living room.

"You guys can stay up, but I don't want to hear anything about you being freaked out or having bad dreams from these horror flicks you're watching."

"We're good," they said, almost in unison.

"Good night, guys," I said, kissing them both before I retreated to my bedroom.

"Good night," they chortled back, as I walked away.

Once in the privacy of my bedroom, I sat on the edge of my bed and reread James's text messages.

I forgive you, but I never want to see you again.

I texted him and then rolled over and went to sleep.

16. Hard Facts

I have left but a footprint on his heart.
I'll never have it, and yet I am eternally fascinated by
him.
One day, I will tell my children of him,
And they will ask why I didn't marry him if I loved him,
And I will tell them,
"So that one day you could ask me that question."
~ Olosunde

Carlos was in a coma for the rest of the week I spent in Puerto Rico. I stayed with him every moment I could, short of going back to his parent's house to collect my belongings, and checking into a hotel near the hospital. His mother refused to be separated from her son, and we provided emotional support for one another as she shared stories of his childhood and the rest of the family. It was healing for us both, but I knew it would be short lived, as I had to return to D.C. to work.

Before Freddie took me to the airport, I promised to return frequently and to call daily to check on Carlos until he woke up. I feared he may never awaken, and leaving him was the second hardest choice I ever had to make — the first being terminating my pregnancy when I was twenty-five.

When I arrived back in D.C., I hailed a taxi back to my apartment. Rico was all over me, mewing and rubbing his entire body up against me. I crumpled to the floor in tears, taking his furry body into my arms. He didn't try to wriggle away or protest as I held him. He just purred and let me hold him, as if he understood what had happened to Carlos while I was away.

Who says cats don't love, I mused as I left my luggage at the door, eventually pulling myself together, and going to take a shower. When I was clean, I slipped into a T-shirt Carlos had left at my place, crawled into bed, and fell into a deep sleep.

***

When I woke in the morning, I showered, dressed, ate a bowl of oatmeal, drank a cup of coffee, and went to work without all the bubble and energy I normally had. I felt like I was trudging through muddy water wearing a taffeta ball gown. I looked like my normal self in every other way except my eyes and the suntan I was sporting. I masked my pain with a smile I had practiced in the mirror, but my voice sounded glum. I wore a nice outfit, but my steps lacked the chipper bounce that was customary to my personality. To anyone who didn't know me well, nothing had changed, but I couldn't hide from Sydney at lunch. She had insisted on meeting me to hear about my trip and I agreed, unable to find the heart to tell her about Carlos' accident and current condition in a text message.

We met at Cava Mezze near her job and she was bursting at the seams with joy when she saw me. She squealed and snatched my hand toward her face to get a closer look at the engagement ring on my left hand.

"Oooh, Girl! That ring is gorgeous! When you sent me that text, I almost died? And he proposed on Valentine's Day? He's so fucking romantic! You must tell me everything! I mean everything! Don't leave out any details!"

I smiled weakly at her, unable to match her enthusiasm. "Syd, I need you to sit down. I have to tell you something."

Her face fell as she released my hand and stepped closer to me, resting a hand on my shoulder. "Journey, what's wrong? Babygirl, why aren't you excited?"

I swallowed hard and forced the tears that were threatening to overflow from the deep well of sadness I had been holding inside for the past few days. I wasn't sure if the well even had a bottom at this point.

"Let's sit, please," I begged softly.

She followed behind me silently and took a seat across from me at a table near the door, as far away from other patrons as I could possibly get. I took a shaky breath. *I can do this*, I coached silently. I could say these words out loud.

"Carlos had an accident at the beach . . ." I began.

Her eyes widened in horror.

"He was riding a Jet Ski when a wave apparently knocked him off and into the ocean," I continued. "He was attacked by sharks . . . he lost a lot of blood and his hand and leg were mangled and . . . and . . . "

I couldn't hold the water in the bottomless well anymore. My face crumpled and I cried into my hands as I said, "He's in a coma!"

I was shaking and nearly hysterical as I envisioned the entire incident playing in my mind like a movie reel on repeat. I could smell and taste the memory of blood in the ocean spray at the back of my throat. Sydney came over to me, and her arms were tight around me as she let me cry. She didn't say anything for a long time, she just held me, rocking me softly until I calmed down a bit.

"I'm so sorry, Journey," Sydney said. "I want to say that I know he will be okay, but I don't want to invalidate your pain with statements that may not be true. What are the doctors saying?"

"He's stable, and they did some reconstructive surgery on his hand, but his leg was so badly mangled that it had to be amputated below the knee," I said between sniffles.

Sydney sat back down. "Damn. I'm so sorry, Girl. I don't even know what to say. I'm here for you if you need anything—and I do mean anything. I don't care if it's as small as a phone call in the middle of the night or as big as taking a couple of days off to go with you to Puerto Rico to visit him and his family so you can have some additional support. Whatever you need, I got you."

"Thanks, Syd. I really appreciate that. I have been feeling shitty for days, and since he's unresponsive, I can't utilize any emotional management tools I'd normally rely upon. I mean, I don't know how long I have to be strong or whether there's a happy ending to this at all."

"Endings aren't happy. Being together with the man you love is happiness, and it's okay to hold on to hope for that. I can't imagine the depths and breadths of what you must be feeling, but I'm here for you. Please don't hesitate to lean on me, and please don't feel like you have to pretend to be strong and endure this alone. You have me."

I nodded silently, wiping my face with a napkin. I knew my makeup was ruined and I supposed that I should probably refrain from wearing it until I could control the crying fits I had been experiencing since Carlos went into the hospital. Sydney   patted my shoulder before getting up and walking to the counter to order food.

She returned with a bowls of delicious rice and vegetables and lentil soup for both of us. I didn't look at her. I just shook my head slowly from side to side, indicating that I didn't want to eat as I pouted and stared down at nothing, feeling so much that I felt nothing.

"Journey, Baby, you have to eat," Sydney coaxed.

I shook my head again. I didn't feel like eating, and my stomach was in knots of numbness. I just wanted to go home and lay in bed. I didn't even want to go back to work. Fuck that class, and fuck those people. Sydney wrapped both of our meals in carryout containers and picked up her cell phone.

"Hello, this is Dr. Sydney Beale calling on behalf of Ms. Journey Richards. I've just seen her today for strep throat, and she's going to need to call out the rest of the day and tomorrow. Yes, I will fax over a doctor's note by close of business today. Thanks so much. Yes, you have a good day also."

I looked up at her and smiled weakly. "You didn't have to do that," I said softly.

"Yes, I did! Girl, you are in no condition to deal with anyone today. You take your food and carry yourself on home. I will fax a doctor's note over to your job and bring referrals for a few therapists I know over to your place when I get off later today."

"A therapist? Why?"

"Because, Sweetie, you're going through a very difficult time and you shouldn't have to navigate this shit alone. Besides, your insurance is great, so I will find one who takes yours."

"Thank you."

"That's what friends are for. Now go on home. I will come see you later. Doctor's orders."

I laughed a little and got up to give her a tight squeeze. She hugged me back and walked me out to my car.

At home, I turned the heat up a little and cuddled on the couch with Rico and a cup of tea. I turned the television on and started watching *Practical Magic* on Netflix.

By the time Sandra Bullock's character began whimpering to her aunts to please bring her husband back from the dead, I found my face filled with fresh tears and decided I should stop torturing myself. I turned the television off and got up, heading for my medicine cabinet.

I pulled down the bottle of melatonin from the cabinet and stared at my reflection in the mirror for a few minutes. My cheeks were ashen and the corners of my eyes had salty residue from the evaporated tears in them. I splashed a bit of water on my face and dried my hands before unscrewing the lid and clumsily spilling almost all the damn clear pills onto the floor.

"Shit!" I muttered as I bent down to scoop them up.

I held them in my hand, I imagined taking them all so I could just sleep forever or until Carlos woke up. I wondered whether I would die, and then dismissed the thought and replaced the fallen pills into the bottle, holding onto just one. I swallowed the little iridescent, pearl-looking pill and crawled into bed with Rico curled up beside me. The curtains were closed, blocking out the early March afternoon sunlight. For the millionth time in my life, I wished I could call my mother and talk to her, but before I could completely picture her face, I fell asleep.

I dreamt I was a beautiful black and golden snake with rainbow colored eyes that looked like jewels. The earth was cool and moist beneath me as I slithered on my belly through tall, green grass. The trees were gigantic around me, towering so high that they nearly blocked out the sun itself. The air was humid and the breeze made the blades of grass rustle against me like a thousand gentle kisses. I moved through the greenery until I reached a clearing that led to a hill where the sun was shining brightly.

Atop the hill in the distance was a woman dressed in a long, white skirt and white top, swaying from side to side with her head slightly lowered. She looked like a beautiful blade of grass herself, with the wind billowing her skirt and hair to one side as she swayed gently. As I neared the woman, I realized she was me. My heart began to beat a little quickly in the snake form as I neared my human form. I could feel the pulse of the Earth begin to synchronize with my heartbeat, and I could also somehow feel the soft breathing of my human form. Soon I was right behind my human form, and as my snake form wound around the leg of my human form, my spirit exited the snake and returned to my human form.

I took a deep breath and dropped my head back into the breeze, the sun kissing my face warmly. The snake wound around my hips and then my belly, making its way to my right shoulder. Against my will, I raised my right arm with my palm outstretched and toward the sky. The snake made its way to my palm, crouched into itself tightly, and sprang into the sky. A rainbow shot from my palm, extending into the distance like a shooting star or comet behind the tail of the snake. There was a whooshing sound that echoed behind the snake and the rainbow, followed by a bright series of explosive lights in the sky, and a strange voice whispered, "Ophiuchus . . . "

I shot up in bed from the dream, and Rico hopped off the comforter, trotting toward the front door as I heard it open and close, followed by the metallic tinkling of keys hitting the granite countertop in my kitchen. I glanced at the alarm clock on the dresser that read 8:44. I assumed it must be Sydney letting herself in. I planted my feet on the floor and walked into the living room to see Sydney . . . and Devin.

"Oh! Hey!" I said awkwardly, "I didn't know you were bringing Devin."

"Hey, J, I'm sorry. I called you a few times to tell you I bumped into Devin at the store, and he was worried about you after I told him about Carlos. When you didn't answer, he demanded to come with me just in case . . . " Sydney explained.

"Yeah, Journey, if it's too much I can go," Devin said, walking over to give me a hug.

"No, it's fine. I just wasn't expecting to see you," I forced a smile as I hugged him back. I cut my eyes at Sydney over his shoulder, and she mouthed an apology holding her hands up helplessly and making a guilty face. I knew how persuasive Devin could be, so I let it go. I sat down on the sofa and wrapped myself in the blanket I had thrown across the back of it earlier.

"Did you eat?" Sydney asked, chastising me with her eyes from the kitchen.

I didn't respond, so she opened the refrigerator and held up the bag of food she had sent me home with several hours earlier. I rolled my eyes at her and sank lower into the sofa indignantly. She put the food back in the refrigerator and came to sit in the chair beside the couch. Devin sat on the adjacent side of the sectional, but nobody said anything.

"Why do I feel like I'm the subject of some whack ass intervention right now?" I asked.

"Well, Love, you just went through something really difficult and your friends are here for you. You don't have to talk if you don't want to, but we're here either way," Devin said.

There was a tender firmness in his tone that I had never heard before. I looked at Sydney, who was just nodding her head silently in support of Devin's statement.

"J, you can't stay like this. I don't expect you to employ your normal three-day rules here, but you have to pull yourself together," Sydney said.

"Why? I've spent my entire life holding it together through painful shit. I think I've earned this moment of losing my shit to the fullest extent," I retorted.

"That may be true, but you can't stay like this. You have shit to do."

"Yes, I had a wedding and a future to plan, and that all went to shit when Carlos was mangled by a shark and went into a coma!"

Devin and Sydney sat in silence.

"You don't have any profound wisdom or intelligence to offer for that, do you? Do you?"

They both shook their heads solemnly. I huffed and wrapped myself tighter in my blanket. We all sat in silence for a few minutes before I looked over at Sydney.

"You brought the referrals you told me about earlier?"

"Yeah, of course."

"Good. I will schedule an appointment for this week. Will that get you off my back?"

"It's a start," she said.

"Fine."

"Don't be mad, Journey. We're just trying to help, Baby," Devin said.

"Do NOT call me Baby," I snapped.

I knew I was being unreasonable, but I couldn't help it. Everything I thought was solid had been snatched from me in the blink of an eye, and I was spiraling helplessly on the inside, sideways falling away from any level of sense and stability I was known for. I was internally thankful that Sydney and Devin were there, but I didn't know how to express that the way I normally would at this moment.

I was just glad that I didn't have to retell the story of Carlos's accident again, since Sydney obviously had. I decided to tell them about the dream I'd just had instead.

"Ophiuchus . . . What's that?" Devin asked.

"I'm not sure." I admitted.

"I remember something like that from English Literature class. It had something to do with bringing the dead back to life, or something like that," Sydney recalled.

"Hmmm . . . I'm going to look it up," I said, my interest piqued.

I got up to grab my laptop and Googled it.

"It's a constellation of the serpent bearer. Apparently, it can be seen in the Northern Hemisphere in late July and early August."

"Hey, that's around your birthday," Devin said.

"Yeah, that's interesting. You're right, Syd, it does have to do with bringing the dead back to life. The symbol is used on medical emblems with the staff and two snakes. I wonder what my dream means."

"That's deep, considering what you're going through," Devin chimed in again.

My arms tingled and the hairs stood up on them. I shivered slightly, rubbing them as I continued to scroll the website about the Ophiuchus constellation. I read the stories associated with it as I pondered the dreams I had been having lately. First, the death of Devin's brother, then the lions and the pyramid, then Olokun, and now this serpent. I wondered what it all meant.

"You guys, I've been having these crazy dreams for a while now, " I admitted.

I told them about the Olokun and lion dreams, and when I was done, they sat on either side of me, openmouthed.

"What does it mean?" Sydney asked.

"I'm not sure. I think I can find out, though."

"How?" Devin asked.

"I think I need to reach out to Carlos' cousin, Carmen."

"What does she have to do with this?" Sydney asked me.

"He took me to her after the dream I had about the lions. I think that she may be integral to finding out what all this means."

"Why?" Devin asked.

"Because she interpreted the dream I had before, and it really resonated with me. I think there's more to this than I know."

"Do you know how to reach her?" Sydney replied.

"I have her number somewhere; otherwise I will just have to visit her."

"Do you need me to go with you when you go to her?" Sydney offered.

"No, I don't think so. I think she will talk to me either way."

"Good. Well, I'm going to go, Journey," Sydney announced, rising from the chair and putting on her shoes.

"Okay. I will keep you posted. Devin, did you want to stay? My couch is really comfortable."

"I would, but I have to be up early for work," he declined.

"Okay, cool. I will let you both out."

When they were gone and my house was quiet again, I brushed my teeth and lay back down in bed. I had run my social battery down faster than my cell phone battery, and I just wanted to sit in silence and listen to Rico purring contentedly beside me.

"Tu gato esta muy contento," I heard as my eyelids felt heavy with sleep.

"Mi Tesoro," I whispered to the shadows as I drifted away.

17. Inside Out

She is the honey and the bee,
A beautifully regal enchantress of my duality.
Her sweetness lures me.
Distracting and overwhelming me with her heartbeat.
A strong and rhythmic African drum.
She snaps her fingers and I come.
She lures me from my lowly vibrations and crowns me
King,
And yet I love her most of all when she stings.
~ Olosunde

I was floating in an abyss of soft underwater sounds and a faint beeping. It was what I imagine it was like being in the womb. There was darkness all around and I didn't know where my limbs were. I tried to wiggle my fingers and toes, but I couldn't. I was floating in the nothingness of a darkness so deep and vast that I had no concept of time or space. I felt no thirst or hunger, no sense of fatigue or pain. I floated and breathed to a rhythm that was foreign to me.

After what felt like years of floating, I blinked my eyes. I had eyes. I could see! The image was a blurry, soft, pink and yellow light, hazy and without structure.

"Carlos ... My son ... "

I recognized the voice of my mother speaking softly over the beeping.

"Mom? Mom!"

I shouted at the top of my voice, but she didn't respond. I heard her weeping, but I couldn't see her. Where was she? Where was I? I heard what I thought was my heart beating amid the water sounds and beeping. How long had I been in this nothingness?

A deep panicking sadness came over me as my mind wandered to the idea of being trapped in this place forever. But what was forever if I couldn't see or feel anything? I tried hard to think back to the last things I could remember.

The beach . . . the warm sun . . . the cool spraying mist of the ocean on my skin . . . the taste of saltwater . . . the feeling of happiness and a loving embrace, but from whom? Wait! Journey! Where was she?

"She's home, mourning you."

The voice seemed like it came from within me, but it was unfamiliar, layered, and not distinctly male or female.

"Who are you?" I asked nervously, unable to see anything but pink and yellow haziness.

"We are many, and we are with you," the layered voice replied.

The tones vibrated and caressed me on all sides, without exactly touching me.

"Come with us and you will see."

"Come with you where?" I was nervous and I didn't like the helpless way I felt. "Where are you?"

"We are everywhere and nowhere. We are with you. We have been watching you since you left us to fulfill your destiny. It is time that you returned with us."

"Can I have a name?" I asked.

"We have had many names; more than you could ever recall in your lifetime, but you belong to us and we belong to you. We are yours and you are ours. Everywhere you go, you take us with you. Every thought you think, we are with you. Every action you take, we are watching. We are the mothers and fathers of your lineage. We are with you."

"Well . . . okay. Where am I?"

"You are in between."

"In between what?"

"You know the answer to your question."

I pondered this for a few moments before asking any further questions.

"How do I get out of here?"

"You must come with us. When you are ready to stop clinging to this life, you will come with us."

"You mean . . . die?"

"Death is merely a part of the journey that is life."

Journey . . . they had said her name, and my heartbeat quickened. The sound of the water rushing and the beeping picked up a bit.

"What if I don't want to go?" I asked.

"You will remain here until you come with us."

I felt a deep sense of longing. I wanted to see Journey again. I wanted to kiss her and hold her close to me while I breathed in her scent.

"You can see her," they told me.

"How?"

The pink and yellowness began to darken and I felt myself being pulled sharply into a deeper darkness. I felt a fear that I had never known as drifted someplace . . . else.

After a few minutes, I could smell a familiar warm, sweet fragrance. A few minutes later found me standing in Journey's apartment. The brown sugar and fig fragrance of her home wafted toward me in a comforting and inviting way. I inhaled deeply as the apartment began to materialize around me. It was dark, and I could hear the city sounds outside. A soft thud made me turn toward her bedroom door where Rico was watching me, his green eyes glowing in the darkness. I told myself that he must have jumped down from her bed. He stared at me for a few minutes before his soft, white paws padded their way toward me, his belly wagging beneath him. He sat down in front of my toes, twitched his whiskers, licked his nose and blinked at me silently before rising and walking away toward her door again, stopping to look back in my direction, almost as if to say, "She's in here."

I followed him, and found Journey lying in her bed sleeping. Her back was facing me, and her shoulder was rising and falling as she breathed softly, quietly. I sat down on the bed behind her and just watched her for a while in silent appreciation of her curls piled on top of her head by her pink satin scarf like a curly pineapple crown. I lay down beside her, pressing my body up against hers, spooning her as I wondered whether she could feel me. I slid one arm around her waist and nestled my face in the back of her neck the way I always did when we slept together. She stirred slightly and released a purring sigh of comfort.

I didn't close my eyes. I was afraid to find myself back in the strange prison of pink and yellow lights. I just held her and listened to her breathe.

"Journey . . . I love you," I whispered into her shoulder.

"I love you, too, Carlos," she mumbled back, letting out another sigh and falling silent again.

Water rose to my eyes as I held her close to me, praying that, somehow, she'd remember this moment when she woke up. Praying that she was dreaming of me the way I wanted to dream of her. Praying that no matter what separated us, she'd never let me go.

Somehow, I had fallen asleep, or what I could only describe as sleep. The womb sound had returned and the sound of the beeping made me painfully aware that I was no longer lying beside Journey. The pink and yellow haze was back, and I found myself wanting to weep and rage simultaneously that she was gone, but it was me who was gone.

I gave in to the nothingness, trying hard not to let the hollow sound of the beeping fill me with despair. I wanted to move, but I still couldn't in this place.

Where was I? Why was I here? Why couldn't I go back to Journey? I had so many questions, and the voices weren't around anymore. I started talking to myself to try to remember as much as I could. I quizzed myself over and over about all the things I could remember: my name, my address, my birth date, the names of my relatives, their birth dates, my favorite foods, colors I liked, places I've visited, and Journey.

I imagined her face, and I smiled. The way her curls were wilder in the center of her head than anywhere else. The symmetrical beauty marks on both sides of her body. The way she smelled. The way she walked like there was a silent song playing just for her. The way her laugh sounded like a little girl's when I tickled her. I sighed as the emptiness filled me like purplish-black ink filling me up inside, staining the pink and yellow haze a unique hue of sadness.

"Are you ready to come with us now?" the voices asked, returning from what felt like years of silence.

"No," I said firmly. "I want to stay with her."

"You will only hurt yourself more. You must transcend this and move on."

"Fuck that! I want to stay with her!"

"She is missing you also, but you've left a piece of yourself with her. A piece of all of us remains."

"What does that even mean?" I asked angrily. "Why do keep speaking in riddles?"

"There is a life within her . . . a child . . . your child, as well as ours."

I was silent for a while as I thought about the time we spent together in Puerto Rico.

"Yes," they said, "it was then that the new life was conceived. She carries us within her."

"Take me back to her!" I demanded.

I needed to be with her, to watch over her instead of sitting helplessly in this place. I wondered whether she knew.

"She is not yet aware, but she will know soon."

"Take me back to her," I said again, with less aggression. "Please, let me see her."

"Very well," they conceded.

The darkness followed by the pulling sensation occurred again, and I found myself standing in the back of the room of the class she was teaching. She was as beautiful as I remembered, only the light in her eyes was replaced by a sorrow that I had never seen.

"Yes, sir, can you please tell me your name?" she asked one of the men attending her class.

"My name is Carlos," he said. "Ms. Richards, I'm confused about the directions on page seventeen. Can you please repeat that section of the module?"

"Carlos? Um . . . Certainly . . ."

She scrolled the slides back and stared at the projection screen that was linked to her laptop, but she didn't say anything.

"Ummm . . . I'm sorry."

She rested her hand on her forehead and then the center of her chest as she took a deep breath. I could hear her heart pounding from across the room as all her thoughts started to jumble in an obvious panic all over her face. Apparently, having someone in her class with the same name as mine was totally throwing her off.

"Excuse me," she said as she laughed nervously and settled herself. "In order to maintain compliance with your company's standards you need to renew your license every five years. To do that, you need to attend quarterly trainings, such as this, every year. To apply for them, you need to visit the home site and enroll in the classes. When you have completed them, you have to bring the validation form to your office manager and have it signed, and then submit it to your project manager for credit. Does that make sense?"

"Yes, thank you," he replied.

"Fabulous! That concludes today's training. I hope that you've enjoyed yourselves and found this very informative. Please complete the survey at the end, and feel free to help yourselves to refreshments in the lobby. Thank you for attending today's seminar, and have a fantastic day!"

She barely finished her sentence before she began scrambling to gather her things. She was rushing to get out of there, and my heart broke for her as I watched her in rare form. I followed behind her, unseen, as she rushed to the ladies' room and slammed the stall door shut behind her. She collapsed against the door and breathed erratically for a few minutes while I stood on the other side. I rested my forehead on the cold metal of the door and listened to her as she began to weep softly. I wished that I could hold her and let her know I was here with her, feeling with her, mourning with her. I felt helpless in my present form.

"She will mourn you, but you extend her pain with your presence. She is a medium and she has the gift of sight. She can feel your presence even though she cannot see you."

"When will this end?" I asked the voices.

"It will end when you are tired of tormenting her and you're ready to move on."

"But I'm not tormenting her. I love her."

"She loves you also. You are connected to her, but you do not need to continue in this way. You can be at peace and allow her to find peace as well. It will take time, but you must accept what is. Either you stay and torment her, or you come with us and let her live on."

"But I'm not ready."

"Then this will carry on."

A sound interrupted the conversation. It was the sound of Journey vomiting into the toilet. She gasped and wretched again before flushing the toilet. When she emerged, her face was pale as she stared through me at her reflection. She spat in the sink and made a face of disgust at herself in the bright lights of the mirror.

She filled her mouth with water over and over, and splashed water on her face before wiping her face and eyes with a paper towel. She sighed and shook her head as she gathered up her purse and computer bag, and walked out the door. I fought with myself as to whether I should follow her or do as the voices said and let her be. Against their advice, I walked out of the building and followed her to her car. I watched her load her bags, get in, and drive away.

"Are you ready now?" they asked me, sounding like wind whispering harmoniously through the trees around me.

"Not just yet."

"Very well."

"Take me with her," I asked.

"As you wish . . . "

Journey arrived on the block where I took her to visit my cousin Carmen. She stepped out of the car and stared up at the tall apartment buildings, squinting into the late afternoon sunlight.

"Hmmm . . . I think this is the one," she spoke aloud to herself.

"What's she doing?" I asked.

"She is looking for answers."

The voices were softer than before, like a breeze on a spring day. I sighed and shoved my hands into my pockets and shivered, although I couldn't feel the cold breeze at all.

Journey walked up to the building I took her to months before, pressed the buzzer for Carmen and waited, tapping her foot in the cold breeze.

"Hello?" Carmen answered.

"Hi, Carmen. It's Journey. I visited you with Carlos awhile back and I just wanted to . . . "

The door buzzed and unlatched, and Journey stepped into the building. She stepped onto the elevator and pressed the button for the ninth floor. When she arrived at the top floor of the building, a middle-aged woman with wide hips and a long skirt was leaning out of her apartment silently waving her down the hallway.

"Journey! Ay, dios mio! What are you doing here?"

"I'm sorry for coming by unannounced, but I left you a voicemail and I've been experiencing some strange things since Carlos' accident. I didn't know where else to turn."

Carmen shook her head and hugged Journey to her chest, ushering her inside with a sad smile. Journey went inside and took her shoes off at the door as she had the last time.

"Please, please, have a seat. Tell me what has been happening."

"I . . . I honestly don't know where to begin," Journey said as she sank into the sofa. "I went to Puerto Rico with Carlos, as I'm sure you know. I met your family there, and Carlos proposed to me."

"Ah, yes, congratulations. I'm so sorry that things took such a terrible turn," Carmen lamented.

"Yes, but since I've been home, I've been having strange dreams again. I think Carlos has been trying to communicate with me somehow. I know how silly that sounds since he's in a coma all the way in Puerto Rico, but it's true."

"You have a gift. He may be trying to reach you," Carmen explained.

"Yes, but I've also been dreaming of some other things that I don't understand. Have you ever heard of Ophiuchus?"

Carmen looked confused. "No," she replied, shaking her head.

"What about Olokun?" Journey asked.

Carmen's eyes widened. "What did you say?"

"Olokun. Do you know that word? Is it a name or a place?"

"I know it," she said, her eyes still wide. "I think you should come with me to my shrine room."

She led Journey down the hallway of her apartment to the small room in the back like the last time we visited her. There were a few books opened with bowls of water and an incense holder with a trail of incense ashes lingering at the bottom resting on the rug that was on the floor.

"I'm sorry if I was interrupting you from something," Journey apologized.

"No, no, it is all right. Just sit."

Journey sat on one of the pillows and pulled her knees up to her chest, rubbing the chill off her shins.

"I was about to put on some tea. Would you like some?" Carmen offered.

"Yes, please, that would be great!"

"Okay, I will be right back."

Carmen walked out the room and came back shortly after with a tray holding two steaming hot mugs of tea, and a jar of honey in the center. Journey stirred the honey into her tea and sipped the mug cautiously after blowing it to cool the surface.

I smiled broadly at her as she exclaimed, "This tea is delicious! What kind is it?"

"It's red raspberry leaf tea. It's good for the womb, and since you're pregnant, you'll want to start drinking it to tone your uterus," Carmen stated matter-of-factly.

Journey choked on her tea and began coughing and sputtering at the word "pregnant," and when she was done coughing, she wiped the water from her eyes and stared at Carmen with her mouth wide open.

"What the hell did you just say?" Journey demanded in between deep breaths. "Did you say pregnant?"

"Oh, you didn't know?" Carmen asked wide-eyed, and then smiled conspicuously into her mug.

"How do you know?" Journey demanded.

"I just know these things. It's a gift. I can tell."

Journey wasn't convinced, but I was immediately frantic when I heard her say, "I'm sorry, but I have to go," as she scrambled up off the floor.

I already knew about the baby, so I wasn't as shocked as Journey was anymore. I wanted her to get her questions answered, though, and I felt an overwhelming sense of panic and something like anger, but not quite. A pile of papers blew off one of the shelves haphazardly, and the broom fell in front of the doorway blocking Journey's exit.

"Someone is here," Carmen said, looking around suspiciously.

"Say what?" Journey asked, whirling around to look at Carmen. "Is it Carlos? I need answers!"

Carmen closed her eyes for a few minutes and took several deep breaths.

"Yes," she said, "It is Carlos. I can smell him and I can hear him."

"What's he saying?" she asked.

"Journey! Journey, I'm here," I said, but she couldn't hear me.

Carmen shivered and trembled slightly as I came closer to her. I rested my hand on her shoulder and showed her the last things I remembered.

"He's showing me that he was riding on a Jet Ski and the water spraying against him. You're on the Jet Ski and I can feel your arms around him. He's filled with an overwhelming sense of love for you. He's happy. Then you got off for some reason and he went off to continue enjoying the ride. A wave knocks him off the Jet Ski and he starts sinking. He's afraid he won't see you again, that you'll forget him."

"Tell him I'm here!" Journey exclaimed.

"He knows you're here. He followed you here from work. You had an uncomfortable experience at work today that made you come here. You vomited in the bathroom before you came here. He knows you're pregnant, too. He ... I lost it ... " Carmen trailed off.

"What? What! Bring him back!" Journey begged.

"I can't. He is gone now. I can't hear him anymore," Carmen said.

I was leaning against the shelves panting and coughing. I'd never experienced anything like that before, and I was suddenly drained. I felt like I was fading. I used my last bit of energy and threw myself at Carmen and hugged her. She moved toward Journey and hugged her, and for a few seconds I felt alive. I was inside Carmen's body, wearing her like a costume, and brushed the hair out of Journey's stricken face with Carmen's hand and made her squeeze Journey tightly again. Journey didn't say anything she just stared, astonished as she hugged Carmen's body back.

"Whew!" Carmen exclaimed, releasing Journey, "That was intense!"

"Yeah, it was," Journey whispered. "I'm going to go. That was a lot for me and I need to go home and process this. Can I call you?"

"Absolutely! Carlos obviously wants to make contact. Please take my card and call me tomorrow. I'd like to do another reading for you and answer some of your questions. You should arrange an appointment with a doctor or midwife soon. I know a few midwives you may interested in."

"Okay," Journey said taking the small piece of cardstock from Carmen bearing her phone number and email address. "Thank you for all your help."

"No, thank you. Carlos' accident was hard on all of us. You're family now, and I'm here for you all the way."

"Thank you," Journey said, as she collected her purse, shrugged on her jacket, and followed Carmen to her front door. They hugged briefly in the hallway before Journey walked away toward the elevator.

I didn't have the energy to follow her, and I felt myself being pulled back into the nothingness. The darkness filled me and dragged me away from them, bringing me back to the pink and yellow haze. I was angry I had been separated from her again, but I waited quietly, listening to the beeping. I realized I must be in the hospital, and the beeping must be the machines surrounding me. I wondered if I'd ever be free of this prison that was my nearly lifeless body.

"You will be free when you decide to come with us." The voices whispered.

"I don't want to go with you!" I exclaimed. "I love her and I want to stay with her!"

"You have to be careful. You're expending a lot of energy visiting her because she's so far away."

"I have to," I replied. "I love her."

"You will always love her, but you will never hold her with your own hands again. When you're ready to stop hurting her, you can leave this place."

My eyes began to water against my will. I hated that I had to be away from Journey and all that she was going through without me.

"You must remain calm. You will exhaust yourself."

The beeping sound increased and there was a strange pumping sound.

"Your body can't handle all this stress. You must remain calm," they spoke in harmony.

"But what about her? She's out there while I'm stuck inside myself."

"She is fortified. She will bend like a blade of grass in the strongest wind. She will bend, but she will not break. We are with her as well as you. Peace, be still."

18. Outer Limits

I once experienced a hurt so great,
I hid it from myself until I could forget.
I covered it with positive thoughts, happy memories,
But each hurt that came after the original pain covered
the core like its own special layer of silent poisonous
association.
Now I remain with onion layers of pain,
And the peeling back of each layer reminds me of what I
tried so hard to forget.

~ Olosunde

I sat in front of the therapist for my third session with Dr. Wilmington, and stared at my hands holding the cup of tea she had offered me.

"Is there anything else you'd like to say?"

"No. That's all."

I had just finished telling her how I lost my parents and how that had led me to being everyone else's source of nurturing and comfort in my life, my three-day rule on dealing with loss, and how it was completely ineffective when it came to dealing with the serious injury of Carlos. Everything was Carlos, and Carlos was everything. She handed me another tissue and didn't say anything as I wiped my eyes for the umpteenth time.

"It seems to me that you've always been trying to save the world. Everyone; your friends, your family, your clients, and anyone else you've ever loved. But then you found out that you couldn't. Then you made Carlos your world, and now you have to accept that you can't save him either. That doesn't make you a bad person, nor does it make you a failure. It merely makes you human."

I pondered this for a few minutes before taking a deep, shaky breath and collecting my coat, realizing that our session was over. My phone buzzed in my pocket while I was waiting by the elevator in the hallway of the office building where my therapist saw her patients. I reached for it to see a text message from Sydney inviting me out for happy hour and some girlfriend time. I side-stepped a man without looking up as I entered the elevator while texting her back that I would meet her in forty-five minutes.

When I arrived at Rose Bar, I passed the smiling hostess and went upstairs to the floor where Sydney was waiting for me. She was smiling, talking to some tall, slender man in a suit. I slid onto the sofa beside her and began to rest my coat on it when she squealed and hugged me.

"Hey J! Journey, this is Otis. Otis, this is my friend, Journey," she introduced.

"Hi, Otis," I greeted blandly.

"Hi, Journey," he said with a smile. "Sydney has been telling me all about you."

"Oh, dear God, I hope she didn't share any embarrassing details," I said with a sarcastic smirk.

"Absolutely not!" Sydney protested, pushing my leg.

"No, she thinks very highly of you. Anyway, I promised Sydney I wouldn't infringe upon girl time, so I'm going to be heading out."

"It was nice to meet you," I said.

"Likewise . . . Call me later, Sydney."

"I sure will," she replied.

He leaned in and kissed her on the cheek before gathering his coat and sliding it on.

When he was out of earshot, I turned to Sydney exclaiming, "Girl! Who was that? He was fine!"

"I know, right? I met him a few weeks ago, before you went out of town. He's really sweet!"

"That's fantastic! I'm happy to see you engaging in cuffing season, however late you may be," I said, genuinely happy for her.

"Girl, I don't have much time for dating with my work schedule. You know how it is out here for successful black women and love. I met him at the grocery store on the off chance that I didn't just have my shit delivered to my house that day."

"Well, he seems nice! He kinda reminds me of a guy I used to see years ago," I said.

"Really? In what way? Have I heard about this guy before? What was his name?" she asked in rapid succession.

"Probably not. I don't talk about him too much, but his name was Lamont. He was fine. I was smitten from day one!"

"Mmmm . . . Do tell! I live for your stories!"

I laughed at that, closing my eyes as I mentally drifted back to that time.

"I met him in Atlanta when I was giving a ride to my roommate's boyfriend. Lamont owned this urban clothing store in the Little Five Points area. The first thing I noticed about him was his voice. It was deep and rich, like being wrapped in a warm velvet blanket. He was tall, slender, and chocolate . . . "

"Just like you like 'em!" she laughed as she wiggled her fingers at me.

"Yes, ma'am! Anyway, we would sit and talk and he always had the most interesting things to share. I mean, he was about ten years older, so his experiences far exceeded my twenty-three year old self."

"Fine and experienced! Yaaaas!" we both chuckled.

"He used to always invite me to spend the weekend with him, telling me to bring my favorite pajamas and fuzzy socks, and sit in a hotel room ordering room service and watching television all weekend. I always declined because I didn't think it was proper, but then one day he set me up . . . "

"Set you up? How?" Sydney was practically on the edge of her seat.

"Girl, listen. This one day, he asked me to come pick him up because he had an errand to run and he didn't have a car. I agreed to pick him up from his store, but when I asked him about where we were going, he just told me that he would give me directions. I thought that sounded strange, but I didn't ask any further questions since he had never given me any reason to doubt him before."

" I was still relatively new to the area, so I used the GPS on my phone to get everywhere, and it was a little unnatural for me to let others give me directions verbally, but before I knew it, we were outside of this mall I'd never been to before. He asked me to park outside of the Macy's entrance and wait in the car for him."

"When he returned, he was holding a little Macy's bag, which he put in my back seat underneath his back pack. Then he got into the front passenger seat and started directing me again. About fifteen minutes later, we were pulling into the parking lot at the Hilton, and he guided me into the parking garage, all the way to the top floor. He had me park near the elevator, then he reached over and turned down the radio before turning to look at me with this expression I had never seen before. It was serious, but tender. He had the most smooth and sincere tone when he said, 'I've been knowing you for months now, and I keep asking you to come and spend the weekend with me, and you keep telling me no. I totally respect your choice and maybe you just don't feel comfortable, but I figured I'd ask you again. I want you to come inside and stay the weekend with me, Journey. If you say no again, I will respect it and never ask you again.'"

"Girl! I was all but shocked! Especially when he told me he'd give me time to think it over. Then he got out of the car and stood outside smoking a cigarette all smooth and shit!"

"What? Sydney exclaimed. "Oh, my goodness! What the hell!"

"I know, right!" I co-signed.

"What did you do?" Sydney asked.

"Hell, I phoned a friend for advice! I called up my girl, Carla, and told her what the situation was because she was a little older and I had no idea how to navigate that shit!"

"What did she tell you?" Sydney asked breathlessly, thoroughly engrossed in my story.

"She told me to get my ass out the damn car and politely ride his dick into the sunset."

We both leaned into one another cackling and swatting at each other like teenaged girls.

I continued, "I hung up with her and got out of the car more bravely than I felt because I had never done anything like that before. He flicked his cigarette away, smiling at me as we walked toward the elevator. I told him we weren't having sex, and he just replied he wouldn't try to make me do anything I didn't want to do. I don't know why I felt like that was the end of it, but whatever. We went to the front desk where he got the keys and then back on the elevator up to the room."

"Daaaaaamn! Did you end up having sex?" Sydney gushed.

"Just listen," I told her with a wave of my hand, knowingly holding her in suspense.

"We got into the room and he pulled bathroom cleaner and a sponge out of his bag and went into the bathroom and started cleaning out the tub. I'm just staring at him thinking he must be a bigger germaphobe than I am. When he finished, he started running a bath. He came back into the room and pulled the little Macy's bag out of his backpack and removed a bottle of bubble bath of the fragrance that I had on when we first met. I was floored when I realized that this was all for me all along, Girl."

"Wow!" she grinned conspicuously, but she didn't press me.

"I know, right? So, he propped a pillow in the bathtub and invited me to get in. I objected that I didn't have clothes to change into, which he dismissed by telling that it didn't matter. I went into the bathroom and got in the tub. A few minutes later, I'm surrounded by bubbles and warm water, feeling nice and relaxed. He tapped on the door and asked if he can come in. I said no, slightly alarmed because, you know, we've never been together like that before. He told me to close the curtain, and that he just wanted to sit and chat. I thought about it for a minute before agreeing, rationalizing that if he wanted to take advantage, he could have already."

"He came in and sat on the floor, and started talking to me about all types of stuff: my childhood, my family, my college experience, my dreams. We talked until the water was cold and my fingers were wrinkly."

"And he never tried to touch you or anything?" Sydney inquired.

"Nope. He stayed on his side of the curtain, and he left when I was ready to get out so I could cover myself. When I was out of the bathroom, I grabbed the bottle of fragranced oil that he had also bought for me and sat down on the bed with it, preparing to moisturize myself. He walked over and snatched the bottle from my hands and told me firmly to sit down."

"When I was seated on the edge of the bed, he poured the oil into his hands and began rubbing it into my feet. He focused on my feet for a long time, never once looking at me. It was like he was studying my responses to his touch."

"When he was finished, I felt extremely aware of the fact that I was naked underneath the towel and I moved like I was going to get up, but he placed his hand on my knee to stop me, saying only 'Let me.' How could I say no to him? I mean his eyes were so earnest . . . He kneeled and rubbed oil onto my legs, massaging my ankles and calves, staring at me intently. I gazed back, feeling myself getting wetter as his hands caressed higher and higher up my legs."

"Ooooh, Journey!" Sydney giggled.

"I'm telling you!" I said. "When he got to my knees, I clamped them together so tight, and he just smiled. He bit his lip and reached under the towel, gripping my hips, and then rubbed his hands all the way back down to my ankles. I shivered a little, and he stood up and told me to turn over. That's when I started internally freaking out because I KNEW if I turned over he would know that there was a small river flowing down the insides of my thighs."

We both laughed at that.

"Journey, you could write a damn book, Girl! Keep talking! This is getting juicy!"

We both giggled again.

"I stood up and turned over, towel still wrapped around me as I lay down on the bed. He continued to massage the oil into the backs of my thighs, touching the wetness I knew was there, and then he rubbed my shoulders and neck, and I opened the towel so that he could reach my lower back. He rubbed me until I was comfortable, relaxed, and my body felt like a tub of whipped honey butter."

"Mmmmph!" Sydney exclaimed.

I continued, "My eyes were closed, and I was totally not expecting to feel his lips on my feet. He kissed me up the backs of my legs before rising and kissing me up my spine to the back of my neck. Then he whispered for me to turn over while he was holding the towel down on both sides of me to keep me covered. I turned over and he kissed my lips until I couldn't resist wrapping my arms around him. He trailed his lips and tongue down my neck to my collar bone and across my shoulder. I was so wet at that point that I knew I was in trouble. He peeled the towel away from my breasts and spent a little time there until I was writhing and trembling underneath him."

I stopped and took a deep breath, remembering the moment, when Sydney swatted at me, "Keep going!" her eyes were wide, as she was fully invested in the story.

"My bad, Girl, I was reliving it," I laughed.

"He kept peeling back the towel, bit by bit, kissing the newly exposed flesh underneath until it was gone and on the floor beside the bed. I had lost all my modesty and had completely forgotten how I told him that we weren't having sex. While he was on one end of the bed with his face pressed into my thigh, licking and nibbling it, I was losing my shit on the other end of the bed. Eventually, my clitoris was in his mouth and I was

LITERALLY climbing the walls. Oh, my God. I was not ready. I managed to get away and was crawling toward the headboard, when he grabbed me by my hips, pulled me back into him and licked my butt."

"Say what?" Sydney's mouth dropped open.

"Yes, Girl, he tossed the entire fuck out of my salad. I was all the way done."

"Was this your first time experiencing that?"

"Yes! How many college guys you know tossing salads out here? I was all of two years out of undergrad! I'd never experienced anything like that in my life!"

"So, I guess it's safe to say you had sex that night, huh?" Sydney guessed.

"Girl, he stroked me until the grey matter was oozing out of my ears. I had never had so many orgasms back to back in my entire life. I was all the way fucked up."

"I bet!"

"When it was over, I was laying there sweating with the upper half of my body wrapped in a sheet, and the lower half exposed. I have no idea how that happened, but he stroked my hip and told me to go to sleep, and I took a deep sigh and passed out until the next morning. It was the best sleep I'd ever had."

"Well, damn! How long did you two date after that?"

"That's complicated. I woke up in the morning and freaked out, snatched on my clothes, and left," I confessed.

"You did WHAT?" she was incredulous.

"I know, I know!" I covered my face in remembered embarrassment. "I literally had a '7:48! Where are my panties?' moment. The stupid shit you do when you're young," I sighed.

"He was probably pissed," Sydney said.

"Pissed isn't even the word. I didn't contact him for two weeks," I said shaking my head.

"Journey! That's horrible! The man gave you EVERYTHING that night and you GHOSTED him? I'm so shocked! I would never imagine you doing that, you're always sooo . . . together."

"Yeah, when I finally reached out to him, we had a few weeks of uncomfortable conversations, and I had to apologize A LOT for being immature. I don't think he ever truly forgave me, but when we started talking romantically again, I couldn't keep my vagina off him."

We both fell into loud, cackling laughter, spilling Sydney's water on the table. We flagged down our server to bring us napkins, and Sydney sipped her cocktail while I sipped my water in silence, looking apologetically at the man who came by with a mop.

"How long did you two date?" Sydney asked after the spill was cleaned and we were alone again.

"On and off for about two years. It was complicated all around, but I loved him."

"More than Devin?" she asked.

"I don't know about more. It was different. He taught me a lot about myself."

"Hmmm . . ." Sydney muttered.

She stayed silent as if she were chewing my words, turning the textures of the sentiments I expressed over inside her mouth. When she finally spoke again, I wasn't ready.

"Journey, what was that drink we had at your last birthday party? Kissing something . . ."

I didn't answer immediately. I couldn't bear the thoughts of Carlos that came rushing back to me. In order to collect myself, I pretended not to remember for a few minutes before finally saying, "It was called the Kissing Frog."

"That's right! Let's order some of those! I liked that! Do you remember how to make it?"

"Yeah, I accidentally learned about it when I went to Carlos's restaurant the first time," I said softly.

She immediately knew that she had triggered me into sadness.

"I'm sorry, Journey!" she apologized. "I didn't know that. We don't have to get that drink."

"It's fine. You didn't know," I replied.

All the sadness I had been avoiding came rushing back and I excused myself to the restroom.

"I'm sorry, Journey!" she called after me, but I didn't turn to respond. I needed to get out of there.

When I was safely inside the bathroom stall, I resisted the urge to cry, leaning against the door while I practiced the breathing techniques I had learned in therapy when I refused the antidepressants that Dr. Wilmington tried to prescribe. I inhaled deeply, held it for five seconds, and then released it slowly for ten seconds, over and over, until my hands stopped shaking and my heart stopped racing.

I heard my phone chime a few times while I took my time peeing. After I came out of the stall and washed my hands, I checked my phone, expecting to see text messages from Sydney inquiring whether I was all right. Instead, I saw five texts and three missed calls from Carlos' mother. My heart began racing again as I hit the button to call her back without listening to her voice message.

"Hello?" her voice sounded frantic.

"Hello, this is Journey, is everything okay with Carlos?" I asked with anxiety in my voice.

I could hear her hesitate for a beat before whispering through tears, "He's gone, M ija. My baby is gone."

There was a loud clattering sound as I heard her start wailing from what sounded like the bottom of a can. I could hear other voices trying to calm her as I held the phone tightly to my ear, frantically waiting for someone to pick up the other end and tell me what happened. The call was disconnected abruptly, but I continued to hold the phone to my ear as I slid down the wall to the cold tiles of the bathroom floor.

There was nowhere for me to run or hide. Carlos was gone, and I wept all the water from the bottomless well of my sadness onto those cold tiles. When I got up off the floor after several minutes, I felt a huge cramping sensation in my abdomen. The cramping was followed by a feeling of pressure between my legs, and I knew that I was miscarrying Carlos' baby. As I closed the door to the bathroom stall again, I heard the main bathroom door open, and Sydney's voice called out urgently.

"Journey, are you okay? I'm sorry for upsetting you. I didn't know."

"I know you didn't. It's okay," I replied through the stall door.

"Are you okay?"

"I just started bleeding. I think I'm going to head home."

"Bleeding? Do you need a pad?" she said with concern.

"No . . . well, yes. I'm having a miscarriage."

"Journey! You were pregnant? Why didn't you tell me?"

"You know why . . ." I trailed off.

She was silent for a second because we both knew what I said was true.

"How far along were you?" she asked quietly, hesitantly, trying to sound more like a friend than a doctor.

"About twelve weeks," I replied through hard cramps.

"Let's get you to the hospital, then. Make sure you're all right."

"I don't want to go to the hospital, Sydney. I just want to go home."

"All right. Well, at least let me stay with you for the night to make sure you're okay."

"All right," I agreed through tears.

I wiped myself, and before I could ask, Sydney handed me a pad under the door.

"All I have are regulars, but something is better than nothing."

"You're right. Thanks," I said as I took the yellow pad from her hand under the door.

I fixed the pad to my panties, then stood to pull them up. I flushed the toilet with my toe, ignoring the crime scene that shone redly in the bowl and emerged from the stall without a tear in sight.

As I washed my hands, Sydney tenderly said, "I need you to visit your gynecologist in about a week to make sure you passed it completely."

"I will," was all I could muster. "Let's go."

We walked silently out of the ladies' room, paid our tab, and then went to our own separate cars parked near each other.

"I'll stop by my place for some clothes, and then come to your place," Sydney said.

"Okay," I said. But nothing was okay. Carlos and everything that was him was gone.

19. Nothing Even Matters

Unsure of future,
Fearing the struggles long past.
Ignoring the levels of the water in the glass.

~ Olosunde

"Mom, I'm sorry I disappointed you," I began.

I needed this exchange to go well, and I wasn't trying to see the hurt expression on her face again. "I know there's nothing I could say to you to make you feel better after me being arrested and all that, but I wanted to at least let you know that I wasn't doing the same thing I've done in the past."

The words were catching in my throat as I fought to find a way past my pride to explain the depths of my most recent screw up. I had shown up at her house unexpectedly and finessed her into a kitchen conversation.

"Erica, it's fine," she said, cutting me off. "Just pay us back the twelve-hundred dollars when you can, and I will just forget it ever happened."

"You don't understand, Mom," I whimpered, sounding like the fatherless child I had always felt I was. "I need you. I need you so much right now. I know that I've always seemed like I was flying by the seat of my pants, and to a certain extent, I was, but this is different. I am navigating uncharted territory, and I don't have a compass. I need you to be my compass until I can be my own. I don't want to repeat this lesson, and I feel like this is an opportunity to get something right."

"What are you talking about, Erica?"

"Mom . . . Mommy, I'm lost. I loved a man that you would have loved, and he hurt me. Now, I know it has been weeks since I talked to you and that you didn't raise me to howl about my broken heart in despair, but that's where I am right now. I feel like I've been repeating the same emotional cycle in my life since my father, and I've rejected you out of anger for so long, but I need your wisdom and discernment now, Mom."

Her face softened from the lines of confusion she had before, to reveal the expression that I needed most of all; softness, protectiveness, and understanding.

"Okay, Baby. I can't promise that I'll agree with everything you say, but I will do my best to listen. Tell me what's wrong."

I told her about Jason's father and how after he denied his son, he left me in the hospital holding a baby that looked just like him. I wept. I cursed. I gave her the rawest version of the story that I could muster.

I owned the guilt I felt about the relationship between she and I at the time, and how I had left Jason for her to raise. I was humble and proud, and the most amazing thing happened; my mother heard me. She saw me. She understood me as a woman in a way she never had before. She hugged me, held me and told me that it wasn't all my fault, and for the first time, I felt accepted by her. I need not be perfect or infallible; I needed only to admit to her that I had made a mistake, and suddenly nothing else mattered.

"I'm not worried about that twelve-hundred dollars," she started. "I would prefer you returned it to us from a place of principle, but I know things are tight for you with Jason. In fact, forget the money. If you want to pay us back, Baby, go be great. Not just for me or even Jason, but for yourself. The best revenge and forgiveness is to be your best self."

When our conversation ended, I felt empowered, and I called Jason to come up from the basement so we could leave. He came bounding up the steps with Leilani in tow, happy to see his companion again.

"Come on, little man, let's go home," I told him.

"Aw, Mom, can we just stay the night? Leilani and I are playing Monopoly and I'm beating her!" he whined in protest.

"Sorry, kiddo, we have to head out. I have to get dinner going before we go to the carnival later."

"I would rather stay here than go to some carnival, Mommy. Can we just stay?" Jason said with big puppy dog eyes.

I opened my mouth to respond, but my mom cut me off, saying, "He can stay the weekend, Erica. Why don't you go on home and have a weekend to yourself? I have to visit someone in the Decatur after church on Sunday, so I will drop him off when I'm on my way there. He's good here. You're welcome to stay as well."

"Are you sure?" I asked, not wanting to be an inconvenience to her in any way.

"Of course! I'm always happy to see my grandbaby, and Leilani could use the company."

"Yes, Big Sister! Please let him stay! Pleeeeeeease?" Leilani pleaded.

I realized I had no choice but to concede, so I just laughed at them and grabbed my keys. Jason and Leilani walked me out to my car so he could get his remote-controlled car from the backseat, and I began the trek back home.

When I arrived home, I hung my keys on the hook by the door, stepped out of my shoes, and padded barefoot toward the sofa. When I slumped down, an unpleasant smell whooshed out of the cushions at me, and I made a face of disgust. Why did my couch smell like growing boy? Ugh.

I rose to get the Febreze fabric spray out of the laundry closet and sprayed the living room furniture down, and then opted to go lounge in my bedroom for a while until it dried.

The weather was starting to cool a bit as the sun went down, and I stepped outside into the August evening, sitting on the balcony. The fireflies winked sporadically in the darkening sky, and I leaned on the second story railing, staring out into the darkness. Children played hide and seek in the complex as the street lights came on, calling some of them home before parents stepped outside to call the stragglers into bright, busy homes. Fireworks shrieked in the distance, even though the fourth of July was long past. A new moon was barely visible among bright stars, and I felt the urge to get out and dance.

I texted Tracey and asked her if she wanted to hang out. When she said yes, I told her I'd meet her at Compound, and went inside to get dressed. After a quick shower, I pulled a gold dress and heels out of my closet. I brushed my hair up in the back and pinned it into itself, leaving the curls at my crown to frame my face the way I had seen Journey style her hair many times before. I brushed a golden bronzer across my cheeks and dabbed a bit of golden-colored lip gloss on my full lips. When I was satisfied with my appearance in the mirror, I clicked my heels out of the house.

Compound was packed, as usual, and I found Tracey lingering near the bar.

"Hey, Girl!" she squealed.

"Hey!" I squealed back.

"It's packed in here! You clearly aren't going to be doing much dancing in here tonight."

"Yeah, that's true. I don't know what I was thinking!" I shouted over the music.

"Well, you wanna get our drinks here, and then find someplace else to go?" she offered.

"Sounds like a plan to me. There's too many chicks in here trying to get chose tonight anyway."

"I know, right? I don't need that. I have a man at home."

"I don't, but the last thing on my mind is penis," I replied.

"Whaaaat? You don't have penis on the brain? Hell must be freezing over!" she chided.

"Shut up!" I shot back laughing.

We got our drinks from the bartender and moved through the crowd until we found a corner of space to stand in while we grooved together to the music. At least the deejay was good, although we couldn't do much more than two-step. When we finished our drinks, we decided to make our way out of there. *Lollipop* by Lil' Wayne pulsed in the background and the asses of random girls began bouncing around us in appreciation as we surveyed the room in silence.

"Let's go to Onyx and show the ladies some love!" Tracey suggested.

"Bet! "I said high-fiving her in agreement. "I'm not making it rain on anyone tonight, but at least we can sit down in there. Maybe Simon still works the door."

We turned together and began walking towards the door.

"I think he does, which means we won't have to pay," Tracey said.

Our conversation was interrupted as we pushed past sweaty people and people wearing too much fragrance until we got to the open space by the door.

We stepped outside and Tracey turned to me to finish her statement.

"Sounds like a plan! Meet you there!"

"Coolio!" I said, as we walked out into the parking lot together. "See you there!" I called as I ducked into my car.

When we pulled up in front of Onyx, the parking lot was packed, but there wasn't a line outside the door. We submitted our purses to security and smiled at Simon as he waved us past the door-girl and her scowl at us for not having to pay the cover. We ignored her and stopped side by side to take in the full spectrum of lovely, brown dancers sashaying and strutting around in their high heels and nearly nothing else.

Three women were working the poles while lap dances were happening at the tables around us. We found an empty table in the back, and rested our purses on the table before we started dancing with each other. A couple of guys eyed us from across the room, but didn't approach. We didn't mind because it was a strip club and there was plenty of ass jiggling around us. We ordered a couple of drinks and a hookah before sitting down to people watch.

A waitress in boy shorts that were two sizes too small walked up carrying our drinks on a tray balanced in one hand and our hookah in the other, set our order down in front of us.

"I like your dress, Girl!" she exclaimed to me.

"Thank you, Baby!" I shouted back over the music.

"You're welcome!" she turned and switched her ass away with a smile.

"You're always flirting with the waitresses!" Tracey laughed.

"I learned from my old roommate. We used to get the best service everywhere we went because she was always sweet to the waitresses in D.C.," I explained.

"Well, you might end up with her number if you aren't careful. I mean, we ARE in Atlanta," Tracey giggled.

"True. It wouldn't be the first time," I giggled back.

We watched a few other dancers take the stage before giving each other the mutual eye slide that said we were ready to go. After we paid our check, we stepped back out of the abyss of ass, titties, and thirsty dudes into the warm night air. The moon was full and bright, and not a cloud was in the sky.

"Let's go to Waffle House," Tracey suggested.

"I'll go with you, but I don't feel like eating that greasy mess right now."

"Well, where do you want to go?" she asked.

I chewed on my lip for a minute before suggesting Café Intermezzo.

"Oh, you're feeling fancy. Okay, let's go!" Tracey agreed.

Two guys stepped out of the door of Onyx as we were turning to walk away.

"Aye, Shawty, where y'all headed tonight?" one of them asked us both.

I rolled my eyes slightly before replying, "To eat."

"Can we come with y'a'll?" the other one asked.

"No thanks," Tracey said back before I could respond.

We walked away from them and to our cars parked side by side. I loved the way Tracey was firm, but sweet at the same time. One day I would learn to have positive boundaries the way she did, but for now I was learning to be quieter and let go of the angry person I once was.

Whenever I spoke the way she did, I felt like I wasn't taken seriously. Maybe it was my tone. Maybe it was my issues with my father. All I knew was I was in a space of learning. Journey had tried to teach me, but I wasn't ready to grow then. She never held that against me, but I was now in a season of growth. Sometimes it was painful and confusing, but sometimes it was beautiful.

We parked in a corporate parking lot across the street from Café Intermezzo and strutted into the place, only to find it packed and a flustered hostess at the door.

"I told you we should've gone to Waffle House," Tracey muttered to me under her breath.

"I wanted dessert," I said back, before smiling at the hostess.

"Two for the first open seats," I requested.

"It will be about thirty minutes," she replied.

Tracey cut her eyes at me.

"Never mind, thank you," I said before turning and walking out with Tracey not far behind.

"Okay, let's go to Waffle House," I conceded.

"Great!" she squealed. "I could really go for some pecan waffles!"

"Ugh! I can't see how you eat that stuff!" I replied with disgust.

"Girl, bring your uppity ass on here!"

We walked back to our cars and drove to the nearest Waffle House. When we arrived, we only had to wait ten minutes for a table. Tracey ordered her pecan waffles, while I ordered the apple pie from the menu.

"I guess this is meant to be . . . " said a man's voice.

We looked up to see the guy who was trying to holler at us outside of Onyx at the next table over.

"Aw, shit. Tracey, let's get our shit to go," I muttered.

"Nah, I got this," she said to me.

Then she turned to him, asking, "How can we help you, Sir?"

"We saw you two at Onyx and we wanted to kick it with you, but we didn't want to be disrespectful. Now we're seeing you again, so I figured I'd shoot my shot," he responded.

"Well, allow me to save you some trouble. We are both in relationships, and we appreciate your compliments and attention, but we won't be taking it any farther than that," Tracey said in a calm, but no-nonsense tone.

"Well, damn! I just wanted to sit and chat with you. My friend and I just like being in the company of beautiful women."

"Check, please!" I said to the waitress when she came near our table.

I didn't want to talk to this man, and I wasn't sure how much more sweetness Tracey had in her, but I was feeling triggered and I wanted to get out of there. The waitress brought us two containers and we paid our bill and left together.

"We didn't have to go, but I understand that you felt uncomfortable," Tracey said as we walked toward our cars.

"After all I've been through lately, I'm just not trying to find myself in any sticky situations that are avoidable," I replied.

"I understand."

"Yeah. I don't feel like calling it a night yet. You wanna come by my place? Maybe watch some chick flicks and sip some wine?" I offered.

"Sure! I might just stay at your place if you don't mind the company."

"Sure, let's go," I said before ducking into my car.

I parked my car in front of my apartment and went inside to get the guest parking pass while Tracey waited in her car for me. When I came back out with the little piece of plastic to hook onto her rearview mirror, I had a strange feeling that something out of the ordinary was going to happen tonight, but I didn't know what it was. The moonlight was shining brightly and it wasn't quite midnight yet. I felt a strange pulling sensation from my chest, but I ignored it and went inside with Tracey bringing up the rear.

"I have Apothic Red Crush, Alamo Malbec, and Gallo Pinot Noir. Pick your poison."

"Alamo," Tracey decided.

"Coming right up!" I walked away to the kitchen and poured two glasses of the fresh bottle of wine.

"Can I have some pajamas to change into?" Tracey asked.

"Of course!" I said as I passed her glass of wine to her. She followed me to my room to get something loose and comfortable to wear. She was a little bigger than I was, but I found her some loosely fitting pants and an oversized T-shirt that I had stolen from James before I decided I never wanted to speak to his ass again.

"Thanks, Girl!" she said in appreciation.

"You're welcome!'

We flopped down on the couch and began flipping through Netflix for a good movie to watch.

After agreeing not to watch any sappy films, we scrolled through the horror genre for a bit.

We decided to watch a horror spoof about a toxic waste spill that turned the beavers in that ecosystem into zombies. We were cackling after about fifteen minutes into the film; yelling at the screen and directing the characters not to walk outside, swim in the lake, or enter certain rooms. We were laughing obnoxiously when the dog was eaten by zombie beavers while swimming in the lake, when Tracey asked me to spark up my hookah.

"Don't forget to add the special ingredients!" Tracey shouted to me while I was in the kitchen.

I shook my head and called, "Okay," back to her while chuckling softly to myself.

Dr. Bronson had referred me to a therapist in Atlanta who had diagnosed me with mild depression and anxiety. Since marijuana had been decriminalized in Atlanta, I've had a prescription for medicinal marijuana for the past three months, much to the enthusiasm of Tracey, who would come by and smoke with me from time to time when Jason wasn't around.

I sprinkled a small amount of the plant into the hookah and lit the coconut coals on the stove. I brought the hookah out while I was waiting for the coals to get hot, and Tracey was starting to look bored with the film, so I suggested we watch *Black Swan* instead.

"Oooh! Is that the one with Natalie Portman as a ballerina?" she asked.

"Yeah, I haven't seen the whole movie, but I think you'd enjoy it."

"Let's do it!" she agreed enthusiastically.

I found the movie on Netflix and went to retrieve the coals for the hookah from the stove. I hadn't seen beyond the part where Mila Kunis's character befriended Natalie Portman's character and showed up at the house.

"Why is she still living at home?" Tracey asked.

"I don't know, Girl, but her mama seems a little crazy," I said.

"Yeah, why is she so pressed to keep her grown ass daughter from going out?"

"Just watch the movie, Girl!" I giggled.

"Ooooh, shit! She's gay?" Tracey exclaimed after a few minutes.

"Well, damn, that was unexpected!" I said in an exhalation of hookah smoke.

"I know, right!" she agreed.

"This movie is wild. I've never kissed another woman," I confessed, passing the hookah hose to Tracey.

"Really? I have. It wasn't weird."

"Wasn't weird? Girl, how do you reconcile having another pair of boobs pressed against yours? I guess that's just not my thing."

"You've never even tried it, so how do you k n o w what it's like?" she asked, exhaling a large plume of smoke.

"I don't," I giggled. "I'm just saying I don't get it."

"It's just like kissing a guy, but with boobs," she explained.

"I don't know, I kinda like having a harder body against my softer lady parts."

Tracey chuckled and shook her head. "Close your eyes, Erica."

I turned and looked at her, my limbs tingling slightly, as she smirked at me from the other side of the couch in a way that I could only describe as flirtatious. I hesitated for a couple seconds longer, but I closed my eyes with my head still turned in her direction. I felt her scoot closer to me, closing the space between us on the couch. She brushed my curls out of my face gently, and I giggled a little.

"Stop being goofy! Just relax!" she commanded.

I took a couple deep sips of air, licking my lips slightly. She walked her fingertips down the side of my neck to my shoulder. I resisted the urge to stop her, deciding to just go with it and prove my point that this whole thing was just awkward and not enticing for me in any way. She slid her fingertips up from my shoulder to the back of my neck until her fingers were entwined in the curls at the base of my head. She tugged my head back gently to expose my throat, and kissed it gently. I felt a shiver run through me as her lips found their way up my throat, to my chin, and finally to my mouth.

The first kiss was gentle and soft, almost asking for permission. She kissed me this way a few times until I found myself kissing her back. When she placed her other hand on my breast and squeezed it gently, I gasped and moaned in spite of myself. Her hands began roaming all over my breasts and thighs, gripping me and squeezing me in all the ways I would normally expect a man to touch me when he was trying to turn me on. I was breathless and kissing back with more sincerity, and then she stopped abruptly, retreating to her side of the couch. My eyes jerked open with surprise as I attempted to fix myself, realizing that she had proved her point.

"That's what it's like to kiss a woman," Tracey said, picking up the hose to the hookah to inhale.

"Hmmm . . . " I mumbled under my breath, as I encouraged my body to stop tingling. We watched the rest of the film in silence, as my mind reeled over the sensations that the marijuana had made more extreme.

When the movie was over, I got up and handed the remote to her.

"You can keep watching TV if you want. I think I'm going to go to bed."

"Nah, I'm coming, too," she replied. "I'm a little tired as well."

We had shared a bed many times before, but Tracey had never kissed me before, and I felt a little apprehensive, but I didn't say so as she followed me to my bedroom after helping me clean the hookah and put the wine glasses in the sink.

I removed the shammed pillows from the bed, pulling back the summer duvet to climb between the cool sheets. She got in bed beside me, and turned off the light on the nightstand.

We lay side by side for a while, not saying anything to one another, until I turned over on my side facing away from her. When she turned in the same direction, I didn't think anything of it. My limbs were still tingling and I was feeling nice all over as I began rocking myself slightly to calm the sensations. When I felt Tracey's hand on my thigh, I didn't push it away. I was partially too sleepy and partially too high, but I realized I liked it. I didn't stop her when she reached her hand underneath my shirt and rubbed my belly softly, her caress slow and circular and stirring me with a sense of urgency. I felt like my entire body was covered in delicious, molten lava that was being stirred and spread all over my flesh.

I didn't stop her when her fingers found their way between my legs and began dancing and stirring in the wetness that was there. I didn't stop her when her lips found the back of my neck, causing me to shiver and tremble against her as she continued to kiss and touch me. Some distant part of my consciousness flashed red lights at me, reminding me that I wasn't into women; that this wasn't my thing, but my body trembled and arched against her in a completely alternative communication.

I felt like I blinked for a long time, and when I opened my eyes again, Tracey was on top of me, pulling my shirt over my head. I writhed underneath her weight as she lowered her lips to my breasts, sucking and licking my nipples, and all the white-hot flesh surrounding them until I cried out, trembling.

When she kissed me down my ribs to my navel, I felt like I would explode, and when she finally reached the place between my legs where the river was flowing warmly, I was officially slayed. Eventually the pleasure receptors firing off in my brain were so intense that I released a noise I had never heard myself make before, and then I blacked out, falling into a dark cataclysmic well of ecstasy that was sleep.

When I awoke in the morning, Tracey wasn't beside me. I crept out of bed, my naked limbs feeling relaxed and light, and tiptoed to the bathroom to urinate and brush my teeth. *Was it all a dream*, I wondered at my reflection in the mirror. Was it some sort of marijuana-induced fantasy, raised to the power of *Black Swan*? I splashed water on my face and rubbed the sleep out of my eyes. When I heard something metal clash in the kitchen, I rushed out into the direction of the sound, heart racing, to find Tracey standing in front of the sink with a skillet and spatula in her hand.

"Good morning, sunshine! I figured I'd let you sleep in and make you breakfast. Did I scare you?"

"A little bit," I admitted sheepishly, "I was thinking last night was just a dream."

"No dream, sweetheart. Although you did pass out after the first orgasm. Is that common with you?"

"No. I guess it was just the special hookah," I replied.

Tracey laughed, "Well, I made you a plate. It's in the oven keeping warm."

"Thank you," I said as I pulled my plate out of the oven. "You didn't have to do this."

"Girl, hush. I woke up starving. I wasn't going to feed myself and let you starve. Although, I could have woken you with another meal." She looked at me suggestively.

"I don't know if I'm ready to talk about that yet," I said, shoveling a forkful of food into my mouth.

"We don't have to talk about it now. Right now, all you have to do is enjoy your breakfast. I have to get going soon. I have some things to do with Chris."

I felt myself bristle slightly, but I couldn't explain why.

"Okay, well, no rush here. Enjoy your breakfast and do what you need to do."

"Oh. I will," she said flirtatiously.

I sat at the table and finished my breakfast, as she continued preparing hers. When she started eating, I cleared the dishes from the dishwasher so I could fill it with the dishes she used to cook.

"I laid out towels for you in the bathroom. Breakfast was delicious. Thank you again," I said.

"My pleasure! I'm going to call you later when I get done running errands with Chris."

"Okay."

I walked out of the kitchen and into my bedroom where I could process my feelings in peace. I didn't know how to react to the experience I had with her the night before, what I was supposed to expect, or how to continue as if nothing had taken place.

"I'm gone, Erica!" Tracey called out from the front door.

"Okay! See you later!" I called back.

The screen clapped loudly behind her, and I thought to rush out to remind her to get the parking pass out of her car, but when I stepped out into the hallway, I saw it sitting on the kitchen table. I turned and went to my bathroom to take a shower, and as the water poured down on me, running ringlets off the ends of my curls, I asked myself the most strange and unexpected question . . . *Am I gay*?

20. Everything You Don't Know

I want to fall asleep to your heartbeat,
Give you all my coolness,
Steal away all your heat.
The dimple in my lip m isses your soft nibble at the tip.
The way you watch the sway in my hip.
The grasp,
The embrace,
T he slip.

~ Olosunde

It had been six weeks since I'd seen Carmen, and my dreams and experiences had been all over the place. After taking time off work to heal from the miscarriage and attend Carlos' funeral, I was starting to feel somewhat like myself again. Sydney and Devin had been swapping shifts to come by every day to check up on me. They made sure I was eating, and provided moral support for the tears and darker moments I was feeling. I had been sleeping a lot, but my dreams were far from peaceful.

I tapped on the door to Carmen's apartment and I wiggled my fingers at the peephole when I saw it darken from her looking through it.

"I didn't know you were here," she said, looking down the hallway suspiciously.

"How did you get in?"

"Oh, I'm sorry, I helped an elderly lady carry her groceries inside downstairs, and I just came up. There's nobody here but me," I explained.

She grinned broadly before ushering me inside. "It's no problem, sweetie, I was just startled. Come in!"

I took my shoes off at the door and began to wiggle my arms out of my jacket. It was warmer that afternoon then it had been in the morning, but my iron levels were still a little out of whack from the miscarriage, and I was unseasonably cold despite the May temperatures.

"Would you like some tea or anything?" Carmen offered.

"Sure, that would be nice."

"How about some mint?"

"Sounds good, thank you!" I said.

I settled into the soft sofa cushions and rubbed my hands together, and then tucked them between my legs. I loved the way her house always smelled warm and inviting, like amber and citrus oils. The tea kettle began to sing a few minutes later, and I could hear Carmen clinking the mugs against the metal tray, preparing to bring it to the living room. She rested the tray that held the mugs, spoons, and honey on the coffee table, and smoothed the black, wavy hair that had managed to escape back into her bun.

"Enjoy!" she offered with a chipper voice.

"Thank you," I said as I picked up my mug and began stirring the honey into my tea. "It smells so nice! I swear you always have the best tea! Where do you get it?"

"There's a little herbal shop that I go to. They make their own tea there. I will give you the card before you leave."

"Thank you! I suppose that's why it's so fragrant."

"Yes, the tea leaves are fresh," she agreed.

"I see! Well, this is the most delicious mint tea that I've ever had!"

"I'm glad you like it! Now, tell me about the things you've been experiencing," she said.

"Well, the dreams have been extremely wild!" I began. "At first I thought it was just the hormones and whatnot, but after I stopped bleeding my life away, and then attended Carlos' funeral, they didn't stop."

"I keep dreaming about this Olokun and what seems like a huge underwater wedding party. I don't understand it, and I find it a little scary and yet intriguing at the same time. I don't know what it means," I finished.

"Very interesting! Olokun is an Orisha; you remember me telling you about the African deities of Benin and Nigeria the first time we spoke. It is the deity of the bottom of the ocean."

"Some people argue about whether Olokun is male or female, but most recognize it as the spirit of abundance and prosperity and the mysteries of the depths of the ocean. As such, it can encompass the energies and processes of life, death, and rebirth. Considering what you've been experiencing lately: the life of the child that you conceived with Carlos, the death of Carlos, may he rest in peace, and the rebirth that you are going through at this time, it would seem to me that this makes sense."

"I have the information about you regarding your birth date and the names of your parents, so if you like, I will divine about whether you need to receive initiation to this Orisha or whether some offering is necessary. If more information is needed, I will consult my godfather to investigate further."

"That sounds like a solid plan, thank you, Carmen, I really appreciate your help," I said.

I exhaled a breath I didn't realize I was holding. I watched silently as Carmen poured tea into my cup. I stirred honey into my tea and as the spoon tinkled against the porcelain, I began feeling way more relaxed.

"You're so welcome," she said. "How are you feeling now with everything? Are you sleeping okay?"

She poured her tea carefully without glancing up at me.

"About as well as can be expected," I said. "Considering . . . I mean this has been a really difficult time."

I held my tea cup and allowed the warmth of the cup to warm me as I waited for the tea to cool.

"I bet it has! You're so strong, my dear. I admire the way you are trying to push through and not allowing all of this to cripple you."

She reached over and touched my face supportively, like a mother would.

"It hasn't been easy," I said into her palm. "Some days, I don't want to get out of bed. Others, I just want to cry. I have been crying a lot less these days, though." I sighed deeply.

"That's to be expected. You've gone through a very traumatic experience. Just take your time and allow yourself to heal."

"I plan to. It's not like I have much of a choice at this point. It's not like I can just check out on life."

I flopped my hands, feeling the very opposite of strong.

"No, you can't," she agreed, pouring honey into her tea with a slow, solemn shake of her head. "You have so much to do and so far to go. Just keep taking care of yourself, keep listening to your body, and if you need to talk, just know I am here for you. Carlos may no longer be with us, but you are. You now have that which you have always craved; a family."

My eyes filled with tears briefly, and I blinked them away. She was right on so many levels, and I couldn't help but wonder how she knew so much about me without me telling her. I wasn't the least bit surprised, seeing as how she seemed to know so many other things before. I leaned in to hug her on the sofa, and as she hugged me back, I felt an overwhelming peace that I hadn't felt in a long time. Once again, Carlos' family had made my spirit feel a sense of being home, although home didn't exactly mean a specific location. It was in the presence of those who truly cared.

After I left Carmen and was driving down the highway, I couldn't wait to get home to Rico and take off the mask of my day. I thought deeply about taking a quick shower before relaxing in my bathtub with a nice bath bomb, candles, and a glass of wine. I hated baths, but I could endure them if I had a shower first. People always thought that was weird, but I didn't care. Who wanted to stew in their own dirt?

Rico was yowling like crazy when he heard my key in the lock. I looked at his empty food dish and realized I had forgotten to feed him earlier that morning.

"I'm sorry, Baby," I said.

I petted him lovingly and poured dried salmon flavored cat food nuggets into his bowl. I mixed some wet food in with it to solidify my apology and then filled his water dish. He attacked his food dish hungrily, paying little to no attention to me.

I padded in my stocking feet to the bathroom for a shower, and then wrapped myself in a plush towel before scrubbing out my tub for my bath. While the water ran, I searched under the sink for a bath bomb and dropped it into the tub. Green and gold, lime and verbena scented glitter exploded in the water as I lit my candles and poured myself a glass of the wine from the bottle I had already brought into the bathroom. I rested the bottle beside the tub and sank into the bubbles that waited for me. I lounged there silently for the better part of an hour before I drifted off into a lucid dream.

I was standing at a kitchen sink, washing baby bottles. I heard a baby cooing behind me, and I turned to see a handsomely chocolate man with a beard smiling at an adorable little girl on his lap. She was smiling a toothless smile up at him and holding the end of his nose in her tiny fist while he talked to her.

"Let Daddy tell you how he met your Mommy . . ." he said to her.

She looked at me with the most beautiful brown, almond eyes. I stepped toward them and extended my arms to the outreached arms of the baby and took her from her father. I held her warm, chubby body close and smelled the sweet, soft baby smell that came from her.

"Come here, Mommy, and sit on my lap," he said to me, gesturing to his lap with a soft pat.

I moved to sit on his lap with the little girl in mine before the image faded away and I opened my eyes in the tepid bathwater. I shivered, rose, and wrapped myself with my towel again and went to my bedroom to moisturize myself and put on some warm pajamas. Afterward, I went back into the bathroom and let the water out of the tub, brushed my teeth, and snuggled into bed with Rico, dismissing the dream.

***

When I woke in the morning, Sydney was calling me. I groaned and ignored her call. I didn't feel like talking to anyone. I rolled over onto Rico, who whimpered his offenses before scrambling out from under me and off the bed to do whatever he was going to do. The phone buzzed again and I continued to ignore it with my head under the pillow without checking to see who was calling me.

A few minutes later, I heard my front door open and close. I scrambled out of bed, and into the kitchen to find Sydney placing her purse on my counter as she took off her shoes.

"Sydney! What are you doing here?" I demanded with a panicked expression on my face.

"I called you to tell you I was here to scoop you up for breakfast, but you didn't answer, and I got worried," she replied.

"Worried about what?" I asked defensively.

"I don't know, Journey, you weren't answering, so I was concerned. I'm sorry."

"It's fine," I muttered blandly with a wave of my hand. "I forgot we were having breakfast together. I was hoping to sleep in a bit."

"Sleep in? Girl, it is BEAUTIFUL outside!" she exclaimed.

She opened the curtains. I scoffed and went back into the haven of my bedroom, leaving her in the living room.

"I hope that means you're getting dressed, Ma'am!" she shouted to me.

"Yeah, yeah, give me a minute," I called back without enthusiasm.

"Don't you give me that!" she shouted back playfully.

"I'm just not in the mood to be around people today," I told her.

"Well, do you want to stay in and have breakfast here? I can cook for us," she offered.

"Nah, I'm going to be ready in a few minutes." I emerged in jeans and a grey sweatshirt with my hair piled on top of my head in a messy, high pony-bun.

"Journey, are you okay?" Sydney asked.

"I'm fine. Why?"

"Because you're attempting to leave the house in something less than the fabulosity that I'm accustomed to," she pointed out.

"Girl, please. Who am I trying to impress?"

"Nobody in that getup," she said with a side eye glance.

"Forget you!" I shot back playfully. "If I take the time to dress the way I normally do, you'll be rushing me."

"True, but it's warm outside. Can you at least find a cute short sleeved shirt to wear with those jeans? I mean your booty is cute in them and all that, but you can do better up top."

I shook my butt at her and she laughed and clapped her hands.

"Aye! Aye! Aye! " She shouted with appreciation as I went back into my room to fish out a shirt with short sleeves.

"Is this better?" I demanded, emerging in a grey shirt that said "bougie black girl" on the front.

"It'll do," she said with a smirk.

We headed out to Chadwick's in Old Town and found the line going out of the door and down the block.

"Dang! I didn't think that it was going to be so busy this morning," Sydney said in a disappointed tone.

"It is breakfast and brunch on a Saturday," I replied.

"Do you feel like waiting an hour to eat, though?"

"Not really. Let's try Warehouse Bar and Grill," I suggested.

"Sounds like a plan."

We walked the few blocks to Warehouse with families and couples pressing past us in the spring warmth. An Asian lady with her hair slicked back met us at the door.

"Welcome to Warehouse! Will it be just the two of you?"

"Yes, thank you," Sydney spoke up.

"Would you like to sit indoors or outdoors today?" she asked.

"Indoors," we said in unison.

I thought of how glad I was that she knew me so well that I didn't have to explain why I didn't want to sit outdoors. We walked further inside, following the hostess to a table by the windows.

A waitress appeared almost as soon as we sat down. "Would you like to hear the specials today?" she asked.

"No, thank you, we know what we are ordering." Sydney told her.

"Very good, then." She pulled her pad out of her apron and waited for us to give her our orders.

"I will have the shrimp and crawfish etouffee," I told her.

"And I will have the New Orleans French toast," Sydney said.

"Very good. Would you ladies like champagne and strawberries, or strawberries and cream?"

"Champagne and strawberries," we said in unison again.

We giggled at our mutual decision as the waitress walked away, and began people watching as we normally did.

"I will never understand why white people feel the need to let their dogs kiss them in the mouth. I mean, there are so many ways to let their pets show them love," Sydney observed with a look of slight disgust.

"I know right! I just can't imagine!" I giggled back at her.

"Awww! Look at that cute baby! I can't wait to find me a white husband and give him some black, ashy babies!"

"Girl, bye! If that's your goal, you can have black ashy babies with anybody!" I responded.

We both chuckled as we sipped the champagne with strawberries the waitress brought us.

"Journey, you always bring me to the most bourgeois place you can find."

"No, I don't. It's not my fault we both like nice things," I defended.

She pointed at my shirt, and we both burst out cackling.

"At least you aren't the type to keep us from having nice things," she said as her giggles died down.

"What does that even mean?" I asked her chuckling.

Before she could answer, a chocolate man with a beard and a gorgeous smile walked into the restaurant followed by a beautiful, caramel-colored woman with long wavy hair. I stared with my mouth slightly open for a few seconds before blinking and looking away when they kissed briefly as he pulled her chair out for her.

"Journey? Journeeeeeey . . . what's wrong with you?" Sydney sang at me, snapping her fingers in front of my face.

"Uhhh . . . nothing," I lied.

"Bullshit! You just turned four shades of white that I've never seen before. What's up?"

I made a sound of slight frustration, "You see that guy?"

"Yeah, so what?"

"I saw him in a dream the other night," I told her.

"The dark skinned dude with the beard?"

"Yeah . . . " I said as I kept sipping my champagne and staring at him over my glass.

"So? Why is that such a big deal?" she asked.

"We were married and we had a little girl."

"Together?"

"Yes! Quit asking me dumb questions!" I whispered sharply to her.

"Oh, uh-uh! You don't have to be nasty. I still don't see why it matters. Care to fill me in?" she replied with a little neck roll.

"I can't explain it. It's a feeling. Like . . . I belong with him somehow," I struggled to explain.

"Uhhhhm . . . You do realize that he's hugged up with that racially ambiguous woman, right?"

"Yes, but my dreams have been extremely on point lately, and this is weird for me."

"What about Carlos?" she asked.

"What about him? He isn't here, and I see the man who was in my dream. I'm not saying I'm going to try to steal him from her or anything, but don't you think that's strange?"

"Of course, but . . . I don't know, Journey, I'm just trying to make sense of what you're saying," Sydney said.

"Well, stop trying and just hear me. I can't explain why I feel what I do toward him, but I saw him in a dream and we were a family."

"You're buggin, Girlfriend!"

"I might be, but this is worth speaking on," I replied.

"I guess . . . " she trailed off.

She ignored me and I stopped watching the man from my dream and the woman he was with. The waitress appeared with our food. We blessed our meals and began eating our food in silence for the next few minutes.

After my etouffee was well mixed and I had eaten about half of the plate, Sydney asked me if she could try some.

"Sure!" I said as I scooped a generous amount of it onto a small plate for her.

"This is delicious!" she exclaimed after the first spoonful, "I might have to order this next time!"

"It's my favorite dish from here! I am picky about my etouffee, but this is the best I've had outside of New Orleans. The shrimp and crawfish aren't overcooked and the flavors blend beautifully!"

"Yeah, I will eat all your food, bourgeois-ass girl!" she chuckled.

"I will karate chop your hand over my food, Missy!" I threatened playfully.

We laughed and finished our food while staring out the windows and people watching for the rest of our meal.

***

A week later, I was sitting at Marvin's Room listening to the live band that was performing there and catching up on some work on my laptop. I was sipping a glass of pinot noir and grooving in my seat to the music, when the door opened and the man from the restaurant, and my dream, swaggered inside carrying a computer bag.

He sat in a seat on the sofa adjacent to mine and began to adjust his suit. He pulled his laptop out of the bag, turned it on and then pulled a little card out of the bag, a n d plugged it into his computer. I watched him out of the corner of my eye, but adjusted my gaze back to my own screen after I realized how much of a creep I looked like.

A few seconds later, I heard him mutter, "Shit!" under his breath, and he began looking along the floor near the wall for what I assumed was an outlet. I watched him silently for a few minutes before he flopped back down on the couch, looking dejected; his smooth, dark brows furrowed in frustration.

"Excuse me, are you looking for an outlet?" I asked him.

"Yes."

"Oh, well, there's one on this wall over here," I gestured.

"Is that an invitation?" he asked with a small, flirtatious smile.

"Um, I guess so. You can sit over here," I replied with an awkward smile.

"Thanks, I'll be right over," he said, his smile growing.

My heart fluttered a little bit, and I scooted over to make room for him beside me.

"The outlet is right there," I told him, pointing to the wall.

He plugged his cord in beneath mine and lowered himself onto the sofa beside me.

"Thanks. I'm Ronald," he said, extending a hand to me.

"No problem. I'm Journey," I said, accepting his hand and swallowing a smile.

"Nice to meet you."

"Likewise," I responded.

"Are you a student?" he asked.

My smile was replaced by a look of confusion in response to his inquiry, but as I pushed my glasses up and nervously smoothed the wildness that was my curls, spilling onto the green, boat-necked FAMU sweatshirt I was sporting, I understood why he would think I was a student.

"No, I'm not," I replied, "I'm about seven years removed from undergrad." I chuckled.

"Wow! Really? I just knew you were about twenty-two. You look like a baby!"

"Thanks, I think," I chuckled.

"I promise, I meant it as a compliment."

"It's cool," I laughed.

"So, what are you working on?"

"I'm just catching up on some reports. I'm a government contractor for a professional development firm."

"Oh, okay! Check you out!"

"It pays the bills," I said. "What about you? What are you working on?"

"I'm a private investigator. I'm just finishing up some documentation and whatnot," he said.

I nodded politely and returned my eyes to my computer screen, not wanting to get too distracted by him or his smile.

Don't look at him, Girl... don't look! I coached myself internally.

I glanced up again at him.

Girl! What did I just tell your ass? Why are you staring at him? He CLEARLY has a girlfriend, and he's here smiling all up in your face like he wasn't just sucking face and rubbing tonsils with that racially ambiguous chick about a week ago! Get your shit together! The last thing you need is some petty tryst with some dude who is already knee deep in the next chick's vagina. Stay focused, mind your business, and do your work!

His eyes seemed to draw me in, and I didn't know why, but I wasn't trying to get caught up in any foolishness while I was still trying to process all the things that had been happening to me lately. He didn't speak to me again for a little while. He moved to the seat across from me where he made and received phone calls, typed on his computer, sipped his drink, and only smiled at me when our eyes met over the screens of our laptops.

Eventually, two other ladies walked in and sat on the sofa adjacent to us, and began chatting and cackling loudly. I was initially thankful for their presence as a distraction, but after their cackling, Ronald and I looked at one another with slight annoyance over the noise interruption. We smirked at one another, simultaneously averting our eyes back to our screens again.

A few minutes later, two more ladies appeared in our little section, apparent friends of the first two, and one asked if she could sit beside me. I opened my mouth to decline, when Ronald interrupted me.

"Why don't you two lovely ladies sit here? I will move over there with her."

I closed my mouth, silently grateful for the low lights, as my cheeks burned slightly. Ronald squeezed past me and plopped down onto the sofa beside me again.

"I guess this is where I was supposed to sit all along," he said with a winking grin.

"I guess so . . . " I replied.

"Do you have a boyfriend . . . or a girlfriend?" he asked.

I laughed loudly. "A girlfriend! Really?"

Oh, so you're just gonna smile in his face like that? Do better and stop being so damn thirsty!

"Hey, these are questions a man must ask these days!" he replied, laughing.

"I can't argue with that!" I laughed. "But, no, I don't have a boyfriend at this time. I don't date women, either."

He smiled and licked his lips, scooting closer to me on the couch.

"In that case, I find you extremely beautiful, and I'd like to exchange phone numbers so I can talk to you; maybe take you out sometime" he said.

"Wait a minute, you don't have a girlfriend?"

"I'm single and dating right now, but I'm interested in getting to know you better."

"Hmmm . . . I must admit I've seen you before. Rather recently, in fact," I revealed.

"Really? When?"

"About a week ago. You were in a restaurant with a woman who had very long hair."

His face went blank for a second, then he recovered with a smile.

"That's a woman I was dating. She and I aren't an item anymore."

"Ahhh, I see. So, you're back on the prowl a week later."

"Not quite on the prowl, but certainly seeing what's out there," he smoothly responded.

"Well, I'm going to respectfully decline, but if we bump into one another again, I'll consider giving you my number."

"How about I give you my number, and if you see me again, you can just text me and let me know?"

Oh, he's a smooth, slippery one...he's probably a Pisces, sis, don't do it!

I laughed, but agreed to take his phone number. He handed me his card, and I tucked it into my computer bag.

"Dang! You aren't even going to put it in your wallet?" He asked with mock disappointment. "I'm going straight to the computer bag?"

"If you become important enough to me, I will know where to find you," I replied with a grin that was friendlier than I intended.

"You're a tough one, huh? Okay, I can accept that. Can I buy you a drink?"

"If you'd like," I said with a shrug.

Girl! Now you know this isn't how Beyonce, Claire Huxtable, or Dorothy Dandridge would handle this. Well, maybe Dorothy as Carmen Jones, but dammit you know what I'm saying here! You know better . . .

He beckoned to the waitress and I asked for another glass of wine. The band took a break, and the deejay got on and began playing *Wobble*. The ladies who were sitting in our section cheered, got up, and started toward the dance floor. One came back and tapped me on the knee, "Come on, Girl!"

I grinned and politely shook my head no, but Ronald removed my laptop from my lap and pulled me from my seat, gently pushing me toward the dance floor. I conceded with a giggle and danced with the group of women I didn't know for the entire song, and I found myself smiling and having fun. When the song ended, I returned to my seat to find Ronald staring at me like I was food.

"You looked good out there."

"Thank you," I replied with a smile.

"I see those HBCU days taught you how to move a lil' bit."

"I didn't *learn* to dance at FAMU," I laughed, wiping the sweat from the nape of my neck and fanning myself, "but I definitely did my share of line dancing while I was there, and I was captain of one of the many dance teams."

"I can imagine that! You were doing a completely different version than the rest out there. Where'd you learn that style of The Wobble?"

"I lived in Atlanta for a while. I don't know any other way to do it," I giggled.

"Check you out! How long have you lived in this area?"

"For a little over six years."

"Oh, okay, I'm from Baltimore, but I've lived in this area for about ten years. I was in the military for a while."

"Oh, cool! What branch?"

"The Air Force."

"Oh, so you traveled a lot."

"Yeah, I've been a few places in my day. My current passport is almost full, and it's less than a year old," he admitted.

"Shoot, I'm trying to get like you!"

"Yeah, I admit that travel has been one of the best perks of my job."

"I can imagine that was exciting! Is that why you're single?" I asked.

"Somewhat," he said. "I was married for a while. I have a six year old daughter. Her mother and I were high school sweethearts. We got married really young, and it just didn't work out. What about you? Have you ever been married?"

See! I told you! He's a divorcee and he has baggage like a motherfucker! He's probably a cheater! Abort mission! Make an excuse to get out of there. Don't let him reel you in!

"No, I haven't," I replied, swallowing a twinge of sadness.

"I can't believe a pretty young thing like you hasn't been wifed up by now. How old are you?"

"I'm twenty-nine. I was engaged not too long ago, but it didn't work out."

"What? Some guy let you get away?" He looked incredulous.

"No, he had a Jet Ski accident the day after proposing to me which ended in his death," I shared.

Nice one! Now he will leave you alone because he thinks YOU have baggage . . . which you do! My girl!

"Oh, shit! I'm so sorry!" Ronald sympathized.

"It's okay, you didn't know. Besides, how common is that?"

"Yeah, it sounds like something out of a book or a movie or something," he said, shaking his head.

"I know, right? I've been feeling like that for quite some time since his death."

"I bet! How long has it been?"

"A few months. I'm still healing from it," I said, taking a breath to steady my voice.

"That makes sense. I can completely understand why you would be guarded right now."

Now he's trying to psychoanalyze me? Dammit!

"I wouldn't say I'm guarded any more than usual, just healing from the loss and unfortunate turn of events," I countered.

"I get it. Well, please give me a call. I'm going to get out of here. Do you want anything else?"

"No, thank you, but I appreciate it."

"Okay, Journey. It was a pleasure meeting you."

"You as well," I replied with a smile as he hugged me politely, paid the waitress, and gathered his things to go.

Good job getting rid of him! Now don't call his ass!

I watched him answer his phone as he walked out of the restaurant with my heart fluttering strangely. Why was I so excited? I shrugged the feeling off and turned my attention back to my laptop, but I was too distracted to work.

After staring at the same PowerPoint slide for fifteen minutes, I decided I was going to get out of there and head home also. I hailed the waitress, but when she arrived she told me Ronald paid my bill as well. I smiled to myself, realizing he paid with the hopes I would reach out to him and thank him.

Slippery ass man...

"Well played . . ." I said aloud to myself as I packed away my laptop and retrieved his card from my bag.

I sent him a "Thank you' text with a smiley face as I walked to my car and tucked my phone into my back pocket. A few seconds later, my rear end began buzzing. I pulled my phone out of my pocket to see Ronald's unsaved number on the screen.

"Hello?" I answered as I opened my car door.

"I hoped you'd give me a call or text," he said.

"It would have been rude not to at least text to say thank you," I said.

"Indeed, it would have. I was testing you," he admitted.

"Testing me, huh? How did I do?"

"Better than I hoped. I didn't think you'd reach out for at least a day."

"At least a day? Oh, you were feeling pretty confident," I said as I settled into the driver's seat.

"Maybe . . ."

"Well, it was nice talking to you, Ronald," I said, preparing to end our conversation.

"Hold on, wait!"

"What?"

"What are you doing tomorrow?" he asked.

"I don't know yet, it's Sunday."

"Sunday, fun day. . . Well, what about going out with me? There's a comedy show at Purple Lounge tomorrow. You should let me take you on a date," he proposed.

"I don't know, it's kind of short notice."

"Come on, rearrange your imaginary plans and let me take you out."

"Imaginary plans? Well, that's presumptuous" I replied.

Rude is more accurate...

"I didn't mean it like that. I just find you attractive and interesting, and I want to get to know you better. Is that okay with you?"

Say no! Say No!

"Hmmm . . . I guess . . . What time is it?" I responded with hesitation in my voice.

Fuck my life! You never listen!

"It starts at seven thirty," he answered.

"I will let you know tomorrow by noon."

"Fair enough," He replied sounding hopeful.

"I'm in my car now. I will text you tomorrow and let you know."

"Okay, cool. Good night, Beautiful."

"Good night."

And just like that, I had a date. I called Sydney as soon as I got home, anxious to share the tea that had been brewing for the past few hours.

"Hello?" she answered.

"Girlah!"I said loudly.

"Hey, Girl! What's up?"

"Remember that guy we saw at Warehouse about a week ago?" I quizzed her.

"The one kissing that woman in the mouth who you were staring at like some creepy, astral plane obsessed weirdo? Yeah, I remember."

I ignored her petty ass details, responding, "Yes! I just saw him at Marvin's Room!"

"Really? Mmmmhmmm...! I'm listening."

"It was like a classic case of kismet!"

"What happened?" she asked.

"We talked. He's single. Apparently, he's not dating that woman anymore. He asked me on a date."

"A date? J, I love you and all, and I hope you don't take this the wrong way, but are you sure you're ready for all that?" Sydney asked in a concerned tone.

"It's just a date."

"Yeah, until he starts asking you those 'when was your last relationship' questions and you start crying and shit."

"I'm not going to start crying. You suck for even saying that!" I protested.

"I'm just saying! You tear up at the very mention of Carlos' name."

"I haven't cried in a while. Besides, he already asked me and I told him my fiancé died."

"Define a while; and you TOLD HIM?"

"Well, damn. I thought you'd be happy that I was branching out."

"I am. I'm just concerned about your heart," she said.

"Well, I'm not trying to fall in love or anything. I haven't even agreed to go on the date yet."

"Okay, give me his stats."

"He's thirty-three, divorced, has a daughter who is six, he's ex-military, and he's a private investigator," I rattled off as I sniffed the air and headed to the kitchen.

"Hmmm . . . He's got some baggage."

See, she picked up on that shit a mile away. Why are you too dumb to see it?

"Who doesn't have some baggage after thirty?"

"True . . . So, what are you going to do?"

"I don't know yet. I mean, I suppose there's no harm in entertaining him. It's just a date, not a marriage proposal," I said as I located the source of the bad smell in the kitchen trash can.

"Yes, but my concern is for your emotional state following the trauma with Carlos and everything associated with it. I mean, he's only been gone for a few months. Do you sincerely feel ready to try dating anyone?"

"Syd, we aren't dating. It's one date. I've mourned my loss; how will I know what I feel if I don't try?"

"You make a good point. Just be careful, okay? Promise me that you'll go slowly at the very least."

"What kind of girl do you take me for?" I asked as I pulled the smelly trash bag out of the can.

We both giggled at that, and I told her I was going to go take the trash out and would chat with her later.

"No, Girl! Call me back! I need to tell you about this dude *I* met!" Sydney exclaimed.

"What dude? I thought you were dating the guy I met when we were at Rosebar a while back."

"We were, but things got intimate and he had poor hygiene, and I just couldn't do it. I met another guy. His name is Cason. He's a physical therapist I met about two weeks ago."

"Aw, snap! I want to hear everything! Let me take out this trash and call you back."

"Black people always coming up with the most random reasons to get off the phone! You better call me back," she said with a huff.

"I will! I swear!"

"Okay, bye!"

"Bye!"

I lugged the heavy bag outside and down the hallway to the incinerator room, holding my breath as I entered, and let the bag slide down the chute. I went back to my apartment to gather the container for my recycling and took it to the incinerator room also. It smelled like spoiled eggs, old broccoli, and feet in there, and I found myself missing Carlos and how he used to take my trash out so I didn't have to. He was so chivalrous.

My heart began racing as I walked back to my apartment, but I didn't know why. I stopped outside my front door and took several deep, slow breaths like the therapist taught me before turning the knob and walking in. I put the tea kettle on and pulled a mug and honey down from the cabinet before calling Sydney back.

"Hey!" she sang.

"Hey, Girl!"

"It took you forever!" she said in a dramatic tone.

"Don't be a diva. Tell me what's up," I said with a slight eye roll.

"So, I went to a party with my friend, Patrice, two weeks ago and I met this guy named Cason. He's so handsome — I mean just the finest man in the entire party. Mmph! Anyway, we sang a little karaoke together and then we exchanged numbers. He walked me to my car, and I went out with him for lunch two days later. We went from the restaurant to a billiards house where I spanked his ass in pool. We had a great time! I had never played pool before and I had so many points!"

I smiled and listened to her without saying anything. It felt good to hear my friend feeling happy, and I was genuinely happy for her.

"You there, J?"

"Yes, I'm listening, Syd, keep talking."

"Okay, well we went to brunch two days after that, and then to this little hookah spot in Bethesda. I spent seven hours with him that day, and we had a really good time!"

"That's great, Girl! If you can spend that much time with someone, then you know there's something worth investigating, right?"

"Right! He wants to take me on a weekend trip next month," she said.

"A weekend? Don't you think that's a little risky?"

"Yeah, but if things continue the way they have been, I'm going."

"I hear that! Well, as long as you're happy and safe, I'm happy for you. Where is he trying to take you?"

"I'm not sure yet. He's planning it."

"Okay. So, it was just two dates?"

"Nah, he got sick after the second date. I initiated the third date. I made him meet me at Calabash, that tea bar spot."

"Yeah, I know the place."

"Yeah, he's Jamaican, and you know they believe tea cures everything."

"It does!" I said, giggling as my tea kettle signaled the water was ready.

"Girl, bye! I was just trying to win cool points for that sorrel tea they have."

"So, how was that?" I asked.

I poured the hot water into my mug and dropped a chamomile and melatonin tea bag in before covering it with a plate to steep.

"He called me two days after that to tell me he felt better. We had a sexual encounter," she divulged.

"Whaaaaat?!"

"Yes, and it was amazing!"

"You little loose booty," I joked.

"I know, right! Ugh! I didn't plan on it. I went over to make him some soup and shit, but he was trying to eat something else instead."

I screamed and laughed at her.

"I know, I know! Don't judge me, J!"

"No judgement here. We all go through our ho phase, and anybody who tells you otherwise is lying."

"Ain't THAT the truth!" I agreed while stirring honey into my mug.

"So, is this a new thing, or is he just another notch on the lipstick case?"

"He's a new thing for now."

"Gotcha. What do you want to see happen?"

"I don't know yet. Right now, I just want to date him, get to know him, and see where it goes."

"Well, why did you have sex with him if you don't know where it's going?"

"It was honestly a moment where he caught me by surprise, and I just went with it. I haven't had any in a long time," she confessed.

"You weren't getting it on with the dude in the suit?"

"No, ma'am! I told you that I wanted to take it there, but he had poor hygiene. I was too grossed out to even try."

"Wow! What happened with that?" I walked to my sofa with my mug of hot tea, and sat with my feet tucked under me.

"He came over after having said he showered and all that, and he had skid marks in his underwear!"

"Ewwwwwww!" I shouted, nearly spilling my tea.

"I know! The worst part was that we had been rolling around in my bed for a while, making out and all that with no clothes on, and he got up to get a glass of water."

"When he got up to do that, I went to the bathroom. When I came back, I lay down in my bed and I saw this stain on my comforter that wasn't there before. I picked the blanket up in my hand to get a closer look and . . . I sniffed it . . . "

"Oh, my GOD! Ewwwwwww!"

"I know, Girl, I know!" she laughed. "I reached down and snatched his underwear out of his jeans and the same stain was there also! It was so gross."

"Ewwwww! How did you come back from that?" I asked, fully engaged in her story.

"I didn't! I lied and said my period had started and I was feeling crampish, and he needed to go home. That was six weeks ago, and I haven't called him back since," she admitted.

"You ghosted him?"

"Girl, how do you effectively tell a man that he has skid marks in his underwear, and then still want to fuck him afterward?"

"Good point! So, you never told him anything?"

"Nothing, J. I was just so embarrassed for him, I couldn't bring myself to do it. He was great on paper, but he doesn't clean his ass well, and I just don't need that kind of nonsense in my life."

"I can't say I blame you," I agreed shaking my head. "You wanted to be his woman, not his damn mama."

"Exactly! So, when I met Cason, I was in a more vulnerable space. Normally, I wouldn't have given anyone the business so quickly after meeting them, but I was in a space of weakness when he put his lips on me and shit."

"I see! Well, at least he seems like he has better hygiene, so hopefully you won't be disappointed by this little trip."

"Yeah, Girl, I'm interested in seeing the real thing because he only kissed it that day. Either way, I think 'she' likes him," she confessed.

I squealed again. "Well, I can't wait to hear all the details, since I'm clearly living vicariously through your sex life nowadays."

"I know, right. Who knew?" Sydney laughed.

"Okay, Lady, I need to get ready for bed. I gotta get up early to finish this work tomorrow," I said.

"Coolio! Thanks for listening!"

"Of course! Good night, Boo Thang!"

"Good night!"

We hung up, and I took a hot shower and put on my pajamas. Curling back up on the couch with Rico, I watched an episode of *Reign* on Netflix and caught up on the latest episode of *Being Mary Jane* before the tea and shower had me feeling sufficiently drowsy. I turned off the television and trudged my way to my room, pulling the blankets up over myself. I giggled slightly to myself as I remembered the skid mark on the blanket story Sydney had told me earlier. I blinked slowly three times, and I drifted into a peaceful slumber.

***

I had agreed to have a date with Ronald on Monday. I walked down the street to the comedy show in Purple Lounge feeling light and free from the crazy work day I had endured. The bouncer checked my ID and waved me in with a smile. I smiled back and strode into the venue where people were already talking loudly over the music and the clinking glasses indicated that it was happy hour.

I stood at the door, surveying the room in search of Ronald, until I found him at the back of the room in a booth under a string of lights. He caught my gaze at nearly the same moment and smiled at me. I smiled back and began heading in his direction. A woman stepped onstage as I reached the table Ronald was holding for us, and I hugged him and sat down beside him.

"How are you?" he asked, licking his lips and sipping his drink.

"I'm well," I said. "I had a really long day and I was looking forward to leaving that office."

"I totally understand. Would you like a drink?" He asked.

"Yes."

He signaled the waitress who came over and asked me what I wanted to drink.

"Does your bartender know how to make a Kissing Frog?"

"Ummm, I can ask." She said uncertainly.

"Never mind. I will just take a glass of pinot noir." I conceded.

At some point I was going to have to stop lingering on Carlos's memory.

"No problem!" she replied sweetly before walking away.

"You missed the first two comedians. They were funny. I'm hoping that these last few are as good too." Ronald offered.

"Me too. I hate when the performance wanes after the first few."

It sounded like a double entendre, but I ignored my gutter minded thoughts and asked a more practical question, "How was your day?"

The emcee interrupted getting on the mic to introduce the next comedian.

"Next up on stage is the beautiful Anna Mae, right here from D.C.! Show her some love and clap her up to the mic!"

I averted my eyes to the stage, while Ronald placed his hand on my middle and pulled me backward into him while he whispered in my ear.

"It was a long day, but it's better now that I've seen you."

I smirked slightly and felt my cheeks warm as I nodded in silent appreciation before turning back to look at him and smile more broadly. I was a lightly boiling pot of energy with him behind me, his hand on my belly, stroking it slightly. I didn't want to push him away, but I felt more open to his advances than I would usually allow so soon, so I rose and strategically made my way to the ladies' room to collect myself. I stepped past two women who were standing side-by-side, stroking and adjusting their weave in the mirror.

"Babe, you saw that chick eyeing me in there?" one said to the other. "She wasn't looking at you, she was looking at me." The other laughed. "We should pick her up and take her home with us."

"The more, the merrier." The second replied.

I chuckled quietly to myself when I heard them slap hands and exit the restroom.

"Let me tell you what just happened!" I whispered to Ronald when I returned. "What?"

"There were these two women in the bathroom plotting on this other woman up in here!"

"Say what?!"

"Yes! They were talking about 'the more the merrier' and I was trying so hard not to laugh too loudly while I was in there!"

"Sounds like they were plotting on your sweet ass."

"I think not!" I laughed, "They were talking about some woman who was watching them out here in the audience."

"Where are they now?"

I scanned the room discreetly until I saw them, "Those two over there with the weave."

We both looked in the direction of the women who winked at us and raised their glasses in our direction, to which we both burst out laughing.

"See! I told you they were talking about you! They were watching you when you walked in."

"Nooooo!" I exclaimed, laughing harder. "I totally heard them say that there was a woman watching them!"

"Aren't you watching them now?"

"I guess you make a good point." I said, as I turned my back to them and leaned into Ronald to emphasize that I was strictly dickly.

He wrapped his arm around me again and we went back to watching Anna Mae who was telling jokes about periods and sniffing a used tampon. Everyone was howling, but more from a place of being grossed out than pure humor. I was watching with a look of disgust on my face, waiting for her to leave the stage. She just wasn't funny to me.

"Are you okay?"

"Yeah, she's just trying too hard."

"Facts." He said with a laugh. "Do you want anything else?"

"I guess I can go for another glass after all her disgusting jokes."

"I heard that."

He waved to the waitress and gestured to her to refresh our drinks.

"Thank you." I told him.

"My pleasure."

We watched two more less than funny comedians before the deejay came on signaling the end of the performances for the night. Ronald and I moved to the dance floor to work it out to a few songs before returning to our seats and conversing about the events of his day.

He had a couple of arrests and a lot of paperwork to complete, but I understood the stres. I shared about the man who attempted to embarrass me in my class earlier that day by harboring on an answer to a question that I couldn't answer about a program I was teaching about and how he complained in his survey at the end of the training.

"I can't stand pompous jerks who try to make a big deal out of small things in front of an audience."

"Exactly. I make it my business to be prepared for every session, and he asked a complicated question that wasn't even in the troubleshooting. He was one of those techy guys who will probably never have a relationship outside of those online catfish dudes in Oklahoma or some shit."

"He must have really upset you!" Ronald laughed

"He did! I was nice to him and all that, but he was belligerent and trying to embarrass me."

"Do you want anything else?"

"No thanks. We can go whenever you're ready. I know you have to wake up early, and so do I."

"Cool. Let me close out and we can . . . head out." He smiled at me mischievously, like he had dirty intentions in mind.

"Okay."

He got up and walked to the bar, rather than hunt down the waitress, who was nowhere to be seen. When he returned, I got up and he helped me as I slid into my coat. We smiled at one another and walked out of the lounge into the cool evening air.

"Will you ride with me to the gas station to get some gas?"

"Absolutely. No woman needs to be pumping gas this time of night by herself."

We walked to my car in silence and I removed my computer bag and papers from my day off the passenger seat and into the back seat of my car to make room for him.

"I see you bending over in your car for me." He said.

"What?"

I heard him, but I wanted to give him a chance to check himself.

"Never mind." He said as he walked around my car to open the door for me.

"Thank you," I said.

"No problem."

We both got into my car and I drove to the gas station across the street.

"What kind of gas do you take?" he asked as he unbuckled his seatbelt and got out of the car to pump my gas.

"Mid-grade." I said with a smile.

It had been a while since a guy had pumped my gas for me, and I was somewhat smitten over him performing such a small task. It's always the little things that makes a woman melt. When he was finished pumping gas, he returned to my car and I poured hand sanitizer in his hands before we drove back to the lounge parking lot where his car was parked. I parked in a space beside his car. He turned to me and looked at me like I was food again.

"Thank you for letting me take you out tonight," he said.

"Thank you for asking me out," I said. "I had a really good time."

"That's all I needed. Come on out and give me a hug."

I took off my seat belt and stepped out of my car and he did the same. He walked around to where I was. He hugged me tightly and longer than I expected, stroking my back and rocking me from side to side. I looked up at him for a second, wondering how long this hug was going to last, when he cupped my chin in his hand and kissed me.

I was so caught off guard by the gesture that I didn't panic. I melted into his embrace and kissed back almost hungrily, as if I would never be kissed again. After a couple of seconds of lip locking, my superconscious self kicked in and I pulled away.

Whew! Damn, Ronald!

"Whew!" I said aloud, echoing the sentiment in my head.

"What's wrong?" he asked.

"Nothing. I just wasn't ready!"

"I understand. Well, maybe we can do this again." He suggested.

"I'd like that." I replied.

"Good. Drive home safely. Text me when you get home, please."

"I sure will." I said, as I slid into my car. He shut the door and walked back to his car. I put my address into my GPS and began to pull off into traffic. When I got to the light, I felt like my car was full of people who were all shouting at me to call him back to me. I mentally tried to silence the noise and sat at the light feeling jittery as I replayed the kiss in my mind. I drove halfway down the block before I felt completely compelled to stop and call him back to me. I pulled into the parking lot of a Days Inn and text him to come there. When he didn't respond after a few seconds, I called him on the phone. It felt like years waiting for him to answer.

"Hello?"

"Come back."

"What?"

"Come back. Meet me in the parking lot of the Days Inn."

"Well aren't you being bossy?" he asked with a hint of lust in his tone.

"I apologize, I just feel compelled to call you back to me right now."

"Don't apologize, I like it. I'm making a U-turn and coming back to you."

"Okay."

A few minutes later, he pulled into the parking spot beside me, and I got out of my car to meet him. I wasn't sure why I needed him to come back so urgently. I was just being obedient to the energy I was picking up from him and the cacophonous chorus of voices I heard insisting for me to bring him back to me. When he neared me, I literally felt like six sets of hands pushed me into his arms and he wrapped me up in the most passionate kiss.

I shivered and moved closer to him, and he embraced me more tightly as our kissing intensified. He reached around behind me and pulled my shirt up and caressed my back. I moaned softly and continued to kiss him, not caring where he touched me.

I wanted to give him everything right then, but I wasn't going to. He reached his hands past the waist band of my pants and slid his fingers into the seat of my panties and rubbed them through the puddle that was collecting there. I gasped in surprise, but I didn't stop him. He broke our kiss and took a step back, putting his fingers, wet with my excitement, into his mouth and closed his lips around them, sucking the moisture off of them and smiling at me.

"You taste delicious." He said to me.

I stood there with my mouth open for a few seconds before covering my face with my hands and giggling.

"Thank you." I replied, blushing and hiding my smile behind my hands like a teenaged girl.

"I'm going to leave before I try to keep you. I'd like to take my time with you." He told me.

"Okay . . . I just couldn't let you leave yet." I confessed.

"That's ok. You get home safe, with your delicious ass."

"Uh . . . You too. I will let you know when I make it."

"Please do." He turned around and loped slowly back to his car and slid into the driver's seat, sending a seductive gaze and suggestive smirk my way. I grinned and got in my car, and we went our separate ways. My body was buzzing and tingling from his touch and I couldn't help but look forward to seeing him again.

When I parked my car in the garage at my apartment and walked into the building, I still felt lightheaded as I reminisced on kissing Ronald. His lips were so soft and his body felt so good pressed up against me while he held me, kissing me until I felt like I could hardly breathe. I was so distracted that I dropped my keys as I tried to unlock my front door. I bent to retrieve them, and I saw a shadow out the corner of my eye, but when I turned to look in the direction of where I saw it, there was nothing. The hairs rose on the back of my neck and my arms as I thought of Carlos.

Immediately, I felt guilty, and I stood and let myself in. Rico was mewing up a storm inside and rubbing against my legs so that I could barely get all the way across the threshold. Suddenly, he cried out loudly as if someone had stepped on his tail or something, hissed and ran away into the apartment.

"Rico! What happened? Where are you going?" I could see his yellow-green eyes shining in the darkness of my living room. I turned on the lights to reveal him hiding underneath the couch; the white and tawny fur of the tip of his tail barely peeked out as he twitched it angrily.

"Well, that was weird." I muttered to myself as I took off my shoes and got comfortable.

I decided to coax Rico out from under the couch with some cat treats, but when I retrieved the plastic bottle of the little treats that normally brought him running, he didn't budge.

"Come out, Baby!" I encouraged, but he still didn't come from his hiding place.

"Okay, weirdo gato." I grumbled with a defeated sigh, replacing his treats to the shelf and heading to take a shower.

I heard my phone chime a text message as I wrapped myself with a towel. I tapped the screen and saw it was a message from Ronald.

> I thought you were going to let me know when you got home, Pretty Lady.

I smiled to myself, and the butterflies I had been feeling since we kissed intensified.

> Sorry, hun. My cat was acting weird when I got home and I forgot.

> You forgot me that easily? I guess I will have to kiss you better next time.

I laughed quietly to myself as I typed out my response.

> If kissing you gets better than it was tonight, I'm not sure I'll know what to do with myself.

> Believe me, my dear, we've only just begun.

> You sound pretty sure of yourself.

> I just know how kissing makes your body respond. I love how you respond to me, and I can still smell and taste you.

> #Speechless

I followed my last text with a shocked emoji with a hand over the mouth. He texted back:

> You don't even know, but in time you will find out.

I smiled hard and bit my lip at his flirtation, glad he wasn't there to see my facial responses, and decided to dial him back a bit.

> I had fun with you. I'm headed to
> bed. Good night.
>
> Good night, beautiful.

I walked back into my bedroom, plugged the phone into the charger, and got dressed for bed. After I brushed my teeth, I checked to see whether Rico had emerged from his hiding place, but he was still glaring at me from the darkness and safety of the underside of my couch.

"Good night, Rico." I called sweetly, but he just winked one glowing eye at me and nothing more.

I closed my door, but left a crack for him in case he decided to climb into bed with me later in the night. I tied my hair into a pineapple with a satin scarf and lay down under the blankets, although it wasn't cold, and soon I felt myself drifting off into a peaceful slumber.

I woke feeling refreshed and unmolested by any weird dreams or visions that I could remember. In fact, I couldn't recall my dreams at all. I did my normal morning routine, humming a little Goapele tune to myself as I stepped into a pair of sky blue slacks. I pulled a cream boat necked blouse with bell sleeves over my head and styled my curls into a goddess twist around my head. I hooked a pair of dangly pearl earrings into my ears and slid my feet into a pair of African print wedges.

I opted against any more makeup than a little black eyeliner and lip glass for the day and, when I was pleased with my appearance, I collected my thermos from the coffee machine and poured in my cream before grabbing my purse and heading out to fight rush hour traffic on my way to my training site for the day.

When I had finished my class on cultural awareness and sensitivity, I began collecting the surveys and extra pamphlets from the tables and headed for my car with my work bag and tote with wheels. I fished my cell phone out of my purse and saw the missed calls and texts on my notification screen. I opened the message from Ronald first because it had come in two hours earlier.

> Hello, Beautiful. I'd like to take you to lunch today if you have time. Let me know if you're free.

I responded:

> I'm sorry I missed this text. I was busy teaching a class. Is the offer still good, or should we meet for lunch another time?

I responded feeling hopeful that I'd be able to see him again. My phone began vibrating in my lap as I turned the key in the ignition, and I let out a small yelp as I grabbed it from between my thighs to look at the screen. Ronald's name showed on the screen and I slid my thumb across the face of my phone to accept the call.

"Hello?" I said cheerily.

"Hey there, Beautiful. How are you today?"

His voice poured through the speakers of my car, and I felt the stressful energy of my day melt away to be replaced by a different kind of energy. Something like stepping under a waterfall on an extremely hot day. I wanted him, but I couldn't figure out why the energy was so intense. Was it just because I needed to fill the Carlos void, or was it something more?

I mentally repressed the internal conversation so I could focus on his words. Had I ever been to Gringos and Mariachis? Did I like Mexican food? Had I had lunch already?

I told him I hadn't eaten yet and that I had never been to that place before, but that I loved Mexican food.

"Perfect! I'm going to send you the address in a text. I will meet you there. I'm about twenty minutes away."

"Okay! I'll see you soon! I'm about thirty minutes away." "Cool, Love, I can't wait."

"Okay, bye."

"Bye."

I had butterflies in my stomach as I drove to the restaurant, and I couldn't locate any emotion that outshone my excitement to lay eyes on him. When I parked my car down the street from Gringos and Mariachis, I noticed the little bounce in my step as

I got out the car and walked toward the place. I was walking on clouds lined in silver and gold glitter, and all the colors seemed brighter than before. The wind ruffled my blouse as I opened the door and stepped inside. I found Ronald waiting for me near the bar. He smiled brightly when he saw me and, in my head, I practically skipped into his arms. In real life, I maintained my cool and sashayed over to him in my wedges, putting an extra little switch in my hips for emphasis. He grinned at me as I neared him and slid his arm around my waist, resting his thumb on the base of my spine as he hugged me to himself.

"Hey Lady!"

"Hey!" I replied, withholding the urge to kiss him, but he leaned in and kissed me openly. I slid my palms up his chest, to the sides of his neck, finally resting them on his cheeks, as I kissed him back like there was nobody else around but we two. The hostess appeared beside us and cleared her throat politely, prompting us to untangle from our embrace.

"I have a seat for you two over here. Follow me, please."

She swallowed a chuckle and led us to a booth in the back.

"Your waitress will be Arianna," she said as she handed us our menus and walked away.

I turned my attention to my menu to try to decide what I wanted to eat and Ronald did the same.

"Have you eaten here before?" I asked.

"No. A friend of mine suggested this place to me a few days ago, and I figured it would be a good place to try with you." I smiled behind my menu as I decided on the lamb tacos.

"I've never had lamb tacos before," he said. "I'm going to try their cauliflower tacos."

"Are you a vegetarian?" I asked.

"No, but I figure we can share."

"Sounds good to me."

When Arianna arrived, we ordered our tacos and commenced to stare at each other, smiling across the table while saying nothing with more than our eyes. I felt like the unspoken desires between us were thick, heavy and almost tangible, but neither of us said a word.

"How was your day?" he asked eventually.

"It was productive. I enjoyed my class. Good questions and solid information about cultural sensitivity. It was a training for administrative staff for a local school system."

"Did you make them do any extra homework?"

"My students don't do homework. In fact, I don't always see them more than once, depending upon the contract."

"Interesting. So how did you get into that?"

"I went to school for education, but I received my Masters in Human Resources. After teaching children for a few years I joined a company that contracts me to do professional development for different companies and organizations. I've been in this role for about six years now. I get to enjoy utilizing my teaching skills to train adults in different ways. No day is quite the same."

"Sweet," he said. "That sounds way more interesting than my job."

"How'd you get into your job?" I asked.

"I used to be in the military, and then when I finished my deployment, I was hired to be a private investigator. I've been doing this for almost eight years now. I like it, but it gets boring sometimes. I get tired of digging and researching people."

"That's too bad! I thought your job was interesting."

"I mean it has its perks. I get to travel internationally sometimes, and it pays well, but I spend a lot of time by myself."

"What about your daughter? How often do you see her?"

"Mostly holidays and school breaks. Her mother is engaged now and her fiancé is good to my daughter, Amaya."

"That's a pretty name, and that's good. A lot of men have a hard time accepting another man's child."

"Yeah, I struggled accepting him at first, but after a while I could see that he was really genuine and only wanted to love my daughter and her mother. I wouldn't have things any other way. If you could see them together, her smile is from the heart, and I would kill any man who hurt my babygirl."

"Kill him? That's excessive, but I understand your meaning."

"I feel that any man who doesn't feel strongly for his child and the mother who created that child is a coward. I'm not going to allow another man to destroy the light in my child's eyes for any reason. As long as he's handling my daughter and her mother with the greatest care and respect, I won't feel threatened and I won't interfere."

"That's noble."

"Everything doesn't always go the way we plan. I've known my ex-wife since high school. I've watched her grow, and her current relationship makes her happier than I ever could."

Before I could respond, our food arrived and my mouth began to water at the smell of the delicious tacos steaming in front of us.

"Aw man, these have onions on them. I don't like onions." I muttered as I began picking the onions off my dish with my knife.

"I didn't see that on the description. Sorry about that."

"It's not your fault." I said, distracted by the task of removing the white, gas inducing onions.

He was almost done with his first taco while I was still picking onions. Once they were gone, I was famished and I wanted to stuff the entire taco into my mouth, but I folded it up and ate slowly instead.
"How is it?" Ronald inquired.

"Mmmm!" I exclaimed as I chewed a mouthful of lamb taco. "This is SO GOOD! You should have one!"

"Let me taste it." He said with a suggestive smirk.

I folded up another taco, after picking off the onions, and held it across the table for him to eat.

"That IS good!" he exclaimed, "I've never had lamb tacos before. I'm going to have to have that again! Good choice!"

"Thank you!" I said, feeding him the last bite of the taco before returning to mine. "Do you want to taste mine?" he asked.

"Sure!"

He folded a cauliflower taco and fed it to me across the table, watching my lips curl around the edges of his fingers as I took a bite.

"Don't bite my fingers off!" he exclaimed with feigned alarm.

I giggled and held my hand over my mouth so as not to spit my food at him. When I finished the last bite, I said, "That was delicious!! I'm going to have some more of that next time I come here!"

"Maybe we can come again sometime."

"I'd like that."

"Good."

After we finished our food, Ronald suggested we go for a walk to an arcade he knew of down the block.

"An arcade? Hmmm . . . I can't remember the last time I was in an arcade."

"If you'd like to do something else, we can."

"No, let's do it. It could be fun!"

"Are you good at any video games?"

"I used to play Gauntlet and House of Terror a lot when I was younger, but I haven't played any video games in so long. I used to beat my brother in the Need for Speed racing games, and I'd watch him play Resident Evil and Silent Hill, but my expertise was in things like Crash Bandicoot or Kirby's Dreamland."

"I haven't heard of those games in so long!"

"I know! When Doom was a computer game, I would play that a lot also."

"Didn't they turn that one into a movie?"

"Yeah, but I never saw it."

"I've seen all the Resident Evils and the Silent Hills."

"Yeah, those were pretty good. I always knew what was going to happen in the games before my brother. He hated for me to watch him play, because I'd warn him and be right."

"Well, are you any good at pinball?"

"I've never played before."

"Perfect! The place we're going has nothing but pinball, so maybe I can teach you to play."

"Awww! Look at you wanting to teach me something new!"

"Somebody has to teach the teacher new tricks."

I smiled and followed his tug of my hand into a dimly lit pizza restaurant where the walls were lined with pinball machines. He introduced me to the man working behind the counter, and exchanged a few dollars for quarters. We walked over to the pinball machines and chose a Guardians of the Galaxy game first.

"So, this is how you play; you pull this plunger handle, and then when the ball comes out, you have to keep it from going into the sides of the board by pressing these buttons that control the flippers. If you lose the ball, another will come out and you can try again. Here, watch me."

He pulled the handle and I watched him intently as he pressed the buttons for the flippers erratically. I didn't think he had much technique, but I didn't say anything. He wasn't exactly watching the ball and where it went, and I felt that he was scrambling with the ball rather than guiding it. It was evident that he didn't realize that he wasn't allowing the ball to touch the edge of the flipper to shoot it with more precision, but I just watched and prepared to try my hand when he was finished.

"See! It's easy! I scored fifteen-hundred points!" he beamed, proud of himself, as the light flickered on the machine and the music blared, "Now you try!"

I stepped behind the pinball machine, resting both hands on the sides of it, and he stepped behind me. I tried to ignore his breath on the back of my neck as he attempted to guide me, reiterating the directions previously given. I smirked a bit, making myself ignore his closeness, the scent of him, the warmth of his pelvis barely grazing my behind, and focus on the game. I could tell he was using this opportunity to press up on me and feign innocence, but I was attracted to him, so I didn't mind. I wasn't going to give him too much encouragement, but I didn't mind.

I pulled the plunger handle and watched the shiny, silver pinball shoot out of the side and into the playfield. I carefully used the flippers to propel the ball into the targets, kickers and slingshots. The playfield was chiming and flashing as I stalked the ball's movements like a lioness stalking her prey. I was flipping the ball across rollovers, through spinners and onto ramps that led to other rollovers and into jackpots. My points were ringing up, but I wasn't watching them; I was focused on keeping the ball out of holes and gutters. Eventually, I lost the ball, but another was waiting to be put into play. I was oblivious to the fact that my turn was taking much longer then Ronald's did, because when I lost the second ball, there was a third one to play. I shot the third ball into the playfield and suddenly six more pinballs flooded it.

"Oh shit! You're in wizard mode," he said.

I didn't say anything. I was trying to keep as many balls in play as I possibly could. The music was playing faster and louder, but I maintained my laser focus. When the last ball slid into the gutter, all the chimes on the machine sounded and the lights flashed erratically enough to trigger an epileptic seizure. Ronald, wide eyed and excited, grabbed me by the shoulders and squeezed me to him.

"Journey, you scored two-hundred fifty-four thousand eight-hundred and twenty-three points! I can't believe it!" he snatched me away from his chest and looked me in the eye sternly, "Are you sure you've never done this before?"

"Never! I swear! This is my first time!" I insisted with a surprised giggle as I waved my hands in front of myself.

"Well, I suppose we have uncovered a hidden skill for you, then!" he grinned and winked.

"I guess so!" I beamed.

I was afraid he would get upset that I had done better than he had, but he was so excited that he didn't seem to mind.

"This has to be beginner's luck! Come on, let's play again." He pulled a handful of quarters out of his pocket, cupped his empty hand underneath mine and poured coins into my palm.

Feeling somewhat confident, I turned back to the pinball machine I had been playing on and dropped two quarters into the slot. The machine came to life, singing "Come and Get Your Love" and as I narrowed my gaze on the playfield, curling my fingers around the plunger and releasing it, I knew I was going to beat my last score.

I committed my focus on the ball, coaching myself to BE THE BALL, as I racked up more than three-hundred thousand points. When the wizard mode started again, my heartbeat increased and I flipped three balls into the jackpot. Ronald appeared beside me, open mouthed, as he watched me winning the game.

"I can't believe you've never played before! You're really good at this!"

"Thanks!" I said as he high-fived me and then scooped me into his arms for a kiss.

"I thought I was going to teach you something new and impress you, but you're better at this than I am. You didn't have to lie, you could've told me that you were a pinball shark on the low."

"I swear I've never played pinball before! You can ask anyone!"

"I'm just joking; I believe you. You're great at it, though. Maybe I can learn a few things from you. What's your technique?"

"Well, when you were playing, I noticed you were more erratic with your trying to flip the ball. You expended unnecessary energy with the flippers instead of focusing on exactly where the ball was going, which would allow you to maximize your precision."

Ronald smiled broadly at me, "I love it when you talk nerdy to me!"

I giggled as he pulled me into his arms and kissed me again.

"Let's get outta here. I think you've done enough showing me up for one afternoon."

"Okay," I said laughing. "I have to start making my way home through this traffic anyway."

"Cool, I'll walk you to your car, then."

The early evening sun was dazzling as we stepped out of the dimly lit arcade, and we both stood still for a few minutes blinking until our vision adjusted. Walking hand in hand, we made our way to my car and Ronald kissed me once more before I ducked into my driver's seat and shut the door. It had been the most fun date I'd had in a while, and I felt a little glowing sensation in my chest as I pulled away. I couldn't wait to see him again.

Forever on my right shoulder,
Never on my left . . .
Always lingers somewhere in between.
I hope, in spite of myself.

~ *Olosunde*

"I had so much fun with him, Girl!" I squealed to Sydney.

"Child, hush!" she grumbled with a wave of her hand as she pulled her eye mask over her eyes to block out the light. "I understand you are excited and that you can't wait to see him again, but I DO NOT want to spend the entire flight discussing your date with Ronald for the umpteenth time. Let's just make it to Puerto Rico in one piece and let these sleeping pills kick in. You know I'm only here because you guilted me by reminding me that I said I would go with you when Carlos first died. I don't even LIKE flying!"

"Well somebody's a grumpy bear this morning!"

I teased her from the window seat. Her silent reply was plugging her ears and leaning her head back onto the head rest.

We were heading to visit Carlos's grave site and his family for the first time since the funeral. I had attended that event alone, but I cashed in on her best friend vow to come with me to Puerto Rico whenever I wanted her to, and she had a fear of flying. My date with Ronald left me feeling like I needed closure from Carlos's death, and I figured that visiting his family and his grave would give me what I needed. The cemetery was near the ocean and his family had a mausoleum there where the family was lain to rest. The four hour flight to Arroyo was uneventful and Uncle Rafael met us at the airport with a ready smile and lots of hugs.

I was immediately reminded of why I liked him so much when I first met him. He was so charming and sweet to the ladies in a way that was uncommon in other places in the States.

"Journey, Heeeey!" he said excitedly. "It's so good to see you again! You look just as beautiful as I remember! Ahhhh, who is this lovely lady?"

He hugged me and kissed my cheek, and then Sydney's.

"This is my friend who is like a sister to me, Sydney. Sydney, this is Uncle Rafael."

"It's a pleasure to meet you Rafael." Sydney replied politely.

"Please, call me Uncle Rafael! Any family of Journey's is family of mine!" he replied as he hoisted our luggage into his truck.

"Is this a new truck, Uncle Rafael?" I asked.

"Yes! The old one died on me a few months ago, and I loved the thing so damn much I bought a newer one in the same color."

We all laughed at that, and Uncle Rafael turned off the air conditioning and rolled the windows down, tossing a grin in my direction.

"I remember how much you love the natural air over the air conditioning."

"Thank you!" I said, returning the smile and feeling the warm sense of familial acceptance and appreciation well up and wash over me. I leaned my head out of the window slightly, letting the wind whip my curls all over my head.

"This place is really beautiful!" Sydney sighed from the back seat.

"You ain't seen nothing yet," Rafael called back to her. "Just wait until we get off the highway and closer to the house."

"How is Mrs. Rivera doing?"

"Ivelisse is fine. She's still mourning Carlos, but she's looking forward to seeing you. I think she's planned to cook a special dinner for you and your friend."

"Aw snap! I can't wait! I'm starving!" Sydney exclaimed.

"She can throw down, Girl," I said. "You're going to be stuffed, believe me! She fed me so much when I visited last time, I was sure I gained five pounds!"

"Well I'm not sure if everyone will be there like the last time you visited, but I know she is impatiently awaiting your arrival and is itching to love you up." Rafael informed with a huge grin.

"I can't wait to see her either. It's been months . . ."

"Well, the room you stayed in last time is ready and waiting for you. What day do you want to go to the cemetery?"

The smile faded from my lips as I remembered that my visit wasn't going to be completely happy. I had come to return the family ring Carlos had given me and make peace with his memory. I knew I would always be welcome, but it just didn't feel right to hold on to such a treasured item. Rafael patted my leg supportively and then held my hand.

"You are not alone. I will be with you as much or as little as you want me to be. You say the word, and it's whatever you need, ok?"

"Thanks, Uncle Rafael."

"De nada." He said, reaching over and grasping my hand, kissing the back of it, then releasing it.

When we pulled up in front of the house, Carlos's mother practically ran out of the house and into the front yard, She made a sound like a squeal and opened my car door, pulling me out of my seat and into a tight embrace, kissing my cheeks in between squeezes.

"Mija, I've missed you so much," she squealed. "I'm so happy to see you! Let me look at you!"

She stretched her arms out with me still in them and looked me over before clicking her tongue, "You haven't been eating! You're too skinny! Come in! Come in! I've cooked for you!"

She pulled me by my hand behind her and called over her shoulder, "Rafa, take the bags to the room, por favor."

"Mrs. Rivera, wait!" I pleaded, "Let me introduce you to my friend, Sydney."

"Ah! Silly me! I forgot you were bringing a friend!"

She turned around, still pulling me by the hand, and walked back to the car where Sydney was finally stepping out of the truck. She embraced her warmly,

"Sydney! How nice to meet you, dear! Welcome! I hope you're hungry too. Come on you two!"

I laughed and grabbed Sydney by the hand and pulled her as Mrs. Rivera turned around and pulled me into the house. She let go of my hand once we crossed the threshold and Sydney and I followed her into the kitchen where delicious smelling food beckoned to us from inside many metal containers.

"What's for dinner?" I asked enthusiastically.

"Mofongo, arroz con gandules, asopao de pollo, and sweet platanos. I'm waiting on Marisol to finish mixing the drinks outside, but I want you two to get comfortable and wash the travel off of you before you eat. Everything is finished cooking. Do you remember where your room is, Mija?"

"Yes, Mrs. Rivera, I'll . . ."

"Listen, you stop it with that Mrs. Rivera business! You are home, Mija, call me Mom!"

"Yes, Mom, I remember!" I said with a sheepish grin, knowing there was no sense in arguing with that.

"That's my girl!" she said as she pinched my chin between her thumb and finger the way Carlos used to do.

I smiled, but my eyes teared up at the gesture, and when she noticed she pulled me into her with a tight embrace.

"Shhh . . . It's ok, Baby. You can cry, but you don't need to. You always have a home here with us. I've missed you so much."

"I've missed you too."

I whispered into her shoulder, inhaling her sweet scent as I hugged her back. We were two women who had suffered the same loss and were desperately holding on to the memory of Carlos through one another. I didn't want to appear inauthentic or presumptuous in any way. I loved his family and I yet I feared my attachment to them because I had lost so much.

"Look at us," she chuckled, pulling me away from her body to gaze at me again, "Carlos would be happy to know that you came here, and you need to always remember that. Promise me?"

"I promise." I said, chuckling and sniffling at the same time, "I'm happy I came back also."

"Good," she said, kissing my cheek, "now go show your friend to the room you'll be sleeping in. I'm sure she's ready to get comfortable and eat."

She popped me on my behind and I giggled as I turned toward Sydney to lead her to the bedroom.

"That was sweet, J." Sydney whispered, "I feel the love up in here! It's good that you've maintained such a positive relationship with Carlos's family."

"Yes, I spoke to her every day when Carlos was hospitalized, but after he passed away it was too painful for us to keep up with each other as much. We would speak every other day, then once a week or so. They're really good people."

"I see! Well, happy homecoming to you." She whispered as she gave me a supportive squeeze.

I showed her where the bathroom was and taught her how to work the shower before stepping away and letting her have her privacy in the bathroom.

I sat on the sofa that faced the bed and closed my eyes, taking a deep breath. I heard a faint giggle, and I opened my eyes and saw a memory of Carlos lying beside me in bed, my hair disheveled from our vigorous rolling in the sheets, as he kissed me on my forehead, nose, lips, and neck. "Te amo . . ." he whispered as he kissed me over my heart.

"I love you too . . ." I whispered back in unison with the memory of us. I closed my eyes and exhaled shakily as a lone teardrop slid down my cheek. "I love you too . . ."

Just as I was beginning to feel the shadows of doubt creep from the corners of the room to join those from the corners of my mind in a feeling that maybe I had made a mistake in returning here, Sydney emerged from the bathroom releasing a deep, relaxed sigh.

"Girl! That shower was EVERYTHING! Your turn!"

"Thanks, Girl." I muttered as I gathered my toiletries and left her in the bedroom alone to get dressed.

Under the stream of water, I felt safe from the shadows, but the memories of Carlos were here too. I washed more quickly than I would have if I had been at home in my own shower, but I told myself that it was only because I was hungry and wanted to eat that delicious food I could still smell all the way from the kitchen.

When I emerged from the bathroom, Sydney wasn't in the room. I slathered myself with shea butter and slipped into a yellow sundress and white, sunflower patterned flip flops. I rubbed detangling curl cream into my hair and used a paddle brush to comb it through, leaving my hair to air dry and making me look like a fluffy lion. I flip-flopped quietly back into the kitchen where I found Sydney opening a fresh Medalla b e e r and then sipping another half-filled one.

"I felt you coming," she said as she handed me the new bottle, "I figured you could use a drink with all the memories up in here."

"Thanks." I said as I took the bottle from her and turned it up to my lips and took a sip. "Was it that obvious?"

"Girl, you're my best friend. You were sitting in a dimly lit bedroom staring at the bed that you slept and made love on with your deceased fiancé in. You can't keep that type of shit from me."

"Facts." I mumbled before taking another sip. "I just need to get through the weekend and give back the ring."

"What ring?" Ivelisse asked as she came into the kitchen through the back door, letting it clap shut loudly behind her. She looked from me to Sydney, and back again, waiting for an answer.

"I . . . Well, I came back to give back the family ring."

She didn't say anything for a few seconds, she just stared at me as if processing what I was saying to her.

"Why would you do that?" she asked. "Carlos gave you that ring as a symbol of his love for you and it has been in this family for several generations."

"That's exactly why I don't feel comfortable keeping it. Carlos is gone, and I don't want the tradition of passing it down to be lost on me when I can't even marry him or pass it on to his child. The younger children should be able to hold on to it for when one of them marries."

"She's right, Ivelisse." a quiet male voice said from the kitchen doorway.

We all turned to see Mr. Rivera standing there, apparently having heard the whole conversation.

"Shut up, Jorge, who asked you?" Ivelisse retorted.

Jorge sighed and walked over to me, wrapping me in a fatherly embrace, "Journey may be family, but she is young and she has her whole life ahead of her. She can't possibly heal and move on with that life if she's holding on to the memory of a union that she will never have."

He turned to look directly at me, "You will always be family to us and you'll always be welcome here, but you have to make your peace with Carlos's memory also."

He returned his gaze to Ivelisse, "It isn't fair of you to cling to our son's memory by expecting her to carry on as if he's still here. Let her return the ring so that the other children can continue the tradition."

He touched my face tenderly, planting a fatherly kiss on my forehead before turning around and walking out of the room.

"I know you mean well and I know my husband is right. I'm just . . . not ready yet. Can you understand?"

"Of course I do, Mom, and I want you to know that I love you and this family. I just don't feel right about keeping such a precious item."

She nodded solemnly, "Let's talk about this later. For now, let's eat and enjoy the fact that you're home."

She assumed a more confident and centered countenance than what I knew she was feeling as she lifted her chin, turned on her heel and walked back out the screen door, letting it clap shut loudly behind her again as she left Sydney and I to linger in the heavy-hearted silence of the kitchen that sought desperately for reprieve.

Dinner was just the energy Sydney and I needed to shift the sadness we were both feeling after the conversation with Carlos's parents. I was embraced, kissed, fussed over, squealed about and genuinely loved by so many people that evening that I couldn't possibly imagine a happier feeling. I truly felt blessed to have been adopted into such a warm and loving family unit, even if the person who was my connection point was no longer there to validate my position.

I was overwhelmed with the feeling of being home, and after all I had endured, I was irrevocably grateful. By the time we finally went to bed, even the coqui frogs had stopped singing and all was relatively silent around the Rivera house. I slid into bed beside Sydney and relished the swimming sensation from all the rum I had that night. I yawned twice, and surrendered to the blanket of sleep that enveloped me; tugging me into dreams and memories that were, for once, more sweet than bitter.

We spent the rest of our weekend catching as much sunshine and doing as much laughing and enjoying the island as we possibly could. When Uncle Rafael dropped us off at the airport, Ivelisse tagged along. As we embraced for my departure again, she made sure to reiterate to me that I was family. She made me promise that I would return to her again and that nothing, short of death, should keep me from coming home to her for as long as I lived.

That good old Latina mom guilt, I thought to myself as I hugged her for the hundredth time that day.

I understood that it was hard for her to let me go because I was the closest person to her son before his passing, and the miscarriage and loss of Carlos left us forever bound in our mourning.

"So, I popped your airplane cherry, Boo!" I sang to Sydney as we found our seats. "Was it as good for you as it was for me?"

"Shut up, Girl! You are so crazy! But, if you must know, yes I had an amazing time and I'm really glad I came along with you."

"Me too. I was a little worried that we wouldn't be able to get past the initial mourning vibe, but I am glad that I saw the whole weekend through. I think this visit was extremely healing for me. I think that I can finally move forward, while still holding space for the family I've chosen in the Riveras."

"Are you going to keep in touch with them and visit like Mrs. Rivera made you promise?"

"Absolutely!"

Sydney made a disapproving face, "Uhmmmm . . . How is THAT going to look going forward? I mean, especially if you get with someone else and start a family? What if he feels uncomfortable with you maintaining that relationship? What if he feels like he's living in the shadow of your ex for the rest of his life?"

"Girl, that's silly. How anyone could feel jealous of a dead man, I won't understand. I don't necessarily need HIM to come visit, but Puerto Rico is beautiful, and family is who you take care of as much as it is blood, right?"

"Yeah, I guess..." she replied, closing her eyes and adjusting her neck pillow.

When she closed her eyes, I pulled my window shade up and stared into the puffy cotton of the cumulus clouds, reflecting on what she had said. What if the man with   whom I chose to make a life decided that he was jealous of Carlos's memory or worse, the Riveras? I decided to cross that road when I got to it and forced the slithering serpents of my overthinking into a black box and mentally dropped them into the ocean where they could hopefully remain in the depths of the unknown forever. I was learning to worry about what I could control, rather than trying to control everything I could imagine a reason to be worried about.

***

As I rolled my suitcase into the house, my phone chimed. I plopped myself down on my couch and pulled Rico into my lap, as I reached for it. I was hoping it was Ronald texting me back, but it was Sydney letting me know that she had arrived home. I made plans to meet her for lunch later in the week and decided to text Ronald again.

He hadn't been replying to my texts all weekend, and I thought that was strange, but I didn't want to seem too thirsty. I read my, "Hey there, I'm home from PR" text and allowed my thumb to hover over the send icon for several minutes before deleting the entire message and tossing my cell on the other end of the couch.

I decided to shower and pick my outfit for the next day instead of allowing myself to linger in the space of wondering, which would undoubtedly turn into overthinking. Maybe he was just busy, maybe he was seeing someone else. Ultimately, it didn't matter. I wasn't his and he wasn't mine and, since we had no ties, that was more than okay.

22. Finding My Way

Beauty that shines from inside,
So purely that it can't be recognized by unworthy eyes
Is of no virtue or consequence to the eyes that cried
Brokenhearted tears
For the vain years during which I tried.

~ Olosunde

It had been a full week since I returned from Puerto Rico and, while my days were busy with work they almost felt like they were running into one another. I kept finding myself wondering what the hell happened to Ronald. I thought we hit it off on our date.

"Maybe he felt like you weren't emotionally available after Carlos." Sydney offered over brunch.

The early summer sun shone through her newly dyed hair and I smiled wanly at her.

"What's wrong?" she asked.

"Nothing."

"You're just gonna lie to me like that?"

"No, I just . . . It's just . . ."

"Just what? I mean spit it out, J!"

"I didn't tell him about Carlos. At least I don't remember telling him."

"Well . . . Whatever, Girl. Maybe he's just not as into you as you thought. That's not all bad. I mean, if he's not right for you, better for him to subtract his dusty ass from the motherfucking equation than drag you along and lead you on!"

She had a look of disgust and contempt on her face.

"Wait a minute, is this about me, or is this about ole what's his name?"

"Cason . . . Ugh! No, although we went out several times and we had that steamy weekend together."

"Mmmmmhmmm! So you've been holding out on the deets!" I joked.

"Nah, Girl, I'm just tired of getting myself worked up over somebody's dusty ass son, only to be disappointed," she said with a small pout.

I could tell her ego was bruised, but I didn't dare say it.

"Awww, Syd," I comforted, pouting back at her from across the table as I tucked a loose curl behind my ear. "I know you'll find the guy who's right for you."

"Yeah . . ." she whispered as she tossed back the last of her pineapple mimosa. "I guess it's just emotional chess out here until then."

We were both silent for a few minutes, as the gravity of her comment filled the silence.

"Well, Honey, in case nobody has told you today, you are beautiful, amazing, intelligent, funny as hell, educated, accomplished and your butt is nice."

She giggled at me and finger waved the waitress over for a refill.

"Yeah, you're right. I can't argue with that one bit. If he's too stupid to see it, I can't help him!"

"That's the spirit! Keep that same energy, and anytime you need me to remind you of how amazing you are and smack that ass for you, I'm down!"

We both cackled at my comment and clinked our glasses together.

"I saw there was a concert in the park over at National Harbor this afternoon. Are you interested?" I asked her.

"Hmmmm . . . Who's playing?"

"I don't know, but I figured it might be a good time either way. I brought my blanket and a couple of bottles of wine just in case. "

"Red or white?" she asked, giving me a knowing grin. "Girl, what's my name?"

"Both" we said in unison, as we laughed again and clinked glasses.

"Well, I'm gonna have to either drink a whole bunch of water between now and then, or we're gonna have to have white. I'm not as young as I once was, so I gotta stick with the girl I took to the prom these days."

"Girl, you are only three years older than I am. I know you're not punking out on me."

"While that may be true . . . I can't go as hard as I did when I was in my twenties."

"Ma'am, you JUST turned thirty! Don't act like that!"

"Yes, but these thirty-year-old aches and pains are showing up for all the realness I have in me. I don't know HOW you can keep that back and forth down when it comes to swapping drinks. My metabolism just isn't what it used to be."

"I guess, Girl, but I'm gonna drink all the wine I can before I start falling into my old lady shit like you."

"Oh, forget you!" she said, flicking water at me from her glass.

"Whatever! You better quit wasting that water and guzzle it down, Miss Thirty and Falling Apart out here!"

We shared a few more glasses of pineapple mimosas and split the bill.

***

We decided it was a better idea to park our cars at my house and Uber to National Harbor, since we both planned to drink our sorrows away into the Sunday sun. We found a good spot overlooking The Awakening statue where we could see the stage and the ships coming in. People watching was the most fun and important part of this excursion, and we wanted to be in the crowd without being of the crowd.

I pulled the blanket out of my bag and spread it out on the fake grass and began pulling the bottle of Skipjack wine out of my bag. I poured the sweet, cool wine into the plastic wine glasses I had pulled out of my sunflower patterned beach bag and we both made ourselves comfortable as we waited for The Roots to come out and perform.

"Thanks for this, J, I needed this day more than you know."

"Oh, I needed it too. Please believe me," I said.

My phone chimed, and I opened an email from my new director, Charisse, informing me that there would be a meeting with the administrative team and the consultants about some changes the owner of the agency wanted to have at nine in the morning tomorrow.

"Ugh, I like her, but I cannot get with these Sunday emails." I complained.

"What's going on?" Sydney asked.

"I have a new manager since Regina got promoted to another office in California. She's very nice and organized, but she sends out a weekly email every Sunday, and I hate that because I'm not trying to think about work on a Sunday."

"She's probably just doing her job, J. You've gotta be more open to change."

"It's not that I have a hard time with change, it's just that . . . Okay, maybe I *do* have a hard time with HER changes, but I like her. It's just frustrating sometimes."

"Well, you know you're the shit, and you're amazing and educated, and you have a nice butt."

She said referencing the compliment I gave her earlier. We both giggle and sipped our wine as the music pulsed and the people milled about around us.

***

In the morning, I sat attentively in an orange dress with a cream blazer and cream colored pumps, waiting for the crew to arrive for our meeting.

Charisse smiled warmly as she entered the room, "Ms. Richards, you're early!" she greeted with her arms full of paper for the meeting.

"Yeah, I hate to be late, so early is my thing."

"That's a good 'thing' to have," she offered absentmindedly as she lay out the stacks of papers at every seat. "We are going to meet the owner of the agency today, so this is really important. Being early is a good way to have your work and professionalism recognized around here."

"Yes . . . Would you like some help?" I offered.

"Sure, thank you!"

I set the pens out for note-taking and followed her to the little kitchen to prepare coffee.

"Why are you doing this? Sistine is the new administrative assistant, shouldn't she be handling this?"

"Oh, haven't you heard?" Charisse asked. She's pregnant."

The words weighed more heavily on me than I expected, but I kept my face free of that emotion.

"No, I had no idea."

"Yeah, she's having a difficult pregnancy, and she's sick today, so I'm doing her job and mine."

"Ah, I see. Well, let me know if I can support you in any way."

"That's really sweet of you, Journey. I'm surprised that you weren't first choice for my position, especially since you've been here for so long."

"Yeah, it was offered to me, but I really enjoy being in the field and teaching the classes," I shared. "I'm just not ready for a managerial move yet."

"That's understandable. If you change your mind, you just let me know. I'd be more than happy to recommend you for a promotion."

"Thank you!" I replied sweetly, "That really means a lot to me, and I'm happy that you recognize my hard work and efforts here."

"Not a problem at all!" she said with a smile, as other training consultants began to file in.

When all the other consultants and administrators were seated, Charisse stood and smiled at the group.

"Good morning, everyone."

"Good morning," we all replied in unison.

"I'm sure you're all wondering why you're here," she said, as heads nodded around the large rectangular table. "Well, the new CEO of our company wanted to come and meet with us and hear about our progress before the fiscal year ends. We have made significant progress and gains in our sessions, and our sales team has been hard at work securing more contracts for us and . . . "

A very tall, dark man entered wearing a well-- -tailored suit, and all eyes turned to look at him.

"Oh! Good morning, Mr. O. we were just about to introduce the purpose of our meeting today."

"Good morning, Ms. Chambers. Thank you, please continue," replied the handsome man who strode to his seat at the head of the table.

Charisse resumed her introduction, "Mr. O. has asked to meet personally with all the head consultants and review our data for the past year. Would you like to introduce yourself?"

He stood, his energy seeming larger than life as he greeted us and thanked us for staying on with the company after his father took ill and many of the proceedings had shifted since his bedrest was mandated by doctors.

"Thank you for the introduction, Ms. Chambers," he began. "I appreciate all that you've done since joining our family business. Some changes have been made over the past six months or so, and I'm just paying a visit to ensure that things are running smoothly and to listen to any concerns that may be held by those who have been here for longer than I've been in charge. It is my hope that everyone has found a place of peace and functionality in the face of the shifts and transitions that I have mandated with the hopes of bringing us into a new space."

I listened, rapt by his handsomeness and the way he worked the room, answering all the questions that everyone asked him with poise and diplomacy.

"Ms. Richards, do you have any concerns at this time?"

His question snapped me out of the way I was staring at him and watching his lips move as he spoke, "No sir, I've made it a point to maintain my flexibility throughout the transitions that this business has experienced. I hope your father is doing well and that your new leadership is a wonderful reflection and a fresh innovation to what procedures and protocols already existed."

"Thank you. I appreciate that. I want everyone who is present today to feel welcome to communicate any concerns or ideas with me directly."

The meeting went on for an hour and a half, with each consultant being called up to share the successes and challenges they'd been experiencing lately in their efforts to provide the most exemplary training experiences to our clients. When the meeting was over, I lingered behind to help Charisse clean the meeting room for the next group of people. Mr. O. stayed behind, listening to feedback from the other consultants, but I felt his eyes on me every time I entered and exited the room.

When Charisse and I were finished, I went back to my office and shared the details with my new Brian, whose name was actually Thomas. He told me that I had a few emails to check in my inbox. When he left, I plopped my weight down into my chair and slid my feet out of my pumps, wiggling sensation back into my nearly numb toes under my desk.

I saw a few emails confirming future training sessions but, while I was crafting a response to one of them, I noticed a new email come through my inbox from a Q. Olokun.

I stared at the highlighted email for a few minutes before hurriedly finishing my email and opening the new email. I was curious because of the last name, and my hands felt cold although the temperature was comfortable in my office.

I read the email:

Dear Ms. Richards,

I'd like to meet with you for lunch to discuss your progress and potential advancement within the company.

Very Respectfully,

Q. O.

I read the email several times before replying that I'd be free to meet for lunch later that day. My whole body seemed to vibrate as I hit send, and I sent Sydney a text that we needed to meet later during happy hour. Somehow, I knew this meeting would be the first day of the rest of my life. I couldn't explain why, and I would likely deny it if anyone asked, but I knew intuitively that this was a very important meeting.

He sent me the address to a restaurant called Lincoln in northwest D.C. and asked me to meet him at 12:30. I had a little over an hour, so I packed my bag so I could make my afternoon class at 3:00 and then drove the thirty-five minutes to the restaurant.

I valeted my car and strode into the restaurant to find Mr. Olokun waiting for me at a high-topped table.

"Good afternoon, Mr. O." I greeted.

He rose to shake my hand and pulled my chair out for me. I thanked him and sat down, and resisted the anxiety brewing inside me as he pushed my chair in effortlessly.

"Good afternoon, Ms. Richards. Thank you for meeting with me on such short notice."

"My pleasure," I said. "Thank *you* for taking time out of your busy schedule for this morning's meeting and for meeting with me for lunch."

"The pleasure is mine." He said in a smooth, crisp voice that was like Kahlua being poured over ice.

We spoke at length about the success of my employment at the company, my thoughts about the changes that had occurred since he took things over from his father, and my future plans. I had decided that I like him well enough, and I thoroughly enjoyed listening to his voice, when he asked me if I was married or seeing anyone seriously.

My cheeks burned a little as I thought about Carlos and even my most recent relationship fail with Ronald.

"No, sir, not yet."

"That must get a little lonely sometimes, although I admire your dedication to the company. How do you maintain a healthy work/life balance?"

I didn't know how to receive his observations, but I replied, "I have a close circle of friends, and I spend time enjoying travel with my extended family in Puerto Rico."

"Oh, so you're Puerto Rican?"

"No, sir. I'm African-American, but I was previously engaged to a man who was from Puerto Rico. He had a tragic accident and died, but his family has been good to me since I have no living family other than my younger brother. Both of my parents were only children."

"I'm sorry to hear that."

"Thank you." I replied politely. "May I ask you a question? I asked.

"Certainly."

"Where are you from with a last name like Olokun?"

"Oh!" he chuckled softly, "You even said it correctly. I'm Nigerian, but I was raised in America. I'm first generation Nigerian-American."

"Really?" I breathed.

"Yes. My father decided to turn his business over to his eldest son, and it didn't hurt that I have an MBA."

"Oh, okay. Excuse me if I'm being too forward, Mr. Olokun. Or should I call you Mr. O.?"

"Not at all. In fact, if I may call you Journey, I'd like it very much if you called me Quest."

"Quest? That's your first name? I wondered what the Q, stood for. I imagined your name was Quentin or Quincy, but Quest is very unique."

"Yes. My parents moved here while my mother was pregnant with me, and they were on a quest for greatness for our family, and that's what they named me."

"Wow! Quest! That's a great story. I'm sure you're a very interesting man."

"Yes, well, my brothers and sister have more traditionally Nigerian names, but I led the way, so they named me Quest."

I nodded, feeling myself being drawn to him and his energy.

"Well, Journey, if you're willing, I'd be interested in seeing you again."

"Really? I was under the impression you lived in San Diego."

"Well . . . I do, however if you're willing to see me again, I'd like to invite you to go out with me on a date. I know most employers don't get involved with their employees, but I find something about you very alluring and I'd like to get to know you better."

"If we hit it off, great," he continued. "If we don't, I promise not to make things challenging for you in your position within the company. I really want to promote you, also."

I hesitated for a few seconds before excusing myself to the ladies' room to give myself a proper escape from the conversation. I looked at myself in the mirror for a few minutes, smoothing my hair back into the curly bun I was sporting that day. Why did I feel so anxious? Was it his name? Was it his handsomeness? I couldn't tell. I smiled at myself in the mirror and checked my teeth for any bits of food before I returned to the table.

"So, what's the verdict, Ms. Richards? Are you going to let me take you out or not?" his smile was warm and slightly mischievous.

"I think I'd like that, Mr. Quest."

I chuckled. He smiled more broadly, reaching for my hand across the table and kissing the back of it. I blushed and giggled slightly, and, just like that, I had a date with Quest Olokun.

23. The Quest Becomes You

I cling to my innocence,
Clutching it to my breast,
Along with my hope, the pieces of me that still
dream without disappointment.
Holding fast with my whole self,
Tooth and nail,
Heart and soul.
I make room with grace,
For harsh words and mistakes,
As I try to release them into the wind, and cleanse them
in the rain, rather than force them down.
Down, down into the deep recesses of myself where they
may spring forth again, unexpectedly.
I tell myself, "They are human," while all members of my
unseen council remind me, "So are you!"
I scoop the bitter memories out of my love,
Slowly spice what remains with cinnamon and sweeten
with honey,
Waiting for the right moment to smear it everywhere,
And in everything so that all of me may heal.

~ Olosunde

One year later

I basked in the light of a full blood moon. It left a path the color of auburn, autumn leaves across the ocean, beckoning to me in the warm breeze. My nipples hardened and I shivered slightly as two warm hands materialized on my hips, caressing me up the sides of my waist, finding their resting place clasped beneath my navel.

Quest's kiss was deliciously moist on the back of my neck, and I closed my eyes, pulling air into my mouth while biting my lip as I clutched the side of the balcony and dropped my head back onto his shoulder. I exhaled into the humid Maui air and leaned into him more as he held me firmly in place, not allowing me to turn around and face him.

When he was certain that I wouldn't attempt to turn around again, his hands drifted up to cup my breasts. He rolled my nipples gently between his fingers and thumb while he kissed my neck and nibbled my shoulder, making me press myself into him more and more, gasping my pleasures into the breeze like so many silent prayers. He placed kisses down my spine, lifting my leg and resting it on his shoulder so he could slide his tongue into the moisture he had created between my legs.

I shivered, gripping the side of the balcony more tightly, not caring whether anyone passed by on the beach below. When my whole body began to tremble, and I began to raise my whole body's weight up on one toe, he stood and pulled me closer, leaning me forward slightly so he could slide inside me. I gasped and arched my back into him, rocking my hips steadily as he stroked me and held me close. I lowered my head in ecstasy, but his hand found its way to my chin, lifting my head and turning my face toward him so he could look me in the eyes while he pleased me. He lowered his forehead to mine and whispered, "I love you, Journey," as I trembled into an orgasm.

"Don't close up, Baby, keep that leg up for me. Mmmm . . . That's my girl. Yesssss . . . " The moisture we created splashed against my thigh and trickled down my leg as he gripped me close and exploded inside of me. He held me tightly, kissing my shoulders and neck, and then my lips. When he withdrew himself from me, he turned around and walked his chocolate self into the villa. I heard the water running in the bathroom sink, and a few minutes later, he brought me a warm towel and wiped me down. When he was finished, he took the towel back into the bathroom and rinsed it, returning wearing a robe, and carrying one for me to wrap around myself.

"I'm sorry round three was so short, but I was watching you under the moonlight and I just couldn't let the moon have you while I couldn't."

"Mmmm . . . I'm not mad about anything, Babe."

We laughed and shared a kiss as we sat on the balcony furniture together.

"This place is so beautiful, Quest. I can't get enough of the sound of the ocean and the warm breezes. I wish we could stay here forever."

He chuckled softly, "We can, Love. When we get married, we can honeymoon for a month if we want to, anywhere we want to."

"Married? Quest, you can't just leave work for a month. Hell, I can't leave work for a month."

"Baby, you're a boss and I'm *the* boss. I don't have to call in for anybody or answer to anybody, and you don't have to answer to anybody either. Now that you're a partner, the only person you have to answer to in my empire, which I hope to make our empire, is me; and I wouldn't have chosen you if I was uncomfortable with you being the voice to speak for me."

"But, Quest, I . . ."

When I turned to look at him, he was on one knee holding out a ring, and my voice caught in my chest.

"Quest!" I breathed, "I—don't know what to say."

"Say you'll be my wife and walk with me to the ends of the earth, swim with me to the depths, and walk with me through the fires that will transform us into one flesh. Say you'll be my partner in this beautiful experience called life. Say you'll carry and birth my children. Say you'll love me, even when it's inconvenient."

He continued, "I know you've been through a lot with Carlos, and in your past you've been hurt a lot, but you're so strong, and I just want to treat you like you're everything to me, because you are. You deserve the crown. You deserve all the riches I can bring, and I just want to share my everything with you. So, what do you say, Journey? Will you be my wife?"

"Yes . . . Yes, I'll marry you," I said through the tears streaming down my face.

I tried not to ugly cry. He reached for my hand and I wiped my face on the sleeve of the robe before rising to embrace and kiss him. The past year had been everything I'd ever imagined a perfect relationship could be, and I knew he wanted to do something special for the anniversary of our first date, but I never imagined that he had planned this.

"Were you planning this the whole time?"

"Journey, I told you months ago that I had been watching you from a distance for a long time. My father always spoke highly of you and your hard work, but when I saw you, I knew I loved you and I told myself that if I ever had the opportunity to meet you, I'd propose to you within thirteen moons. Well, love, this moon is the thirteenth, and you still shine more brightly."

He said, "The very sun itself is jealous of your light. You were meant to be treasured as the crown and the jewel. My family loves you and they already knew that I planned this moment. My mother is already planning a huge Nigerian wedding, and you ain't seen nothing till you've seen a Nigerian wedding! My father wants to send us on a month long honeymoon so he can spend some time sitting on his throne again for a while."

"So you mean to tell me that this entire thing has been in the works for months?"

"Months? Baby, I told my father I wanted to marry you after we had been together for three months and we traveled to Haiti for the relief conference. You were so well received and the people there loved you so much! I still get emails about how amazing you were. I knew I needed you by my side for the rest of my life. I was so impressed by your kindness, nurturing and diplomacy and I you were worthy of a crown."

"That's really sweet, Quest."

"By the way, how do you feel about a chieftaincy title?"

"A what?!"

"A chieftaincy title. I didn't tell you my father is a chief back home in Nigeria, and when we marry, my wife and I will receive a title as well."

"What? Wait, so you're like a prince?"

"Well . . . Not really, but sort of. Are you mad that I didn't tell you?"

"No! I'm just shocked. I always knew you had a different energy about you, but I never knew what it was."

"Well, now you know. Don't worry, there will be enough time for you to adjust to the role that you'll play in that regard, and nobody will be expecting much from either of us except to show face at certain events once in awhile."

"Quest . . ." I whispered, "I'm a little scared. I feel like I'm in some modern version of *Coming to America* right now."

"That's okay, Baby. I will keep you safe, love you like a brother, protect you like a father, and respect you like a friend for the rest of my life. Now go and tell Sydney and whomever else you want to that you're getting married."

He popped me on my butt, and I giggled as I rushed into the living room to search for my cell phone.

"Sydney . . . Girl, I'm sorry for waking you up like this in the middle of the night, but I need you to get ready to be my maid of honor because I'm getting married!"

She squealed and screamed in my ear for about two minutes before she collected herself and said yes.

***

In the morning, we lounged on the beach and enjoyed beach service over kisses and sunshine. It was the happiest I'd been in a long time. I texted Ivelisse and showed her the ring Quest had given me. She video called me almost immediately and demanded details from a totally maternal place.

"I knew he was going to propose soon, but, madre de dios, that's a beautiful ring!"

"Wait! Mom! You KNEW he was going to propose?! You didn't even tell me!"

I looked over at Quest, who lowered his sunglasses and winked at me and placed them back on his face.

"Si, Mija! He called us and asked our permission as your surrogate parents about a month ago. We were just waiting on the big moment! We are so happy for you!"

"We? Wait! Who else knew? Dad?"

"Yes, Mija! You think I kept such an important detail from him?" she clicked her tongue.

"Oh my goodness! Well, look who was out here being traditional and shit!"

"Hi, Ivelisse!" Quest called from beside me.

"Hola, Quest! Congratulations! You guys enjoy your vacation! I can't wait to squeeze some beautiful grandbabies!"

"I know! We'll get to work on that directly!" he said. I swatted him with my beach hat and he laughed.

"Okay, Mija, enjoy yourself! We love you!"

"I love you all too! Talk to you soon!"

"Okay, bye!"

When she hung up, I turned and looked at Quest. "Babe ?"

"Yes, My Queen?"

"You did all this for me?"

"I'd do anything for you, Journey."

I was silent for a few minutes as I sipped my mimosa, processing the past twelve hours. All of a sudden, I felt queasy and my saliva tasted strangely unpleasant. I took a deep breath and exhaled.

"Babe, I think I'm sick."

"What's wrong, love?"

"I don't know. I think I ate something that didn't agree with me."

I coughed and gagged slightly.

"Whoa, you don't look good. You look a little pale. Do we need to go back to the villa?"

"Yeah, I think I'm going to go in for a bit."

I didn't make it to the room before severe nausea set in. I ran ahead of Quest the rest of the way to make it to the bathroom. When he finally made it to me, I was heaving into the toilet, holding my curls out of my face. Quest came into the bathroom and held my hair back with one hand and rubbed my back with the other while I gripped the sides of the toilet and retched again. When I finished, I was out of breath.

"I'm sorry, Babe, I don't know what happened." I rose and began brushing my teeth. "It's ok, Love. I do."

"What do you mean?" I asked over a mouthful of toothpaste.

"Journey, we've been together for a year now, and we've been having unprotected sex for at least three months. Baby, you're pregnant."

"No, I'm not." I said after I spat the last of the toothpaste out, "I'm on the pill. I have regular periods, and they're . . ."

"They're like the moon . . . you always bleed during the full moon. The moon is full, Journey, and you're not bleeding. You're pregnant, and I've known it for a couple of weeks."

I stood looking at him with my mouth open. I closed my mouth, then opened it again twice, but no sound was coming out. Quest walked away to the bed room and returned with a pregnancy test, handing it to me.

"Here. Check if you don't believe me."

I took the test from his hand and tore open the shrink wrap without bothering to ask him why he had it to begin with. That was a question for a later time. I sat down on the toilet and he handed me a mouthwash Dixie cup from the counter. I urinated in the cup and dipped the test into the cup before wiping, flushing and washing my hands. We both waited, practically holding our breaths, until the test began to change colors.

When the pink plus sign appeared in the little result window, we both screamed. My response was terrified, although his was excited. With tears in both our eyes, we hugged and kissed and screamed again, this time both screaming with joy.

"How did you know?!"

"Remember a few weeks ago when we had that night in the hot tub?"

"Yes," I said with a little naughty smirk. "You were amazing."

"Thank you," he replied with a laugh. "Anyway, you had a little spotting a few days later. Then when we visited my parents, you didn't like the smell of the egusi soup, and you LOVE egusi soup. My mother said something to me then.

When I was packing for this trip, I was preparing to propose to you, and my mother suggested that I bring a test along with me. You know she's a midwife and a doctor, so she thinks about that sort of thing. We had a talk about your cycle and things I had been noticing about you being tired lately and wanting to sleep a lot, so I was a little bit aware."

"But you let me drink."

"You don't drink enough to hurt a baby this early in the game, so I knew it wasn't an issue. Like I said, my mom is a midwife and a doctor and she thinks about those things."

"Wow. Quest, I don't know what to say."

"I love you, Journey."

"I love you too."

"Can I make a request?"

"Of course."

"I'd like to name our child Golden if it's a girl and Ahjai if it's a boy."

"I like that."

"Good. Although, I'm hoping it's a boy."

"I'm sure." I laughed. "Ahjai, Olokun. That sounds like a good, strong name."

"And he will be," he said, lowering himself to my belly and kissing it.

I looked at myself in the mirror over his shoulder and smiled at our reflection. I was going to marry Olokun after all and, although I still didn't know what the Ophiucus thing was about, I knew I would eventually find out, and that was enough.

For the first time in my life, I felt like I was enough for myself and someone else too. I knew I didn't have to pretend to be more than what I was to please Quest and make him happy. Even though I didn't know anything about all the things he'd been planning for me and for us, I was happy about where I was in this place.

I had kissed enough frogs and I didn't have to fix Quest, put him together, heal him, or wonder about him. I didn't have to worry about my love being thrown back in my face. I didn't have to worry about being abused. I didn't have to guard my heart, because he truly protected it and he wanted to give me his everything. After all I had been through, I was finally happy.

Acknowledgments

I would like to thank: my parents for telling me I could be and do anything I wanted, but not being too disappointed when I blazed my own path. Mama Banks (Leslie Esdaile Banks) for encouraging me to keep writing, and telling me that my stories and voice needed to be heard. My sister circle for the influence of their stories, their support, their accountability and all the love they poured into me when I was going through the trials that periodically clouded my creative focus. My book proof crew for incrementally reading my work and always giving honest feedback. My ancestors, Orisa and Olodumare for literally waking me from my slumber and forcing me to write until my eyes were too weary to make sense of the words on the screen. My son, Jameson, for the inspiration of his existence. You are magic personified.

About the Author

Jessica Lynn is a proud graduate of the Florida Agricultural and Mechanical University undergraduate program for Elementary Education and Clark Atlanta University's Master of Educational Leadership and Administration program. She began her career teaching elementary school and has worked as an educator for over a decade. In 2014, she published, *Love, Like Water in a Basket*, a compilation of poetry written over the course of 13 years. Jessica began writing Kissing Frogs: The Thirteenth in 2017, after the birth of her son, Jameson. Many details are tribute to her mentor and favorite author, Leslie Esdaile Banks, who encouraged her to keep writing during her early twenties. Jessica is a Chicago native, now residing in Washington, D.C. with her son and favorite feline fur baby, Rico.